Everything and More

Everything
and More

GEOFF NICHOLSON

THE OVERLOOK PRESS
WOODSTOCK · NEW YORK

First published in paperback in the
United States in 1999 by
The Overlook Press,
Peter Mayer Publishers, Inc.
Lewis Hollow Road
Woodstock, New York 12498

Library of Congress Catalog-in-Publication Data

Nicholson, Geoff, 1953–
Everything and more / Geoff Nicholson
p. cm.
1. Department stores—England—London—Fiction.
2. London (England)—Fiction   I. Title.
PR6064.I225E94   1999   823'.914—dc21   99-10238
ISBN: 0-87951-710-7
Originally published in Great Britain by Victor Gollancz
First U.S. Hardcover edition published as A Wyatt Book for St. Martin's Press in 1995

Manufactured in the United States of America
1 3 5 7 9 8 6 4 2

Fiction provided me with many valuable ideas
and some very real incentives to success.

H. GORDON SELFRIDGE

1 · THE GRAND OPENING

The store rests in darkness, waiting for opening time, for the human presence. The escalators are still, the air-conditioning is silent. The carpets are vacuumed and ready for business. It is all here. The preparations are complete. The merchandise is all laid out for you; of good quality, eye-catchingly displayed, attractively packaged.

The shelves and hangers and rails and spinners are heavy with goods. Each floor, each department, each aisle and counter is well stocked and arranged to offer up its best; from pocket calculators to bridal wear, from the tartan shop to the heel bar, from pets' accessories to the mother and baby room, it is all in order, accessible and schematized. The staff have worked hard. The systems are in place; systems of accounting and stock control, of safety and security, of supply and demand.

It is all for you. We are here to serve. We assure you of our best attentions. We thank you for your continuing support in these difficult times. You are our favoured customer. You are always right.

Don't be afraid to touch. Feel the quality, feel the breadth. Feel free to browse. Take an unhurried wander through each and every department, turn it into an occasion, make a whole day of it. Wallow in the luxury. Breathe in the balmy air of the perfumery and the enticing smells from the bakery and the Mr Cappuccino Coffee Shop. Throw away your cares. Let yourself be pampered. Spoil yourself, live a little. Live a lot.

Arnold Haden, the only surviving Haden brother, reclines in the austere whiteness of his penthouse at the top of the department store that bears his name. He is a large, soft man, weak but not frail, youthful though not young.

He says, 'It's the old story. The lunatic sets up his easel and decides to paint the whole world and everything in it.

'He works diligently and makes good progress until the moment he realizes that in order to complete his task, the painting will need to contain a self-portrait of himself painting the whole world and everything in it.

'Not only that. He will then need to paint himself painting himself painting himself and so on. I believe this is known as a regress, and it might well drive him mad if he weren't mad already.

'And it's very much the same with a department store like Haden Brothers. We like to say that the store contains everything and more; that's our slogan, our sales pitch. If you want a pin, an elephant, a Ron Arad Big easy chair, an Aldo Rossi La Conica stainless-steel coffee maker, we've got it. But can you come here and buy a department store in which you can buy everything and more? Well, we do have a real estate department, but no, not really. And can you come here and buy a department store in which you can buy a department store in which you can buy a department store in which . . . ? And so on. Another regress.

'At Haden Brothers we have not quite reached that state of philosophical purity, nor have we yet been driven mad, but I will say this for us: Haden Brothers is everything that is the case.'

The call comes via Arnold Haden's secretary, and the message is that Miss Vita Carlisle would at long last like to see him in private. She has come to a decision and she suggests that the meeting take place in his penthouse at seven o'clock that evening, after the store has shut.

For Arnold it's almost too good to be true. At first he thinks his secretary may have got the message wrong, though normally she is absolutely efficient. It's just that he can't quite believe it. He's waited so long. Then he wonders if it's a tease, a delaying tactic to be followed by more frustration and more rejection. And yet he suspects not. To date that hasn't been Vita Carlisle's style. She doesn't seem to be given to acts of deliberate cruelty, but he has nevertheless been hurt by her indifference. So perhaps his campaign has finally succeeded. She has succumbed, she is ready to submit; or at least she will be at seven this evening. His persuasiveness, his pleas, and certainly his patience have finally paid off. Nevertheless he needs some confirmation and so makes an internal phone call to the department where he knows she's working.

She answers the phone and says, 'Furnishing fabrics.'

'Miss Carlisle?'

Of course she recognizes the voice at once but she doesn't reply.

'Vita?'

'Yes, Mr Haden.'

'I got your message, Vita. Does it mean what I think it means?'

'Please, Mr Haden, I'm in the middle of a crowded shop floor.'

'I'm sorry. I know I shouldn't ring you at work, even if it's my work too. It's just that if it does mean what I think it means, then I can't tell you how happy I am.'

'Can you not?'

'Well yes, I can if you'll give me a chance.'

'Perhaps you'll tell me later.'

'At seven, yes certainly, if you like, but really, why wait so long, why not come up right now?'

'I'm afraid I do have customers waiting.'

'Of course you do. It's very conscientious of you, it's just that, I was wondering . . . '

'I'll be happy to deal with all that for you later,' she says, and he detects a sudden coldness.

'What is it? Can you not speak? Is the buyer standing next to you? Don't worry about her.'

'Yes, seven o'clock. Thank you for calling Haden Brothers.'

She doesn't exactly hang up on him but suddenly the line is dead and she's moved on swiftly and efficiently to her next customer. Arnold Haden's mind throws up intriguing pictures of her at work in the furnishing fabrics department, being attentive and efficient, gently coercive, making a lot of sales. Then the pictures become distorted and fantastical. As though in a dream sequence he sees her naked, yet still going about her duties in the department, operating the till, showing swatches of cloth to customers who are completely oblivious to her nakedness, immune to the white perfection of her body. He is not so immune.

The rest of his day is spent in a barely controlled frenzy of anticipation. He remains in a state of adolescent nervousness and arousal that nothing can quell. As the afternoon wears on, he showers more than once, has a manicurist and hairdresser sent up from the store to make sure he's trim and presentable. He selects his newest, cleanest, whitest clothes, ensures that his stocks of chilled white wine and champagne are more than adequate, has maids come in to hoover his white carpets, put fresh white lilies in the vases, put crisp white sheets on his bed. He is not naive enough to believe that Vita Carlisle is a virgin, and yet he feels there will be much about this meeting, this event, that will be fresh and virginal. He sends his secretary home early. His staff are told he is incommunicado. The phones are muted. Nothing is going to be allowed to intrude on his pleasure with Vita.

A little before the appointed hour he hears the whirr of his private lift. The commissionaire at ground level has been told to admit nobody except Vita Carlisle, so it can only be her. He waits in the plain, sparse ante-room into which the lift opens. He positions himself by one of the panoramic windows and adopts a pose that he hopes looks nonchalant and unstudied. The suspense is killing.

The lift arrives, its doors open and suddenly she's there with him. Although her every feature and repertoire of gestures is imprinted on his memory, there is still something fresh and surprising about her. She is no longer in her work clothes, but is wearing a long, pale, loose cotton dress, summery and chaste; not that it has a chastening effect on Arnold Haden.

'Hello, Vita,' he says.

'Hello, Mr Haden. Arnold.'

'Thank you for that,' he says. 'I think it's time we were on first name terms.'

She makes no reply. She looks serene and self-possessed. Arnold Haden's instinct is to make a spirited if clumsy lunge at her, to ravish her on the threshold of the lift, but he knows she wouldn't appreciate that. She is a sophisticated young woman, she must be granted her own time and her own space. He remains stuck in his pose and doesn't move as she crosses the room, not approaching him but heading instead for one of the windows, where she stands some ten feet away from him and looks down to the street below, at the people, the taxis and the parked cars.

She taps on the window with the knuckle of her right hand. 'Armoured glass?' she enquires.

He finds it a surprising question but nods in confirmation.

'I suppose you feel secure up here,' she says.

At this moment he feels insecure to the point of dementia. The muscles in the rear of his knees have developed a neurotic, twitching life of their own, but he admits that being here gives him a much needed sense of safety and detachment.

'Even if a bomb went off in the street you'd be safe up here, wouldn't you? You might feel a shock wave, a painting or two might fall off the wall . . .'

'There are no paintings on my walls,' he says hastily.

'But nothing could touch you, could it?'

'I wouldn't say nothing. That is, I wouldn't want to put it to the test, but yes, the general idea is that I should be safe.'

'I don't blame you at all,' she says sweetly.

He's pleased that she understands, seems to care about his safety. So many people consider his isolation to be a rich recluse's eccentricity.

'So terrorists hold no fears for you?' she continues.

'I wouldn't say *no* fears.'

'But why? I mean look at those cars down there, say the blue Ford Escort, the red Hillman Imp, the white Renault; even if every one of those cars was packed with explosives, and even if the police weren't given a tip off, and even if they exploded, and even if there were bombs in the store itself, say incendiary devices, smoke bombs and nail bombs, and even if the whole lot went off, well, you'd be all right, wouldn't you, Arnold? You might lose a few customers, a few members of staff, a certain amount of stock, but you'd be fine, it wouldn't make any difference to you, would it?'

Arnold Haden is finding this conversation unnecessary and anything but erotic, nevertheless he doesn't want to ignore her apparently real concern.

'I care very much indeed about our customers and staff,' he says. 'And I'd hate to lose any stock.'

'Come on, Arnold, stop sounding like the staff manual.'

He smiles, enjoying her sudden playfulness. He takes her garrulousness as proof that she is every bit as nervous and apprehensive as he. He doesn't mind that at all, yet he decides it's time to take the initiative. He moves towards her but she has her back to him and doesn't turn round, just continues to look out of the window. He puts his hands on her neck and although she doesn't resist, neither does she react. That doesn't please him. He'd like her to thrill at his touch. He wants her to submit, but he doesn't want her to be inert.

'I've been waiting a long time for this,' he says.

'I know. Me too.'

'But I think it was probably worth it; the pleasures of delayed gratification and so on.'

'I think I know what you mean.'

'I realize I have no right to ask this, Vita, but tell me, what made you change your mind?'

He begins very gently to massage the nape of her neck and he convinces himself that there is a dim ripple of pleasure in her body.

'I mean, was it simply my persistence? Or a sudden realization? Or did something happen in your own life?'

'All the above,' she says, offhandedly, and he takes it as an evasion, a reluctance to answer.

'Not that it matters now you're here,' he says to let her off the hook.

He moves very close, presses his body against her back. Her buttocks fit into his pelvis, her head rests against his shoulder and her blonde hair presents itself to his face. He inhales deeply. His hands snake around her, make straight for her breasts. He holds them just for a moment, clenches them, realizes he's rushing things, pressing too hard, releases them, and yet he can't stint himself; his hands descend down her ribs, to her waist and then to her belly, and that's where things start to feel very wrong.

There is something strange under the loose cotton of the dress, a lot of webbing and strapping. He thinks at first it might be some kind of corset or item of structural erotic underwear. That would be very thoughtful of her, although in fact it would not suit his particular tastes, and yet his instincts tell him he is not touching anything as simple as underwear, and as his hands continue their descent they encounter something hard and cylindrical, something that at first feels distinctly phallic. 'Oh my God, don't tell me I've been trying all this time to seduce a transvestite or a transsexual.' But there's nothing fleshy or sexual about this cylinder and he can feel there are several of the damn things located in a row across her abdomen. He takes his hands off her and steps back.

She turns towards him. The dress still hangs too loosely to tell him what's beneath, but obligingly she reaches down and grips the hem, slowly, tantalizingly lifting the skirt above her knees, then above her thighs, then to her waist to reveal a form of undergarment he has never seen before, a form that is not a real undergarment at all.

The hard cylinders are, in fact, three sticks of dynamite, held in place by tape and belts, with detonators and a tangle of electrical wiring that leads to a switch located by her navel. He wonders if he's misread Vita Carlisle completely, that she isn't some fresh young thing and that she's offering him a part in some bizarre and arcane sexual game, a piece of perverse role playing that he would never have expected from her. Yet in his heart of hearts he knows this is not the case. This isn't simply about sex.

She says, 'There's enough explosive here to blow us both to smithereens.'

He doesn't doubt it. 'Do you *want* to blow us both to smithereens?' he asks.

She considers this for a moment. 'I don't know yet,' she says. 'But it's definitely an option, isn't it?'

'Yes, it is,' he admits.

'If you attempt to call security or make a dash for it, or try to overpower me, then I'll do it without a moment's hesitation.'

'I wouldn't dream of doing any of those things.'

'That's very sensible of you,' she says.

'Are there any other options?' he asks gently.

'What?'

'I mean is it possible that you *won't* blow us both to smithereens?'

It's a genuine enquiry, a request for information.

'I suppose so,' she says, but she sounds neither convinced nor convincing.

'Is there something you want from me?' Arnold Haden asks. 'Money maybe?'

'No, I don't think so.'

'Or is there something more specific you need, some service, something I can do for you?'

'I'm not sure. Possibly. I'll have to think about it.'

Arnold Haden looks at her with an expression that he hopes conveys concern.

'Take all the thinking time you need,' he says, and he doesn't sound pleading. It doesn't sound like a delaying tactic. He genuinely doesn't want Vita to be rushed.

'I must say, Arnold, you're taking this terribly well,' she says sarcastically.

'I am, aren't I?'

'How come?'

'Because I've been expecting this, Vita. I've been expecting it all my life.'

ARNOLD HADEN: Yes, it's true that I liked to have sex with pretty young women. The fact that some of them, most of them, tended to be Haden Brothers employees is not so very surprising. Haden Brothers is my world. It's where I have my being. I didn't go out much in those days. I wasn't a very socially adept person, I admit it. It's not a crime.

And if you were to say that these sexual encounters were not particularly meaningful or spiritual or uplifting, well, I would probably have to agree with you. But equally I would say that they were harmless and not particularly exploitative. I told the young women exactly what I wanted, and I didn't want anything so terrible. I wanted sex. I didn't make any sort of pretence. I never pretended I was in love with the girls. I didn't promise to marry them or say I could advance their careers at Haden Brothers. I was very straightforward with them. That's how I always try to do business.

And yes, I know it could be said that my tastes were a little humdrum, a little predictable. I liked the girls to be young, innocent, fresh, blonde, unsullied, clean; I was always very particular about cleanliness. I went for the natural look, unadorned, and certainly Vita Carlisle fitted the bill, the pattern, was almost a Platonic model, an ideal of the kind of young woman I like. But it wasn't that simple.

On the surface it might look like Vita Carlisle was just another of Mr Haden's girls, and at first that's all I wanted her to be, but as time went by, the longer she resisted, she became, in my own mind if nowhere else, something quite different; something special and unique and really rather wonderful. Not to put too fine a point on it, and not wanting to sound too pathetic, I fell in love with her.

VITA CARLISLE: As a person he disgusted me, obviously. How could he not, a man of his age, not very attractive, not in very good shape, not witty or charming or intelligent, despite his own high opinion of himself. I thought Mr Arnold Haden was a very inadequate human being, and I can see why he would have problems forming mature relationships with women.

In theory I don't see prostitution as a particularly pernicious form of human interaction. At least its rules are clear. A medium of exchange is established; the power relations, at least for the time of the transaction, are clear cut. If Arnold Haden had simply hired a string of call girls I would have had some sympathy, and considerably more respect for him. What disgusted me was that he chose to involve some of his female employees (invariably the younger, more vulnerable, less experienced ones) in a set of relations where the medium of exchange was distorted to his infinite advantage. Perhaps some of the girls would say that they were happy enough to have sex with him, perhaps they got something out of it that they needed, but that isn't to say they weren't exploited. How could they be equal partners in a transaction where the power relations were so monstrously unequal?

I thought Arnold Haden was a user and an abuser. He was, among other things, corrupt, sick and dangerous. But actually, that had nothing at all to do with why I went to his little white penthouse at the top of his store and threatened to blow him to smithereens.

CHARLIE MAYHEW: The quest for meaning is, arguably, the quest for structure. Novelists, in particular, often feel the need for a rigid, supportive, guiding framework in their books. This may be mythological and/or ironic and/or arbitrary. So James Joyce has the *Odyssey*. Primo Levi has the Periodic Table. Georges Perec has his Parisian apartment building. And so on. Some of these structures seem a lot more supportive than others.

So I thought to myself, why not structure a book like a department store? There would be ease of access, fancy window dressing, a bargain basement, loss leaders, information points, knobs and knockers, free tastings, gift wrapping, puzzles and games, a grotto at Christmas, everything clearly signposted and lots of fire escapes and emergency exits.

But more than that, a department store is a great depository of stuff. It's a world of objects. Perhaps not all human life is there but there's not much lacking in the way of desirable consumer items. And the store divides up this world of objects in ways that are essentially arbitrary, into floors and departments and sub-departments, and occasionally into franchises or stores within the store, so that each area contains its own categories of experience and knowledge, its own slice of the world. This is, arguably, a fairly serviceable structure. This is, arguably, what all art does.

And of course there are people in the store; the more or less fixed population of staff and the more or less fluid population of shoppers. They exist within the structure. They animate it but they are also subservient to it. Structures are controlling mechanisms for people as well as for works of art.

At the centre of my imagined book there would be a pun which might seem highly significant or rather lame depending on your attitude. The pun would be on the word 'retailing', which suggests both the selling of goods and the telling of tales. An author is indeed a seller of goods, and a department store is indeed a place full of stories, even fictions.

If one were not careful this could all too easily turn into some kind of sub-Chaucerian compendium featuring the bought-ledger clerk's tale, the stationery sales assistant's tale, the wife of the customer in the delicatessen department's tale, and so, boringly, on. This would be a structure but not an appealing one.

It is clear that stories are important to us, and can in themselves be a form of structure, but they aren't the only thing that's important. Significance may lie in a graffito, in a colour scheme, in an arrangement of tableware, in the purchase of a new flip-top bin. Light fading through shop windows, the angle of a spotlight, the shape of some point-of-sale packaging; all these things contain meanings but they are not stories. We need a structure that can contain these too.

The book would contain a linked but smaller and more localized pun on the verb 'to shop', which can mean to buy goods, or in slang terms, to betray, to turn someone in to the authorities. (Of course, one may do this by 'telling tales'.) I'm not sure that this second meaning would make sense in American or Australian or South African English, to say nothing of the translations.

But structure is never wholly arbitrary, and it is always allied to function. The structure of a department store draws in the customer, allows a wide range of goods and services to be stocked, displayed and sold. It keeps both staff and customers under control. And if this is done with some efficiency the store may shift a lot of units and show a profit.

At best, the structure of a novel draws in the reader, allows a wide range of themes and ideas to be stocked, displayed and, in some sense, sold. It keeps both the author and his subject matter under control. And if this is done with some efficiency he may shift a lot of units and show a profit. If he's really lucky his novel may even be on sale in department stores.

It sounded like a great idea to me, but it took me a long time to realize what was possible, and by then it was far too late.

I never wanted to work at Haden Brothers at all. I thought it far too snobby, far too grand. I would have said it was full of overpriced, useless rubbish. I thought the staff were probably all morons and the customers even worse. Until I went to work there I wouldn't have been seen dead there, but you know how it is, paupers can't be choosers. I wouldn't have worked at all if I could have helped it. It sounds silly, but I wanted to be an artist!

I said this to Vita Carlisle the first time I met her. And strange as it may seem, as soon as I set eyes on her I had a feeling that my fate and hers were going to be inextricably connected and, at the time, like a fool, I thought that was going to make me happy.

2 · PERSONNEL

It was a long time ago that Charlie Mayhew first walked across the threshold of Haden Brothers, and he knew immediately that he had entered a different world. A uniformed commissionaire held the plate-glass door open for him and said, 'Good morning, sir,' an act that Charlie found deeply embarrassing.

He stood in the vast and imposing entrance hall. Certainly it beckoned and drew him in, but it was perhaps too grand and large scale to be truly welcoming. There was polished, smoke-coloured marble under his feet, and above his head etched mirrors and columns and chandeliers and escalators ascended in a relentless surge of glitter and optimism and artificial light. This hall was a portal, a city gate. It gave access to whole realms of opulence and expense. It was a Monday morning in February and the air outside was freezing, but inside the store even the air was different. It was a hot blast of centrally heated warmth, processed and perfumed, unlike any air he'd ever breathed before.

A loose wave of customers broke around him, unEnglish complexions, distant accents and unfamiliar, fussy clothes. They all looked purposeful yet leisured, casual yet well-heeled. These people professed high standards and taste and equally high disposable incomes. There he stood in his fashionable suit (a powder blue Hugo Boss linen number bought in a sale but still costing a fortune) with his sharp haircut, his hand-painted silk tie, his DMs, and he felt very ambivalent. He could see how easy it would be to stroll through a few departments, picking up trinkets, collecting gewgaws, ordering rattan sofas and new winter outfits. It would be simple enough to shed a few thousand pounds in the course of an afternoon's unruffled shopping. He would have no difficulty with that.

The problem, the unfortunate truth, was that he was not here to do any shopping. He was here looking for a job. He was wearing his fashionable suit, his only suit, because he was on his way to the eighth floor of the store, to the personnel department for an interview. And if the interview went well, and if he was offered a job, he knew it would pay him the kind of weekly wage that would, at a pinch, buy one modest decanter from the glass department, or half a cashmere sweater in men's outfitting. This did not make him especially happy, but neither did it make him bitter. He could afford to swallow his pride. He was just passing through. There were better times of untold prosperity and success around the corner. Surely. The Fates surely didn't intend that someone of his obvious talents should languish for long so low down the pile. In fact he found it fairly incomprehensible that the Fates intended he should languish there at all, but there was no doubt they did, and it looked as though he was going to have to live with it.

He had arrived in London six weeks earlier with a little bit of money and the addresses of half a dozen friends from college who had some time ago assured him that there was always a bed, or at least a floor, waiting for him if he ever came to London. Only one of these offers had survived his arrival. The others had claimed they had mothers visiting, that the landlord wouldn't approve, that their flats were already too small and overcrowded. For all he knew these excuses might have been genuine, but he doubted it. Only after some serious emotional blackmail had he succeeded in imposing himself on Keith and Sarah, a couple he hadn't even known all that well at college. Their flat was small too, but they had been prepared to squeeze him in, and he was currently camping out on the sofa in their living room. Keith worked for a record distributor. Sarah was temping as a secretary. Each evening they would come home from work tired and stressed. They would eat, drink a lot of cheap wine, smoke some dope and watch TV until the early hours. They would occupy the sofa, Charlie's bed, while they did all this. Only when they'd vacated the sofa and gone to their own bed was Charlie able to turn in for the night.

He had been sure that this too was going to be a temporary arrangement. He thought it would be no time at all before he established himself in London, found his niche. This, as far as he was concerned, involved falling in with a group of like-minded creative types. They would be artists and models, rock musicians, collagists, poets, jewellers, independent film-makers, actors, writers of experimental prose; and they would recognize him as one of their own and clasp him to their collective bosom. There would be parties, readings, gigs, private views, book launches. It would be bohemian and faintly (though not dangerously) decadent. He would make friends, find lovers, be invited to stay in great houses and country cottages. He would become a picaresque hero.

More to the point, he would become an artist. Charlie had always been creative in a general, undifferentiated sort of way. At college he had been involved in student drama, screen printing, a writer's workshop and, although he'd always known it was a bit naff, a folk club. Each had provided him with entertainment, even, as he liked to put it, with spiritual nourishment, and yet he couldn't see himself as an actor, a screen printer, a writer, and certainly not as a folk musician. His true art form was waiting for him somewhere, rich and fecund, and as yet undiscovered. Perhaps it would even be an art form of his own invention. He felt certain that London would provide him with the inspiration and the contacts to forge this new artistic self.

He knew six weeks was not long to accomplish all the above, and so he wasn't too dispirited to find that the bohemian world as yet remained closed to him. But six weeks was long enough to run through almost all his money. He was prepared to play the starving artist for a while, but even the most unmaterialistic and disapproving member of the consumer society (and he never claimed to be that) needed a bob or two to survive in London. London was an expensive town. More pressing, Sarah had made several stinging remarks about his failure to contribute to her and Keith's household budget. Charlie liked to think he had the ability to charm women, but Sarah remained uncharmed.

'What do you want me to do?' he asked. 'Go out and mug somebody?'

'It's worth a thought,' said Sarah. 'I suppose getting a job and a flat of your own would be asking too much.'

And indeed it would, but at least he was prepared to go along to a variety of social security offices. It was an eye-opener. The waiting rooms of the social security offices hung heavy with desperation and mania. Undisguised hatred bounced back and forth between the claimants and officials. The clerks sat at counters, behind glass that was streaked with unidentified fluids, and questioned the authenticity of any statement the claimants made, of any document they produced. On the other side, voices slurred with drink and anger made lurid but impotent threats. Young drunken men pissed in corners. Fat but hyperactive children ran wild along the corridors. Everyone was trying to smoke themselves to death. After spending an edgy hour and a half waiting in what, even at the time, he suspected was the wrong office in the wrong building, he fled. This was not for him. He was too cool for this place. He realized a job was the only way out.

Sarah told him he should go into marketing or softwear design, or, failing that, why didn't he train to be an accountant or a solicitor? He hoped she was being ironic. There was a variety of shift work that offered itself to a man in Charlie's position. There was the possibility of working as a security guard, a cinema usher or a domestic cleaner. None fitted his sense of *amour propre*. So he gradually started to think about Haden Brothers.

If you had to do a job you didn't want to do, Haden Brothers appeared to be a reasonable place to do it. Haden Brothers was London's, probably the world's, most prestigious and most expensive department store. OK, so it might be argued that it sold useless, overpriced tat to a bunch of snobs, tourists and people with more money than sense, but Charlie was prepared to suspend judgement for a while. If you wanted solidarity with the working class you could always try getting a job in Woolworths. Charlie didn't want solidarity with the working class. Haden Brothers, he hoped, would provide a rich and exotic backdrop to his own personal, unfolding drama. Perhaps there would even be like-minded souls there, other aspiring artists who had to work for a living, just like him. And once he hit his stride as an artist he would, of course, get the hell out.

So he phoned the personnel department and somewhat to his surprise they said he should present himself as soon as possible for an interview. They made it sound important and urgent. They had asked remarkably little about him, and Charlie suspected that when he got there it might well prove to be a wild-goose chase but he went anyway, and that was what he was doing walking into Haden Brothers that cold February morning.

He wandered through the store until he came to the lifts. After a short wait one came and he stepped inside. It was bigger than any room in Keith and Sarah's flat, far more elegant and better decorated too, with walnut panelling, bronze fittings and filigree work. And he didn't have to share it with anybody except the lift attendant. He too was uniformed, although as far as Charlie could remember it was a different style of uniform from that worn by the commissionaire who'd welcomed him in. This one looked like an antique from some long forgotten war. It even had medals.

The attendant wearing it was old and white-haired, but very tall and straight-backed. Charlie didn't pay much attention to him at first, not even when he asked what floor Charlie wanted. He said, 'Eighth,' and the attendant said, 'Ah, personnel,' and he pressed a button, there was a hydraulic wheeze, the doors slid shut and the lift began ponderously to ascend. But as it did so, the lift attendant turned towards Charlie and sniffed. Charlie was taken aback and somewhat annoyed, and he glared at the man in what he hoped was a withering sort of way. But the attendant couldn't appreciate Charlie's glare, nor could he glare back. From the way he gazed off into some clearly non-existent distance, Charlie realized the poor old guy was blind. He felt bad about being annoyed.

The lift reached the first floor. The doors opened and the attendant began to announce, 'First floor: bedding, linens, furnishing fabrics, gentlemen's shoes . . . '

Charlie listened politely, but he wasn't sure why the attendant was bothering. As the only occupant of the lift, and having said he wanted the eighth floor, he didn't see why he needed to hear a recitation of the store's various departments. But he could hardly tell the man to shut up. Nobody got in the lift and at the second floor much the same happened again. The attendant said, 'Bridalwear, ladies' smalls, *prêt-à-porter*, British collections, gift ideas.'

Still nobody entered the lift. As they approached the third floor it dawned on Charlie that the job of lift attendant was an unusual one for a blind man, and the more he thought about it, the more unlikely it seemed. It presented so many problems. He looked at the buttons that operated the lift and said to the attendant, 'I hope you don't mind me asking, but those buttons, do they have the floor numbers on them in braille?'

'Oh no, sir, that would be cheating.'

The lift stopped again. 'Third floor: toys and games, babywear, teddy bears, mother and baby rooms, telephones, camping equipment.' Charlie remained the lift's only occupant. When the attendant had finished reciting, the lift closed and moved again. It would have been easy to travel in silence, but Charlie was interested now.

'So how do you know which floor you've got to?' he asked. 'Presumably you can't see the little illuminated numbers.'

'No, I certainly can't.'

'So how do you do it? Just by remembering? You know you're on, say, the first floor, so if you go up two you'll be on three, then if you go down four you know you're in the basement. Is that how it works? Even so, it must get confusing.'

'It certainly would if I did it that way.'

The lift stopped again.

'Fourth floor: pasta machines, books, sporting guns, lighting, estate agency, theatre tickets, travel agency, glossy magazines.' Then off again.

'Are you really interested in this?' the attendant asked. 'You're not just being polite?'

'I'm really interested,' said Charlie.

'Fine. Well, it's partly to do with air pressure. The higher we go, the lower the air pressure on the skin, the mucous membranes, the inner ear. It's very subtle but, as you know, the body compensates somewhat for the loss of sight by sharpening up the other senses.'

'That's fantastic.'

'Fifth floor: pet shop, grand pianos, motoring accessories, florist, hairdressing, executive trinkets, funeral service.'

This time someone attempted to get in the lift, but, of course, the attendant couldn't see him, and closed the doors as if precisely to frustrate the attempt.

When they were moving again Charlie asked, 'And then do you just learn off by heart what's on each floor?'

The attendant shook his head. 'That would hardly work at all, sir. The truth is, this store is in constant flux. Departments are always being moved around, opened, closed, rearranged, having their names changed. Before you'd learned it all by heart it would be out of date.'

'Then how?' Charlie asked.

The lift stopped again, the doors opened and the lift attendant took a large, exaggerated sniff of the air outside.

'Sixth floor,' he said. 'Gift stationery, bath salts, tapes and CDs, major and minor electrical, export bureau, credit control.'

He waited a moment while nobody got in or out of the lift, then made it ascend once again.

'You *smell* which floor you're on?' Charlie asked.

'Not exactly. I smell the *contents* of each floor. If I smell beeswax I know it's the furniture department. If I smell leather I know it's the luggage department.'

'But isn't there a fair amount of leather in the shoe department, too?'

'Yes, but no beeswax. And if I smell dark roasted Arabica coffee beans, then I know I'm on the floor for the food department.'

'Or the coffee bar.'

'No,' the attendant said patiently. 'There are twelve different eateries in Haden Brothers from the Tropicana Blue Mountain Café to the Blackamoor's Head Olde English Pub. Each uses an entirely different blend of coffee and each is instantly distinguishable to the trained nose. Seventh floor: furniture, beds, sofas, tables, pouffes, sideboards.'

Even before the door was closed this time Charlie said, 'And when I got in the lift you smelt me?'

Casually, deliberately, the attendant pressed the button for the final time on this trip. 'Yes,' he admitted, 'but only after you'd told me you wanted the personnel department.'

'I don't follow.'

'You see, sir, only a certain type of person is suited to work at Haden Brothers. The personnel department is very good at identifying and accepting that type, and only that type. For them it's a question of looks, dress and body language. I can't make decisions based on those criteria so I have to rely on smell.'

'And how do I smell?'

The attendant took a perfunctory final sniff, just to confirm an opinion he had obviously come to some time before. 'Oh yes, sir, you definitely smell like one of us,' and then in the same breath he said, 'Eighth floor. Personnel only.'

'Oh well,' said Charlie, a little bemused, 'thank you very much.'

He was unclear what he was thanking him for, and he wondered if you should tip a lift attendant, but he didn't. He shook the attendant's hand, although that too seemed inappropriate, and he said he hoped to see him around, which seemed worse.

Charlie stepped out of the lift and walked through frosted, swinging glass doors into the reception area of the personnel department. It was full of air and daylight. There were pale carpets and hessian wallpaper, a drinking fountain, feathery potted plants and a number of soft, oatmeal coloured sofas.

He gave his name to a shining young male receptionist who was uncannily friendly and welcoming, and he was asked if he'd please be kind enough to take a seat just for a moment until someone could see him, it wouldn't be a moment really, and thanks for his patience. Charlie sat down. He felt strangely at ease. It was partly the receptionist's manner but it had more to do with the lift attendant's assurance that he had the right stuff for Haden Brothers. He wondered exactly how he smelt to a blind person, having spent a long time in the bathroom that morning trying to make sure that he smelt of nothing at all. A lift attendant was hardly an unimpeachable source on matters of company employment policy but somehow Charlie trusted him. He started to feel a great respect and then considerable sympathy for the man. Someone with a fine nose like that should be working as a wine taster or a perfumier, not in a lift. It seemed a criminal waste.

These finer feelings were interrupted when another person entered the reception area. It was a young woman, a girl even, perhaps no older than nineteen or twenty. That she was beautiful he had no doubt, but more than that, she was obviously special. She was rare and warm and sexy yet she also looked extremely business-like. The clothes and the manner said confidence and clipped efficiency, yet there was no apparent aggression or hardness to her. He immediately assumed she had to be some high-flier in the Haden Brothers organization. However, she announced herself to the receptionist – he heard her say her name was Vita Carlisle – and when the receptionist spoke to her in much the same way that he'd spoken to Charlie, it became clear that she too was there looking for a job.

She sat down on a sofa that was a reserved, respectable distance away from Charlie. He caught her eye and flashed her a smile that he hoped was attractive and winning. She smiled back, but her smile was less committed than his, less warm, less calculating too. He knew it was bad strategy to start chatting to her immediately; that looked too obvious, as though he did this kind of thing all the time. He hoped they would be kept waiting a good long while, which would give him both opportunity and reason to begin talking to her.

But they had barely been seated together a minute or so when the receptionist strode over and handed them each an application form. 'Perhaps you'd be good enough to fill in these while you're waiting,' he piped, charmingly. He offered to give them pens, but she declined, having her own gold-nibbed fountain pen. Even Charlie had one of his own but it was a chewed and wretched thing compared to the elegance of hers. She rested the form on her briefcase, while he had to make do with a copy of the *Economist* taken from a pile on a nearby table.

The form was dispiritingly long. Details of birth, education and marital status were straightforward enough, although the form didn't allow enough room for all the information it demanded. Then there were pages and pages for previous employment, with boxes for inserting exact starting and finishing dates, job title, full job description, responsibilities, details of training and promotion, and starting and finishing salaries. Then there was an ominously large expanse with the legend, 'Give full and precise reasons for leaving former employment', followed by another, equally large, headed, 'State what you achieved in your last job in terms of skills, responsibilities and self-growth'.

Vita Carlisle began filling in her form with an energetic fluency. For Charlie it was different. He had only had three or four jobs in his life, and they had been temporary, part-time or terrible; or all three. He had picked up no skills, had been given no responsibilities, had certainly not experienced any 'self-growth', and had generally left under a cloud. Both starting and finishing salaries had been pitiful. He did his fumbling best to spread disinformation through these sections of the form.

There was then a series of questions requiring yes/no answers, in which he had to state that he suffered from no wasting or contagious diseases, had no history of mental instability, that he belonged to no illegal organizations, and that, in the event of being given a job at Haden Brothers, he would be prepared to sign some local equivalent of the Official Secrets Act. Then there were some questions about his religious beliefs, political affiliations and sexual preferences, although these were labelled 'for reference only'.

Charlie would have been happy to storm out of the personnel department in a fit of feigned if justifiable outrage at these intrusive requests for information. Who did Haden Brothers think they were? But he could still picture the horrors of the social security system and, just as bad, he could imagine Sarah's scathing anger if he said he'd thrown away his chance of a job. And for that matter he would also lose his chance of chatting up Vita Carlisle. So he continued filling in the form as best he could. However, he ground to a complete halt at the question, 'Why do you want to work at Haden Brothers?' There were two whole blank pages for his answer.

He looked at Vita Carlisle. Her knees were pressed tightly together.

Her head was tilted in thought, her hair tucked behind one ear. Her creative juices were really flowing. Her pen was dancing relentlessly across the form. She was writing an essay, a dissertation. Charlie felt inadequate but tried to remain cool. Ater a long pause for thought he gave his reasons for wanting to work at Haden Brothers as, 'Because it's *the* place to work!!!' He hoped there would be marks for conciseness. He closed the form and sat silently looking around him; the exam candidate who's either got everything right or everything wrong.

When at long last Vita had finished, her form was a mass of blue-black italic script, compared to Charlie's few ballpoint jottings. Now she allowed herself to smile at him. It was a sweet smile. He raised his eyebrows as if to say, 'What a lot of nonsense this form is, eh?' but she didn't seem to understand. She certainly didn't respond. Separately they got up and gave their completed forms to the receptionist, and returned to their seats. Now it seemed possible for them to talk.

'Nice fountain pen you have there,' he said.

'Thank you,' she replied graciously, no doubt accustomed to far more significant compliments.

'It looks very handsome,' he said.

'Yes, it's a Parker. A Presidential International from the Duofold collection. It makes writing a pleasure,' she said. 'It was a present from my mother.'

'Oh, right.'

'She got it here at Haden Brothers, actually.'

'Now there's a coincidence.'

'Not really,' said Vita.

They sat in silence for a while, a silence that Charlie found more oppressive than she did.

'I say,' he said suddenly and jokily, 'do you come here often?'

He laughed, not because he was given to laughing at his own jokes, but because he wanted her to know that he was being ironic, that even minutes before a job interview he could be funny, irreverent and urbane.

'Well, not for a job, obviously' she said, missing his joke. 'Though I do shop here quite often if that's what you mean. Or were you joking?'

He made a big open-handed gesture with which he attempted to imply that his remark could be taken seriously or facetiously depending entirely on her whim.

'I think you *were* joking,' she said. 'I suppose it's rather funny, isn't it? As if we were at a dance or something.'

Charlie smiled broadly, encouragingly at her.

'But if you're being serious,' she continued, 'I suppose I've been coming to Haden Brothers all my life. My mother says she first brought me here when I was six weeks old. I just love it here. Working here would be a dream come true.'

'Did you put that on the application form?'

'No,' she said. 'I thought it might sound too gushing.'

'Could be,' he said.

'Haden Brothers has always seemed to me the very ideal of what the shopping experience ought to be like,' she continued.

'Hey,' said Charlie, 'you're not in the interview yet. You'll peak too soon.'

'Perhaps you're right.'

Despite Charlie's efforts to be suave and charming, they made awkward and desultory conversation until at last the receptionist said, 'Our Mr Snell will see you now.' Both of them gave a 'do you mean me?' look and the receptionist nodded back and said, 'He'd like to see you together.'

This put them firmly on the same side, a development that Charlie thought could do no harm. The receptionist led them from the bright reception area down an increasingly mean and gloomy corridor until they came to a small, scratched, dirty little door labelled, in self-adhesive black and gold letters, Mr Derek Snell. The receptionist knocked and then whisked himself away before the room's occupant opened the door and popped his head out like a large, gloomy cuckoo.

Derek Snell was no fashion victim, or at least he had been victimized in about 1975 and had never entirely recovered. He wore a brown Viyella suit with wide lapels and deep turn-ups, a chunky knitted wool tie, a shirt with a flapping collar and a pattern of tiny veteran car motifs. He was a toothy, slim-chinned man, about forty-five with a lot of gingery hair that curled round his head like a tarnished halo. He did not look especially pleased to see them.

'Welcome to Haden Brothers,' he said mournfully and unconvincingly, and he beckoned them into a surprisingly tiny, shabby, disordered office. There were three chairs of unmatching heights. Snell took the tall tubular one that might have come from a breakfast bar. Vita sat down on the most orthodox, a grey plastic stacking chair, although it had one leg alarmingly shorter than the other three so that the slightest change in weight distribution sent her and the chair lurching and pitching dangerously. Charlie descended into a broken, squashed, corduroy armchair that put him some two feet lower than Snell.

'I'm Derek Snell,' he said unenthusiastically. 'I have responsibility for personnel, though in fact my brief is much, much wider than that.'

Vita and Charlie saw no reason to respond to this statement.

'Oh well,' Snell continued, 'first of all I suppose I have to take a couple of snapshots of you both. Nothing sinister, just for the records, for the ID cards, and so I can remember you.'

He pulled an old Polaroid Swinger from his desk drawer and from his high perch took pictures of Charlie and Vita. Then he held out the prints for their perusal as the creamy images coalesced out of the blackness. Even in a half-developed Polaroid Vita looked luminously beautiful to Charlie, in contrast to the bleached, pasty face that was being made out of his own features. When they were fully developed Snell looked at them, spending conspicuously more time gazing at Vita's picture than at Charlie's. He wasn't happy with the results so he took two more shots of Vita. Then he tossed the photographs on to the cluttered, coffee-stained, ash-strewn surface of his desk.

'Well,' said Snell, 'I've been perusing your application forms and they're both absolutely fine. So which departments would you like to work in?'

He said it quietly and lifelessly, and Charlie, having envisaged a rather more rigorous selection process, thought he must have missed something. He asked politely, 'Are you really offering me a job? Just like that?'

'Yes, of course. Aren't you pleased? Oh dear, didn't you think I would?'

Snell attempted a laugh, but his heart wasn't in it. It was the laugh of a man who had been practising the art of laughter, despite having no natural talent for it.

'I just thought it would take longer, that's all,' said Charlie.

'Oh dear no,' said Snell. 'Time is money. We can spot the Haden Brothers type without going through a lot of time-wasting routines.'

Charlie wondered if Snell and the lift man were in communication. Maybe the lift man's olfactory interrogation had been all that was required.

'So which department?' Snell repeated wearily.

'Mr Snell,' said Vita, 'it would be an honour and a pleasure for me to work absolutely anywhere in this great store of yours.'

Charlie thought this was plain nauseating and he couldn't believe that a personnel man would fall for it, but Snell looked well satisfied with her answer. Then he turned to Charlie. 'And how about you, Mr Mayhew? Where should we slot you in?'

'Well, you see, the thing is,' said Charlie, 'I don't really plan to be at Haden Brothers forever.'

'Who amongst us does?'

'But I'm talking very short term. You see I have ambitions in other directions. I'm creative. I intend to make my way in the world of the arts and media. I just think you ought to know that.'

'Thank you for sharing it with us,' said Snell, and Charlie wondered if he was being mocked. 'So which department?'

'Let's be honest about it,' said Charlie. 'I can't exactly see myself selling ladies' twinsets.'

'No?'

'Well, no. And I'd just as soon not work in the sports department because I'm not a very sporty person. And I can't really see myself measuring inside legs or selling soft furnishings.'

'Do you know anything about car accessories?' Snell enquired.

'No,' said Charlie.

'Or costume jewellery?'

'Not really.'

'Or hi-fi?'

'Possibly,' said Charlie, realizing it might be as well to make some sort of positive noise.

'Or binoculars?'

'Conceivably.'

'Let me think about that for a moment,' said Snell and he rubbed his temples and gazed sadly at a noticeboard on his wall. Charlie felt some burdensome responsibility for this sadness.

'There is one special option I have up my sleeve,' said Snell.

Charlie, and Vita too, willed him to find some crumb of happiness in that option.

'You see, even in a store as efficient and well-regulated as Haden Brothers,' said Snell, 'little crises still occur from time to time. Staff go on extended holidays or suffer from industrial injuries. New departments are set up, sudden outbreaks of stock shrinkage may occur. There may be shortages in the tills. Members of staff may suddenly discover they can no longer tolerate working together. Push may come to shove between rival assistant buyers. There may be a suicide attempt. There may be improper goings on in the stockrooms. Oh dear, it all sounds a bit bleak, doesn't it? It's not, believe me. At other times there may be special sales promotions or we may need staff to dress up as furry animals.

'And not any old member of staff can slot into a delicate situation like that. So we have a team called the Flying Squad; specially able and gifted employees who are diplomatic, skilful and hardworking. They receive a great deal of trust and respect, and they get to wear a special lapel badge. How does that sound, Miss Carlisle?'

'It sounds like a wonderful challenge,' she said with what appeared to be utter sincerity.

'And, of course,' said Snell, 'it makes for a very good grounding if you're hoping to go into management one day.'

'I am, actually,' she said.

'Well, Miss Carlisle, in that case, please consider yourself the latest member of the Flying Squad. Start tomorrow. Report to staff entrance F at 8.30 a.m.'

'Yes, I'd be prepared to give that a go, too,' Charlie piped up.

'Oh dear,' said Snell. 'I don't want to be hurtful, but are you sure you're ready for the Flying Squad, Mr Mayhew?'

'I think so, yes.'

'Do you? Oh dear. I'm not so sure.'

Charlie had been frantically trying to think of any department in which he actually did want to work. If he wasn't going to make the Flying Squad he thought he'd better come up with an idea pretty soon or it might be too late.

'OK then,' he said, 'if not the Flying Squad then maybe there'd be something for me in publicity or public relations, or advertising, or even working on the staff newsletter.'

Derek Snell shook his head glumly.

'Oh dear, I really don't think so, but I have thought of a niche for you,' he said. 'I can just see you as a junior furniture porter. Start tomorrow. Report to staff entrance F at 8.30 a.m. Don't bother to wear the suit.'

Minutes later, bemused, depressed and with a slim pamphlet in his hand entitled 'Haden Brothers – Your Part in Their Continuing Success', Charlie was back in the lift, Vita Carlisle beside him, the blind lift attendant going through his paces as they descended, stopping at each floor. It seemed to Charlie that the attendant was sniffing out an entirely different set of departments on the way down from the ones he had announced on the way up.

'Well, that wasn't too painful, was it?' said Vita cheerily.

'Not for you,' Charlie replied.

'Nor for you, I would have thought. You got a job, after all.'

'I got offered a job as a junior furniture porter. That's fairly painful. I accepted it, that's more painful still.'

'I'm sure being a junior furniture porter can be very rewarding,' she said.

'Oh sure.'

'And if you're good at it you'll be promoted.'

'To what? Senior furniture porter?'

'The young lady's quite right,' the lift attendant chipped in. 'It's just a first rung on the ladder.'

'But what's at the top of the ladder?' Charlie said.

'A first-rate career with a retailing giant,' said Vita.

'Or possibly,' said the lift attendant, 'the ladder has no top.'

'I see,' said Charlie. 'It's a Zen ladder, right?'

'It's what you make it,' said Vita.

Charlie, now at least as gloomy as Derek Snell, said, 'I just can't see it.'

'Don't be depressed,' said Vita. 'How about a cup of coffee?'

Charlie said farewell to the lift attendant and they went for a cup of coffee in the Sissinghurst Cafeteria. In other circumstances this invitation from Vita might have been a dream come true – the woman making the running – but Charlie was too fed up to think in those terms. Once seated at a corner table in the cafeteria, Charlie let it all come out; that he needed this job but didn't want it, that he needed the money, that he needed somewhere to live, but that he needed to be an artist even more.

'What sort of artist? A painter?'

'No,' he said definitely, 'although the visual arts would surely come into it. I suppose I'm hoping to achieve a synthesis: music, language, the plastic arts; put it all together, make it new, make it my own.'

'Sounds terrific.'

'Sounds better than being a furniture porter, right?' he said. 'You see, virtually anything can be art. Bricks can be art, fat and felt can be art, leaving a block of ice at the corner of a city street, throwing some gold leaf in the river, that can be art. It's all there waiting to be discovered.'

'Well then,' she said brightly, 'maybe working as a furniture porter could be art.'

'No,' said Charlie, 'I don't think so somehow.'

When they'd finished their coffee he asked for her phone number. She hesitated. She was about to write it on a paper napkin for him, then she said they'd probably see each other tomorrow morning anyway, and thereafter they'd be working in the same store, so they would be sure to run into each other from time to time. Charlie didn't try to persuade her. There were days when he might have taken her refusal as a hurtful snub, but today he preferred to see it as a sign of commendable caution, an old-fashionedness, a desire on her part to be courted and wooed. It was a day for grasping at straws.

Up in his office on the eighth floor Derek Snell was rereading Vita Carlisle's application form, and again confirming to himself that it was a beauty. He loved the part which said she was head girl at her boarding school on the Sussex coast, and the part where she said her hobbies were church music and horse riding. It said that her father was a doctor, that she had gone to university precociously early and had studied geography. She had been, in her own words, a 'live wire' in the university orienteering society.

Her previous work experience was brief but classy: researcher for a Tory MP and personal assistant to an antique dealer. Snell didn't recognize the name of either MP or dealer, but he liked the sound of it. His pleasure was so profound that it did not occur to him to question why someone with a CV like that would be applying for a shop assistant's job, or to check whether any of the information was true, but then he had other things on his mind.

He looked closely at the handwriting, a silky flow allied to a firm, regular pressure; so revealing, so in character, so naked. He folded the form neatly and slid it into his inside pocket. And he looked again at the Polaroids of her and confirmed that she was perfect, ideal. He pocketed those too. Later he would find private uses for both form and photograph.

Charlie's application form remained on the desk, becoming part of the sediment that would eventually be transferred to an out-tray, to be misplaced by some incompetent filing clerk.

When Charlie got home from the interview he felt in his jacket pocket and discovered it contained a fountain pen, Vita Carlisle's Parker. He hadn't the slightest idea how it had got there but he supposed he must have picked it up without thinking, probably after they'd filled out their application forms. In a way it was fortunate. It would give him an excuse to seek out Vita, and he was starting to think that he wanted to seek her out very much indeed. It wasn't love at first sight or anything convenient and literary like that, but he found himself in some admiration of her. She had glided through the interview process with an ease that he could not possibly hope to emulate. She had charm and talent, and she told lies with an efficiency that he had to envy. He hoped that if he got to know her a little better some of those manifest skills might rub off on him.

ARNOLD HADEN: It was perhaps in the nature of terrorism that terrorist acts should be irrational, inscrutable and above all unpredictable. The bomb in the school bus terrifies far more effectively than the one in the army barracks. Yet to launch an attack on a department store is surely not entirely illogical.

Terrorism, it could be argued, is some late, dark and diseased flowering of dispossession. This dispossession may be crude or subtle but is inevitably concerned with history and economics. Terrorists inevitably feel unconnected to, uninvolved with, the society they choose to terrorize, even if that society is their own. They have no vested interests. They have nothing to lose. This is not where they make their home. They are just passing through.

The world of exchange, of transaction, of retailing, of the buying and selling of goods, the world of (for want of a better word) shopping is precisely one of connection and involvement. Shoppers have vested interests in what they buy. They have a lot to lose.

This, of course, sounds banal. Do freedom and democracy exist merely to safeguard such humdrum pleasures as the joys of home and hearth, the new bedroom suite, the tea set, the picnic hamper? Well, on balance, probably yes. Perhaps that's what winning the war against terrorism buys us; the right to live in peace, to shop in peace, to gather to us those objects which make us feel secure and accommodated. It is the terrorist's avowed role to subvert that security and accommodation; and there are those who are stupid enough to say it is the artist's role too.

3 · KNOBS AND KNOCKERS

Vita Carlisle has been sitting motionless for some time now. At first it seemed she was deep in thought, but the longer she sits the more blank she appears, as though she's doing nothing more than day-dreaming. She doesn't look like the sort of woman who might blow herself up, though Arnold Haden realizes that looks may mean nothing in a situation like this.

At last she says, 'I know what you may be thinking, Arnold. You may be thinking that this dynamite isn't real.'

As a matter of fact that thought has not occurred to him at all. He needs no convincing about the reality of his situation.

'You're thinking, where would a young woman like me get hold of real dynamite. It's not as though you can walk into a department store and buy it.'

'That's true,' says Arnold.

'Well, let me tell you it's very easy indeed,' says Vita. 'It gets stolen from quarries, from demolition sites, from army bases. It happens all the time. You need a few contacts, a few friends in the right places, but it really isn't so hard to come by.'

'I'm sure that's true, too,' Arnold agrees.

'Not that logically it makes any difference as far as you and I are concerned. The fact that I *could* have got my hands on real dynamite doesn't necessarily mean that I did, does it?'

Arnold Haden nods. Yes, he can see the logic of that.

'But maybe that's the nature of terror,' says Vita. 'Uncertainty is a valuable weapon. *Fearing* you're going to be blown up could be just as terrifying as *knowing* that you're going to be blown up.'

'Not quite, I don't think,' says Haden.

'No, perhaps not quite. And in any case, you can take my word for it. It *is* real dynamite.'

'I believe you. Really.'

'I thought of using a gun,' she says matter of factly. 'I thought of coming up here and threatening to blow your head off with it. But something told me I might not be able to do that. I thought that when I got right down to it my hand might shake too much and I might miss. That would have been a disaster. It's much easier with dynamite.'

'Is it?' he asks. 'Is killing us both really going to be easier than just killing me?'

'Oh yes,' she replies confidently.

'Isn't that a little odd?'

'It probably is, but I suspect we're talking about self-hatred here,' Vita admits.

'I suspect we are,' he agrees and he looks away, falling into a silence of his own. Self-hatred, as he knows only too well, is a massively destructive force. Vita joins him in his silence and they sit in mute melancholy for some time. Then Arnold says, 'This isn't just about sex, is it?'

She looks at him dismissively and with distaste, but he wants to talk this through.

'I know I tried to seduce you,' he says, 'and it's true I wanted to have sex with you; in fact I suppose I still do. All right, that might not be exactly what you want. I know I'm not an attractive man but my feelings for you are genuine. I know I'm not a young girl's dream, but in the world of desire and exchange, I honestly thought we could have come to an arrangement that would have satisfied us both.'

'Did you really?' says Vita.

'And even if I disgusted you, and even if you think I pursued you too hard, and even if you think I abused my position as an employer, and even if that made you angry and caused you to want revenge, and even if you think I'm some sort of monster, well, I still think you're overreacting a little here.'

She looks at him thoughtfully, giving his words due consideration before saying, 'You're right. This isn't just about sex.'

Arnold Haden is glad to have established that.

'In that case,' he says, 'is it about what we might call capitalism?'

She perks up a little at that and shows a glimmer of interest. Arnold Haden is encouraged.

He says, 'Is it perhaps something to do with the fact that I'm an employer? I know Haden Brothers doesn't treat its staff so very well. We have no unions. I know that some of our staff, particularly the ancillary workers, have a lot of trouble making ends meet on the wages we pay. I know a lot of them aren't happy.'

'No, it's not that,' says Vita.

'And then you could condemn Haden Brothers' position in the wider world,' he continues. 'We buy from countries where the workers are abused and exploited. We deal with corrupt and repressive regimes. We buy cash crops. Is that it?'

'Don't be silly,' says Vita. 'You don't kill somebody because of things like that.'

'Don't you? Some people do.'

'OK, Arnold, I'm sure you know more about this than I do.'

He tries again. 'I couldn't argue with you if you said that Haden Brothers fills people's homes with a lot of tawdry goods which they neither need nor want, nor can truly afford. You could say we foster blind acquisition. You could say we supply so-called luxury goods to a crowd of undiscriminating, soulless consumers. You'd get no argument from me.'

'Oh come on, Arnold. What do you think I am?'

'I don't know what you are. Why don't you tell me.'

She shrugs, and for a moment she looks girlish, almost childlike. Arnold Haden finds that very attractive in a woman, and his love for her wells back, and for a moment he finds it difficult to believe she really wants to kill him at all. Difficult, but not impossible, and Vita is clearly not about to tell him her reasons. He has to carry on.

'Maybe you want to be a martyr, a folk heroine like Astrid Proll or Patty Hearst or Ulrike Meinhof. I can sympathize with that too.'

'Who?' she says. 'Who are these people?'

'You've really never heard these names?'

'No, who are they?'

Arnold Haden feels some relief. She may be a mad revolutionary but at least she doesn't know her history.

'Well, a lot of people would call them terrorists,' he says. 'But they were ordinary women, much like yourself, women who took a wrong turning somewhere, met the wrong man or had a bad experience of society and decided to take their revenge. Personally, I find it easy to think of them as victims.'

Vita smiles. She appears to find that a satisfying concept.

'Is that it, Vita? Have you been victimized? Are you part of some liberation army? Have you been brainwashed? Forced to do this against your will?'

'No,' she says. 'I don't represent anybody but myself.'

'Really? You have no allies, no party, no organization?'

She knows it would help a lot if she could claim revolutionary comrades and an underground movement that was all set to mobilize, but she can't bring herself to lie to Arnold Haden, not any more.

'Why would I tell you that?' she says.

'Why indeed?' Arnold agrees. 'But I do think you ought to tell me why you're doing this?'

'No,' she says. 'Not yet.'

'But eventually you will?'

'I suppose so. I suppose I'll tell you before I kill you. Before I kill us both.'

'Thanks. I'd appreciate that.'

'What is the *matter* with you, Arnold?' she shrieks. 'I know you're supposed to be a bit of a weirdo, but here I am threatening to blow you up and you're treating it like a sixth-form debate. That's really crazy, Arnold!!'

'I'm sorry,' he says. 'I really am. But the simple fact is, I'm not frightened any more.'

'Jesus,' says Vita.

'But do you think you could grant me one last request?'

'Possibly,' says Vita.

'Let's go through into my penthouse and have a little drink.'

4

Haden Brothers
YOUR PART IN THEIR CONTINUING SUCCESS
Beginner's Guide and Staff Manual

Hello. Welcome to the exciting and challenging world of retailing at Haden Brothers.

And congratulations! If you're reading this booklet it probably means you have just been offered a job in our great store. Well done! You're one of us now. Whether you're planning to stay with us for a couple of months or whether you're intending to start a long and glorious career, you're equally welcome.

But be careful. Many of those who thought they were just passing through have found themselves here for life. And what a rich and fulfilling life that has always turned out to be!!

What is Haden Brothers?

Haden Brothers is a store of contrasts where the ultra modern rubs shoulders with the ultra traditional.

Once our customers arrived by horse-drawn carriage to purchase jodhpurs and top hats. Today they arrive by Ferrari to buy state-of-the-art televisions and CD players. But they can still buy jodhpurs and top hats too!!!

Haden Brothers is for many an Aladdin's cave, a cornucopia of good things. Haden Brothers is another planet, a sunnier and better place, for staff as well as shoppers. It is indeed a kind of Eldorado, a little glimpse of shoppers' and shop assistants' heaven.

» • «

The first thing to remember is that Haden Brothers is big! It has nine floors above ground level and several below. It has 400 departments and 200,000 square yards of selling space. That's BIG!! It makes Harrods or Selfridges or Macy's or Bloomingdales seem like small potatoes.

At any given moment *Haden Brothers* contains enough carpet to furnish over 600 three-bedroomed houses, enough light bulbs to decorate 6,500 full-size Christmas trees, enough staff to form over 700 soccer teams or 500 rugby union sides (including substitutes).

There are enough ballpoint pens to write out the complete works of Shakespeare 20,000 times over, enough paper bags to wrap Buckingham Palace 150 times, enough shoes, socks and casualwear to provide the entire British Civil Service with complete new wardrobes.

In the event of a power cut *Haden Brothers* has its own generators. It has its own printing press, its own in-house recycling plant, and its own water supply thanks to an artesian well deep below the gardening and DIY department.

It has an on-site medical centre where staff can receive medical, dental and chiropody treatment. There is a team of counsellors and therapists, and a chaplain.

Many places that are proud to call themselves cities contain fewer facilities, splendours and people than *Haden Brothers*. And it is an open city. All are welcome. There are no passports, no customs barriers, no quotas, no quarantine requirements.

Haden Brothers is a real community. You will find people of all beliefs, all ages and classes and races and sexual persuasions working in this store. Of course there are limits to this. Nobody wants to buy a Versace suit from some working-class oik, nobody wants to buy Paracetamol from some Christian Scientist, and nobody expects people of colour to want to demean themselves by selling polo or croquet equipment.

» • «

It wouldn't be true to say that you can buy absolutely anything at *Haden Brothers*. There are certain items that obviously we simply cannot stock but we are always happy to take special orders.

Nevertheless, *Haden Brothers*, as far as most people are concerned, and for all working purposes, contains everything and more.

But who are the Haden Brothers?

Alas, there is currently only one Haden Brother, Mr Arnold Haden. His brother Mr Timothy Haden died in a tragic road accident along with Mr Arnold's wife. Mr Arnold has never married again so at present there are no heirs, no Haden brothers of the future.

Mr Arnold Haden is the third generation of Haden brothers to spearhead our organization. His grandfather and his great uncle established the business on another site and in rather humbler premises in 1899.

Mr Arnold Haden is in many ways a legendary figure, but you should not believe all you have read or heard about him. He is a warm and lively character, a shrewd businessman yet also friendly and approachable. He is a proper gentleman. He is as English as roast beef, as Shakespeare, as the Queen of England.

Organization of the store

A structure as large and complex as *Haden Brothers* is never going to be easy to explain, or to understand. But here, in layman's terms, is an outline.

At the very pinnacle of the organization is Mr Arnold Haden. Beneath him is a group of senior executives, creative executives and special executives. Also at this level are a number of quasi-autonomous controllers, administrators, supervisors and promotions managers who report to heads of budgeting, advertising and publicity.

There are marketing and departmental managers, and there are a variety of permanently sitting 'retail committees' which constantly review sales, profits and image.

Moving down in descending order we pass through merchandise managers, section managers, department and floor managers. They work hand in hand with buyers, deputy buyers, assistant buyers and trainee buyers. Then there are shop assistants in grades one to five, members of the 'Flying Squad' occupying the highest level.

Supporting this basic structure are hundreds of secretarial and accountancy staff, display girls, store detectives, drivers, carpenters, electricians, handymen, etc., etc. . . .

Finally there are the ancillary workers: cleaners, bin emptiers, dish washers, right down to such lowly people as junior furniture porters.

Every one of these employees has his or her place in the scheme of things and they will do well so long as they remember exactly what that place is.

What *Haden Brothers* can offer you

1) Security
Haden Brothers isn't some fly by night operation.

2) Training
We at *Haden Brothers* are deeply committed to training and education, and a small hierarchy of specialist personnel takes care of our in-house training and educational needs.

At *Haden Brothers* you'll be given skills training, commodity training, systems training, human relations training, to name but a few. Our induction training is second to none. After a while you might experience retraining or re-education.

Quite simply, our training is the best! That's why we make our employees sign a contract stating that they won't work for another retailing organization within six years of leaving our employment. Though frankly, after you've worked at *Haden Brothers*, where else is there to go?

3) Welfare
We'll see you all right.

4) Money
Yes, we'll even pay you to work at *Haden Brothers*, though many of our employees swear they'd work here for nothing. Some would even pay to work here!! Which is a good thing, since we don't want staff who are only in it for the money.

5) Unions
We are all one at *Haden Brothers* and see no need for organized labour.

Disciplinary matters

We run a necessarily tight ship at *Haden Brothers*. We believe in discipline and responsibility, in fair play and straight talking.

The following offences can and will result in instant dismissal: pilfering, bad time-keeping, use of telephone for personal calls, stealing office stationery, unauthorized use of xerox and fax machines, prolonged and non-work-related conversations with other members of staff, excessive or unnatural use of the toilets, working under the influence of drink or drugs, insubordination, political activism, talking to newspaper and/or television reporters, sexual dalliance on company time, physical or verbal abuse of customers or superiors.

Alas, we have had to dismiss staff for all the above offences in recent times. There are no second chances at *Haden Brothers*.

The customer and you

Just about anyone and everyone can be our customers. We serve kings and queens by Royal Appointment. H. G. Wells and Kirk Douglas are just two of our many account customers of the past.

We serve tardy schoolboys who want to spend their pocket money wisely in our toy department. One of those schoolboys may grow up to be a captain of industry. That impecunious couple who are today buying a humble pair of twisted gold Creole earrings from our jewellery department may one day be furnishing a whole house in Cheyne Walk.

A final word

If you play your cards right, *Haden Brothers* can offer the new employee everything and more, and is it unreasonable that we expect the same thing in return?

» • «

A NOTE ABOUT OUR BUILDING

The current *Haden Brothers* building was erected between 1930 and 1933. The original intention had been to employ Frank Lloyd Wright, but he proved to be too expensive and too uncommitted. Eric Mendelsohn, in many ways the father of modern department store design, was then approached. He did complete some preliminary sketches of what would have been an imposing and elegant structure with wide glass expanses, slender metal frames and bronze window sills, but the project came to nothing. In some haste the commission was given to Edward Zander, an architect often referred to as a 'maverick visionary'.

It was his conception that the store should resemble Bruegel's painting of the Tower of Babel, a conceit that even in 1930 might have seemed to be asking for trouble. Bruegel's image was based on his observations of the ruins of the Colosseum in Rome, and any depiction of the Tower of Babel must inevitably produce thoughts concerning the vanity of human wishes. A structure that would bring down the wrath of God and send its makers into uncomprehending disarray might not be thought of as the ideal design for a successful department store, but the plan went ahead nevertheless.

Of course the building is not literally a replica of the ruin depicted in Bruegel's painting. If nothing else, having an asymmetrically shaped island site on which to build would have prevented the building having the necessary circular ground plan. But its general form and outline show an unmistakable resemblance. Certainly the building seems to have nine floors for no other reason than because Bruegel's tower did, and the curious, unfinished look is clearly harking back to the divine interruption.

However, Zander's building has few of the rhythms, repetitions or classical form of its supposed model. Rather it suggests a series of multiple codings, elements of Russian Constructivism, Italian Renaissance and stuccoed Baroque. It is decked, as though at random, with crenellated parapets, pantile roofs, ogee arches, steel balconies, oriel windows and flying buttresses. Carved into the fabric of the building are angels, putti and mythological beasts. There are gargoyles, caryatids, mosaics, expanses of Moorish tiling and some magnificent stained-glass. Zander had envisaged a menagerie on the ninth floor and wanted the whole building to be painted blood red, but he was talked out of these schemes.

There are numerous architectural jokes within the building; disorientating effects achieved with mirrors, false perspectives and *trompe-l'œil*. And it is rumoured that the store was built with a number of secret chambers and passages, but, if so, they have remained secret to this day.

Zander claimed that this diversity of architectural feature was a conscious echo of the diversity of goods that would be on sale inside. The building was ahead of its time and yet its quirky beauty is timeless. It has been hailed as an Ur-Post-Modern triumph by Charles Jencks, while Pevsner called it a 'wilful accumulation'. More prosaically it has been described as a cathedral of consumerism and few could argue with that description.

The interior of the store has been remodelled and refurbished many times since its inception and its architect would recognize little of his design there. Nevertheless, his expansive use of space and light, the grand sweeping internal balconies, the central hall with its fountains, plaster centaurs and marble busts of Clara Bow remain untouched.

It is one of the few sad footnotes to the *Haden Brothers* saga that this building was the last Edward Zander ever worked on. Perhaps knowing that his masterpiece was complete he slipped into obscurity and poverty and was never heard of again. *Haden Brothers* remains his monument.

5 · HARD FURNISHINGS

Charlie reread the pamphlet as he rode the tube on his way to his first day at work. He was not dreading this day nearly as much as he might have. For one thing the promise of 'induction training' seemed to augur well. He guessed it would involve sitting in a lecture room while some minor flunky from the personnel department went over company policy, staff rules, fire regulations, that sort of thing. If there was then a question and answer session, the procedure could surely be dragged out to take up most of the day. This would be much, much better than working. But, more importantly, the day would also give him the chance to see Vita again, and that was enough to drive away any dread he might have of work.

To his great delight and considerable surprise, he saw her the very moment he emerged from the tube station. The street was dense with commuters but she moved through them with a cool serenity. He thought there was no crowd in which she would not stand out. But she did not see him. She sailed on in the direction of Haden Brothers, swift and determined, and he had to push his way robustly between bodies in order to catch up with her, then he touched her gently on the shoulder and said an enthusiastic hello. He immediately feared he'd been a little too enthusiastic and not nearly gentle enough. She spun round as if stung and stepped back as though Charlie was some foul and repulsive drunk.

'It's me,' he said brightly.

She stared at him, examining him closely but noncommittally. 'Oh yes,' she said appearing only dimly able to place him but inclined to be polite. 'And how are you?'

'I'm really fine,' he said. 'And you?'

She continued to scrutinize him and gradually she seemed to recall who he was and how they'd met, and her good nature returned slightly.

'Oh, it's you. You look different without the suit,' she said, by way of explanation.

'I guess so.'

'I suppose you're like me, terribly excited to be starting the new job,' she said.

'Oh sure,' he replied.

'I thought you'd have got used to the idea of being a furniture porter by now,' she said.

'Afraid not.'

'You'll soon discover whether or not you can cope with the work. And if you can't, well the only decent thing to do is resign.'

'It sounds simple when you put it like that.'

'It's not so very complicated,' she said.

He didn't believe her, and he was aware that his half-heartedness wasn't doing his cause much good. If he really wanted to impress her perhaps he ought to be as enthusiastic about work as she was, but that would have been asking too much.

'Maybe the two of us could have lunch together today,' he said.

'Well hardly,' she replied. 'Not today, not on our first day. I think there'll be far too much going on to accommodate a lunch date.'

He thought it best to agree, and consoled himself with the thought that at least he could make sure of sitting next to her throughout the induction. He had her fountain pen in his pocket and he intended to return it to her, but he didn't do so yet. It was an insurance policy, a way of ensuring that he still had a reason for seeing her again.

They arrived at the store and they took a side street that led round the rear of the building to the several staff entrances. Staff entrance F was a wide, square doorway with a rolling metal shutter for a door. This was down and locked shut, and there was a crowd of people standing around waiting to be let in.

'I suppose we just hang about,' Charlie said.

'Well no, *I* don't,' said Vita. 'You see I received a phone call from Mr Snell last night telling me there'd been a slight change of plan and to report to staff entrance A, instead of F. There it is over there.'

Charlie turned his eyes towards entrance A. There was a small but ornate glass porch around the doorway, gleaming white steps, a commissionaire and two meticulously clipped bay trees in terracotta pots. A red carpet would have been perfectly in keeping.

'So I'll possibly see you again one of these days,' she said.

'I do hope so, maybe we could . . . ' but she had left and was

46

walking towards the entrance without a backwards glance. The commissionaire saluted her and the glass mouth swallowed her up. Charlie was glad he hadn't mentioned the fountain pen.

Charlie stood at the edge of the crowd that mooched around outside staff entrance F. They were, to put the kindest possible interpretation on it, a chequered bunch; sullen, dowdily dressed with an air of inadequacy, of incompleteness about them. They lacked teeth and fingers, though they tended to possess limps, hunched backs and unappealing facial birthmarks. A few had only one arm or one leg, and a great many had twitches and tics. The only ones who looked whole were a small group of noisy, loutish, tough-looking young men who were standing around wearing only thin T-shirts despite the bitter coldness of the February weather.

Charlie didn't feel that any of these people were likely to become close and trusted colleagues. If anything, they frightened him, not because they looked particularly violent or threatening, although some did, but because they looked so utterly dispossessed. Despite his present lack of funds he had little experience of dispossession and he wanted to keep it that way.

He did his best to distance himself from the others by trying to look confident and capable, not like a loser, but he felt that nobody was likely to be deceived. He realized that to a casual passerby he might even look like one of them. The metal door showed no sign of being opened. He decided to walk round the outside of the store, to pass some time and to put some physical space between himself and the other plebs. He would look in the store's windows and familiarize himself with the kind of thing they sold at Haden Brothers.

The first window he came to was surrounded by a gang of cleaning staff. The window display showed a beach scene. There were canopied deckchairs, purple and gold bath towels and a family of mannequins in flowery swimming costumes. Their heads and arms were twisted at bizarre and often impossible angles, and they were adorned with exotic sunglasses, divers' watches, and, in the case of the mother of the family, a bloodstone tiara.

The cleaning crew were going at the window with a vehement determination and dedication, and after a moment Charlie saw they were doing their frantic best to remove a graffito that someone had spray-painted across the wide expanse of glass. But the crew's hard work hadn't achieved much and the words were still clearly legible, if not entirely comprehensible. Charlie might have expected the name of some football team, a political slogan perhaps or just somebody's scrawled initials, but instead the message read 'Hamnet was here'. Charlie stared at it for a while, in case he'd misread it, or in case the cleaning crew had already erased some vital part of the message that would have made its meaning clear, but this obviously wasn't so. He couldn't imagine what it meant, but neither did he imagine that it mattered much. In this, as in much else, he was mistaken, but he continued with his tour of the store's perimeter.

It took much longer than he would have expected, and after ten minutes he realized he ought to be getting back to staff entrance F. However, it seemed to him that he must already be more than halfway round the building, so it would be quicker to continue than to retrace his steps. But he was mistaken again. Even though he hurried, eventually breaking into a run, it was another fifteen minutes before he again arrived at the entrance. By then he was hot and flustered, and of course the door was now open and the crowd of employees had gone in.

He hurried inside. He would have preferred to have been on time but he was not so very disappointed to be late. He liked to think it showed a certain independence of spirit, and in any case the induction training would inevitably be slow to start. Surely the most he would have missed were a few minutes of general introductory chat. For Charlie there was no commissionaire and no salute. He found himself in a dark vestibule that smelt of disinfectant, and there was an old, angry-looking porter who immediately barred his way.

'Excuse me,' said Charlie, huffily. 'I'm starting work here today and I'm late already.'

The porter yelled at him. It was so loud and passionate that Charlie couldn't make out any of the words. 'Sorry?' he said, and the porter yelled something entirely different but equally incomprehensible. Charlie listened carefully. The man did not seem to be speaking English, nor any other language Charlie had ever heard. In fact, as he went on it sounded as though he might be speaking some entirely invented tongue, perhaps pidgin Esperanto, or possibly one that he was making up as he went along. Charlie looked at him questioningly and shrugged to show that he couldn't understand. This didn't make the porter any sweeter-tempered, but at least his bawling then became accompanied by gestures. He pointed at a number of racks on the wall that contained time cards and at a clock for clocking-in. Charlie went over to the racks and searched among the cards for his name. He couldn't find it. The porter came up behind him and yelled in a way that Charlie somehow recognized as a demand to know his name. Charlie told him. The porter looked along the row of cards and came up with one belonging to somebody called Maynard. He snapped it towards Charlie with a look of sneering triumph.

'But that's not my name,' Charlie said.

This stirred the porter to new heights of shouted ferocity, so Charlie took the card and clocked in with it. He hoped that there would be an opportunity to sort this out with the wages office later.

It seemed futile to ask the porter where he was supposed to go next, but the man waved his arms purposefully and shooed Charlie towards the rear of the vestibule into a long corridor with glossy walls painted a deep shade of mauve, ending in flapping rubber swing doors. Gingerly Charlie negotiated these doors and pushed his way into a dim, cavernous stockroom. It was chilly in there, and there was another smell, something more organic and potent than disinfectant, perhaps rotting vegetables or dirty towels. At either end of the stockroom there were towering massed rows of metal shelving. The ones to Charlie's right were completely empty, while the ones to his left were all stacked full of large, unlabelled cardboard boxes.

Charlie looked around him. He could see no way in or out of the room except through the swing doors and the place looked deserted. But he couldn't be absolutely sure so he walked up and down between the rows of shelves in hope of finding some sign of life. When he had thoroughly convinced himself that he was alone, there was an abrupt clap of hands behind him and he turned around to see a small black youth looking at him with real, if exaggerated, contempt. He looked incredibly young, barely into his teens. He was slight, even flimsy, and very short, though he had a cocky, obnoxious manner that might have belonged to someone much older, much bigger and more threatening. He wore a badge that said his name was Loz.

'Where've you been, man?' he demanded of Charlie.

Charlie didn't even try to tell him. In fact he didn't see that he owed any sort of explanation to this little urchin.

'I think I'm probably in the wrong place,' said Charlie.

'You're in the right place, all right.'

Charlie didn't see how this could be true.

'See those boxes?' said the youth. 'See those empty shelves?'

'Yes,' Charlie admitted.

'Well, put 'em together.'

'Look, I've only started work today. I mean I haven't started work at all. I haven't been told what to do.'

'I just told you what to do.'

'But I haven't been given any training.'

'How much training do you need to shift boxes? So shift 'em.'

'You mean you want me to take the boxes off the shelves they're on now and put them on those empty shelves at the other end of the room?'

The kid turned and walked away. Charlie took that to mean yes. He was left alone in the stockroom. He thought about walking out. Things were starting badly. He did not like being shouted at in strange languages and he didn't like being told what to do by obnoxious kids who looked too young to be in legal employment. He considered whether there was any element of racism in his resentment of the black youth, but cleared himself of all charges by deciding he'd have been equally resentful of being bossed around in such a manner by anyone, regardless of racial group. He was glad. Equally, he did not think it was because of a poor attitude towards authority. He recognized that in any job certain people had the right to tell you what to do. All he demanded was that they should tell him civilly. He hoped this wasn't going to be a problem. However, if it was, he saw that the resolution of his problem was simple enough. Vita had said it and it was even in the handbook. He did what he was told or he got out. But he was neither brave enough nor cowardly enough to get out quite yet.

The full boxes and the empty shelves beckoned. They were not enticing, not alluring, but they imposed themselves powerfully. He tested the weight of a box. It was very heavy but just about liftable. The empty shelves were some forty or fifty feet away from the full ones. Carrying the boxes across that distance would be back-breaking work. A trolley would have made the job much easier but there was no trolley to be seen. He thought Haden Brothers must be possessors of any number of trolleys, maybe even of fork lift trucks, but he didn't know where to look for one and there was nobody to ask.

He lifted the first of the boxes and carried it painstakingly across the length of the stockroom to a waiting empty shelf. He repeated the procedure with another box, and again with a third. He stood panting from the unaccustomed effort and he looked at his watch. It had taken him some ten minutes to complete these three journeys. He began counting the total number of boxes. A rough calculation told him there were over five hundred. Further mathematics told him that at his present rate it would take him at least three days to move all the boxes, and he knew that his present rate would slow down considerably as the day wore on and he became increasingly worn out.

He thought he had every reason to be angry, but in the event he just felt fed up. It felt like his first day at school, but there was no Mummy to run home to. He heaved a couple more boxes across the stockroom, glad that the sheer physical effort drove out the wimp in him. Then after a couple more boxes he began to feel self-righteous. Damn it all, they'd told him he was going to be a furniture porter. This work he was doing now hardly constituted furniture portering. He had envisaged carrying a small console table here, a standard lamp there. He had not been expecting relentless, solitary toil. And all right, even his version of being a furniture porter wasn't the most glamorous job in the world but it ranked considerably higher than what he was doing now. He thought they had a duty to give him the job they'd promised. He thought they had no right to treat him like this. At the same time he was aware that he didn't know precisely who 'they' were.

He worked on and he thought of Vita. No doubt she was now doing something cushy and comfortable; operating a till, doing a stock check, being nice to customers. Perhaps for people like her there really was induction training, although Charlie wasn't so sure. Already it seemed to him that Haden Brothers was a big sham, a place where reality and appearance failed to mesh, a place of broken promises. He also found it pretty galling that Derek Snell had phoned Vita at home.

He threw himself into the work again. He heaved the boxes around angrily and banged them down on to the shelves. And if there was something fragile inside them, and if he happened to break that something, he didn't care. It was only then that he began to wonder what was inside the boxes. They were robustly sealed with staples and tape but Charlie was determined to open one of them. When he had fought his way in and had rummaged through the paper and polystyrene chips inside, he discovered that the boxes contained a lot of much smaller boxes, perhaps four inches square, each printed with the Haden Brothers logo. He levered one of these out and opened it. Inside, swathed in tissue paper, was a souvenir of Haden Brothers, a snow storm scene. Inside the little water-filled, plastic dome was a minute model of the Haden Brothers building, and as Charlie shook the scene, flakes of white litter danced and swirled around the tiny, enclosed Tower of Babel.

For some reason he found that funny. He found it pathetic and stupid and meaningless too, but he allowed himself to be wryly amused. Carrying huge boxes of tiny toy versions of Haden Brothers from one set of shelving to another came very close to a perfect definition of meaningless toil, yet he felt it might have been worse. Had he been moving boxes of cutlery, or gardening tools or hand-carved chess sets, that would somehow have been even more insulting. The fact that he was involved in something so abstract and trivial impressed him with its basic, elemental rightness. This did not make the work any easier, of course, but for a short while he lost track of the time.

Somehow he got through the morning. By the end of it he was clammy with sweat and his back and arm muscles ached with exertion. He had never worked so hard. He had thought he was probably entitled to a tea break halfway through, but he had worked on, punishing himself to show his toughness. It was early afternoon before he started to crave lunch. On cue the black kid returned.

'You get half an hour for lunch,' he said, then surveyed the work Charlie had done. Charlie had no desire to please Loz but he thought there was no denying that he'd done a good morning's work.

'I could have done a lot more if someone had given me a trolley,' he said.

The kid didn't reply. He just stood shaking his head and looking superior.

'Hey,' he said. 'You got shit for brains or what?'

Charlie remained silent.

'I said shift the boxes didn't I?' the kid asked.

'Yes,' Charlie agreed.

'I never said nothing about shifting what's inside 'em.'

Charlie stopped dead. 'Are you really saying you wanted me to shift the boxes but not the contents? Are you?'

The kid said nothing.

'You wanted me to open the boxes, take out the contents, then stack the empty boxes on the shelves over there? Is that what you're trying to tell me? Is it? Then why the hell didn't you say so? Eh?'

'I don't owe you an explanation,' the kid said.

He was too cool to have a conversation, too cool to explain anything, too cool to say what he meant.

'After lunch you can do it right,' he said as he walked away.

All through his lunch break Charlie seethed with impotent anger. He trudged out of the stockroom, walked along the corridor that led to staff entrance F, the entrance now having become an exit. He left the store and found a local cafeteria where he ate a lonely, dry sandwich in resentful silence. Even if he had known how to get to the staff canteen, he wouldn't have used it, not even if he could have been sure of seeing Vita. He ate his lunch. He had no desire to return to work, then or ever, but there was one little thing he intended to do.

The half-hour passed all too quickly and Charlie dragged himself back to Haden Brothers. He stood in the middle of the stockroom, looked at the boxes and the shelves, gloomy in the dim light. He smelled the dubious smells. If the bloody kid couldn't tell him what he was supposed to be doing then how could he be expected to do it? Or was the kid just being obnoxious? Perhaps Charlie's work would have been wrong whatever he'd done. But by now he didn't care. He had decided to do nothing for the rest of the day. He spent a long afternoon slouched between the shelves, sometimes thinking, sometimes dozing, waiting for clocking-off time, or more specifically for the return of his tormentor.

Charlie had almost given him up when, at six o'clock, the kid came into the stockroom. Charlie stood up and tried to look as though he'd been working all afternoon. The kid surveyed the scene and obviously didn't think much of it, but it was a studied response. He would have sneered regardless of how much work Charlie had done. And he was obviously unaware that Charlie had done nothing all afternoon.

'You can piss off home now,' he said to Charlie.

'Oh, can I?'

'Yeah, and then tomorrow you can come back and put it all back as it was.'

'Oh, can I?'

'Yeah.'

'Why would I want to do that?' Charlie asked.

'What you want doesn't come into it, dickhead.'

'Oh, doesn't it?'

Charlie looked at the kid steadily and then in one smooth movement grabbed him by the throat, picked him up off the ground and pinned him to a wall of the stockroom.

'See here, Loz, you don't talk to me like that,' Charlie said. 'I don't

53

want you ever to talk to me like that again. Nor to anybody else. Not ever again? Do you understand me, Loz? Am I making myself clear?'

He held the kid's windpipe just long enough and tight enough for the kid to think he might actually have murder on his mind, and then he let go. The kid slumped to the ground and appeared to be laughing. Charlie looked around as half a dozen young men came into the stockroom. He thought they must be some kind of security men, come to arrest him and throw him out for getting into a fight on his first day. Instant dismissal could not be far away. That suited him fine. Then he realized they were the same group of loutish, T-shirt-wearing young men he'd seen waiting outside staff entrance F that morning. Strangely enough, they didn't look particularly malicious now, and he had hopes that they'd let him walk out in one piece. As he looked more closely they even seemed to be smiling.

'Nice one, mate.'

'Well done, old son.'

The kid was now on his feet, looking humbler but still pleased with himself. He walked towards Charlie offering a hand to be shaken.

'That's not bad,' he said to Charlie. 'That's not bad at all. You only put up with one day's shit. That's pretty good. Some of the ones who come through here take a couple of weeks before they turn on me.'

'What?' said Charlie.

'We were just testing you,' said Loz. 'If you hadn't turned on me you'd have been no good at all. We were seeing what you're made of.'

'You're OK,' said another. 'You're one of us. We're furniture porters. We don't take *no* shit.'

Charlie couldn't really feel that he was one of them, chiefly because he didn't know who or what they were.

'We're going home now. We'll see you tomorrow,' said the kid. 'Then we'll tell you what's what.'

They started to leave. Charlie saw then that they each had large Haden Brothers carrier bags. He was certain they hadn't been carrying them that morning. They reached inside and pulled out silk shirts, cashmere sweaters and designer jackets, and put them on. At first Charlie thought it might be pay day and in some unlikely and expensive act of company loyalty they'd spent a large slice of their wages in the store. It took all of ten seconds for him to realize this was absurd and that what he was actually witnessing was a grand act of group pilfering. They ditched the bags and the packaging, and wore the clothes as if they owned them, which in every sense they now did.

He followed them at a distance as they went out of the stockroom, along the corridor to the time clock. He looked along the row of cards and saw that his name was now among them and that someone, very generously, had clocked him in that morning.

The others hurried away and he slowly walked alone round the outside of the store. He hoped he might be leaving at the right time to catch another sight of Vita, but that would have been asking too much. A group of cleaners was again working hard on one of the windows. At first he thought they might have been there all day but then he saw that the graffito they were trying to erase was a new one and somewhat different from the one he'd read that morning. This one said, 'Hamnet is still here.'

Still blissfully unaware of what that meant, Charlie returned to the tube station, and eventually to Keith and Sarah's flat, to another night on a sofa in a place he was not wanted.

TRACEY FORD, retail display trainee: In my opinion, everybody's an artist. I think everybody's like Leonardo when they're born, but then their parents and school and society and stuff just knock it out of them until they're not fit to do anything creative at all.

I'm lucky really. I work in a department store and I like it a lot. They call me a retail display trainee, which is a bit like being a window dresser but a lot more creative. Not that it's all plain sailing. I keep coming up with some absolutely amazing ideas but it's very hard to get those ideas taken seriously. But that's not surprising. That's how it's always been for artists.

For instance we were doing a jewellery window, and jewellery is never an easy thing to display because it's small and the windows at Haden Brothers are big. So my idea was to take one of those big windows and half fill it up with broken mannequins and parts of scrapped cars. Then I was going to spray it all matt black so it looked as though there'd been a car crash and then a fire. So you'd have this all-black display but here and there you'd have a couple of eternity rings or a diamond choker, and they'd be spotlit so they'd really stand out. So I put it to my boss and he goes, 'It's a great idea, Tracey, it's just a bit morbid.' I mean really.

Then I had this idea for cutlery which isn't easy to display either. I thought we could turn the window into a sort of sealed fish tank and fill it with red jelly. Then when it's set we'd stick the knives and forks into the surface of the jelly. Simple but very effective I thought. My boss thought that one was 'naive'.

I suggested putting a live wolf in the window surrounded by state-of-the-art hi-fi equipment. Then I wanted to get half a dozen naked people in the window and have them smear each other with jams and preserves from the food hall. And then I wanted to fill a window with hundreds of fresh lemons and leave them there until they rotted. And my boss is like, 'What's that supposed to be selling?' And I said art doesn't have to be selling anything, but as a matter of fact I thought it might shift quite a few fresh lemons actually.

I'm no fool. I know we're in business to show off the merchandise to its best advantage so that we can sell it. But that doesn't mean you can't be creative, and it doesn't mean you can't have ideals. I know all about good design, about the importance of composition and colour and shape. But sometimes you just want to throw it all away and start again.

I mean, things are difficult enough without having someone daubing graffiti all over the shop windows. It's not as if 'Hamnet was here' actually means anything. It was just sort of stupid and ugly and antisocial and it completely spoiled all the hard work I'd put into that window display of a beach scene.

But I'll tell you this; people looked at that window more than they ever looked at any display I'd ever done before. Their eyes were caught by the graffiti and then they looked at the goods behind the glass. And that gave me a lot to think about. It occurred to me that whoever had painted that slogan on the window might actually have had Haden Brothers' best interests at heart. In fact, I almost wished I'd done it myself.

ARNOLD HADEN: In the old days a lot of people used to ask me what Haden Brothers was like. I was never lost for an answer. I used to say that Haden Brothers was like a confederation of independent states, with each department proud and autonomous, and yet coming together for the common good. Or perhaps it was like a whole society with its plebeians, its aristocrats and its outsiders.

Or I'd say it was like a beehive in that many of the workers were unthinking drones, and yet they still managed to produce the honey of profit.

I used to say Haden Brothers was like an encyclopedia, each department offering a different form of knowledge, wisdom and expertise. Yet each was cross-referenced and drew the customer on to other, related 'entries'.

I'd say it was like an orchestra, a harmonious group of talented individuals who played together, merging their personalities in one composition, all working in a common key and tempo and thereby making very sweet music.

I'd say it was like a good, well-balanced meal, a *mélange* of textures and flavours, strong tastes and subtle aromas, sweet and savoury, the raw and the cooked. Then I'd say it was like a kaleidoscope, an ever-changing pattern of light and shade, of shapes and colours that delighted the eye and the imagination.

And certainly Haden Brothers could be said to be like an army, a pyramid, a circus, a chorus line, a holiday camp, a plate-spinning act. And to me it sometimes looked very much like a model of entropy, but I always kept that to myself.

It would have been nice to have said that Haden Brothers was all things to all men, but in the end I concluded that all similes, all metaphors, all resemblances were essentially false. Haden Brothers was unique. It was essentially and quintessentially and only itself. It was everything and more, but it was like nothing else.

6 · BEDDING

A tiny, circular lift, barely large enough for two people, took Vita from staff entrance A, slowly and whisperingly all the way up to Arnold Haden's penthouse on top of the Haden Brothers building. The lift had only one operating button and it served no other floor. Soon the lift stopped, the doors slid open easily, and Vita stepped out into an empty ante-room that was consciously tasteful and neutral, and which refused to state precisely what kind of room it was. It was not quite an office, not quite a waiting room, and it was uninhabited. There was no receptionist to greet her, no commissionaire to salute her, no desk, no sofas, no telephones. There were, however, large panoramic windows that looked out over the rooftops of London. The air in the room was warm and still.

A white metal door, massive and solid and completely out of place here, was the only exit except for the door to the lift. The lift had now gone and it was not at all clear what she should do next. She waited several minutes before knocking on the metal door. She listened carefully for noises of life. No sound came from behind it, but after a while, as she was wondering whether it would be appropriate to knock a second time, she heard the handle rattle, the door eased open and a large, distinguished but dishevelled man in a white suit was revealed. He bustled into the empty room and closed the door behind him.

'I'm Arnold Haden,' he said immediately and shook Vita by the hand. His touch was warm and dry, his hands big and extraordinarily soft. Vita needed no telling who he was. Arnold Haden was decidedly camera-shy but she had done her research before applying for this job and she had tracked down a couple of newspaper photographs of him. But it was strange to see him in the flesh, stranger still when he said, 'And you're Miss Carlisle, of course,' thereby proving to her considerable surprise that he knew who she was too.

Arnold Haden was wearing a white shirt, white tie and white shoes with his white suit. The effect was curious, as if he might be a member of a religious cult or part of an all-singing, all-dancing chorus line. The suit was expensive, even stylish, but it refused to fit him. It hung like a damp bathrobe, and he moved inside it awkwardly and at odds with the cloth. Vita guessed he had once been boyishly good-looking. He still had the remains of a head of floppy, sandy hair. It was greying and thinning now, but it hadn't been entirely harnessed and it sprang up here and there in defiant tufts. The face was round and undefined. It was possible to imagine that it had once been delicately cut and rather fine, but the years had blurred and softened it. The cheeks and mouth were now loose, there were bags under the eyes, and there were jowls where they had once been a jaw line.

'I'm honoured to meet you,' said Vita warmly.

'I imagine you're a little surprised, too.'

'A little, yes.'

'You expected some drudge from personnel, not the boss.'

'I did expect some induction training.'

'Yes, of course you did. But instead the lift brought you here, which is precisely what I had in mind.'

He smiled at her, then shyly looked away out of the window. What he saw out there clearly didn't please him.

'You're young, Miss Carlisle, perhaps you look out there and see an impressive skyline: a series of 'sights', landmarks, tourist attractions. Perhaps you see signs of exuberant life. Perhaps you see a great city, overlaid with the patina of history and culture.'

He stopped, and she was about to tell him what she *did* see but just in time she realized he did not want any word from her.

'But that's not what I see,' he continued. 'I see warring tribes. I see Barbarians, Vandals, Philistines. I see the enemy. I see a vision of hell. That's why I keep the drawbridge up. And I keep my powder dry. Always.'

'That's very interesting,' said Vita.

'Of course, you don't see it that way, I know. You're young. It takes time. But you'll see it my way eventually. Everybody does. Things are terrible out there, believe me. And the one thing I'm sure of is that things are bound to get worse. God save me from the rabble.'

'But they're not *all* rabble, surely,' Vita said charmingly.

'Aren't they?'

'Surely some of them are, well, Haden Brothers customers.'

That cut no ice with Arnold Haden.

'And it seems to me,' she continued, 'that the values espoused by Haden Brothers have a genuinely civilizing effect on the public.'

'You mean that if they buy a Wedgwood bowl from Haden Brothers then they won't go home and start a race riot?'

'Well, it's a possibility, isn't it?' said Vita.

He laughed, though not at her. 'You're a fascinating young woman, Miss Carlisle,' he said, 'but, of course, I knew that already from your CV.'

Together they gazed out of the window again and, in their different ways, looked at the view. Far below the city looked like a model of itself, lovingly scaled down, the details meticulously observed and recreated. Vita was aware how calm and quiet this room was. It was above the dirt and the noise, above many things.

'Well,' said Arnold Haden, 'I'm sure this isn't exactly the kind of conversation you expected to be having on your first morning in employment. Let's get down to business.'

The white metal door opened and Derek Snell entered the room.

'I'm very happy to meet you again, Miss Carlisle,' he said, though of course he didn't look at all happy.

'I've been talking to Miss Carlisle about the state of society,' said Haden.

'I couldn't help overhearing, sir. It was all so very profound, so very true.'

Arnold Haden looked at Vita and said, 'You see, Miss Carlisle, I'm surrounded by flatterers. But then perhaps we surround ourselves with what we need. What do you think, Vita?'

'I don't think a man of your obvious abilities needs to be flattered, Mr Haden,' said Vita.

'Not a bad answer,' said Haden. 'No, I don't need flatterers, but I do need people like you.'

'Like me?' she said modestly.

'Oh yes.'

'For the Flying Squad?' Vita enquired.

'Perhaps.'

'Meaning perhaps not?' she said. 'Mr Snell didn't lead me to believe there was anything provisional about the job offer.'

'And there isn't,' said Arnold Haden. 'But please listen. Working for the Flying Squad is a perfectly acceptable way of making a living. It's socially useful, it's tolerably varied, not too dull. The wages are slightly above average and the prospects of advancement are reasonable. But, let's be honest, when all's said and done, you're still only working as a shop assistant.'

Vita was aware that Derek Snell was watching her intently. There was a twitchiness, an air of expectation in his gloomy demeanour. Vita saw that he was holding a Polaroid between his fingers. It was of her, one of the ones taken at the interview, and it looked ominously grubby and well-thumbed.

'What Mr Haden is saying', Snell said, 'is that there are other options.'

'Yes,' said Arnold Haden. 'Basically I'm saying that I'd like to have sex with you.'

Snell averted his eyes in an act of coquettish but false modesty, as though he was trying to spare Vita's blushes, as though he wanted to distance himself from Arnold Haden's lack of subtlety. But the effect was lost since his mouth simultaneously slipped into a prurient, idiotic leer. It was some time before he looked at Vita to see how she'd reacted, but she had not reacted at all. She was nodding and looking thoughtful. Arnold Haden took this as a signal to press on, and Snell's leer widened.

'You see, I don't get around very much,' Arnold Haden said. 'You could say I'm an agoraphobic, but that's just a word. Simply putting a name to something doesn't necessarily explain it. But whatever you call it, the simple truth is I haven't left this place for the last ten years. I order what I need from the store. It gets delivered. God knows it doesn't have to come far. I consume it. Perfect.

'I don't have to go out. I don't need to, and God knows I don't want to. I have no taste for parties or clubs or social gatherings of any sort. Consequently I don't meet many women, and I wouldn't know how to deal with them even if I did. I suppose I could invite prostitutes here, but that really isn't my way. I don't have a way. It can make life difficult at times.'

Vita nodded sympathetically.

'Fortunately Mr Snell is a great help to me in these matters. He knows what I like. He can spot talent. He spotted you. You're my type. I believe you could make me very happy. What do you say, Miss Carlisle? Can we do business?'

Vita was deadly quiet and both Haden and Snell still feared she might react badly and erupt with indignant rage. That had happened before with other girls, despite Snell's careful vetting, and the law of averages suggested that it would happen again from time to time, but they both hoped desperately that it wouldn't happen with Vita. They both saw a great and special potential in her. Even if she wouldn't go along with their plans, they still didn't want to lose her, and they felt a great need to placate her.

'You'd be a proper member of staff in every way,' Snell said. 'You'd be a proper member of the Flying Squad too. The job security, the pension rights, the staff discount; all that would still apply. You'd work as normal but every once in a while there'd be a telephone call. That would be from Mr Haden or from me or possibly from one of his staff. We would ask you if you wanted to do any overtime, and that would be a sort of code. Then, at the end of the day you would report to staff entrance A as you did this morning. The lift would convey you here where you would satisfy Mr Arnold's demands.'

'My demands have always been described as modest,' said Arnold Haden.

'And they're entirely orthodox,' Snell added reassuringly, but Vita did not seem to be in need of reassurance. She looked entirely at ease, entirely comfortable with this proposition.

'Tell me, Mr Haden,' she said, 'are you a married man?'

'Certainly not,' said Snell on his boss's behalf. 'This would not be adultery.'

'And would you take precautions?' she asked.

'Safety first, that's Mr Haden's motto,' said Snell.

'And would I be free to have other men friends?'

'Within reason.'

'And this would all be very discreet?'

'Of course.'

'And the pay?' Vita enquired.

'You'd be paid exactly the same as you would on the Flying Squad,' Snell said. 'But we would give you a generous allowance of Haden Brothers gift vouchers.'

Vita looked thoughtful. 'Well,' she said, 'it's certainly tempting, for a variety of reasons. I find you a very attractive man, Mr Haden, and it's got nothing at all to do with money or power, though I appreciate that you're well endowed with both. And certainly the idea of being the plaything of a Haden brother is very appealing indeed.'

Arnold Haden was already starting to look disappointed. For all her encouraging words he knew there was a 'but' coming, a qualification ending in refusal.

'Do you know my only reason for hesitation?'

Haden shook his head, and Snell joined in.

'The pay and conditions of your kind offer might be attractive, but there's the question of prospects.'

The two men looked confused.

'You see, I'm an ambitious person,' she said. 'I want to get on in life. Being a shop assistant is admittedly a modest job, but a shop assistant can aspire to becoming a buyer, or a floor manager, or even in the fullness of time, a member of the board. But what could the boss's concubine hope to become? The boss's wife? It seems unlikely, doesn't it?'

'Er, well . . . perhaps,' Haden muttered, while Snell knew enough to keep silent.

'It may sound old fashioned but I really do want to get to the top in Haden Brothers,' Vita continued. 'In the end, Mr Haden, you could say that I even want *your* job. And I realize that along the way some patronage from above will be extremely useful to me. But more than that I want your respect. And I don't think I would get it if I agreed to have sex with you at the first time of asking.'

Her answer only made her more attractive to Arnold Haden. He was impressed by her delicacy, her suppleness of mind, her tone of voice. He liked her ambitiousness and directness. And he especially liked the hint that subsequent times of asking might meet with less firm refusals.

'So, I'm afraid I'll have to say thanks but no thanks,' Vita said solemnly.

Disappointment seeped into both the men's faces. She wanted to tell them to cheer up, to look on the bright side but she resisted her natural urge.

Two hours later Derek Snell had personally briefed Vita on company policy and company rules, informed her about the security systems, trained her in till procedures and given her a special Flying Squad lapel badge. He had also installed her in the toy department where there was an urgent vacancy caused by the sudden nervous collapse of a senior sales asistant.

As he said his farewells Snell suddenly added, 'If you ever have second thoughts . . . '

'Then you'll be the first or second to know,' she said.

'Things change,' said Snell.

'Certainly,' said Vita.

'I hope you weren't too surprised by Mr Haden's forthrightness.'

'I was charmed.'

'You're a remarkable young woman,' said Snell. 'And I suspect you know it.'

As Vita entered the toy department, an unruly gang of children, not obvious Haden Brothers customers, were wrecking the radio-controlled toy cars by staging complex, high speed collisions. Vita spoke to the children in firm but understanding tones, and before long they had become much less destructive and were using the model vehicles to demonstrate courtesy and good road manners. Vita smiled beatifically at them, while she in turn received jealous and hostile looks from the rest of the toy department staff.

7 · LOSS LEADER

Arnold Haden was never sure exactly what frightened him so much about the world. But perhaps it was not anything exact. Perhaps he was frightened because of his own innate and undifferentiated timidity. He was frightened of his own shadow and of all other shadows too. He was frightened by aggression and violence, by conflict. He was frightened by boorishness and barbarism. He hated noise and vulgarity and bad taste. He was frightened of tight corners and of wide open spaces. He was frightened of men, but more of women. But these were only symptoms. He was like a man with an allergy who cannot discover what he is allergic to because he is too busy sneezing.

Perhaps if he had been more ordinary, or at least more poor, he would have been forced to confront his fears. He would have had to go out into the world, to make his way, at the very least to make a living. But being frightened and being a recluse were so much easier if you were rich, and if you worked for the family business, if you *were* the family business, and easier still if there was a penthouse above the shop where you could hole up.

In the early days he had spent a certain amount of time in the store. It was part of his work, although his exact role and job were always unspecified. Those who felt well-disposed towards him said he was a troubleshooter, a man with a sharp eye for detail, full of all the right questions, taking nothing for granted, even something of an iconoclast in the world of retailing. He never communicated directly with the lower orders, but there were one or two senior executives, his father and brother while they lived, with whom he could speak freely, who would listen to him, and his 'suggestions' more often than not trickled down through the hierarchy and proved to be useful. Even then he liked to tour the shop before or after trading hours, when it was devoid of people, when it was still and empty. He was not sure who he was more eager to avoid, the staff or the customers.

In those days he was married and lived what most people would call a normal life. He lived in a large, interior-designed apartment in Kensington, within easy walking distance of the store. He lived surrounded by beautiful things. He and his wife collected modern paintings and African tribal masks, and they bought early pop art and medieval oak furniture. They travelled, missed very few London theatrical or operatic first nights, were often seen at Ascot and Arnold played cricket for the Lord's Taverners.

But after his father died, of natural causes, and after his wife and brother died young and tragically, he decided all that had to go. He wanted his life to be spare and hard. The ninth floor of Haden Brothers contained an awkwardly shaped storage area that Edward Zander had intended to be part of his proposed menagerie. It had lain empty for decades. Arnold Haden claimed it as his own and turned it into his home.

Now he wanted none of the clutter of his previous existence, no works of art, no collectables, nothing beautiful. Arnold Haden's penthouse was to be as austere and barren as a monk's cell, though considerably more spacious. Walls, floors and ceiling were all white, and what little furniture he had was white too; a white leather armchair, a white bed. Kitchen and bathroom were plain expanses of white tile and porcelain and enamel. There was nothing comforting here, no products, no household names. He wanted anonymity and featurelessness, an absence of objects, an end to anything he might attach himself to.

He was able to withdraw completely from the shop floor. He spent more and more time in his penthouse and the store survived perfectly well without him. His role became increasingly abstract. He would sit up there considering questions of image, public relations, company philosophy, the future of retailing. He would write reports and memos on these matters and they would be widely circulated, though not widely read. The people who *did* read them noticed that as the years went by they seemed to have less and less to do with the reality of running a department store. They read, indeed, like reports written by a man who never set foot on the shop floor, who never left his all-white penthouse.

His isolation didn't mean that he was impregnable. They were still able to get at him, whoever they were. They would spray graffiti on the store's windows. They left messages on his answerphone: a disguised, muffled voice that repeated the words 'Hamnet was here'.

There was even a Hamnet computer virus that popped up from time to time and stripped files bare, swallowed major orders and turned memos and reports into gibberish.

There was a balcony attached to Arnold's penthouse. It was narrow, sloping, with a terrifyingly low parapet, and it might have been designed to pitch yourself from. It had been one of Edward Zander's more questionable architectural jokes. At one time it had been open to the public, but far too many had succumbed to its lethal potential. It had been christened Suicide Ridge. Now it was closed off, made part of Arnold Haden's territory. He was the only one who might throw himself off it, and there were many evenings when this seemed like a perfectly sound idea.

Then there was the business of sex. As he had explained to Vita Carlisle, his social skills were far more limited than his libido. He needed sex and saw no objection to paying for it. However, he wanted to keep his purchases in-house. He did not want street walkers or call girls. He wanted good-looking, wholesome working girls, the kind who worked in Haden Brothers. Derek Snell was able to keep him informed about likely new recruits. By and large the system worked satisfactorily, but Arnold knew it was not entirely healthy.

Arnold was aware that rumours circulated about him. Some said that he was mad, or that he marauded around his penthouse in a stupor of drink and drugs, that he favoured sex with boys or geriatrics or amputees. He thought this said more about the paucity and vulgarity of the popular imagination than it did about him, but it still hurt, and was, incidentally, totally untrue. And now he had decided to do something about it. He had agreed to be interviewed by a member of the press, a sympathetic female journalist, a woman who said she worked for friendly features departments on the less demanding Sunday papers, a woman called Lesley Crane. He had never heard of her but that didn't matter. He did not want to be confronted by a personality journalist. He planned to appear calm, warm, frank and above all normal. He knew it was going to be quite a performance.

The interview was to take place in the anonymous ante-room in which Arnold Haden had first met Vita Carlisle. He had no intention of letting any journalist see the blank splendours with which he surrounded himself in his own penthouse. Derek Snell had offered to sit in on the interview but Arnold Haden felt proud of himself for having the strength to face this alone.

He stood waiting for the lift to arrive, to deliver Lesley Crane to him. He posed casually by the picture windows and hoped that he looked neither too posed nor too casual. He wanted to show that he cared about this interview, but he didn't want to appear to care too much.

Then the lift arrived and he lost his composure completely and dashed across to it, and as the doors were opening he said, 'Hello, Miss Crane. I'm Arnold Haden. So pleased to meet you.' They were shaking hands before she had even stepped out of the lift, and in fact she couldn't step out at all since Haden was blocking her way, and as they stood there with outstretched hands, the doors closed again and grabbed his arm, and though they opened again immediately, their rubber edges left two sooty grey bands on the sleeve of his white suit. He laughed unconvincingly and pretended it was nothing, then ushered his interviewer into the room.

Now he was able to see her properly and she was not at all what he had been expecting. She was bonier and less motherly than he had been hoping for, more robust and formidable and serious. She was dark-haired, tanned and heavily made up. Her lips were the colour of raw liver. She frightened the life out of him, and the fact that she was clearly doing her best to appear unthreatening only threatened him all the more.

They sat down, separated by a long low table. Chairs and table had been brought to the room specially for this occasion. There was a full cafetière placed at the centre of the table, but Arnold Haden was too nervous to offer his interviewer any coffee. Lesley Crane produced a pocket tape-recorder and set it between them. Arnold Haden did the same with a recorder of his own, as though making a countermove in some complex board game.

'Can't be too careful,' he said.

'I understand,' she replied.

He waited, expecting to exchange a few ice-breaking remarks, but she was having none of that.

'Well, Mr Haden,' she began, 'I'm pleased to see that the rumours aren't true.'

'Rumours?' he said disingenuously.

'Yes, that you're a mad recluse, or that you're horribly disfigured or a drug addict . . . '

She listed a few more colourful possibilities, most of which he had heard before. However, he didn't want her to know that, so he simply looked blank.

'Have you never heard these rumours?' she enquired.

'I don't get around much,' he said.

'But, as I can see,' she continued, 'you're a perfectly ordinary man.'

'Yes,' said Haden. 'That's exactly the image I want to put across. I mean it isn't an image. I really am perfectly normal.'

'I realize that,' she said. 'So let's talk about your love life.'

That had him reeling. He had made up his mind that he was prepared to let out one or two little hints about his private life, but he certainly hadn't prepared himself to answer any such direct question. He found himself unable to reply.

'My readers will want to know all about your love life,' she added.

'Will they?'

'Yes. Specifically they'll want to know why you're not married. Why you don't have a steady girlfriend. Why you don't have children. They'll want to know if you're a homosexual or a paedophile or a celibate, or what.'

'Will they really?'

'Yes, they will. I appreciate you may not want to talk about it, and you have my sympathy, but let me put it this way, if you don't say anything about your love life they're only going to imagine the worst.'

'Are they really?'

'I know my readers.'

He believed that she did. She waited a while, long enough for him to offer up some juicy bit of information, but he was clearly going to take some prompting.

'Obviously you're heterosexual,' she said.

'Oh yes.'

'And you used to be married, but that was a long time ago. Since then you've obviously chased quite a few women, and no doubt you've caught a great many of them. But you've never found Miss Right and so you've never remarried.'

'Yes,' he said. It was more or less the truth.

'Is there someone in your life now?'

'Well, in a way.'

'You probably don't want to tell me her name.'

'That's absolutely right.'

'I understand that, so could I write something about a secret love?'

'I think that might be going too far,' he said.

'Or what if I referred to a mystery girl?'

'Oh no, really.'

'A *femme fatale*?'

'No. Please no.'

'She's more homely than that?'

'Well, homely has some rather negative connotations, doesn't it?'

'Would you like her to be the mother of your children?'

'I don't think I can answer that.'

'There were no children in your marriage were there, Mr Haden? Why's that?'

'My wife and I, we simply . . . didn't, and since then obviously I wouldn't have children if I wasn't married.'

'I'm sorry, Mr Haden, in today's world that just isn't a good enough reason. Perhaps if you were to say that the modern world is such a terrible place it would be wrong to bring any more children into it.'

'Yes,' he said, 'I think I could agree with that.'

'You're not very at home in the modern world, are you?'

At last she said something with which he could feel at ease. The modern world and its horrors was a much less difficult problem than his private life.

'Is it so obvious?' he said.

'It wouldn't be obvious to everyone,' she said, 'but it is to me. And is that why you never leave this penthouse?'

'I do leave it sometimes.'

'Good. When did you last leave it, Mr Haden?'

'Recently. I think it was some time in the early eighties.'

She said 'Mmm' in a meaningful fashion, and then demanded, 'How much are you worth, Mr Haden?'

He was flustered again. This was another thing he had not prepared himself to talk about. He opened his mouth but nothing came out.

She said, 'I was thinking I could push this angle of Arnold Haden the eligible bachelor. And let's face it, in today's world eligible means rich, doesn't it? So how much?'

'My accountant would have a much better idea than I would. Really.'

'Come, come, Mr Haden, there's no need to be coy. I'm sure a sharp business mind like yours could tell me instantly to the exact penny.'

'Well, you know, modesty forbids.'

'All right, let me ask it another way. Obviously it would be accurate to describe you as a millionaire.'

He agreed.

'Would it be accurate to call you a multi-millionaire?'

'Well, I suppose so.'

'And would it be reasonable to call you super-rich?'

'Well, it's not a term I'd ever use.'

'No, but if I called you a super-rich multi-millionaire eligible bachelor, would I be getting somewhere in the vicinity?'

He had to think for a while but before long he said, 'Yes. I don't mind the sound of that at all.'

'And how do you feel about shopping malls?' Lesley Crane asked.

'I don't think I understand.'

'Surely, Mr Haden, fewer and fewer people visit department stores these days. Instead they'll go to a mall, take the family, spend the whole day, have a leisure shopping experience. Surely the days of the large independently owned department store are well and truly numbered.'

'Well, I don't know, I've never . . .'

She stared into his eyes as though looking for his answer, as though attempting a feat of mind-reading. Then triumphantly she said, 'But of course you wouldn't know anything about shopping malls if you've only left the store once since the early eighties.'

She was pleased with her deduction, yet she wasn't gloating. Haden could see it was pointless trying to deny it. He gave her a pleading look.

'There are some things you know are terrible without experiencing them directly,' he said.

'And shopping malls fall into that category?'

'I think so, yes.'

She said, 'Well, what if I were to say that shopping malls are vulgar and modern and soulless, and that Haden Brothers is upholding standards of taste and decorum and quality.'

'Yes,' he said. 'That sounds reasonable.'

'And I could quote you as saying something about Haden Brothers being an oasis, about the decline of standards, about Philistines at the gate. Would you trust me to put something together along those lines?'

'Yes,' he said. 'I believe I would.'

'And could I say that's the reason why you never leave Haden Brothers? That you find the world a filthy, noisy and violent place, and that you want no part of it? That you find people dangerous and uncouth and troublesome and you like to put an iron curtain between yourself and them? That you think the world is in decline, that it has no hope and no future?'

'Yes,' said Haden, 'that's all true, just so long as you don't make me sound cranky.'

'I wouldn't do that to you,' she said, and he believed her.

He suddenly noticed the coffee. By now he liked his interviewer well enough and was relaxed enough to pour a cup for each of them. He was looking forward to her next question.

'Well, that's it,' she said abruptly. 'It wasn't too painful, was it?'

'No,' said Haden. 'But is that really all?'

'Yes. We're not talking about in-depth here, are we?'

'Oh, I suppose not.'

Suddenly she was on her feet and at the lift, the doors had opened, she had stepped inside and was about to descend. Haden hurried after her.

'There's just one more thing,' she said, holding the lift door open.

'Yes?'

'I got an anonymous phone call last night.'

'Oh?' said Arnold.

'Yes. It said I should watch what happens to your face when I say the words "Hamnet was here".'

Arnold's face did its best to do nothing at all, but strange shapes moved beneath its surface, shapes of anger, fear, panic; the forms of old bones and skeletons; shadows of hatred and deception and death.

'Thank you,' she said. 'I think you've told me everything I need to know.'

The lift doors hissed shut. It was a long time before Arnold Haden's face was back to anything like normal.

8 · YARNS

Charlie, arriving early for his second day at Haden Brothers, found staff entrance F shut, just as it had been the previous day. But this time he did not take a walk around the perimeter. Instead, he found the group of furniture porters and joined them.

They didn't look very pleased to see him. The suggestions of *bonhomie* they had expressed upon bursting into the stockroom to rescue Loz had been forgotten. Even Loz scarcely acknowledged Charlie's presence. The group discussed things and people that Charlie knew nothing about. They left no room for him to join in. He tried not to be concerned. He kept looking towards staff entrance A, hoping he might see Vita, but she did not appear.

When the metal door was finally raised, Charlie tagged along with the rest of the porters. He clocked in and then followed them as they went along corridors, up flights of stairs and into a service lift, and finally to the furniture department. He was not altogether surprised that their earlier offer to 'show him what's what' came to nothing. They sat around in a back room in a corner of the department playing cards, reading the tabloids, apparently waiting for something to happen, definitely not talking to the new boy. Occasionally they would belch, fart or let fly with an obscenity. There was a sort of foreman, a young man called Anton Heath who had chiselled good looks, long tousled blond hair and a definitely posh accent. He found it necessary to fart, belch and swear louder than anyone else. Charlie felt painfully out of place.

It was halfway through an entirely idle morning before anybody addressed any words directly at him. When they came, the words were, 'How about the Cerebral Lobes?'

'Sorry?' said Charlie.

'Or how about the Aorta? Or the Broken Ankles?'

The porter saying these words was a lanky, round-shouldered boy with a lot of shaggy black hair and chunky, horn-rimmed spectacles. His name was Douglas.

'What do you mean?' Charlie asked.

'I'm trying to think of a name for a rock band, OK? And I was thinking of naming it after a part of the human body, OK?'

'OK,' said Charlie.

'I can see you're not that impressed. What if I named it after a film? How about *Gentlemen Prefer Blondes* or *Strange Cargo*? How about *Carry on Cowboy*?'

Charlie was willing to get involved. He said, 'Well, it's hard for me to know if they're good names or not. I mean it all depends on what kind of music you play.'

Douglas looked at him contemptuously.

'No, it *doesn't* matter what kind of music, actually,' he spat.

'Oh, OK,' said Charlie, not looking for an argument so early in the day.

'What if I called my band the IRA?' Douglas suggested.

'Well no, I don't really think you can call a band the IRA,' Charlie said.

'Why not?'

'Well, you know, at the very least it's in bad taste.'

'But rock music's all *about* bad taste.'

'But not like that I don't think,' Charlie said.

'Then how about the Black September? Or the Shining Path?'

This was very nearly a conversation about art, his first in a long time, and Charlie wasn't going to hold back.

'I think the problem is', he said gently, still trying to avoid an argument, 'that these people, the IRA and so forth, go around blowing people up, killing people. I don't really think you can go on stage named after organizations like that and then try to entertain an audience. I don't think people will accept that.'

'Well how about the Tamil Tigers? Or Prima Linea? Or the Red Brigade? They have some great sounding names these terrorist groups.'

'That may be true,' said Charlie, 'but the names have implications.'

'Hey,' said Douglas, 'wouldn't it be a giggle if I came up with the name of a rock band but everybody thought it was the name of a terrorist group. Like Hamnet Was Here.'

Charlie was suddenly interested.

'What does that name mean?' he asked.

74

'I don't know,' said Douglas. 'I saw it sprayed on a window yesterday.'

'So did I. Is it the name of a rock band, then? Was it just a publicity stunt?'

'Well, it could be, couldn't it? I happen to think it's a rotten name for a band. But I don't blame the person who did it. Any publicity's great publicity.'

'Yes, but is it really just the name of a band?'

'How the fuck would I know?' said Douglas, then he slouched away sulkily.

This business of communicating with the porters was a tricky one. Charlie hoped that having made this slight, if spiky, contact with one of their number the others might start talking to him. By and large they didn't. There was a moment late in the morning when a message came through that half a dozen circular dining tables had to be carried from one end of the department to the other, and just enough communication took place to tell Charlie what he had to do, but conversation was kept to a minimum. He tried to shrug it off. After all, he was there to earn a living, not to establish a social life.

Just before he went to lunch Douglas said to him, 'Well, what if I used a newspaper headline as the name of a band, like the High Price of German Unity, or Training Budgets Severely Underfunded? Or how about Alert Sounded on Plutonium Threat?'

Charlie said, 'They sound terrific,' and thus he made Douglas very happy.

The lunch hour came and went, and in the afternoon Charlie was required to do a little more light portering. At five o'clock it looked as though the whole day might pass and his only human contact would have been two conversations about the names of rock bands. However, a little before they went home, Anton Heath, the blond foreman, beckoned Charlie over for a chat.

Anton leaned on the packing bench beside the giant rolls of adhesive tape, next to the array of Stanley knives and the endless rolls of bubble packaging and said, 'You'll have to forgive Douglas. He's a failure. He's never had a rock band. He's never learned any songs, never learned to play an instrument. He can't sing. He just likes to think up names. Pathetic, isn't it?'

'Well, sort of sad,' Charlie agreed.

'Don't let it happen to you,' said Anton.

'I don't intend to.'

'Good. Because my instinct is that you've got failed artist written all over you.'

'No, not me,' said Charlie.

'Good. You like art though, don't you? I can tell.'

'Yes, I do as a matter of fact.'

'You know,' said Anton, 'Just about anything can be art,' and Charlie was able to agree with him, but then he said, 'Smashing windows can be art. Destroying files can be art. Assassinating a politician can be art. Bombing a children's hospital can be art. Wouldn't you say?'

'Well no, I'm not sure I would.'

'Art isn't about rationality,' Anton continued, and again Charlie could only agree with him. But then he said, 'And it isn't about morality. It isn't about order. A workers' strike could be a work of art. Bringing Haden Brothers to its knees, that would be a great work of art. That's what we furniture porters are here for.'

The furniture department occupied all of the seventh floor of Haden Brothers. It consisted of a long series of interconnected, over-furnished rooms, each full of numerous pieces of furniture that only vaguely matched each other. These rooms came in all styles, from Antique to Avant-garde, from Rustic to Retro, and resembled every-thing from country cottages to Imperial boudoirs. Some showed understated elegance, others bragged loudly about money and ful-filled ambition. Charlie would come to spend a lot of his time passing through these rooms, finding them increasingly sad and ghostly. Dining tables were laid for meals that would never be eaten. Armchairs clustered around fake fireplaces where people would never gather. The bed department was like some vast artificial dormitory where nobody would ever sleep.

Most prevalent, it seemed to Charlie, were the sofas and three piece suites. They came with hardwood frames and coil springing, with scroll arms and serpentine back cushions. There were traditional leather sofas coloured chestnut or claret or buff or antique green, with deep buttoned arms and backs, with Queen Anne legs. There were classic designs equally at home in the modern apartment or the English country house, filled with feather and down, with fire resistant foam, in damask or linen, in plain or patterned Dralon, in floral prints and flat weaves. There was contrast piping, tassel fringing, box pleats, split valances and bun feet. There were futuristic settees all asymmetry and acid colours, made of suede and steel and animal skins.

Next came the tables. There were dining tables in oak and pine and ash and mahogany, in marquinya marble and black travertine. Some were circular, some extendable, some drop-leaved. There were coffee tables and hall tables and lamp tables, and some even came in nests. There were chairs to go with the tables: diners and carvers, chairs that rocked and reclined, spoon backs, ladder backs, slipper chairs, swivel and campaign chairs. There were also the stools: bar stools, footstools, tudor stools, saddle-seat stools.

Beds came in all sizes: king size, queen size, three-quarter, single. There were circular beds and water beds, divans, bunk beds, orthopaedic beds, futons and four posters; beds with posture spring-ing; brass bedsteads, and head boards in padded velour and forged iron.

There were chaise longues and love seats and day beds. And there were wardrobes and dressing tables and free-standing bookcases and dressers and servers and armoires and bureaus and commodes. There were fine materials and finishes: burl and rosewood and chestnut, cane and wicker, intricate wrought iron, glass and lacquer, tubular chrome, verdigris, inlays, veneers, stencillings. And there were all those little accessories that make a home complete: bedside cabinets, magazine racks, hat stands, scatter cushions, mirrors, pouffes.

Charlie would have liked them all a lot more if it hadn't been his job to porter them around.

The furniture floor was stalked by roaming salesmen. They were independent characters who liked to hunt alone, and to pounce ruthlessly on likely looking browsers. They were polite and helpful enough, but bluff and anything but servile. If a customer wanted a special finish or an unusual fabric or a custom-made item, the salesmen would say firmly, and with a certain pleasure, that it was not available, that it could not be done. Their pleasure did not come from simply denying the customer what he or she wanted – that would have been pointless and petty – rather it came from the knowledge that special orders required extra work while earning no extra commission, thus by saying no they had saved themselves from unnecessary, unpaid effort.

The salesmen were backed up by a series of 'consultants' who worked for the various companies that manufactured the furniture on display. The consultants were always female, always suntanned, always on a diet. They were not as young or as pretty as they had once been. They knew it and it didn't make them happy. They were brittle and moody, tended to use unconvincingly 'posh' accents, and Charlie found them hideous. In his first week at Haden Brothers, one of them asked him to move a plum-coloured leather banquette for her, to a spot she thought was more likely to produce sales. Charlie did as she asked and she watched him so critically, so clearly expecting him to scratch the leather, or knock over a lamp, or tear the carpet, that he succeeded in doing all three.

Charlie gradually discovered that Anton's and the other porters' desire to bring Haden Brothers to its knees was heartfelt but patchy. It manifested itself in the extravagant pilfering of clothes, as he'd already seen, taking very, very long lunch hours and tea breaks, stealing more pens, pencils, notepads and envelopes than they could possibly use in one lifetime, and making lavishly expensive phone calls at the company's expense.

As the days passed, the porters slowly began to talk to Charlie, and mostly it was to encourage him to join in their subversion. He was happy enough to extend his lunch and tea breaks and he did make one or two phone calls, though they were not nearly as frequent or as long distance as the others would have wished. 'Don't you have any friends in Australasia?' Anton would ask, but Charlie didn't. Neither did he bother stealing stationery because he didn't need it, and he didn't get involved with the stealing of clothes. He couldn't altogether have said why not. He thought of himself as indifferently honest, and if he had been in great need and presented with a great temptation, he would undoubtedly have succumbed. But his need for silk shirts and cashmere sweaters was nonexistent, and although his need for money was considerable, he didn't want to steal them just in order to sell them on, the way some of the porters did. Essentially he didn't want to be a thief.

He didn't bother trying to explain any of this to his fellow workers, and they didn't try too hard to coerce him. They felt sure he would come round to their way of thinking before long, and then act accordingly. They would have said it was not a matter of need or temptation but of revenge. Their thievery was motivated by a sense of grievance against Haden Brothers for the terrible way they considered themselves to be treated.

They also engaged in petty but vicious acts of sabotage around the store. If they were on the shop floor and someone asked them for directions, they would give minutely detailed instructions which would take the customer to entirely the wrong place. In the washrooms they would leave hot water taps running so as to waste water and energy. They delighted in pushing the emergency buttons that stopped the escalators, since they knew it would cause maximum disruption and irritation to both staff and public. Charlie took no part in these activities, and although he never said anything he almost hoped the others could sense his disapproval.

He soon learned the ropes of his job. Typically he and a couple of other porters would be called upon to take a three piece suite or a dining table or a room-divider from the shop floor to the packing room, where they would wrap it in protective polythene sheets, then take it to the loading bay where it would go into the back of a van and be dispatched to some waiting customer. Then they would perform this process more or less in reverse as new stock came in from the suppliers. It took Charlie no time at all to see the disadvantages of having a furniture department on the seventh floor. But he never again saw the dark stockroom where he had spent that first miserable day. That, he supposed, remained in wait for the next unfortunate new recruit.

For all that Charlie would have preferred not to work, or at least to have worked at his art, he really couldn't see what was so terrible about being a furniture porter at Haden Brothers. That small, hellish glimpse of meaningless toil they'd given him on his first day bore no relation to the actual work. True they sometimes had to move heavy or awkward items, sometimes there was a rush job or a busy patch, once in a while a furniture salesman would treat them a little snottily; but in general the work was not too strenuous, not too hurried, certainly not too difficult. It offered very little future, but it made, in his opinion, for a perfectly tolerable present.

Even though the furniture porters were a cynical, aggressive and arrogant bunch, they were curiously well-liked around the department. Although they weren't foolish enough to admit to the various acts of theft or sabotage they committed, they made no secret of their contempt for Haden Brothers and all its works. They were mavericks and people admired them for it. People always had a piece of banter and a dirty joke for a furniture porter. The salesmen liked to share laddish repartee. The girls from the furniture office flirted with them. Even the less brittle of the consultants were prepared to give them the time of day. Because he was in their company, Charlie was treated as though he was one of their ilk but he was becoming increasingly certain that he wasn't.

They invited him to go out drinking after work, but he always said no. He said there was a cooking rota in his flat and he had to be there to participate in it. This was, of course, completely untrue, and even as he said it he knew it sounded unconvincing. In truth he always got a cheap take-away on his way home and ate it alone in the kitchen while Keith and Sarah occupied the living room.

Friday came. His first week at Haden Brothers was over and he got his first wage packet. It contained exactly the amount of money it should have, but Anton insisted that Charlie should come along with the rest of the porters who were going to the wages office to query their pay. Their wages were every bit as correct as Charlie's, but waiting in a queue to see some wages clerk who would then explain some abstruse point about how holiday entitlement was accrued, or how National Insurance worked and then confirm that their wages were perfectly correct, was, Anton assured him, guaranteed to waste a couple of hours, and this was an opportunity not to be missed. Charlie tagged along, but it seemed stupid and futile to him. He was happy enough to avoid work, but sometimes it appeared that the amount of energy that went into skiving was more exhausting than actually moving furniture around.

A couple of hours were duly wasted. Finally, after some hapless clerk had explained to each porter in turn all the things they already knew, they happily left the wages offices. Once back on the furniture floor Anton decided it was too late to do any more work that day, and they were all going home. It was only three o'clock however, and they explained to Charlie that someone would have to stay behind until six and then do the clocking-out for all of them. Charlie was the chosen one. He was sure this must be an offence for which he could lose his job, but he did as asked. As he spent three long hours hanging around he realized this could have been a great opportunity for getting on with his art on company time, but instead, still having claimed no art form as his own, he read the papers, did a quick crossword, made a few cups of coffee. At one point he was even called upon to move a small cocktail cabinet.

The day eventually ended. On his way home he bought a couple of litres of Bulgarian wine and a family-size packet of potato crisps. This would be a way of celebrating his first wage packet. It would be a peace offering for Keith and Sarah, not that war had been declared or fought, but he thought it wise to pay his reparations in advance. He had also agreed to give them a fair slice of his wages for the continuing pleasure of sleeping on their sofa.

'Look,' Sarah had said, 'obviously we could let you continue staying here for free, but that way there'd never be any incentive for you to find a place of your own, would there? This way, if it costs you as much to stay here as it would to move out, then you'll be highly motivated to move and that'll make you happy, right?'

Charlie knew it wasn't that simple. Even renting a tiny bedsit in some outlying part of London required an enormous outlay of money. A month's rent had to be paid in advance and then landlords always wanted the same amount again paid as a deposit. The idea had been that once he was working he would start saving up this deposit, but it was obviously going to be a lot more difficult to save anything if he paid rent to Keith and Sarah.

He got home at about seven. He could hear voices coming from the living room. The television wasn't on; an unusual situation in Keith and Sarah's household. He went into the kitchen, opened one of the bottles of wine, put it and the crisps and three wine glasses on a tray and waltzed into the living room. He called out, 'Party time!' as he pushed open the door. However, Sarah was already engrossed in a party of her own, and it was not one to which Charlie, nor Keith for that matter, was invited.

Sarah was in the living room having sex with some man Charlie had never seen before. They were both naked and glistening fiercely with sweat. Sarah's ankles were somewhere up around the man's neck and he was pumping into her with an athletic seriousness, as though he was participating in some sort of highly specialized endurance event. Sarah looked far more voluptuous than Charlie would have imagined her to be, not that he had ever seriously tried to imagine what she would look like naked. Her unexpectedly large breasts flowed rhythmically back and forth across her chest in time with the man's movements. He was a rugged, hairy-backed specimen who looked the sort you would not want to cross. Charlie found himself staring at the scene with some fascination, not because he was more than averagely voyeuristic, but because they were using the sofa, his sofa, his bed, as a platform for their coupling.

They were at least as surprised to see him as he was to see them. Perhaps they thought he was Keith returning unexpectedly. The man immediately disentangled himself from Sarah but things had reached such a pitch that as he withdrew he inadvertently spilled his seed all over the cushion where Charlie lay his head every night.

'You fucking idiot!' Sarah said, and at first Charlie thought she was addressing her lover, who after all had been guilty of a certain idiocy, but it became clear she meant him. It was not the moment for lengthy discussions, and there was barely time for a few hasty apologies before Charlie fled the flat in embarrassment.

It was a cold February night. He found himself sitting alone on a park bench using the red wine he'd brought with him as insulation against the cold. He felt sincerely sorry for himself. He felt like one of London's unfortunates. There were people all over London who were jobless, homeless and penniless. He was, in the strictest sense, none of these things, but he experienced a sudden, brief affinity with the rest of the poor naked wretches.

It did not seem to him that he was asking too much out of life. He wanted a roof over his head, some friends, a girlfriend (Vita Carlisle, if he was given a choice) and the chance to become an artist; that was all. It now seemed supremely presumptuous ever to have hoped for any of these things. He was alone and miserable and hurting and it occurred to him then that the furniture porters at Haden Brothers, much as he felt himself to be different and separate from them, were perhaps the best friends he'd got. This realization only drove him a little closer to despair.

He didn't see how he could ever return to Keith and Sarah's flat, but then it began to rain and he saw precisely how he could. Sarah was alone watching television when he returned. The stranger had gone and Keith was still out. Sarah turned casually towards him as he passed through the living room but kept half an eye on the television programme.

'What you saw tonight,' she said, 'it never happened, right?'

'Oh, OK,' said Charlie.

'And, if you ever mention it to Keith, you're dead.'

Charlie said OK again.

'I'll call you a liar,' Sarah continued. 'I'll call you everything under the sun. And I'll kick you out of this flat so fast you won't know what's hit you. Got that?'

'Got it,' said Charlie.

He went into the kitchen and drank some of his Bulgarian red from a tumbler. He owed no particular loyalty to Keith but he couldn't help feeling a little guilty. On the other hand he did not want to be dead, neither literally nor figuratively, and humble though it undoubtedly was, he still didn't want to lose his bed. For a while at least, things could remain as they were, though from now on he would be sleeping with his head at the other end of the sofa.

9 · PURCHASE ASSEMBLY

Vita Carlisle is sitting in a white leather armchair in Arnold Haden's all-white penthouse. Her bare feet rest in the deep-pile white carpet, and the dynamite rests reassuringly on her stomach. Arnold is drinking a glass of blanc de blancs, which he is showing every sign of enjoying. Vita thinks this must be an act of bravado. Can he really have the sangfroid to enjoy wine in a situation like this? At his insistence she has taken a glass herself, and she wonders if he's trying to get her drunk.

'This is a very white place you've got here,' she says.

It is now an hour or so since Arnold Haden's rendezvous with Vita began and he still has only the sketchiest idea of what's going on or why. Vita has said that she's not a terrorist, but that doesn't mean much. That she's a disturbed young woman he has no doubt, but that means even less.

'Vita,' he says gently, 'I'm not trying to tell you how to do things . . . '

'Good,' she says.

'But it seems to me, we're not getting anywhere with this. Now, because of the position I hold and because I'm interested in that sort of thing, I have made a bit of a study of how terrorist acts, hostage-taking, kidnapping, sieges and so forth, are supposed to work.'

'Have you really?'

'Yes, I have. And it seems to me there are one or two areas where you're going slightly astray.'

'Is that right?'

'You see, the way I understand it's supposed to work, you begin by taking the hostage or hostages, you confine them, you threaten and scare them, break them down and make sure they know you mean business. And so far that's worked just fine. I'm here, I'm scared and I know you mean business. But what now?'

Vita does not respond to his question.

'Next,' he says, 'I think you're supposed to call the authorities, the police, the security forces, the anti-terrorist branch, the bomb squad, get the place surrounded, get some professional negotiators in, take it right to the top. Then, and perhaps most important of all, you bring in the media, some of whom may even be sympathetic to you and your cause; but even if they aren't, it doesn't matter, because at least your cause is being aired. You become something of a figure, you might even get a few supporters and followers.'

'I'm not sure that I want followers,' says Vita.

'Well, that's not particularly important, but what *is* important is that you then make some demands. These can be very vague or very specific. They can be reasonable or totally absurd. They can involve money, property, getaway cars, helicopters, aeroplanes, new passports, releasing prisoners from jail, the calling of an amnesty. Anything like that.'

'I don't have any demands,' says Vita. 'I just want you dead.'

'That's a shame,' says Arnold Haden. 'Tell me, have you ever heard of the law of diminishing marginal utility?'

'What?'

'It's a term from economic theory. I'd like to tell you about it. Why don't you have another drink?'

She refills her wine glass and lets Arnold talk.

'As I understand it,' he says, 'utility, in economists' parlance, is the satisfaction derived from the consumption of goods or services. You buy an apple, you consume it, you derive some satisfaction: that's the apple's utility. But there's a problem if we have a lot of apples, because it's generally argued that three apples don't contain three times as much utility as one apple. If the first apple has satisfied your needs, the second apple, by definition, can't satisfy them as completely. In fact, the more apples you have, the less utility each apple is likely to contain. But I know what you're thinking: what if you had an apple and an orange?'

Vita glares at him. No, that is not what she was thinking.

'That changes things,' he continues. 'If you had one apple and one orange, they might well each contain similar amounts of marginal utility, but since they would satisfy different needs, the *total* amount of utility would be higher. I believe this is known as the substitution effect.

'Now, it seems to me that this law of diminishing marginal utility may be relevant to our current situation.'

'You don't say,' Vita sneers.

'Yes, Vita, because you'll derive a certain, quantifiable amount of satisfaction from killing me. The act will contain enormous utility as far as you're concerned. But I'm wondering if the substitution effect might apply here and if there are any means by which you could increase the total utility you derive.'

'I can't see it, Arnold,' she says. 'I really can't see what would make me happier than killing you.'

'Please don't get me wrong, Vita. I'm not begging for my life here. I assume you're going to kill me, and that's fine; I accept that. But if you blow us both up, then you'll be dead as well, and I'm not sure that you could derive any utility at all if you were dead.'

Vita looks at him suspiciously. It just sounds like a ruse to her.

'I would hate it if you killed yourself, Vita.'

'Oh really? And why's that?'

'Because I love you, Vita, you seem to keep forgetting that.'

10 · FIRST AID

The toy department buyer was a raw, lean, adrenalin-driven young man called Carl Laughton. Although he was youthful enough in years, he had been chosen and had styled himself to appear as serious and as unplayful as possible. The selling of toys was a serious business and had to be seen as such.

On Vita's first full day in the department he took her aside and told her, 'We sell a lot of merchandise here on the basis that we're educating the little fucks, stimulating their imaginations, fostering hand-eye co-ordination, that kind of crap. The truth is, what we're struggling to do here is sedate and socialize a generation of would-be Adolf Hitlers.'

Vita looked at him uncertainly but still managed a smile.

'The thing to remember is this,' Laughton continued, 'all children are thugs, fascists and megalomaniacs. There was a time when they wanted scaled-down versions of the real world: toy animals, toy soldiers, dolls, building blocks to make miniature cities. Then they pulled the eyes out of the animals, tore the dolls limb from limb, massacred the soldiers, razed the cities.

'These days, they play with computer games, and they can play at destroying whole life forms, whole planets and galaxies. They take to it like ducks to water. It all comes perfectly naturally to them. And they genuinely believe that when they grow up they'll be able to do all this stuff for real. But when they do grow up they discover, with one or two important exceptions, that they *don't* get to blow things up at all, and that really hurts them. It's a discovery nobody ever quite recovers from. I know *I* haven't.

'That's why toys are so attractive to adults, why they carry so much nostalgia with them, because they remind us of a time when we were power-mad, conscienceless dictators.'

Vita smiled at him again and said, 'Oh, I'm sure you don't really believe that. I'm sure you're just using your cynicism as a way of denying the child inside you.'

He hated her for saying that, and it took no time at all for everyone else in the toy department to hate her just as much. There were any number of reasons why they might feel that way, and different members of staff chose the different reasons that best suited their personalities. The mere fact that she was so punctual in her comings and goings would have been reason enough for some, while others honed in on the precision of her till procedures, her helpful manner and her relentless enthusiasm, her propensity in any spare moment to start cleaning and dusting, what is known in the retail trade as 'house-keeping'.

More galling still was the fact that she was so good with customers. She was able to sell them armfuls of merchandise, things they hadn't even dreamed of buying when they first entered the department. She achieved this in an effortless, guileless way. She didn't appear to be trying. She certainly wasn't using any hard sell. It was simply that her enthusiasm for Haden Brothers and all its products seemed so boundless and so contagious that it rubbed off on hapless shoppers.

But what could galvanize even the most generous-spirited of souls into hating Vita Carlisle was her way with children. She could produce smiles and placidity in any child, however savage and wilful. She would talk to them and sometimes read to them. They loved it, and the other staff had to admit to a grudging respect for her skills. But when she was caught, on the morning of her second day, actually singing 'A Spoonful of Sugar' to one small, bawling slime-cheeked infant, it was universally agreed that she had gone too far. For this she earned the nickname Julie Andrews.

What made hating Vita a particularly subtle and convoluted business, was the fact that she was so bloody nice. Despite everything, she was actually quite hard to hate, but that didn't make her any easier to like. Carl Laughton found it particularly hard because she was so good for business.

She got on well with her superiors, but she didn't crawl, and she was genuinely friendly towards the other assistants. She wasn't all high and mighty and smug with assumed superiority the way some members of the Flying Squad were. She was genuine, honest, enthusiastic, cheerful, in some profound sense even pleasant, and the whole department felt they had no choice but truly to despise her for it.

'Shouldn't we send some flowers to the lady who had the nervous collapse?' she asked Carl Laughton. 'You know, the lady whose job I'm doing.'

'A Venus fly-trap maybe,' he suggested.

'Didn't you get on with her?' Vita asked.

'You could say that.'

'Well, this would be as good a time as any to start being friends, wouldn't it?' she suggested.

'Why? It was me who brought on her nervous collapse. It took some doing.'

'I'm sure that's not true.'

'It bloody is. And if she ever comes back I'll do my best to see it happens again.'

'I know you don't really mean that,' said Vita.

Laughton insisted that he did, explaining that the lady in question had been so bad at her job that she had frequently cost him his monthly bonus, but Vita continued to see the best in him. It drove him to a fury and he began contemplating some way to make Vita collapse too, though he could see she was made of considerably stronger stuff than his previous victim.

On Wednesday, her third day in the department, Derek Snell visited the toy department to see how his protégée was settling in. He asked her how she was finding it and she said she was blissfully happy, though he knew, and she reminded him, that she would have been equally happy to serve anywhere else in the organization. He conspicuously failed to consult other members of staff on her suitability for the department and that riled them too.

Nevertheless, there was something appropriate about her working in the toy department; not that she was childlike, but rather that she was toy-like. For all her genuineness, she seemed curiously unreal. In the sense that a teddy bear is a safe, soft, clean, odourless version of a wild animal, so Vita appeared to be a tame, sanitized version of a human being. She was too neat, too well laundered, too perfect. There was a growing feeling in the department that something had to be done about her, and sooner rather than later.

Vita was no fool. She knew how they felt about her. That night she phoned her mother from the hostel where she lived.

'I think they all hate me,' she said.

'Well, of course they hate you, dear,' her mother replied calmly. 'You're better than they are.'

'Well yes, but I do my very best not to show it.'

'Why shouldn't you show it?'

'Because I think that will make them hate me even more.'

'But if they hate you anyway, what difference would it make?'

'Oh, I don't know . . . '

'And how do they express their hatred?'

'Oh, you know, they mock the way I talk, they go quiet if I try to join in with their conversations. They don't invite me to go on coffee breaks with them.'

'If that's all that being hated means, what's wrong with being hated?'

'It makes me rather miserable, Mummy.'

'Does it? I don't see why it should.'

Vita sometimes thought her mother was wonderful when she said things like that. It was as though she was cleverly devising a fresh way of looking at a problem, of showing up its smallness and absurdity. But at other times it could seem that her mother was so totally out of touch with the rest of humanity that she really couldn't see why being hated should make someone miserable. Vita could think of nothing to say.

'Well, at least you'll be moving on soon,' her mother said.

'Yes, I suppose that's another good thing about working in the Flying Squad.'

'I didn't mean only the Flying Squad.'

'Oh, Mummy, here we go again.'

'You're not going to stay in that job forever, are you? Before very long I'm sure the scales are going to fall from your eyes, Vita, and you're going to get a sensible job in television or advertising.'

'This is a perfectly sensible job, Mother, and we've already had this conversation. I want to work at Haden Brothers and I'm going to work there.'

'Well anything you say, dear, so long as it makes you happy.'

That kind of sarcasm only made Vita feel worse. 'I don't see why you disapprove so much,' she said. 'Haden Brothers is your favourite shop.'

'And diamonds are a girl's best friend, but I wouldn't want my daughter working in a diamond mine either.'

'Mother, you're not being an awful lot of help.'

'Well, is there something specific I can do? Do you need money? They can't be paying you much at that place.'

'Money isn't the problem.'

'Shall I send you some flowers, or some champagne?'

'That's kind, Mummy, but it wouldn't help.'

'It doesn't sound as though anything would.'

Vita hesitated a moment, getting up the courage to deliver her next sentence. 'Couldn't I come home?' she asked.

'Of course, you're welcome any time. How about coming over for brunch one of these Sundays?'

'I mean to live.'

A profound chill was magically transmitted down the phone line from mother to daughter.

'Is there something wrong with the hostel? It came very highly recommended.'

'It's all right,' Vita said, not wanting to get shunted into a side issue.

'Are the other girls agreeable?'

'Probably. They don't talk to me much. But you see, most of them are in the hostel because they want to work in London and they have families in the north or Scotland or somewhere. It seems a little strange for me to be there when my mother lives in a flat just round the corner from Haden Brothers.'

'Oh, Vita, I don't think you could call it a flat. It's barely more than a *pied-à-terre*.'

Vita thought there was no standard on earth by which her mother's flat could be considered anything less than palatial.

'Oh, Mummy,' she sighed.

'And I know how much you value your independence,' her mother continued.

Vita couldn't quite bring herself to say that she didn't value her independence very much at all, but she knew what was coming next.

'Then can't you find yourself a nice boyfriend to move in with? Or a sugar daddy?'

'I don't know that would make me any less miserable,' said Vita.

'Or how about getting together with one or two of the other girls from work and sharing a flat together?'

'But they all hate me,' Vita said pathetically.

'Poor old Vita Carlisle,' her mother said. 'Nobody wants to play with her.'

It was not meant to be unkind, but like much else in her dealings with her daughter it was seriously miscalculated. Vita was too overwhelmed by misery to say anything more to her mother. She put the phone down. She was calling from a pay phone in a corridor of the hostel. She turned round to see there was a short queue of girls waiting to use it. They all pretended quite hard not to notice that Vita was crying.

Vita woke on Saturday morning, showered, dressed, made up, steeled herself for another day of hatred. Even so, she arrived early at Haden Brothers. And she smiled at everybody she met: the security men who checked her ID on the way into the building, the waitresses in the staff canteen where she had a solitary cup of coffee before work, the people she saw on the escalator on her way up to her department.

She was there among the toys a good half-hour before the store opened, and she immediately set about her housekeeping. She took her duster, her J Cloth and her spray of Mr Sheen, and began polishing all the shiny glass and chrome surfaces she could find, driving away all traces of smears and fingerprints. It was almost soothing.

Some time later she looked at her watch. The store was due to open in five minutes and she was still the only one to have arrived in the toy department. This was very unusual, but she supposed she could manage on her own until someone else came; or if some mysterious bug had made them all too ill to come to work, then members of the Flying Squad would no doubt be drafted in, and that in itself might be a change for the better.

A couple of minutes later Carl Laughton arrived. He looked strangely unconcerned at the absence of staff. 'Vita, could you help me move this cabinet?' he said the moment he saw her. He pointed to a long glass-fronted display cabinet that was used to house extremely expensive robots and dolls, collectors' items rather than toys. It was a heavy cumbersome thing, and Vita wasn't sure the two of them would be able to lift it, but she went willingly enough. She offered to empty the cabinet to make it lighter but Laughton didn't want that. They each grabbed an end and attempted to lift it. It was a struggle. They both grimaced with the effort, and the cabinet moved barely a couple of inches. They tried again. This time Laughton threw himself into it, and grunted and panted as though to demonstrate just how hard he was trying.

Suddenly, without saying anything, he dropped his end of the cabinet. His face looked white and pained. He gasped for breath and held a hand to his chest. Vita thought at first he was rather exaggerating the degree of his exertion, but his face continued to look agonized, his breath refused to come and he folded at the knees. Vita

92

watched with horror. Could it really be a heart attack? That's what it looked like. He was so young and lean and active, but then again he did suffer from stress. Laughton meanwhile had sunk to the floor and lay on his side, his face pressed to the industrial-quality grey carpet. He looked imploringly at Vita, and if he had been able to speak he would surely have begged her to help him. She stood over him helplessly. She knew a little first aid but the knowledge was largely theoretical. It had never been called upon. She looked around for help, and saw all the rest of the toy department staff suddenly arriving *en masse*.

'What have you done to him?' one of them asked.

'I've done nothing,' Vita protested. 'I think he's having a heart attack, don't you?'

'Could be. Have you called an ambulance?'

'There won't be time for that,' said another. 'It's artificial respiration or nothing. Does anyone know how to give the kiss of life?'

Vita, it was rapidly established, was the only one with even the sketchiest idea of how to give the kiss of life. By now Laughton was lying still, his eyes were closed, and Vita wasn't even sure he was still breathing. This was no time to be hesitant. She knelt beside him, turned him on his back, and began administering the kiss of life as best she could. Nothing happened for the first couple of breaths, but at the third attempt she felt Laughton's body twitch, and the muscles round his mouth moved slightly. She breathed into him again and suddenly his arms came up, grabbed her tightly around the waist and shoulders, pulling her on top of him. His pelvis pumped up and down, while his mouth wrapped itself around hers, and his tongue delivered Vita a long, dirty, slobbering French kiss.

The rest of the staff continued to stand in a semi-circle but now they were laughing and jeering, and when Laughton finally let go of Vita, they gave her a round of nasty, mocking, derisive applause. Vita fought her way up from the floor, dishevelled and flushed with embarrassment and anger. She turned towards her tormentors who at once broke ranks and went nonchalantly to their places in the department.

'I won't forget this,' Vita called after them. 'You won't get away with this.'

But nobody really believed that, not even Vita.

It was a long and ragged Saturday with more than the usual number of complaints, returns, difficult customers and requests for refunds. Vita did not speak a word to any of her colleagues all day, not even to

Laughton when he came close to apologizing to her. What he actually said was, 'All right, so maybe I was a bit out of hand.' Vita remained calm and silent, turned her back on him and went to serve someone. As far as the customers were concerned she remained herself, the perfect shop assistant. She was too proud and professional to let her feelings get in the way of her job.

It was nearly closing time when an old gentleman in an astrakhan coat came into the department, holding the hand of his tiny, lively granddaughter. He asked Carl Laughton for help which he only grudgingly gave. They gathered up a few rather old-fashioned traditional toys and games for the granddaughter: a spinning top, a simple jigsaw showing a map of the world, a box of snakes and ladders. The old man put them down at the till, said 'You've been very kind, sir,' and began to search for his wallet.

He felt around inside the big black coat and a moment later began clutching his chest. He let out a low, faint wheeze and hit the ground with a soft thud, like a roll of carpet thrown off the back of a van. He was the only customer in the department by now, and the assistants gathered round, all except Vita who was keeping her distance. Carl Laughton immediately smelt a rat.

'Oh come on, Vita,' Laughton shouted to her across the department. 'If you want to get your own back you'll have to come up with something a bit more original than this.'

Vita said nothing. One of the younger male assistants pushed the toe of his shoe into the old man's flank. 'Get up, you old bugger,' he said. The old man writhed a little and his granddaughter began to howl. The assistants made caustic remarks about what a brat she was and about the old man being a lousy actor. A couple of girl assistants got helpless attacks of giggles. Only Vita remained impassive.

It was then that Derek Snell walked into the department. He saw the congregation of staff and heard the giggles. He did not like to see his staff congregating or giggling. Then he saw the old man on the floor in obvious distress, and heard the child scream.

'What on earth's going on here?' he demanded.

'It's just one of Vita's little jokes,' Laughton said. 'I don't know who the old geezer is. Her boyfriend probably.'

The others hooted with forced, mirthless laughter. It was then that Vita grasped the situation. She ran across the department and fell to her knees beside the old man. She began to give the kiss of life for the second time that day, but this time it was genuinely needed. Derek

94

Snell picked up a telephone, uttered a few clear, concise instructions and a minute and a half later security and first aid men and a nurse arrived. They let Vita continue with the kiss of life since she was doing it so efficiently. Soon the old man was breathing again and he was carried off on a stretcher. The nurse offered the opinion that Vita had probably saved his life. Vita picked up the small wide-eyed granddaughter and held her tight.

Carl Laughton and the rest of the staff edged away from Vita and Snell, and even though it was now time to go home, they found important chores that suddenly needed doing around the department.

'Are you all right, Miss Carlisle?' Derek Snell asked.

'Of course,' she said.

When he was sure that she meant it he turned towards the rest of the staff and said sadly, 'Oh dear. None of you will ever work in Haden Brothers again. I'm afraid you're wretched, pathetic scum. Leave now. Don't return. Your wages will be forwarded to you. Don't expect a reference.'

He said it firmly but without anger. It was just something he had to do. It was part of his job and he took no pleasure in it and, as a matter of fact, neither did Vita. She could find no vindictiveness within herself. Nevertheless, as she returned to her hostel that evening, she was pleased and a little surprised at the extent to which her habitual misery had abated.

11 · MAKING UP

REBECCA O'HARE, beauty consultant: The first thing I ever ask a potential customer is, 'Do you use soap?' Because if they do, then the second thing I always say to them is, 'Stop it. Stop it right now!'

I believed in my company's products, of course I did, and I wouldn't have said I was unhappy in my job. I wasn't one of those very ambitious women you sometimes meet, who'll do anything to claw their way to the top, but I did want to get on in life, of course I did. Who doesn't?

It's been said by various people at various times in my life that I'm a bit of an easy lay, and I deny that very vehemently indeed. I'm not inhibited and I'm not ashamed of my body. I think it's a beautiful thing and an instrument of pleasure, but that doesn't mean I'm just anybody's. I know my worth. I'm attractive, and thanks to the careful use of beauty products I've made the very best of myself.

Yes, I wanted to sleep with Arnold Haden, I don't deny that. Is it a crime? It looked like a good career move to me. There are very few things I won't do for the right man. But when I heard what Arnold Haden wanted from me there was no way I could possibly oblige him. No way at all.

It was the uniforms that Rebecca O'Hare hated more than anything else, and the fact that her company kept changing them so often. One season she'd be required to dress like a lab technician in a high-necked white smock. The next she'd have to look like an air hostess in a severely tailored grey suit. Then she'd be required to put on pastel-coloured shorts, T-shirt and baseball cap as though dressed for some strange, unspecified sporting activity. She wished they'd make up their corporate mind.

Nor was she keen on having to approach people cold, complete strangers, customers who were eager to get past her to some other department, and ask them if they'd like to try an exciting new fragrance, or tell them that if they bought fifty pounds worth of beauty and grooming products they could have a stylish free gift: a sportsbag or a shorty towelling dressing gown. Sometimes she felt like a beggar, sometimes like a streetwalker.

Of course, she always wanted to look her best, to be an advertisement and an ambassador for her company. She was good at applying makeup, to herself and to others. When she started the job she tried to be subtle about it, to use cosmetics sparingly and economically. But since the products were always to hand, always free, always inviting, there was a temptation to keep slapping on a bit more blusher, to darken the eye shadow, to add extra gloss to the lips. She submitted to the temptation. Her face became a living and lurid mask of makeup, skilfully applied but unmistakably, thickly artificial. The mask could be used to hide all sorts of flaws: wrinkles, spots, bags under the eyes, her tiredness, her discontent with the job.

Derek Snell passed through her department at least once a day. He looked to her like a man in need of a whole new approach to skin and hair care. She felt she could easily have given him a male fragrance to enhance and improve his personal style, but she didn't want to be presumptuous. She always gave him a winning smile and exchanged a few words, and she was keen to show good *esprit de corps* whenever he was around. But she had no ultimate interest in Derek Snell. He was just a middleman, a means to an end, someone who could give her access to Arnold Haden.

She'd heard the stories about Arnold Haden's eccentricities, but she felt sure they were exaggerated. And even if they were not, even if he was a smelly, dirty, long-haired, long-nailed nutcase, and even if he had some highly unsavoury sexual tastes, she would still be prepared to oblige him for the sake of her career. She wanted to be bedded by the boss, a simple ambition, but she had to get to him first.

It was acknowledged in some unspoken way that this sort of thing went on; that Arnold Haden regularly had his pick of Haden Brothers shopgirls, and although Rebecca hadn't been able to find anyone who admitted to having done the dirty deed, she didn't find that necessarily discouraging; if anything the reverse. She suspected that a great many of the store's female supervisors, buyers and departmental managers owed their positions to having slept with Arnold Haden, and she reckoned they were silent about it for that very reason.

She finally took matters in hand. Derek Snell was making one of his regular sorties through cosmetics. Rebecca stood at the corner of the counter holding a spray filled with Eau de Juissance and as Snell drew level she contrived to bump into him and to pour the contents of the bottle all over the front of his shirt.

'Oh no!' she shrieked. 'I'm so clumsy. I'm such a fool. How can you ever forgive me?'

In fact, Derek Snell was not much put out by the accident. These things happened. He would get a replacement shirt from the menswear department. But Rebecca O'Hare was busily dabbing at his shirt with her handkerchief and making ever more frantic apologies. Then she looked up into Derek Snell's face and stopped dead in well-rehearsed horror.

'Oh dear,' she said. 'I see open pores.' And she looked very carefully at Derek Snell's cheeks, touching the skin lightly with her fingertips. 'Now tell me, do you use soap?'

'Yes,' said Derek Snell.

'Well stop it. Stop it right now.'

'Oh yes, all right,' he said unconvincingly and tried to move on, but she had a secure grip on his arm.

'I'm a professional, Mr Snell,' Rebecca said firmly. 'I hate to see a skin tone like yours, especially when there are readily available techniques and products that can solve the problem.'

'No, I don't think so,' said Snell.

'Oh, come on, hop into the chair for a moment. A quick herbal scrub never hurt anyone.'

Derek Snell tried hard to hide the fact that he was a killjoy and a spoilsport. He could see there were certain economic advantages to be derived from entering into the spirit of store life. Besides, he *had* noticed Rebecca smiling at him every day and he was not completely blind to her attractions. With a game reluctance he climbed into the high chair which Rebecca used for her demonstrations. There was a small TV screen beside her showing dry skin in hugely magnified detail. She peered intently into Derek Snell's face and said sadly, 'There's a fair amount of flaking, I'm afraid. And a lot more sebacious secretions than I like to see.'

She smattered his face with lotions, scrubbed it with cotton wool, massaged it, rubbed oils and creams into it, slapped the cheeks briskly. A small crowd gathered to watch the show and Rebecca started her patter.

'Now, I know a lot of men probably think it's a bit pansified to pamper themselves like this. Well, let me tell you, a man who knows how to pamper himself probably knows how to pamper a woman too.'

When she'd finished with Derek Snell's face she said, to him, 'We've got a delivery of a special fennel and juniper skin balm due in later today. I'll pop some up to you, all right?'

'Don't go to any trouble.'

'Trouble? That's my middle name,' she flirted.

Late that afternoon Rebecca O'Hare went to Derek Snell's small dishevelled office. She gave herself an extra layer of lip gloss, some extra frosted eye shadow, a new coat of nail varnish. Derek Snell was surprised to see her. His days were crowded and it seemed a very long time since he had sat in the cosmetic department, but then he remembered her promise to deliver the skin balm. He welcomed her politely but coolly. She placed the jar on his desk in front of him and he thanked her. 'It contains liposomes,' she said. She smiled a lot and sat on the edge of his desk, showing no willingness to leave.

'Is there something I can do for you?' Derek Snell asked.

'I'm sure there is. And plenty I can do for you.'

'I'm sorry?'

'Tell me, Mr Snell, what sort of man is Arnold Haden?'

It was a question he was used to being asked. His reply was practised and not overburdened with sincerity.

'He's a very ordinary person really. I'm not saying he isn't a little eccentric, and of course he's very shy, but there's nothing at all sinister about him. In fact, he's one of the most intelligent and charming men you could ever hope to meet.'

'That's just it,' said Rebecca. 'I do hope to meet him.'

'Mr Haden sees almost nobody.'

'Almost, but not quite, I understand.'

'Well . . . '

'I'm sure you could arrange an introduction for me, couldn't you, Derek?'

'Well, I suppose I could . . . '

'This skin balm,' she said moving more firmly on to the desk, closer to her prey, 'it's not just for the face. You can apply it all over your body, or get a friend to. You might need a friend to help you apply it to all those little out of the way places.'

'I see,' said Snell.

'I'm glad you do.'

She swooped across Derek Snell's desk, and rapidly unbuttoned his shirt, a clean one that was not soaked in Eau de Juissance, and began to run her hands across his chest. She moved her head forwards and kissed his nipples. Her lipstick prided itself on being smudge free, nevertheless she left its traces all over his pectorals.

'I'm not asking much, Derek, and I'm prepared to give a lot in return.'

For the next hour or so she gave her all, using up the whole jar of skin balm. At the end of the hour a flushed, perfumed and moisturized Derek Snell sat exhausted in his chair, while Rebecca O'Hare painstakingly reconstructed her makeup and put on her uniform again.

'So when do I get to meet Arnold Haden?' she asked.

Derek Snell was the kind of man who kept his promises.

'I'll arrange it for next week,' he said. 'But let me give you some advice. Mr Haden likes the natural look. No jewellery, no rings, no necklaces. Forget the makeup, the perfume, the long painted fingernails. Wear your hair down; no mousse, no gel, no hair spray. Basically, try not to look as though you work on a cosmetics counter.'

Rebecca O'Hare glared at Derek Snell in complete disgust, as though he had made the grossest, most indecent suggestion imaginable, and she slapped him hard and accurately across his clean-pored face.

'Let a man see me without makeup!' she bawled. 'I'd rather commit suicide.'

'Now, that's something you'll have to arrange for yourself,' said Derek Snell sadly.

12 · ADULT GAMES

The year is 1929 and we are in the directors' suite of the old Haden Brothers building, a serviceable but essentially grey edifice on the edge of Kensington. The two current Haden Brothers, Matthew and Frederick, Arnold Haden's father and uncle, are there to have discussions with Edward Zander, the man they hope may be able to create new, more prestigious premises for them. His reputation precedes him. A few years ago he built a yew maze at a country house close to Matlock Bath. On the day it was officially 'opened', a high-spirited, twelve-strong party of house guests entered the maze. Two hours later, their spirits were much lower and they had come nowhere near finding a way out. After four hours, when all the women and many of the men had been reduced to tears, workmen were called and a section of the outermost hedge had to be cut away, otherwise they might never have got out at all.

Zander had neglected to tell them that there was a spring-loaded section of yew that rose out of the ground once visitors had turned the first corner of the maze. Once in place, it looked exactly like all the rest of the hedge. It formed a continuous run of yew, thereby creating a maze without an exit. This was the kind of playful, conceptual, almost philosophical aspect of Zander's work that entertained everyone except those trapped in the maze.

Edward Zander brings a steamer trunk with him to the Haden Brothers directors' suite. This is his 'portfolio'. After formal greetings and a glass of sherry he begins to take items out of the trunk and to show them to the initially reserved Hadens. At first he produces a series of papers; nothing so simple as a ground plan or sketches of buildings, but rather optical illusions, puzzle pictures, photographs of Indian bungalows, of Polynesian body decoration, cut-away drawings of steam engines and motor cars. There are monographs of Arcimboldi, Escher and Bruegel, on Boullée and Ledoux. There are fossils, a brass pyramid, a glass eye, a set of Russian dolls.

The Hadens are drawn into the spirit of things, slowly at first but with increasing willingness. When Zander performs conjuring tricks with a box of matches, a silk handerchief and a fountain pen, they are astounded by the quickness of his hands. When he produces building bricks, and then a lump of modelling clay and invites them to roll up their sleeves and show him exactly what kind of building they have in mind, they become coy and deferential and say, 'No, no, *you*'re the architect.' Zander smiles as though he has pulled off his best trick yet.

Before long the floor of the office is strewn with clockwork toys, model garages, spud guns, paper aeroplanes, a Noah's ark. Zander shows an architectural boardgame he has devised. The brothers find themselves kneeling on the floor, jackets off, hair and ties askew. If anyone had burst in now they would have been hard pressed to insist that this was a business meeting. It doesn't feel at all like hard work. Would it have been like this with Frank Lloyd Wright?

Zander talks about Freud, about Clara Bow, about ancient Egypt. Then he produces a wooden box. It is a small four-inch cube. It has a hinged top and one tiny brass catch on the front. Still with the air of a magician he opens the lid but holds the box so that the Haden brothers can't see the contents. He places it on a table at the end of the room, and the brothers scramble to their feet and hurry over to see this new object of delight.

Zander reaches into the box and pulls out something light, intricate, made of balsa wood but painted and polished and veneered to look solid as though made of stone. It is an exquisitely detailed model of Bruegel's Tower of Babel. Zander holds it in the palm of his hand, spins it around, then tosses it up and catches it. He is a man who can juggle buildings.

'This is it, gentlemen,' he says. 'This is the building I'm going to construct for you.'

They peer closely at the model, at its eccentricity and singularity. It is a beautiful example of the modelmaker's art, but is it really what they had in mind? No, it is not, but they are so entranced by Zander, so in thrall, that it suddenly seems to be the building they always wanted, or at least the one they always *would* have wanted if only they had possessed the imagination. And before long it is the only building they could ever conceive of having.

Matthew Haden peers in through the model's tiny windows and is amazed to see a perfect miniature department store in there. He can see a furniture showroom, a jewellery department, a food hall.

'It's really rather marvellous,' he says, a little embarrassed by the extent of his own enthusiasm.

'It's witty,' says his brother. 'It's modern yet classical. It's strange, yet strangely familiar.'

'It's a building and a half,' says Matthew Haden.

'Yes, I think it's everything we've always wanted.'

'Yes,' says the other.

Zander smiles at them indulgently. 'It's everything and more,' he corrects.

13 · TOILETRIES

Charlie Mayhew had been a porter for a little over a month. He was sitting alone in the staff canteen, a cavernous, vaulted place that had been conceived as a grand medieval banqueting hall. There were oak beams crossing and recrossing the space, shields and battle axes mounted on the stone-clad walls, an open fireplace big enough to roast an ox. And as Charlie sat eating his toast at a long refectory table he was looked down on by a row of stuffed animal heads; deer and stags, but also more exotic creatures: a tiger, an orang-utan, a giraffe. Charlie might have found these dead creatures alarming or revolting, but they looked so obviously artificial, so crassly striving for an effect they patently failed to achieve, that it was impossible to take them seriously, much less be offended by them. The fact that they were genuine made no difference.

Charlie was reading a newspaper so he wouldn't have to talk to anyone. That was not much of a problem since the majority of the staff were icily unfriendly to new faces, but he was taking no chances. When a big man in a security guard's outfit sat down on the bench a few feet away from him Charlie merely buried himself deeper in the paper, as though he had suddenly been gripped by a news item. But the man was hard to ignore. His bulk was imposing and perhaps even threatening, and his uniform was not so much that of an artisan security guard as of a five star general. And simply looking away didn't work since a potent cloud of aftershave billowed out from the man. Charlie lifted his eyes a little and immediately looked down again, but it was too late. The man had caught his glance and was determined to engage him in conversation.

'How's it going, lad?' he asked.

Charlie now took a good look at the man. He was hefty, solid, but he looked soft-centred. His voice and demeanour might have be-longed to an enthusiastic but ultimately unsuccessful scoutmaster.

'Fine, thanks,' said Charlie and returned to his paper.

'The name's Chalmers, Ray Chalmers, Head of Internal Security,' and he leaned a long way over towards Charlie to shake his hand.

'Hi,' said Charlie.

Chalmers looked at the lapel of Charlie's overall and read his name on the security badge.

'Pleased to meet you, Mr Mayhew. I know you have to be new here because I don't recognize your face. I make it a point to recognize faces.'

'Oh well,' said Charlie with a light-heartedness he did not feel, 'don't try too hard to remember mine. I probably won't be here for very long.'

Chalmers looked shocked by this casual admission of disloyalty.

'I've heard a lot of people say that,' he said. 'That makes me want to remember them all the more. You're in the furniture department.'

'That's right.'

'So you know our friend Anton Heath.'

'Well, he's my boss. I work for him.'

'Yes. And who does *he* work for?'

Charlie thought he must be missing something here so he remained silent, but Chalmers seemed to take the silence as tacit agreement.

'I understand why you wouldn't want to call Anton Heath a friend,' Chalmers said. 'He's no friend of anybody but himself.'

'I really don't know him,' said Charlie. 'I've only been here a month or so.'

'A month's a bloody eternity in this game,' said Chalmers. 'It's more than enough time to make up your mind about the likes of Anton Heath. Time enough to know he's a troublemaker. In a fair world I could sort out somebody like him. I could take him aside, give him six weeks of boot camp, get him to take orders, give him some extended latrine duties and make a decent lad of him. My current remit doesn't allow for that, alas.'

Charlie had no idea how to respond to this sort of intimation. In the event he just smiled, partly in embarrassment and partly in the hope that Chalmers was joking.

'I can see it must be hard for a lad like yourself to have to take orders from the likes of Anton Heath,' said Chalmers.

Charlie started to nod in agreement, then stopped himself unsure what else he might be agreeing to.

'I can see you're a good lad, Charlie,' Chalmers continued. 'I could see that right away. You're obviously trustworthy, upright, respons-ible. What's more, you've got an honest face. I like that in a lad. I can't for the life of me think why they made you a furniture porter.'

Charlie could agree with that, and for a moment he wondered if Ray Chalmers was in a position to offer him a way out, get him moved to some job where his creative talents would be more useful.

'That furniture department is an absolute breeding ground for subversives and malcontents,' said Chalmers. 'They're like bugs under a rock, maggots breeding inside a dead dog. Present company excepted. They think I don't know what they get up to, and the sad truth is I don't, not exactly; not that I can't guess, but nothing I can prove. You follow?'

Charlie wasn't at all sure that he did.

'For a long time now,' said Chalmers, 'I've thought we should smash that department open like an overripe watermelon. We should sack a few people, have a bit of blood letting, have some show trials, encourage the others. But first I'd need something tangible.'

He looked at Charlie and then his face lit up as though some shiny, brand new idea had just that instant struck him. 'Have you noticed anything a bit dodgy in your department?' he asked.

The dodginess in the furniture department, at least amongst the porters, was so conspicuous that for Charlie to simply say he hadn't noticed it would suggest that he was a complete moron. But having Ray Chalmers think he was a moron didn't seem so terrible. He shook his head.

'No? Well, perhaps that's understandable. An innocent like your-self mightn't even notice some of the things that go on there.'

Charlie nodded in mild though hesitant agreement.

'For instance, have you heard them talk about a character called Hamnet?'

'No, but I saw it sprayed on one of the windows the day I started work here.'

Chalmers tautened as though someone had yanked a spring inside him. 'Shush!' he yelled loudly, and he moved very close to Charlie so they could huddle like conspirators.

'I think you may be a very bright lad,' said Chalmers and he put a hand on Charlie's knee. 'Brighter than I gave you credit for. Subtle too, I'll bet. All right, Charlie, I'll make you a deal. I want you to go back to that department, say nothing to anybody. If you ever see me on the shop floor you'll pretend you don't even know who I am.

You'll carry on working like before, the only difference will be, you'll be my eyes and ears in that department. Yes? I can make it worth your while. Do we have a deal?'

His grip on Charlie's knee became tight and painful. Charlie wondered if it was supposed to be a trial of strength, that he was supposed to pretend it wasn't hurting. He was having none of that. 'That hurts,' he said, and that made Ray Chalmers quite happy and he released the knee.

'What would these eyes and ears be looking and listening for?' Charlie asked.

'Oh, little things. Small but significant nuggets of information. Whether our Anton has any weak spots, any neuroses, any interesting habits, any Achilles' heel. I think you can guess the kind of thing I'm interested in.'

Charlie thought he could. 'When you said you'd make it worth my while, what did you mean?'

It was not that he was thinking of betraying Anton. He had no intention of spying for Ray Chalmers or anyone else, but he was interested to know what stakes they were playing for. Chalmers grinned and put an arm round Charlie's shoulder.

'The sky's the limit for the right bit of information.'

'Money?'

'If that's what you want.'

'Enough money that I could stop working for Haden Brothers?'

Chalmers looked at him harshly. For a moment he wondered if this little toe-rag was taking the piss. Maybe he'd got to him too late and the porters had already made him as base and corrupt as themselves, and yet the expression on Charlie's face still looked open and innocent enough. For the first time, Chalmers was uncertain.

'That really would have to be some piece of information,' he said haughtily. 'But I like a lad who thinks big.'

He slapped Charlie crisply round the back of the neck, stood up and left the table. Charlie went back to his newspaper and wondered if he should tell Anton about this conversation he'd just had, but in the event he kept it safely to himself.

RAY CHALMERS: I'm not trying to say it's like Vietnam out there, but in a sense it is. It's a jungle. The enemy's hard to spot. The terrain is difficult and we don't always get all the backing we need. There are goons. There are traitors and double agents. There are men from our side who've abandoned discipline and gone native. At least in Nam they were allowed to use defoliant, napalm, cluster bombing. I wish we could do that at Haden Brothers. That would shake the buggers up, flush them out so they could be punished with loads of prejudice.

Obviously a part of my job is concerned with shoplifters, though that's not a word I ever use myself. I think that's a pathetic euphemism. I call them thieves. I call them vermin. Sometimes I lose my rag and call them evil scumbags. Give me half an hour with a so-called shoplifter and a Duncan Fearnley cricket bat and I don't think we'd get too many persistent offenders.

I think of shoplifting in much the same way as I think of male homosexuality in public toilets. Some people say that by having enticing goods on display we're encouraging people to steal. But I say it's like a bloke who goes into a Gents and sees some other bloke standing there waving an enormous erection around. Now if the first bloke lays hands on the second bloke's erection and then the second bloke turns out to be a copper and arrests him, that first bloke's going to feel a bit hard done by and say he's been tricked. But I say tough. There's no mystery about it. You shouldn't nick things from shops and you shouldn't grab blokes' tools in public toilets, however tempting and mouth-watering they might look. It's as simple as that.

Then there's credit card fraud. Maybe I'm a Luddite, but if it was up to me I'd do away with credit cards. They're nothing but trouble. I remember the seventies. I remember the Arabs coming over here in their robes. They'd sit cross-legged on the floor of the furniture department, talking to the salesmen, doing a bit of haggling, taking their time, waiting till the terms of the deal were just right. Then they'd reach inside their robes and pull out a bunch of fifty-pound notes as big as your head. *They*'re the kind of customers we ought to be encouraging, never mind your easy terms and your low deposits and your interest-free credit. Who needs it?

But what about the enemy within? What about the filthy, stinking, treacherous employees who are happy enough to accept Haden Brothers wages and then try and undermine the company by stealing from it? What about stock shrinkage? Oh that's another smashing little euphemism, isn't it? What about till fraud, what about those till operators who can't keep their hands off other people's money? When I catch scum like that my solution would be to chop a hand off first and ask questions later. I'd like to see them get their grubby little fingers in the till after that.

What about computer fraud? What about vandalism? What about litter? What about double payrolling and fraudulent invoices? Yes. It's a war out there, and I don't necessarily see myself as part of the peace-keeping force.

I'm not saying I don't occasionally have a certain sympathy for some of the people I catch. A lad can go astray, of course he can. In general, it's because he hasn't had any discipline. A bit of firm handling could have made all the difference, but hey, there's a war on. It's too late to start feeling sorry for the little bastards.

But frankly, I wish I only had the *little* bastards to worry about. There's big bastards around too. It's a matter of historical forces, big movements. We don't have to name the enemies, but we can: socialism, liberalism, anarchy, the big lies. Terrorism.

There are plenty of people around who'd like to blow up Haden Brothers because of what it represents. It represents order, commerce stability, civilization, family values, tradition, the status quo, the Rule of Law. I could go on. A terrorist outrage in Haden Brothers would be a real feather in the cap of some cowardly ethnic son of Satan. They can call themselves freedom fighters. They can call themselves a liberation army. They're all the same to me. I call them all Charlie.

All right, so my job description at Haden Brothers doesn't include combating international terrorism, but that's not to say I couldn't do it if I was asked. Give me the ammo and I'll finish the job. Or let me step outside with one of those so-called men of violence. Let's square up to each other. Let's strip down to our wrestling shorts, get a bit of a sweat going, have it out once and for all. We'd soon see what they were made of. They don't want that, of course.

Vigilance is everything in my job; vigilance, surveillance, watchful-ness. I always say that my staff – and they're a great bunch of boys – I always say a lot of them do nothing all day but watch television. That's just my little joke. In fact they watch monitor screens all day, keeping an eye on every square inch of Haden Brothers. Not much slips by them, I can tell you.

We also run an intelligence unit. We have a network of, well, I won't call them spies exactly, more informers, people who keep their ears to the ground, who know what's going on in the store. Sometimes the information isn't wholly reliable but that's all right. Knowledge is power in this game.

I try to run a tight ship at Haden Brothers but, hey, I live in the real world. I understand human nature. People steal stationery, they use the telephones for personal calls, they use fax and xerox machines without authorization. They have prolonged and non-work-related conversations with other members of staff. Sometimes they work under the influence of drink and drugs, or they get involved with undesirable political organizations or read subversive literature or they go to art galleries and see degenerate art. They have affairs. Sometimes they become insubordinate. That's where I come in, and believe me, I can be subtle about it. I understand how easy it is to make a mistake. Just because somebody errs once, I won't necessarily come down on them like a ton of bricks. No, I'm far more likely to save that mistake for a rainy day.

Naturally enough, I had a pretty hefty dossier on Mr Arnold Haden. Naturally, we had hidden cameras in his penthouse. He didn't know about them, obviously. If he had they wouldn't have been hidden. Personally, I always agreed with Derek Snell that Arnold was a bit of a liability. He was a nice enough guy, but I mean a man of his age, dressed all in white, not married, no children; well, it made me wonder. I know he used to knock off a lot of the pretty young sales assistants; as a matter of fact I've got film of some of it, but I always thought that could just be a cover.

I was well aware he'd gone overboard for this Vita Carlisle woman and I didn't like the sound of that at all. I didn't like her, didn't trust her. She was friendly, polite, good at her job, very attractive. I always suspect that sort of thing.

When I looked at the monitor screen and saw she was in Arnold Haden's penthouse with her skirt up and three sticks of dynamite strapped round her waist, well, I turned to one of my colleagues and laughed and said, 'I told you so.'

14 · SOUVENIRS

Most of Erica Carlisle's therapists said that her condition was not an unusual one. She simultaneously felt that she was dying and that she'd never lived. Inevitably the therapists wanted her to talk about her past, her childhood, and yes, she could remember a time when she was young, with all her life before her, when she'd had dreams and aspirations, and a belief that her life would be full, interesting, passionate and special. Now, aged only a little over forty, with the possibility of three or even four decades still to be endured, it seemed to her she'd had no life at all.

She had brought up Vita by herself. There had been no father to help, no house in the suburbs, no happy family group. But it had seemed enough at the time. It had kept her occupied, too occupied to reflect or complain. But now, with Vita grown up, she had more than enough time for introspection, and she felt that her whole life had been a detour, something to pass the days until the real thing came along. But that real thing had remained unreal. It had remained absent. If this road was the detour, she had no idea where the main road was, nor where it led.

Her own parents had been generous, she had worked when she could and the social services had occasionally been called upon to help. There had been regular shortages of money but no real poverty. The flat she now lived in was nice enough, but little more than a *pied-à-terre* she always insisted. Still, there were no money problems now, apparently no problems at all. Her life looked a little empty but she was intelligent enough to do something about that. She had friends. She took holidays. She was able to take lovers, and did so, though mostly because she thought she ought to, and they gave her little real pleasure. Vita disapproved, but then Vita disapproved of so many things.

Erica Carlisle did not think she had an addictive personality. Drink had never impressed her, drugs were not part of her world, not even tranquillizers or sleeping pills. She was definitely not addicted to sex. Nevertheless, she could see the attractions of having a habit, an addiction, of being in thrall to something that killed the pain of being alone and inert.

She became briefly interested in exercise. She jogged, she swam, she played squash, as though 'getting in touch with her body' might be a solution. She tried yoga, but she soon realized she was looking for something far more concrete and earthbound than any kundalini.

Then she tried therapy. It began as an experiment and turned into a hobby. No doubt most of the therapists she met were well meaning and, if she had not been who she was, some of them might even have been able to help. They brought with them a whole train of presumptions and methodologies that as far as she could see never quite fitted her particular case. They talked of Jung and Adler and Janov, and of gestalt and of projection and denial, and one or two referred to Freud, though only dismissively. Some had tried to seduce her, and she had resisted, although she certainly hadn't been offended. She couldn't see anything wrong in therapists sleeping with their patients. It seemed no less likely to be of benefit than any of their other strategies. She just didn't want to try it.

But ultimately nothing did any good, and she wondered if perhaps her real addiction was to her own pain. In the evening following a therapy session she would, there was no point in denying it, often feel a little better, despite the session having changed or solved nothing. And she wondered if it was precisely the fact that nothing was changed or solved that was really making her feel better; that she liked to wallow in her angst. She didn't think this was the case, but it took a long time before she realized what was really helping.

She always scheduled her appointments for the afternoon. She would spend an hour in the therapist's office, then head for home. But she never wanted to go straight home. She always needed another hour or two to herself before she could return to quotidian life, and in those hours she went shopping. She would go to a clothes shop, or a shoe shop, or a china shop, and buy herself a hat, or new boots or a new punch bowl. They were presents to herself, treats that she deserved for having explored her psyche so diligently.

The best therapist she ever had was a severe, bearded Canadian psychiatrist who had an office round the corner from her flat. In the evening following a session with him she sometimes felt truly elated. However, between the end of the therapy session and her return home, she invariably spent some time in Haden Brothers, and one day it occurred to her (and it was a moment of the most intense and profound revelation) that the elation came not from the therapy but from the being in Haden Brothers.

Erica Carlisle had ambivalent feelings about Haden Brothers. She had worked there briefly before Vita was born. That was not so unusual, so had thousands of girls. She had hated working there and she didn't want her daughter following in her footsteps, but returning as a customer was different. Before long she abandoned her doctors, psychologists and cranks. Instead, whenever the clouds of depression and misery rolled in, she simply went to Haden Brothers.

For all that Haden Brothers was a store full of high prices and big mark-ups, this appeared to be an economically sound decision. The money saved on therapy would pay for any number of little luxuries. And shopping was pleasantly impersonal. It required no self-revelation. It healed wounds rather than opened them. It was an activity full of certainties whereas therapy thrived on doubt and ambiguity.

It became her habit to visit the store once or twice a week, browse for as long as she needed to, feeling good the whole time, and at last she would settle, apparently at random, on some small, pleasing object – a pearl cluster brooch, a silk square, a space-saving wine rack – and make it hers. Each new thing carried with it a certain glow, an aura of pleasing newness. This would be enough to make her happy for a while. Eventually the aura would fade, there would be a grey sky gathering on her horizon, and then she would know it was time for another shopping expedition to Haden Brothers.

Things were simple in Haden Brothers. You knew that quality was high, that the standard of service was excellent, that there would be no quibbles over replacing faulty goods, and that complaints would be dealt with quickly, politely and in the customer's favour. Haden Brothers was a realm in which everything was clearly labelled and clearly priced. Here were brand names you could trust, international reputations for excellence. And all of it could be hers so long as it fell within her budget.

But her budget was inevitably limited. Her desires were inevitably greater than her means. She wanted more than she could afford, and this was a frustration for her, one that threatened to ruin the good that Haden Brothers was doing her. And then she saw the way forward. It was a simple and age-old solution. She decided to steal things. She became a dedicated, efficient, if entirely unschematic, shoplifter. The things she stole were symbols, tokens that satisfied complex, subterranean desires.

She would probably have admitted, if asked, that there was some sexual component to this activity. Desire was followed by possession. Then a brief period of satisfaction ensued before appetite renewed itself. When, all in the same week though on separate visits, she discovered she had taken two candlesticks, a fountain pen and an oyster knife, she thought there must be something Freudian going on. But that didn't matter any more. Now that her activities were no longer policed by doctors and therapists she felt free for the first time in her life. And that was one reason why she didn't want her daughter working at Haden Brothers, but it was by no means the most important one.

15 · INSTANT DISCREDIT

A tall black man entered the hardware department. He looked around for an assistant to help him. He appeared nervous and ill at ease, but then he spotted Vita Carlisle who was rearranging a display of mops and brooms. It was one of her less glamorous Flying Squad assignments.

The man was big and his skin had the dark gloss of polished wood. His face and body were wide and he was wearing a tan-coloured sheepskin overcoat that looked wild and shaggy, but beneath it he wore a neat, immaculately cut charcoal grey suit. He walked with dignity towards Vita and said in a soft, smoky tone, 'Do you think you could help me?'

The voice was impossible to place. There were hints of an African accent, but also an American twang, and the vowels had a studied English aristocratic timbre to them.

'I hope so,' said Vita.

'Yes, I'm sure you can,' he said. 'I want some things for my kitchen.'

'Yes?'

'I need saucepans and oven-proof dishes, a colander and a cutlery drainer and a flip-top bin and a folding step stool, and a washing-up bowl, and a bucket or two, and a soap dish and a scrubbing brush and a sink tidy.'

'I think we can supply you with all of those,' said Vita pleasantly and she showed him the items he had asked for, and he chose the styles and colours he wanted. He was satisfied with his choice but there was something troubling him.

'I also need a fridge and a cooker and dishwasher, and a kitchen table and chairs, and possibly some carpet tiles.'

'You'd have to go to a different department for those, sir.'

'I see,' he said, and his shoulders dropped a little and he looked sad.

'Is there something else I can help you with?' Vita enquired.

'Yes, there is,' he said. 'Everything.'

'I'm sorry?'

'I need everything,' he said. 'I don't just need things for my kitchen, I need everything for my whole house.'

'I see.'

'I think not. I don't want to burden a young person like yourself with my problems, but to put it briefly, I had to leave my own country rather rapidly. There was a coup of sorts, a change of government policy. It was necessary for me to get out. I had to leave everything behind. Everything. I arrived in your country with only the clothes I stood up in. It was sheer luck that I had one or two off-shore accounts that are enabling me to rebuild my life here in England. I'm starting from scratch.'

'That sounds terrible,' said Vita.

He adopted a brave facial expression. 'I can't pretend it's what I would have chosen,' he said. 'And yet it's the chance for a new beginning. I've bought my new house and now I have to fill it with objects. And you know, the best of it is, I want everything in my new house to have come from Haden Brothers. Quite a luxury, I think.

'So what I'd really like to do is go through the whole store and be able simply to point at anything that catches my eye, and to know that I can have it. And I don't want to have to go to each separate department and explain this whole melancholy business to a different assistant each time, so what I need is somebody, a representative from the store, to accompany me on my wanderings, to take note of what I choose, to smooth the whole operation for me. Then, when I'm finished, this person would arrange for all my purchases to be delivered to my residence.'

He paused dramatically. 'I'd like you to be that person,' he said.

'I'm not absolutely sure if I'm allowed to do that,' Vita said. 'I'm not sure that I'm supposed to leave my department.'

'My dear,' said the man, 'I'm going to stock a whole house, buy all the accessories for a whole brand new life. Even by Haden Brothers standards I shall be spending a small fortune. If I want you to accompany me while I do it, I think it would be very short-sighted of the management not to allow that.'

Vita was sure he was right. Nevertheless she checked with Mrs Chesterton, the manager of the hardware department.

'How does he intend paying?' said Mrs Chesterton.

Vita found out that he wanted to pay in cash. She thought that was an odd way of doing things, though she assumed it had something to do with his off-shore accounts. Mrs Chesterton simply chuckled. She seemed delighted with the arrangement.

'You see,' said Mrs Chesterton, 'this is what it's like to work in Haden Brothers; colourful characters with lots of money, interesting work, a hint of eccentricity and luxury. You wouldn't get that in some stores I could name. Off you go, Miss Carlisle.'

Vita and the customer did a tour of the store. Vita had with her an order pad, and each time he saw something that pleased him, she would note down the department and stock number. Later, after he'd gone, she would have to begin the enormous job of filling and co-ordinating the order.

They went through the furniture department, through the furnishings and fabrics, through rugs and carpets, mirrors and decorative home accessories, through the bathroom shop. He found a lot that he liked. His decisions were made swiftly and firmly, and his tastes were consistent. He liked plain designs and strong colours. Vita thought the finished effect might be stunning. They went through tableware and silverware, through television, video and hi-fi, to the hospitality department for drinks trolleys and bar accessories, to smokers' requisites where he ordered several years' supply of cheroots and Havanas. He was hovering on the brink of the riding shop where he was considering acquiring a couple of saddles, but Vita gently suggested there might be other priorities, that the horse tack could come later.

He said to her, 'You know, many of the people in my country are very poor indeed. Now, I'm not one of those people who likes to blame that entirely on the white man, but I think it's true that when a nation has nothing then its people become very unhappy. Lack of possessions breeds disaffection, and political extremism begins to flower like a rare orchid. My people are a simple race. In the absence of consumer durables they embrace strange doctrines; communism, fundamentalism. For my part, I like to demonstrate the redeeming power of money. I like to show that a man may be rich, that he may embrace possessions and yet still not lose his soul. I have always tried to be a role model for the people of my country.'

'What is your country, actually?' Vita asked.

'My country is the whole world,' and he laughed a deep, honeyed laugh.

He ordered a baby grand for his music room, a dozen English

watercolours from the art gallery, some all-weather garden furniture, a barbecue, a hammock, a strimmer. He selected a four-arm rotary clothes airer, a scroller jigsaw, two ironing boards, a fifty gallon water butt. He didn't always choose the most expensive option but he never chose the cheapest, and Vita knew the final bill would be astronomical. He said he had plans to lay in some fine wines, to collect modern sculpture, to acquire a few important pieces of Meissen porcelain. Vita said she wasn't qualified to help him in those areas but she was sure there were specialists in the store who could.

'You know,' he said longingly, 'the more I walk round this great store of yours, and the more high-quality goods I see, the more I want to buy. I'd be very happy to have it all. I want everything.'

'Everything and more,' Vita quoted.

'Yes, indeed.'

It was nearly six o'clock and Vita had spent almost the whole day with her customer. There had been no break, no lunch, not even a cup of coffee. His capacity for acquisition was inexhaustible and he had worn out Vita. They were now standing near the floristry department.

'Yes,' he said, 'I think I want to flood my whole house with flowers every day. And in my new home I think I ought to wear all brand new clothes. And perhaps I will employ the Haden Brothers interior design service to decorate the house for me. And of course I will need new luggage, and perhaps I should buy some nursery furniture for when I find the right woman with whom to raise a family. But I see you're tired. Here, Miss Carlisle, please accept this tip . . .'

He waved a large, multicoloured bank note in her face. She couldn't see which country it came from, nor what the currency was, though she could see it had a high denomination. She was about to insist that she couldn't possibly accept a tip but he put it away before she had the chance to say anything.

'You're right,' he said. 'I didn't mean to insult you. In that case I will terminate our arrangement for now and I'll be here promptly at nine tomorrow morning and we'll continue our adventures in shopping.'

'Fine,' said Vita, and he moved as though he might be about to kiss her, but in the event he simply swept past her without a farewell and left the store. Vita returned to the hardware department where Mrs Chesterton was waiting. To Vita's surprise Derek Snell was there too. He smiled welcomingly.

'How did you get on?' Mrs Chesterton asked.

'Rather well,' said Vita. 'He wants to buy everything. He wants to spend an absolute fortune.'

'I bet he does,' said Mrs Chesterton. 'I bet he does.'

Derek Snell took the order forms from Vita, gave them a cursory look and handed them to Mrs Chesterton. She gave them a similar scrutiny and tossed them into a waste paper bin. Vita watched in disbelief.

'Did he offer to marry you?' Mrs Chesterton asked.

'What?' said Vita.

'Often he asks the assistant to marry him after she's taken the order.'

'Well, I haven't quite finished. He's coming back tomorrow,' Vita said, confused.

'No, I'm afraid he isn't,' said Derek Snell.

Vita looked at him, at Mrs Chesterton who was smiling in a smarmy, superior way, at the order forms which represented a whole day's work and which were now resting in the bin.

'I don't seem to follow,' she said.

'He *will* be back,' Derek Snell said. 'But not tomorrow. He'll be back in about three months, when he'll find some other new assistant and start all over again.'

'I still don't understand.'

'What's to understand?' Mrs Chesterton said viciously. 'The world is full of people who aren't what they pretend to be. Your man just likes to pretend he's rich. Coming into Haden Brothers and making out he's some sort of millionaire makes him feel good. He's not a millionaire. I suppose he's a bit of a lunatic really, but as forms of lunacy go I think he's quite harmless.'

'But if you knew, why did you let me waste all day with him?' Vita said.

Mrs Chesterton shrugged unhelpfully.

'Was it really a waste, Vita?' Derek Snell asked. 'You may not have made any sales, but wasn't it a learning experience? You visited dozens of departments, saw how they work, what they sell. As a form of training I think it was really rather good. Cost effective, too.'

'You've also learned never to trust a damn thing customers say to you,' said Mrs Chesterton.

Vita looked bitterly disappointed.

'If the work doesn't agree with you,' Mrs Chesterton added, 'there are easier ways of making a living.'

Vita wondered if the woman was in cahoots with Snell, making sure her work was hard and meaningless in an attempt to push her towards Arnold Haden's bed. But if that was the case, they were being casual about it. Snell's face revealed nothing and Mrs Chesterton's vileness seemed offhand and unforced. Vita smiled thinly, bade them good evening, collected her handbag and left the department. She felt weak and tired, and abused from all sides. Yet she did not feel nearly so vulnerable as she once might have.

She went to the Ladies, let ten minutes elapse, then returned to the department. Snell and Mrs Chesterton had gone. She reached into the waste paper bin and took out the discarded order pad. Then she moved over to Mrs Chesterton's desk where there was the rubber stamp that buyers used to authorize orders. She picked it up and, without fully understanding her own motives, meticulously stamped each and every page the customer had made her fill in. If she were now to take the pad along to central requisitioning and place it in their in-tray, a whole series of transactions and operations could be set in train, and hundreds of man hours could be wasted, consumed in attempting to satisfy this non-order.

She was tempted, God was she tempted, but in the event she threw the order pad away again. She couldn't quite bring herself to commit such a shabby, destructive, subversive act. Nevertheless, the realization that such acts were possible, were even quite easy to accomplish, was one she found strangely empowering and nourishing. She had planned to phone her mother that evening and have a good moan, but she suddenly felt she had nothing much to moan about.

16 · CALCULATORS

Anton Heath stood in a public telephone booth adjacent to the food hall on the ground floor of Haden Brothers, urgently and furtively trying to make a call. The aromas of freshly baked bread and recently ground coffee floated around him and a man dressed as a toreador offered him a tray containing biscuits and cheese inviting him to try 'a taste of España'. Anton accepted, hoping that a full mouth would help disguise his voice. He finally got through to the main switchboard.

'Is that Haden Brothers?'

'Yes, sir,' a chirpy girl's voice replied.

'I need to speak to someone in security.'

'We don't have a security department as such, sir.'

'Yes you do. I know you do. I want to speak to Mr Ray Chalmers, head of internal security.'

'I see, sir. You're very well informed. What do you wish to talk to Mr Chalmers about?'

'It's a private matter.'

'Involving security?'

'Well obviously,' Anton snarled.

'This wouldn't be a bomb threat would it?'

'It could be something like that, yes.'

'Or should I say a bomb hoax.'

'This is no hoax.'

'We get so many, you see. Yours isn't even the first of the day.'

'This is perfectly authentic, believe me.'

'So what kind of bomb is it?'

'I don't think I want to discuss that with a girl on the switchboard.'

'I mean, how many pounds of explosive? Is it Semtex or gelignite? Is it a nail bomb or an incendiary device? What kind of detonator? What scale of casualties are we envisaging here?'

'What I have to say is for Ray Chalmers' ears only.'

'And where is the bomb located exactly?' she continued.

'Look, I'm not at liberty to tell you that.'

'Well, this is a bit difficult for me, isn't it? You ring up to tell us there's a bomb in the shop but you won't tell us where it is or what kind of bomb it is. And you know, why bother to plant the bomb in the first place if you're then going to ring up and tell us it's here? It sort of takes away the surprise element doesn't it? I mean, I'd have thought any self-respecting terrorist . . . '

'I have my reasons,' Anton blurted.

'The reason is, you're a bit of a wanker, right? There isn't really a bomb is there?'

'Listen, a lot of people could get hurt if you don't put me through to Ray Chalmers.'

'Oh sure.'

'I can't be held responsible for the consequences if you don't put me through.'

'If you were a real terrorist you wouldn't be worried about the consequences, would you?'

Anton was momentarily lost for words.

'Look,' the operator said, 'if you're one of our regular hoaxers then you'll know that genuine bombers always use a codeword that proves they're authentic. I tell you what I'll do. I know you're not a real terrorist but if you can guess the codeword I'll put you through to our Mr Chalmers. I can't say fairer than that, can I?'

Anton had been here before. It always came down to trying to guess this bloody codeword. He tried to think of a likely word, though he knew of course that it would probably have been chosen for its very unlikeliness. In the past he had tried his luck with things such as bomb, shopper, emergency, 007, Mayday, SOS, mayhem, casualty, suspect, Mona Lisa; all to no avail. Finally he said, 'Cold war.'

'Rubbish,' said the operator. 'Not even warm. Bye now.' And she put the phone down on him.

He had failed once again, but it had occurred to him that she might say he had failed even if he did get warm, perhaps even if he said the actual codeword. Or perhaps it wasn't a question of the word itself but of intonation or accent or some other separate and apparently unconnected factor. And of course he knew that it must change from time to time. Sometimes he wasn't even sure why he kept trying, except that it had now become both a challenge and a habit.

He also knew that there must be some not too difficult way of finding out what the codeword was. Obviously certain people in the store knew it, not least the switchboard girls. It ought to be possible to charm or seduce one of them into giving him the word, but his powers of charm and seduction had so far failed him. Equally, there must be some computer files or a series of secret memos that contained the information he needed. If only he could crack that codeword then he could complete the bomb hoax, then he could . . . well, he could at least cause quite a bit of inconvenience to quite a few people.

It seemed to Anton that the first duty of the aspiring terrorist was to erase God from the picture. If God did not figure then there was no day of reckoning, no ultimate authority. Actions were therefore *ad hoc*, pragmatic, only meaningful in the here and now. If a well-placed bomb in a children's playground got the job done then that was a good thing. If there was no final authority, there was no final morality. People might condemn the bomber, might even take revenge on him, but in the absence of damnation and eternity, what could they do except kill him? And death meant nothing without God.

Without God it was easy, perhaps too easy, but Anton had not yet rid himself of God. He had not quite cleansed himself of a belief in that day of reckoning. He thought a day might well come when God would demand of him, as his own father had frequently done, 'What on earth do you think you're doing?' There was enormous scope for bravery here although he hadn't displayed much of it in his dealings with his father. A certain kind of soul might turn to God and say, 'Push off. I don't owe you any explanations. I did what I did. I am what I am.' Then, if God condemned him to eternal damnation, he would shrug his shoulders and say, 'OK, do your worst.'

Anton feared he was not that kind of brave soul. Not yet, anyway. And for the moment he was scarcely in the damnation stakes at all. Making hoax bomb calls was about the summit of his wickedness. He had also raised a few fire alarms, and he had made a few abusive and obscene phone calls to Derek Snell, and then there was all the general, casual mayhem he got up to with the other furniture porters. It wasn't much as yet, but he hoped and believed that his day was yet to come. He had goals. He had ambitions.

As he went from the food hall to the furniture department he tried hard not to listen to the muzak seeping out of the tiny speakers hidden somewhere high above his head, in the very fabric of the walls or ceilings. He knew what that muzak was for. Ostensibly it added warmth and atmosphere, its rhythm might even speed up traffic flow and footfall, but he knew it contained more sinister messages. For a start it told customers to buy, and didn't just tell them, but forced and cajoled and coerced. That's why people got home and their wives or husbands would ask them why on earth they'd suddenly got it into their heads to buy a matching set of coathangers, shoe trees and trouser press. And they wouldn't know why!! They had been brainwashed, made to desire and to consume. It made Anton sick and angry.

There were other messages too, to make them hungry and thirsty so they'd spend money in the restaurants and snack bars, and there were messages that tried to talk them out of shoplifting. Those messages also worked on the staff. Employees were supposed to become placid, well-behaved, malleable. He wondered how he could get his hands on the muzak and implant his own messages, messages that would tell staff and customers to rebel, to steal and destroy, to run riot through these poisoned groves of consumerism.

Of course, he and the other porters worked hard to disobey the constant brainwashing, and by and large it seemed to him that they succeeded, but it was difficult to judge. Yes, they seemed to be creating little pools of anarchy, but perhaps if it weren't for the muzak they'd have created total chaos by now. Certainly the other porters displayed a commendable solidarity, but there was this problem with the new boy, this Charlie Mayhew. He'd been with them for a while now and he wasn't coming along nearly as quickly as Anton wanted, and he thought he should do something about that quite soon.

'Hey Charlie,' said Anton, 'if you had to plant a bomb that would go off and bring this country to its knees, where would you plant it?'

'I wouldn't plant a bomb, Anton, really I wouldn't.'

'Come on, Charlie, don't take things so seriously. This is theory we're discussing here. This is political make-believe. Go on. You want to be an artist. Use your imagination.'

Charlie tried to think, but he was unsure of the terms of reference, unsure what Anton wanted him to say, and he came up with nothing.

'I'm sorry,' he said.

'All right,' said Anton, as though he were dealing with a dull four year old, 'we'll try it a different way. I'll suggest one or two potential terrorist targets and you tell me how they sound.'

'OK,' said Charlie with the greatest reluctance.

'How about the Houses of Parliament?' said Anton.

'I think it's been done,' said Charlie. 'Guy Fawkes.'

'Good,' said Anton. 'You know your history. Then how about Buckingham Palace?'

'Well yes, I suppose it's a major terrorist target,' said Charlie. 'But I assume it's pretty well guarded.'

'You don't think there might be a problem though, that if you blew up one or two members of the Royal Family there might be an immense upsurge of pro-monarchy feeling that would set the cause back decades?'

'I don't know what the cause is,' said Charlie.

Ignoring this Anton continued, 'How about the Old Bailey? How about Scotland Yard?'

Charlie agreed these were the sort of places that terrorists might well want to blow up, though as Anton himself had obliquely pointed out, it was far from clear how the destruction of these institutions would necessarily bring the country to its knees. Anton went on to suggest a Wimpy Bar, the Baltic Exchange, army recruitment offices, Harrods, and finally Haden Brothers.

'No, not Haden Brothers,' Charlie protested, though he was unsure quite what he was protesting against or why he was bothering. 'Not Haden Brothers. I'm getting to like it here.'

'Of course you are,' Anton sneered. 'You've been sucked in, haven't you? You've become part of the establishment.'

Charlie found it hard to think of himself as part of any establishment. Members of the establishment did not work as porters in department stores and sleep on their friends' sofas, surely.

'OK,' said Anton. 'Now it's your turn. You try.'

'Oh, all right,' said Charlie. 'Eton College.'

'Blow up Eton!?' said Anton incredulously. 'Blow up the old school? Come on, Charlie, I think that would be going a little too far.'

17 · GROOMING

'You're staring at me, Arnold,' Vita says.

She's still in the white leather armchair. The wine bottle is empty but neither of them feels any better or any worse for drink.

'I'm sorry,' he says at once, eager not to give offence.

'It's all right. I don't mind,' she says. 'I just wondered why you were doing it. Puppy love? Or so you might be able to describe me to the authorities.'

'If you blow us both up there'll be nothing to describe.'

'That's so true,' she sneers, and then her mind hops in a different direction. 'You know, I really hated working for Haden Brothers. I really despised it.'

'I'm sorry,' Arnold Haden says again. 'You didn't look as though you were despising it.'

'I'm quite the little deceiver, aren't I?'

'Yes, you are.'

'I hated the rest of the staff,' she says. 'They were such a bunch of work-shy, grasping parasites.'

Arnold Haden has always found his staff a disturbing and un-attractive bunch, but he doesn't necessarily want to condemn them all out of hand. He keeps his mouth shut.

Vita says, 'Some people live to work, some people work to live. Haden Brothers is full of people who live not to work. You wouldn't believe the amount of creative energy that goes into skiving off in Haden Brothers. You wouldn't believe the satisfaction your staff get for every little fiddle and scam they can pull off.'

'Oh, I think I would,' says Arnold Haden.

Yes, maybe he would. Vita can see that Arnold, for all his separateness, isn't totally unaware of human nature.

'Every extended coffee break,' she says, 'every visit to the wages office, every day off sick, every dentist's appointment, it gives them such pleasure.'

'I've never wanted to deny my staff pleasure.'

'And I hated the customers, too,' Vita continues. 'I hated the ones who came in and said they didn't know what they were looking for but they'd know it when they saw it. I mean, that's so, so stupid. And worst of all are the clothing departments. Women come in and they try on a dress and afterwards they say, "I like it but it's not me." I always wanted to scream at them, "Of course it's not *you*. It's a fucking dress." But you'll be pleased to know that I didn't scream at your customers, Arnold.'

'I'm glad,' he says.

'And I hated the building. I found it oppressive and pompous and yet at the same time frivolous and whimsical. I hated the man who built it, what was his name, Zander?'

'It sounds like you hated just about everything.'

'Everything and more,' says Vita. 'But I wouldn't want you to think that had anything to do with why I'm going to kill you.'

'Kill both of us,' he corrects her.

She smiles and concedes that she got it wrong that time.

'So tell me, Arnold, what do you think would happen if a terrorist bomb blew a hole in the side of Haden Brothers?'

'Well, the security forces would be alerted and . . . '

'No, not that. I mean, how do you think the public would react? Obviously there's confusion, there's panic, there's a big hole in the side of the store. Do the customers run away screaming? Or do they run in and start looting?'

'They probably wouldn't run in,' says Arnold. 'They'd be scared there was another bomb somewhere in the store.'

'That's a nice point, Arnold. They wouldn't risk their skins for a few consumer items. But is that the only reason? You don't think they might simply believe that looting is wrong?'

'No doubt some would, but the fear of being blown up by a second bomb would be a far greater deterrent. And, of course, a lot would depend on whether they thought they might get caught for the looting.'

'OK then, Arnold, what do you think would happen if by some chance the doors to Haden Brothers were left unlocked one night?'

'What do you mean?'

'One night all the assistants would go home and the security staff would simply forget to lock up, the doors would be left open and anyone could just walk in, get what they needed and walk out with it.'

'Who would know they were unlocked?'

'Anybody who walked past. You could put a sign on the open window if you liked, "come on in and take what you need."'

'That's ridiculous,' he says.

'Go on, Arnold, indulge me. Would people get the same thrill out of shopping at Haden Brothers if they didn't have to pay for things?'

'I don't know,' says Arnold. 'I really don't know.'

'And I thought you knew everything.'

'I never said that,' he insists.

'When I was a child,' says Vita, 'I believed in Father Christmas, and every year he came and left me lots of presents, but I never took care of them. I just tossed them around, broke them, used one of them to smash another. And when my mother asked me why I did it, I had a good answer. I said, these toys don't matter, they're just free stuff that I got from Father Christmas.

'Later, of course, I discovered there wasn't a Father Christmas, that my mother had bought everything. I felt terrible. She'd worked so hard to get me what I wanted. And as a matter of fact she'd got most of it from Haden Brothers.'

Arnold Haden takes a certain pleasure in imagining the child that was Vita Carlisle. He would have liked to comfort her, to have explained things to her.

'And how about *after* the bomb?' she asks. 'What then? Would people stop coming to Haden Brothers?'

'Some would, of course,' Arnold Haden says. 'But I think you'd find that most people would continue to shop here. They'd come back because they'd want to show how unafraid they were. They wouldn't want the bombers to win.'

'And what if the last surviving Haden brother got blown to smithereens in his penthouse by a disgruntled member of staff?'

Arnold Haden only has to consider for a second before he says, 'I should think that would be about the best publicity stunt any department store has ever had.'

18 · ARTISTS' MATERIALS

ANTON HEATH: This is a true story. It's the first day of the Haden Brothers sale, right? They draft in a lot of extra staff, so lots of new faces turn up all over the store, and they get extra tills in all departments to cope with the rush.

So the shop opens and a delivery man arrives in the china department carrying a till, and he asks where they want him to put it. The buyer of the department says she isn't expecting another till, and the delivery man says isn't that just typical, but the people upstairs have told him to bring it and he's already carried it up three flights of stairs and he's buggered if he's going to carry it back down again.

So they keep the till and since they've got it they decide to use it, and all day long they're clocking up the sales on it, taking the money and putting it in the till, and then about four o'clock in the afternoon, the delivery man comes back and says the people upstairs gave him the wrong instructions, this till ought to be in the kitchenware department. So he picks up the till full of money, walks out of the shop, puts it in the back of his van and goes home.

Of course, he didn't work for Haden Brothers. It was his own till. He was never seen again. Brilliant. The man was a genius. You couldn't do it these days. That delivery man was an exponent of an art that's died.

Time passed. Charlie got to know the ropes. He knew which of the managers and buyers and salesmen and office staff were good people and which were complete pains in the bum. There were very few in between. Charlie made no friends, but he did find one or two people with whom he could talk and thereby pass an idle few minutes. He found one or two women he fancied, but his fancying was a purely theoretical activity. He never contemplated asking any of the women out. For one thing they were all office workers or furniture consultants. He knew they would never go out with a mere junior furniture porter, and he was alarmed by the extent to which he was already defining himself in terms of his job. But he never saw any woman who appealed to him the way Vita had, and he had never seen Vita since that first day. That was a disappointment but scarcely a surprise. Given the vastness of Haden Brothers it might take a lifetime before they met again. If they did meet, he would be ready. He still carried her pen – the Parker Presidential International – with him at all times, so he would be ready to return it. She would undoubtedly be grateful. She might even wish to show her appreciation. But the fact remained, Charlie would still be a furniture porter and he knew that meant she would not be interested in him.

By now Charlie had discovered just how little work was required of him. The management seemed unaware that the whole gang of furniture porters remained only intermittently occupied. A gang half that size would have been fully occupied and, in Charlie's case at least, considerably less bored. But the work got done, nobody ever complained, Haden Brothers continued to prosper, and who was he to rock the boat?

He discovered the joys of wandering around the store with a piece of paper in his hand. He knew it was an old trick but it still worked. From the beginning he had been faced occasionally with illegible dockets or order forms written out by a salesman or consultant, and he would have to take the offending document back to whoever had written it and ask them what it said. Sometimes the salesman would be busy with a customer or on his break, and Charlie would have to wait around, occasionally for a long while. If anyone ever asked what he was doing he would wave the illegible docket or order form and that would explain everything. But only rarely did anyone ask. Usually they saw he had a piece of official looking paper in his hand and assumed he was about his rightful business.

It didn't take long for him to work out that this official-looking piece of paper was his passport to skiving off and exploring the entire store. So he would take an order form in his hand, then meander around the floors killing time, looking at merchandise, browsing just like a customer.

On these wanderings he tried to think about art. He found himself surrounded by language, by signs that gave customers directions, instructions and information. Some of them were simply illiterate. They never contained apostrophes, so it was mens casual shoes, childrens clothes, the mothers and babies room; and there were odd, invented department store terms, like menswear. Did it mean 'men's ware', as in hardware, or was it a portmanteau word telling the public that men in these areas were given to bad language? And there were large surreal signs that said 'Trouser Event' or 'Quality Shirts', as though an object could be an event, and as though an object could be without qualities. But his favourite linguistic tic was a half-obscured notice beside the coat hooks in the Noah's Ark wine bar. It said simply, 'The management cannot take responsibility.'

It occurred to him that Haden Brothers could be thought of as a series of Duchampian ready-mades. Choice could be art. All he need do was select an object and sign it, and an act of artistic creation would have been completed. He thought of taking Vita's pen and scrawling his signature on a piece of lavatory equipment or a pack of household goods, say some Brillo pads. But he couldn't escape the feeling that this had already been done.

But art could be combination as much as selection. He wondered if there was a role for himself as an interventionist. If he took a mackerel from the fish department and inserted it in an open-toed ladies' sandal, did this say something about foot fetishism? If he knocked over a pile of carefully arranged 'Apache-design' head scarves, was this a comment about the pernicious effects of imperialism? He wasn't sure.

However, he was certain that Haden Brothers could make a great stage set, an environment for a large-scale piece of performance art. He could easily imagine sixteen cleaning ladies hammering out chopsticks in the piano department. There would be fertility dances amongst the wedding dresses, a score of disc jockeys in the stereo department each with a separate sound system, all creating conflicting noise. There could be book burnings in the paperback department, fire eaters in the ice cream parlour, blood and offal rituals in the butchery, orgies just about anywhere, with nudes descending Edward Zander's wonderfully ornate staircases.

The extravagance and wildness of the building added to the pleasure of Charlie's wanderings. At first he was just interested in the grand effects, the rows of unmatching columns, the marble floors, the light filtering in through abstract stained-glass windows, the way mirrored walls were arranged to create regresses and curious effects of scale. But increasingly he saw details: strange faces and African masks carved into the woodwork, wrought iron archways with swastikas and pentagrams, staircase finials that looked like simple spheres but turned out to be intricately carved globes of the world. It was a backdrop and an adventure playground that cried out for big, overwrought dramas.

Charlie imagined a tribe of wildmen from another wholly alien culture, who would run amok through the store. They might well find the objects on sale to be very attractive and desirable, but they wouldn't understand their meanings. They wouldn't know what they were 'for'. A handbag might be used as a hat, a Spode tureen might become a chamber pot. Silver knives and forks would become drumsticks. They would misunderstand and misappropriate the culture.

Then he looked at the actual Haden Brothers customers and wondered if perhaps they weren't all wildmen and wildwomen in disguise. He wondered how easily their veneer of politeness and good manners might be stripped away, how quickly their needs and desires might turn them into naked savages. He wanted to be there to see it.

19 · CUSTOMER DISSERVICE

A lone customer walked up to the central information desk on the ground floor of Haden Brothers and said hesitantly and without anger, 'I have a complaint.' He was a quiet looking man with frayed grey hair, and he was dressed neatly though not smartly in shades of fawn. He had under his arm a Haden Brothers carrier bag containing a recently bought camera and all its packaging.

'A complaint?' said the assistant at the counter, her voice containing shocked awe. 'I'm so very sorry to hear that. Please step this way.'

'It's only that . . . '

With a sweep of dutiful regard, the assistant guided the customer away from the counter, off the shop floor into a plush corridor, the walls and floor of which were covered in salmon pink carpeting. There was soft illumination though it was hard to tell where it came from. It had the quality of strong sunlight seen through closed eyelids. The corridor might have been considered womb-like and comforting but the customer was not visibly comforted. He looked lost and confused, the more so when he realized that the assistant from the information desk had disappeared and been replaced by someone else.

'Hello, I'm here to deal with your complaint,' she said soothingly. 'My name's Vita Carlisle. Let me take your bag for you. Let me take your jacket.'

Although she was polite and softly spoken she was forceful and there was no arguing with her. He let the jacket and the bag be taken from him and once she had them she quickened her step and led the way forward.

'Complaint is one word we hate to hear,' she said with heavy sincerity, and if the customer said anything in reply she did not acknowledge it.

He trailed along behind her, hurrying to keep up, swiftly ascending a couple of flights of stairs, becoming short of breath, until they reached an arched doorway. It was large and ornate, showing a Moorish influence, and had thick, blood red brocade curtains drawn across it. Vita Carlisle plunged through the curtains beckoning the customer to follow. He got wrapped up in the heavy flaps of material but at last managed to push his way through.

'Come in and sit down,' said Vita. 'Loosen your tie, take off your shoes.'

He wanted to be co-operative but he was too entranced by the room in which he now found himself. The carp pool was undoubtedly the most imposing and unexpected feature, but then he had not been expecting the Persian tapestries either, nor the ornamental fountain, nor the parakeets on their perches, nor the bejewelled mirrors and tables and fireplace, nor the ornately carved golden couches on to one of which he was now being guided. It was impossible to sit on these with any degree of formality and he found himself lying back, reclining like some Roman hero.

It was hot in the room and loosening his tie seemed reasonable enough. He would have preferred to keep his shoes on, but Vita was now removing both tie and shoes for him. At the same time something cool and soft touched his temples. He looked round to see a woman in a sort of white tunic, possibly even a toga, standing at the head of the couch. She smiled at him amiably and her soft cool hands began to massage his head and neck. It was pleasant, he couldn't deny it, but it all seemed to be a distraction and beside the point.

He became aware of music playing, a harp unless he was mistaken, and the tune was 'Solitaire', one of his very favourite songs as it happened. Then Vita was serving him a drink. It came in an earthenware goblet and it tasted like nothing he'd ever encountered before; a herbal tea of some kind, perfumed and tangy and savoury and honeyed all at the same time. It slid down easily enough, and his discomfort began to slide away too. The music swelled a little, the light in the room dimmed somewhat. The plash of water in the fountain was soothing, the couch seemed more comfortable than any bed he had ever slept in. He knew that Haden Brothers liked to look after their customers, but this was really something special. There was now a cat in the room and it came and rubbed itself affectionately against his feet.

He closed his eyes for a moment and he realized he must be drifting into sleep, for he suddenly heard a man's voice and was snapped back into wakefulness.

'What seems to be the trouble?' the man was asking.

'Nothing at all. Everything's fabulous,' said the customer.

'Don't you have a problem concerning a purchase from Haden Brothers?'

The man asking the questions was Derek Snell. His suit looked considerably less glamorous or luxurious than the rest of the surroundings but he was doing his best to sound mellifluous and warm.

'Oh, that,' said the customer. 'Yes, well, it's a bit silly really.'

'I think we'd better be the judge of that,' said Snell suavely. 'Was it perhaps a member of our staff who failed to treat you with the respect you deserved? Tell us the culprit's name and department and we'll deal with him or her appropriately.'

'The service was fine.'

'Then the goods? Were they shoddy? Our quality control is absolutely rigorous but just once in a while a low-grade item slips through. When it does, our suppliers get a real rocket, believe me.'

As Snell spoke, Vita Carlisle stood beside him, apparently hanging on his every word. This was not simple admiration. She was being trained, or at least tried out, in the complaints department. Her temperament suggested to Derek Snell that she might do well here.

'We want you to feel good about Haden Brothers,' said Snell to the customer. 'That way we can feel good about ourselves.'

'Are you feeling good?' Vita enquired.

'Well, I'm feeling much better, anyway.'

'Of course you are,' said Snell. 'Tell us what's wrong. Don't be shy. We'll soon sort you out.'

'It's this camera I bought,' said the customer.

He looked about him to see what Vita had done with the carrier bag, and seeing his consternation she proffered it to him. He made no move to take it, so Snell grabbed the bag and removed the contents. He tossed aside the packaging and held the camera up to his eye. Inadvertently the flash went off and the electric winder spun noisily, indicating that it had just taken a photograph of the now dazzled customer.

'It seems to work,' said Snell. 'What's wrong with it?'

'Oh the camera's fine, absolutely perfect,' said the customer. 'The problem is that I've developed this strange skin condition on my hands and I can't hold a camera properly any more.'

'But you said you had a complaint.'

'Yes, I do have. It's a strange skin condition on my hands.'

Snell snapped to attention. The background music ceased immediately and the fountain fell dead. The parakeets squawked, the masseuse made snorting and tutting sounds and the customer's shoes, jacket and camera were briskly returned to him.

'So I was wondering if I could have a refund . . . ' he said weakly.

Moments later he found himself in a large, overcrowded, fetid office with flaking orange walls and nowhere to sit. Scores of people stood around looking blank and hopeless, as though they had been there for some days. They were holding numbered tickets and multipart forms, and they stared at a video screen that flashed up numbers, apparently at random, a signal for one or two individuals to shamble over to a small cashier's office where a long and thorough cross-questioning took place. This was the refund department, and the customer did eventually receive his money back, but the staff had been trained to ensure that this was a long, tedious procedure.

The lone customer eventually staggered out of the office feeling weak, tired, disgruntled and angry. He was about to go back to the information desk on the ground floor and say, 'I have a complaint,' but he thought better of it.

In the room with the pool and the parakeets, Derek Snell and Vita remained alone. Snell looked unusually sad.

'I'm afraid that was a rather disappointing episode,' said Snell. 'But life is full of disappointments, isn't it?'

'I suppose so,' Vita agreed.

'I think we should talk,' he said. 'About what we talked about before with Mr Haden.'

'I thought we'd rather exhausted that subject,' she said.

'We may have exhausted one possibility, but that's all. Mr Haden remains very disappointed.'

'That's a shame.'

'It's all right. Mr Haden's life is fuller of disappointments than most. But I sense that your life isn't that way, Vita. And neither is mine. I'm afraid it's part of my job to ask you again if you'd like to take up Mr Haden's offer. And I already know what you're going to say.'

'Then there's no need for me to say it.'

'Fine. I want you to know that I understand exactly how you feel. You're not the kind of girl who's taken in by money and power and possessions. You're above all that. I know you wouldn't sleep with a man just because of what you could get out of him.'

'No, I wouldn't.'

'But at the same time, I sense you're no prude, Vita. You're normal and healthy. You're a bit of a sensual woman, aren't you?'

Vita raised an eyebrow but said nothing.

'I sense you're at home in your body. I'm just thinking that I could be at home in your body too.'

Vita scowled.

'Just a joke,' said Snell. 'Just a joke. You probably like the subtle approach. You probably like to be wooed. Let's put it this way, Vita, I'd be very prepared to woo you.'

Vita looked at him wearily.

'No,' she said.

Derek Snell was not deterred.

'I think you're a very smart young woman, Vita,' he said. 'But I think a woman can be too smart.'

Vita let that one hang in the air for a while, before replying, 'I'm not sure that I'm smart enough to know what you mean by that, Mr Snell.'

She gave him a smile of cloying sweetness. Snell saw no point in forcing the issue, and to show there were no hard feelings he invited her to accompany him to the staff canteen. Vita agreed. The canteen was crowded and they were wedged in at a small table adjacent to a crowd of older women from the outsize-corsetry department. Vita waited for a lull in their conversation, then said loud enough for half the canteen to hear, 'Look at it this way, Mr Snell. If I'm not prepared to sleep with Arnold Haden for money, I'm hardly likely to sleep with you for free, am I now?'

20 · BARGAIN BASEMENT

Charlie Mayhew was lolling on a packing bench trying vainly to look alert when Anton said to him, 'Let's go.' Charlie had no idea where they were going but he followed without question. He assumed there was some special piece of furniture to be moved, or, more likely, some special piece of idling to be done.

They went to some distant corner of the furniture floor, and Anton pulled back a William Morris wall-hanging to reveal an old service lift that Charlie had never seen before. They got in and Anton shut the concertina gate and cranked some ancient brass machinery that made the lift descend. Above the gate, an ornate golden finger moved round a dial to show their downward progress. There were far more points on the dial than there were floors in Haden Brothers and that confused Charlie. Anton told him they were going all the way, but Charlie had no idea what he meant.

'Well, Charlie,' Anton said next, 'you've been here a while now. What do you make of us?'

Charlie thought that was a strange question but he said he was enjoying himself.

'What do you enjoy?' Anton wanted to know. 'The work?'

'Yes, it's not so bad really, is it?' said Charlie.

'Or is it the people?'

'Well yes, the people aren't so bad either.'

'We try, Charlie,' Anton said laconically. 'We do try.'

'I'm sure you do.'

'The problem is this, Charlie. We've been very good to you. We've shown you what's what. We've offered you our friendship. We've invited you to socialize with us. But we don't feel you're really one of us yet. We detect a certain reserve. Are we mistaken?'

Charlie knew he had no answer that would satisfy Anton. Weakly he said, 'I suppose I've always been a bit of a loner.'

The lift heaved and juddered to a halt. Anton pulled open the door and Charlie looked out into a great void, a gaping darkness that lay before them.

'It takes a while for your eyes to get used to the lack of light,' Anton said.

Charlie blinked into space and could gradually see that they were in a vast storage area, an underground warehouse at least as big as any floor of the store, and a series of distant, receding arches, corridors and tunnels suggested that it might extend far further, burrowing wide and deep under the surrounding streets. The ceiling was high, the air was cool, and there was the noise of a hard-worked air-conditioning system. There were long rows of shelving packed tight with boxed merchandise. They stretched out in all directions like a maze or a hall of mirrors, the vanishing point impossibly far away. Charlie could see no sign that anybody worked in this region.

'Not many people know about this place,' Anton said conspiratorially. 'You're one of a privileged few.'

Charlie did not feel privileged.

'What is it exactly?' he asked.

'You tell me. It's not on any of the floor plans, not on any map. It's not mentioned in any of the company histories. As far as the world is concerned it doesn't even exist.'

'I don't understand,' said Charlie.

'Well, neither do I entirely. There's canned food down here, drink, water, clothes. You could survive for a long time here. It wouldn't be such a bad place to be when the nuclear disaster happens. Or don't we worry about that sort of thing any more?'

Charlie couldn't tell if Anton was being serious or not. He thought it best to smile. Certainly this place had something in common with a bunker or a fallout shelter, but then he supposed all sub-basements did.

'Let's you and me have a little drink,' said Anton and he went to a nearby shelf which was stacked with crates of wine. He opened one and selected a bottle of something old and French with an expensive label, and he opened it with a corkscrew that was hanging on a cord. Then he went to a different shelf, unpacked a pair of new, unused crystal wine goblets, and poured two generous red glassfuls. Charlie was reluctant to accept.

'Are you sure about this?' he asked.

'What's your problem?' Anton demanded. 'That it's wrong or that we might get caught?'

'Well both, I suppose.'

'This is what I mean about you not being one of us, Charlie. Not yet anyway. Are you a cigar smoker, Charlie? No, I didn't think you were.'

Anton strolled the few yards to another nearby shelf containing boxes of cigars. Very deliberately he selected one and slowly lit it. He blew a cloud of smoke up towards the ceiling and flicked his match on to the floor. He drained his wine in one gulp and tossed the glass over his shoulder so that it shattered against the bare concrete behind him. 'Plenty more where that came from,' he said. Charlie continued to be ill at ease. His own wine glass rested unhappily in his hand. So far he hadn't taken a drink from it.

'If you think it's wrong,' said Anton, 'why don't you do something about it?'

'What could I possibly do?' Charlie said.

'Why not reason with me? Perhaps I'll see things your way.'

'I don't think so.'

'Or why not report me? Why not go along to Derek Snell or Ray Chalmers and tell them about it, or about all the other terrible things the furniture porters get up to?'

'I wouldn't do that,' Charlie said quickly.

'Why not? The morality would all be on your side wouldn't it? And Ray Chalmers would probably give you a medal.'

Charlie didn't answer. He wasn't all that strong on morality and he didn't want to tell tales. He didn't like what he'd seen of Ray Chalmers. It wasn't any of his business and he wanted a quiet life. Somehow it was too difficult to explain this to Anton.

'Come on,' said Anton, 'let's take a ride.'

Charlie followed him as he threaded his way between the rows of shelves, and finally they came to a miniature railway line. The track was rusted and little more than eighteen inches wide, and the small motorized 'engine' was not much larger than a bumper car. Anton took the controls while Charlie squeezed into the passenger seat beside him. Anton threw a switch and the car jolted forwards. Once in motion the car drove itself, which was fortunate since Anton had both hands occupied with his cigar and the rest of the bottle of wine which he'd brought with him. His hair trailed behind him in a wild and decorative manner. It felt to Charlie as though they were completely out of control on some dangerous, subterranean, white-knuckle ride.

As they sped along corridors and tunnels, between banks of shelving, accelerating all the time, Anton played the tour guide. He would point vaguely at sets of shelves and boxes and say, 'Over there tinned food. Over there protective clothing. Over there the guns and ammo.' Since the boxes were sealed and unlabelled, Charlie had no way of knowing whether or not Anton was telling the truth. Even before this expedition had started he had suspected Anton of living in a world of paranoid fantasy. For all Charlie knew the boxes might contain nothing more alarming than old till rolls, invoices and VAT returns.

'What I think we need', Anton said ominously, 'is some way to put you firmly on the same side as us.'

'I don't really take sides,' Charlie protested.

Anton thrust the wine bottle at him as though it were a weapon. 'Take it. Take a drink, for God's sake,' he said. Charlie accepted it and took a small mouthful. He hoped it might be enough to confirm that he was on Anton's side, but he didn't really think it would be.

'We need you to commit yourself, to make some small but significant and unequivocal gesture. What do you say, Charlie?'

'I don't know.'

'Well, *I* do.'

The car came to an abrupt stop against a set of brightly painted buffers. Charlie was thrown forwards in his seat, glad that the ride was over. He was feeling travel-sick already and he staggered out of the car.

They were in a wide, hexagonal vestibule. The roof was high and vaulted, and there was a strange spherical thing suspended from the very apex of the vault. It appeared at first glance like a giant balloon, some six feet in diameter, or perhaps like some outlandish, oversized lamp shade. But it was solid, not translucent, made of metal, and as he looked more closely, Charlie could see that a map of the world had been painted sketchily on the sphere's surface. And yet it was not the world as we visualize it, rather something ancient and mythical. The outlines and coastlines of countries were more jagged and ornate than those to be found on globes of any real world. Charlie looked at Anton in the hope that he might be able to explain this weird object, but Anton only shrugged. Then he put his arm round Charlie.

'I want you to do something very simple for me,' Anton said.

For a moment Charlie thought Anton might be about to demand some sexual favour from him, but it wasn't quite *that* simple.

'All I want you to do is make a phone call for me,' Anton explained. 'I want you to phone the switchboard of Haden Brothers and tell them there's a bomb in the store.'

'I couldn't do that,' Charlie said.

'Of course you could. It's no big deal. They get them all the time. Mostly they just ignore them.'

'Then why do it?'

'So I can record you.'

'What?'

'I have here a little pocket tape-recorder, and I'm going to record you making a bomb threat to the Haden Brothers switchboard. Then if you ever decide you're not on the same side as the rest of us I'll play the tape to Derek Snell and see what he thinks about it.'

'You don't need to do that,' Charlie insisted. 'I won't ever betray you.'

'I'm not calling you a liar, Charlie. In fact I tend to believe you, but this way there can't ever be any doubt about it, can there?'

'I really don't want to do this.'

'I can see that, but you *will* do it because if you refuse, then I can absolutely guarantee that your life in Haden Brothers won't be worth living.'

Charlie didn't like being pushed around, and he didn't want to be blackmailed. He didn't think a time would come when he'd ever want to tell tales about what the furniture porters got up to. He certainly didn't want to make bomb threats, hoax or otherwise. Nevertheless, he had no doubt that Anton could and would ruin his working life if he refused, and without a working life he would have no life at all.

'Nobody's going to get hurt, are they?' he asked.

'How can they?' Anton demanded. 'There's no bomb, is there? They ask for a codeword. You say whatever comes into your head. It's not the right word. They hang up on you and that's the end of it.'

Anton took Charlie to some dark alcove where there was an ancient, but working, telephone. He set his tape-recorder running, dialled on Charlie's behalf, then passed him the receiver.

'Haden Brothers at your service,' said a voice at the other end.

'Er, hello. I'm ringing to tell you about a bomb in Haden Brothers.'

The operator was much less chatty than the ones Anton was used to. 'What's the codeword?' she asked flatly.

Charlie was struck dumb for a moment, his mind was a blank as he tried to think of a word, any word that he might say and thereby bring this nasty little game to an end. Abruptly, and for no good reason, he said, 'Hamnet was here.' At which point an emergency siren sounded and all hell broke loose all over the store.

Klaxons sounded, lights dimmed, then flashed erratically as the auxiliary power circuits kicked in. Escalators shuddered to a halt, lifts stopped at the nearest floor and disgorged their confused passengers. Throughout Haden Brothers a mechanical voice that someone must once have thought reassuring softly ordered customers to leave the store at their earliest possible convenience. And so the evacuation procedure began.

In-store demonstrations abruptly ceased. In the cafés and eateries customers gathered up the remains of their meals as they were shepherded out. Tills locked shut. Phone lines died. In the changing rooms, in the dim, flickering light, people rapidly put their own clothes back on. In the beauty salons hair was left half-cut, faces were left half-moisturized, hands left half-manicured.

People moved swiftly with the calm, uncomplaining efficiency brought on by being genuinely scared. They sensed that something dangerous, important and large scale was going on. There were muttered hints about bombs and fires and hold-ups, but mostly they preferred not to name their fears. Store detectives moved among them, ever-vigilant, ensuring that the evacuation was not used as a cover for shoplifting.

All over the store well-drilled staff directed customers to emergency exits and to corridors that had hitherto been designated staff only. Throngs of people flowed downwards and outwards, towards the store's many doors, towards the street and some version of imagined safety.

Even in Arnold Haden's lofty and impregnable penthouse a chill was felt. Arnold was petrified. This was a black alert, the most extreme of a whole rainbow of alerts, yet he knew there was nothing he could do. He remained paralysed by unspecified terrors, and he stayed put.

As departments were cleared, assistants began security searches though unsure precisely what they were looking for. In-house sniffer dogs emerged to begin truffling in dark, musty, inviting corners. Security men found it necessary to make urgent, loud calls on their walkie-talkies. Ray Chalmers strode about imagining himself to be a colossus.

Backroom staff emerged from their offices and stockrooms and mingled with the departing customers. The furniture porters took it coolly and in their stride, but they moved more swiftly than most, unwilling to be incinerated or blown up in the service of Haden Brothers. It did not cross their minds to ask where Anton and Charlie were.

In fact they were feverishly trying to get back into the store from the sub-basement. Down there the klaxons were sounding with ear-damaging intensity. There was no reassuring voice. All the lights were out except for a few tawdry orange emergency bulbs. Charlie wasn't sure what the panic was all about, but when Anton panicked he felt obliged to follow suit.

'This is serious stuff,' Anton told him urgently. 'If they find out we know about this sub-basement, I think we're in trouble.'

Charlie didn't doubt his word. He accepted that their need to get out of the sub-basement was a serious and urgent one. Nevertheless, there was a certain exuberance to their panic. Charlie could hardly believe that all this mayhem was caused entirely by him. It seemed so unlikely that three simple words like 'Hamnet was here' could produce so dramatic an effect. He had no wish to cause such mayhem, yet he felt strangely pleased with himself. Anton was even more pleased with him.

The little railway was no longer working and they ran back to the service lift in a blind rush. Mercifully, the lift was still in operation. It rose with painstaking slowness, but at last delivered them to the furniture department. There was a security guard patrolling the area and he might have been alarmed at their sudden appearance, but Anton remained so cool, so matter of fact, that he accepted their arrival as completely normal.

'Better hurry along there, lads,' he said.

Charlie wanted to make a dash for it but Anton said calmly to the security guard, 'Don't worry, it will just be another false alarm.'

'No,' said the guard. 'This is the real thing.'

But he was wrong. Once the store was empty and after the police and the bomb squad arrived, several suspect packages were discovered. These were investigated, considered and dismantled, and were found to contain a teddy bear, an avocado and bacon sandwich, a computer game called Street Sweeper, and a family-size pack of suntan oil.

Charlie and Anton stood on the pavement outside Haden Brothers. But Anton's sense of being pleased with Charlie had disappeared. He was suspicious now. Something felt wrong about this whole business.

'What was that all about?' he said to Charlie. 'What the fuck was that all about?'

They were at the appropriate assembly point as dictated by the departmental fire drill regulations where they were to report to the floor manager. There was a dense crowd of unhappy evacuees around them, but no sign of the floor manager.

'I don't know,' said Charlie quietly so the people around him couldn't hear. 'I just did what you told me.'

'But how did you know that was the codeword?'

'I didn't. I just said the first thing that came into my head.'

'But why did you say Hamnet was here?'

'I don't know. I saw it painted on a window, that's all.'

'What does it mean?'

'Nothing. I don't know. I mean I think it's just a slogan like Kilroy was here.'

'But who's Hamnet?'

'The only Hamnet I've ever heard of was Shakespeare's son.'

'What are you talking about?' Anton demanded. 'Are you trying to make me angry?'

Charlie shrugged to indicate that he didn't know what he was talking about and that he didn't want to make Anton angry.

'You want me to believe it was just a lucky guess?' said Anton.

Charlie looked at the empty store, at the mayhem around him, at the crowds of police and firemen and said, 'I don't know that it was lucky at all.'

'You amaze me, Charlie, you really do,' said Anton with some disgust. 'You're a continuous source of wonderment and surprise.'

Charlie knew this was not a good thing. Anton was not the kind of man to relish surprises.

'I'm glad I've got you on tape, I really am,' said Anton. 'I'm glad I can prove you did this.'

With some reluctance Charlie said, 'There's another possibility.'

'Is there really?' said Anton dismissively.

'Perhaps the evacuation had nothing at all to do with my phone call.'

'Don't be absurd. I was there. I heard you.'

'Maybe something else happened at exactly the same time and that set off the alarm.'

'Like what?'

'Like the fact that maybe the smoke from your cigar went up to the smoke detectors in the sub-basement and *that* triggered things off.'

For a moment Anton looked as though he was about to hit Charlie for being so stupid and contradictory, but then something about the idea obviously appealed to him.

'You mean *I* could be the one who caused all the mayhem?'

Charlie nodded and Anton's face settled into an expression of the most supreme self-satisfaction.

Clearing the store had taken eight and a half minutes, a minute or so longer than Ray Chalmers would really have liked, but it was within acceptable limits. There were those who thought the incident a fortunate reprieve, in that there was no bomb and that the evacuation had gone so smoothly. Others thought it a potential catastrophe in so far as it indicated that somebody might have cracked the security code. Arnold Haden wondered if he should have new bomb proof doors and a reinforced steel floor added to his penthouse. The store was closed for a total of three hours, resulting in an estimated gross loss of some half a million pounds. The incident did not make the national news.

21 · ACCESSORIES

A day later Charlie sat in the canteen, beneath the stuffed head of some sad, horned, bovine creature. He was eating toast and minding his own business as usual. When he saw Ray Chalmers come into the room he lowered his head so that his eyes could see no further than the edge of his plate. Nevertheless, he was well aware that Chalmers was approaching rapidly and when he sat down at the table, so close that their outer thighs slapped together, there was nothing for Charlie to do but smile awkwardly and say, 'Hello there.'

'You're a disappointent to me, Charlie,' said Chalmers.

'I'm sorry?'

'I thought you weren't like the other lads. I thought you were my friend.'

Charlie figured the man must be crazy. He couldn't think of a suitable reply.

Chalmers continued, 'You looked like the sort of lad who'd come up with the goods for me. I thought you'd help me nail our friend Anton Heath. But you haven't have you? You've let me down. People don't let me down more than once.'

'I haven't let you down,' Charlie said softly.

'What about that little fiasco with the bomb hoax.'

Perhaps he wasn't so crazy after all. Maybe he knew something about Charlie's phone call.

'I don't see how I let you down over that,' he said.

'Don't play dumb with me, soldier, it doesn't suit either of us. Tell me what you know.'

'I don't know any more than anyone else,' Charlie said nervously. 'I heard the sirens and I left the building like I was supposed to.'

'Tell me about Heath.'

'He left the building too.'

'I know that. We saw you talking to him on the street after the evacuation.'

'Well yes, he's my boss. We work in the same department.'

'Don't get frisky with me, Charlie. You're not telling me what I want to hear.'

'I don't know what you want to hear.'

'I want to hear that it was Heath who created the false alarm.'

So perhaps he didn't know very much at all.

'I want to hear that you saw him do it,' Chalmers added.

'But I didn't.'

'Didn't you?'

Since he was still unclear about what exactly had caused the alarms to sound, Charlie wasn't sure whether he was lying or not when he said, 'No, I didn't,' and since Chalmers looked anything but convinced he added, 'Believe me.'

'I want to believe you, Charlie, I really do. If you told me you saw Heath starting the so-called false alarm, well, I'd believe you like a shot.'

'I didn't see Anton Heath starting any false alarms,' said Charlie. 'I don't think he would. OK, I know he's a bit bolshy and difficult but . . . '

'Oh shut up, you little toad,' said Chalmers.

He moved his face to within millimetres of Charlie's. 'I've been thinking about you,' he said. 'And I've been thinking about art.'

That was just about the last thing Charlie would have expected him to think about.

'In my opinion art's all about vanity and ego. And I think I tend to subscribe to the theory that art is a form of neurosis, a manifestation of a pathological problem.'

'Do you really?' said Charlie, now genuinely contemptuous. This was his ground, this was an area in which he felt able to fight back, not that Chalmers would allow him much opportunity to speak.

Chalmers said, 'I don't see why any normal, healthy lad would want to be an artist. Artists, Charlie, what are they? They're all drunks, or depressives or drug takers or wife-beaters or sexual inverts of one sort or another. Is that the type of lad you are, Charlie?'

'No.'

'Then maybe you're not much of an artist, after all.'

There seemed to be no way of arguing with him, and Charlie

abandoned any attempt, but then he found Chalmers grinning at him. The effect was truly disturbing.

'Derek Snell tells me that you haven't found your art form yet,' said Chalmers.

'I suppose I did say that, yes.'

'But I think the problem might be elsewhere. Maybe you just haven't found your patron yet. A lad needs a bit of patronage, a bit of sponsorship, especially at the beginning.'

He peered enquiringly at Charlie but Charlie didn't respond.

'Or have you thought about this? Maybe the problem is you're too comfortable in your present existence? Your job and your home life might just be making things a little too easy for you. Maybe a bit of economic necessity, a bit of hardship; say if you were out on the street and out of work, maybe that would inspire you. Maybe you're not hungry enough.'

'I don't think so,' said Charlie.

'Well, maybe you won't have to find out.'

'What do you want from me?' Charlie said hopelessly.

'I want Anton Heath. I want you to give him to me on a plate. I want you to shop him. And I want you to shop him soon, otherwise you might find yourself getting very hungry indeed.'

22 · MOTHER-TO-BE

ARNOLD HADEN: Kleptomania is a fascinating concept. It lies at an absolute crux of class and gender. I mean that men who steal are not kleptomaniacs and neither are working-class women: they're thieves. But kleptomania is supposedly different. Like all manias – like pyromania or nymphomania – it implies a loss of control, an involuntary response.

The term was invented by a French physician called C. C. Marc in the 1840s. (Incidentally, I don't think it's a coincidence that the French also invented the department store.) But the phenomenon was soon widespread throughout Europe and the United States. Department stores gave women a novel kind of freedom. The department store was a place where, for the first time, women were allowed to move freely, unaccompanied, unattended by shop assistants and without being accountable to anyone.

Marc and many others after him, conceived of kleptomania as a kind of moral disorder, as a form of mental dysfunction, perhaps connected with the menstrual cycle. It seems naive and insulting to us now, but these doctors were doing their best to wrestle with a phenomenon that they genuinely found incomprehensible: why middle-class women who led otherwise blameless lives should suddenly commit unreasonable acts of theft. The doctors liked to think of it as a disease because that way it was forgivable. But there were problems with this. It asserted that middle-class women weren't really criminals, but it did mean they were weak, feeble-minded and neurotic. Personally I prefer not to think that way about women.

A short, discreet, quietly stage-managed disturbance had broken out at the side door of Haden Brothers, the one adjacent to the ladies' glove department. A plain-clothes store detective, a uniformed security guard and a nervous, temporary counter assistant converged smartly on a middle-aged female shoplifter. Her handbag was wrested from her and she was firmly ushered, coerced, though not manhandled, off the shop floor, down a set of narrow corridors to a large, windowless room where, in the normal run of events, she would face Ray Chalmers and eventually the police. But things did not run normally.

It took a little while for Chalmers to arrive and the woman was left alone in the room. It seemed improbably large and impenetrably dark. There was only one piece of furniture and that was a kind of high desk that looked a lot like a mortuary slab. Light came from a recessed overhead spotlight that produced a dim column of grey illumination, in which the woman stood. It was not easy to see to the other end of the room but she thought she could make out an arrangement of chains and electrical apparatus.

At last a door rattled behind her and Ray Chalmers waded into the room. He wore aviator shades and a toothpick danced erratically in the corner of his mouth. He whipped off the shades and gave the woman a disgusted look that he reserved for the low-lifes and parasites and bottom feeders who got caught attempting to steal from Haden Brothers.

'Anything to say for yourself, sister?'

'I want to see Arnold Haden.'

'I bet you do.'

'I want to see Arnold Haden.'

'You're not in much of a position to do any wanting if you ask me.'

'I want to see Arnold Haden.'

Even Ray Chalmers had to acknowledge that this was an unusual demand from a shoplifter. Tears and threats and sob stories and occasional outbreaks of real violence were common enough, but this was something different. The woman was calm, was not protesting her innocence, and her request to see Arnold Haden was not some skittish demand to speak to the boss, to appeal to some higher authority. She made it sound like a reasonable request, like something she was entitled to expect. She wasn't saying that she was a personal friend of Haden or any of that boloney, but there was something about her that made Ray Chalmers decide to take her seriously. He asked her a few more questions but she would only reply that she wanted to see Arnold Haden.

'I'm going to have to think about this,' said Chalmers, and he left the room to begin a series of phone calls that would take him along the chain of command, via heads of department and via Derek Snell, eventually to Arnold Haden.

'Why would a shoplifter want to see me?' Arnold Haden asked naturally enough.

'I don't know, sir.'

'What's she stolen?'

'She tried to steal a pair of gloves, sir.'

'Worth how much?'

'Not very much, sir.'

'What's her name?'

'She won't tell us, sir.'

'Do you imagine she'll tell me?'

'I think it's a possibility, sir.'

'Don't you have procedures for dealing with this kind of thing?'

'I do, of course, sir. But sometimes you can't play it absolutely by the book. I've got a gut feeling, sir, if you really want to know.'

Arnold Haden believed in gut feelings, and he had reason enough to trust Ray Chalmers. For all his idiosyncracies, the man was good at his job. Since the bomb hoax Arnold Haden knew there were strange things going on in the store these days, and it paid to be aware of them. Much as it pained him, he said that he would go down to the interrogation room and speak to the woman. Fortunately he was able to get there by a private staircase, not meeting anyone on the way. He entered the room silently, and he expected the woman to be startled when he came up behind her and said, 'I'm Arnold Haden.' But she was not startled. She simply said, 'I know.'

'It appears you want to see me,' Arnold Haden continued. 'And it appears you've been trying to steal from me.'

'Not from you, personally, Mr Haden.'

'Well, I'm afraid I do take this kind of thing rather personally.'

'I'm sorry,' she said, but she didn't sound very penitent.

'Why did you want to see me?'

'Because you're a Haden Brother.'

'Yes. And?'

'And I believe in going to the top. And because I thought you would understand.'

'What's your name?'

'I'm not prepared to tell you that.'

'Perhaps you'll tell the police.'

'I don't really think it will come to that. I'm not a common criminal you know. I'm not a shoplifter.'

'Then why did you steal the gloves?'

She shrugged a little insolently. 'Perhaps I'm just a kleptomaniac.'

'No, that doesn't really answer anything as far as I'm concerned. You're not terribly poor are you?'

'Well, I'm not terribly rich.'

'But you had enough money to pay for the gloves.'

'I suppose so, yes.'

'You see, if you were poor and hungry and you stole a loaf of bread from us, well, I'd find it hard to feel very angry about that. And perhaps the same would apply if you'd stolen some children's shoes, or perhaps a blanket to keep out the cold. But somehow I don't feel you're in that position, are you?'

'No,' she admitted.

'And let's face it, stealing a pair of ladies' gloves is hardly the same thing as stealing bread or children's shoes.'

'I'm not trying to say that I stole out of absolute necessity,' she answered calmly. 'But that's not to say that I didn't have a passionate need for the thing I stole.'

'Tell me more,' said Haden, thinking that here was an intellectual trail he might profitably stumble down.

'We live in a complex society,' she said. 'Our needs are similarly complex. Once our simple desires for food, shelter and clothing are taken care of we develop more equivocal, more ambiguous needs. We need not just transport, but a good car. We need not just a break from work, but a dream holiday.'

'If you're implying,' said Arnold Haden, 'that none of us is as rich as we might like to be, that we can't buy everything we want . . . '

'No, I'm not saying that at all. It's not a question of being rich. It's a question of having aspirations. I come into your store, Mr Haden, and I discover desires I never knew I had. I see things that I barely even knew existed – like a novelty sponge in the shape of a squid or a froth enhancer for a cappuccino machine – and suddenly I want them. And you may say that I had enough money to buy this particular pair of gloves, but to buy all the things I see and want in Haden Brothers would cost more than any person could possibly afford. The simple answer is I liked what I saw, I wanted it, I was tempted and I gave in.'

'But look at it this way,' Arnold Haden insisted. 'Consider the goods in Haden Brothers as prizes that you might award yourself for having succeeded economically in the world. The more you've succeeded the bigger and better a prize you can afford. Now, if all these goods were free, or even very cheap, they would not be worth having because they would lose their status as prizes. Do you follow?

'Now, I don't deny that you were tempted. I don't even deny that it was our intention to tempt you. But we were trying to tempt you into buying, not into stealing. You wanted a prize when you hadn't won the game. And in any case, however strong the temptation, and I don't want to get too theological about this, there is such a thing as free will. Or don't you think so?'

She didn't answer. She looked as though she had been sunk by his barrage of words, defeated by an argument she couldn't even follow, and that suited Arnold Haden very nicely.

'And', he said, 'I still can't for the life of me think why you wanted to see me.'

'I wanted to ask you to let me go.'

'No doubt. But why should I do that?'

She looked pained but resigned. What she was about to say would clearly be an effort, but it was an effort she had to make.

She said, 'You see, many years ago when I first left school, I came to work here at Haden Brothers. I was very young then, thinner, blonder, far more attractive, far more your type.'

Arnold Haden raised a hand to stop her speaking, to say this was all irrelevant, but she would not be interrupted. 'I was naive, empty-headed, gullible. When the boss showed an interest in me I was very flattered. How could I not be? But the interest was limited, wasn't it, Mr Haden? Or perhaps you don't even remember me. Perhaps you don't recall that you had me a couple of times, roughly, briefly, clumsily, on a pile of rugs in the carpet department one evening after the shop had closed.'

'What are you saying?'

'You fucked me, Mr Haden. It wasn't a great fuck. It obviously wasn't very memorable for you, but I can't seem to forget it.'

'I don't know where this is leading.'

'Don't you? Now, personally I don't hold a grudge against you. These things happen. You were a lot younger then. Why should you feel guilty? I certainly don't intend to blackmail you emotionally or otherwise, but I do think you owe me a favour.'

He examined her face and his own memory. Until that moment he would have been prepared to swear that he had never set eyes on her before, but that proved nothing. He would certainly not claim to be able to remember all the shop girls he had plundered. That would require a ridiculously grand feat of memory. It was perfectly possible that he had once had sex with this woman, but it was equally possible that she was trying to con him. Maybe she was a cleverer, more experienced criminal than she looked. Perhaps she had heard of his taste for young blondes and perhaps she had fabricated her story as an elaborate bid for clemency. He did not like to be conned. There was one comparatively easy way for him to be sure, a little detail that she would know about if she really had been a sexual partner of his. But he didn't need to test her. Unbidden she said, 'If you hadn't had sex with me how would I know that at the moment of orgasm you always shout, "Hamnet is coming".'

He released her without exchanging any more words. Ray Chalmers' instincts had been right again. It was only after she'd gone that Arnold Haden realized he still hadn't discovered her name. He wondered if he'd ever known it.

23 · CONFECTIONERY

The signing session was due to start in the books department at one p.m. on Wednesday afternoon. Julian Temperley, the author of immensely popular and occasionally well-reviewed novels, was coming to sign copies of his latest book *The Coldest War*. It appeared to be an event that could not fail. In addition to his popularity, Temperley had a certain authorial mystique. His public appearances were rare. He didn't do the rounds of TV and radio programmes plugging his work, neither did he do signing sessions for any old bookshop. He could only be coaxed out of his isolation for a really special establishment like Haden Brothers.

Annette Morrell, the buyer of the book department had ensured that the event was well publicized. There were ads in the press and she'd had publicity leaflets printed. There had been a number of telephone enquiries from customers who couldn't make it to the shop on the day and wanted a copy reserved. But for most people the whole point of the event was to meet, or at least see, Temperley in the flesh.

Temperley had no particular reputation for being a prima donna, but he was a serious, substantial, no-nonsense kind of a man. He had a stature and a gravitas about him that his books never achieved. He took pride in not suffering fools.

Annette Morrell was looking forward to the signing session and she was determined that everything would be just right: the chair, the pen, the bottle of wine she provided. She would not be flippant or excessively breezy. She did not want him to think she was a fool. But she felt perfectly able to cope. She had not got where she was today without being able to handle difficult customers. Besides, she would have a member of the Flying Squad helping out in the department: Vita Carlisle.

At twelve noon on Tuesday the telephone rang in her office and a woman on the other end identified herself as Jean Temperley, the author's wife.

'He's on his way,' she said.

'Oh good,' said Annette Morrell without thinking, but even if she'd thought about it, she would have assumed that Julian Temperley lived out of town and was coming up the day before to spend a night in London.

But Jean Temperley said, 'So he'll be with you in about forty-five minutes.'

Julian Temperley was coming to Haden Brothers on the wrong day, a day early. Annette Morrell explained this to his wife but she was unmoved.

'Well,' said Jean Temperley, 'he wasn't exactly in a sunny mood when he set off. When he realizes he's made a ridiculous mistake there'll be the most terrible scene. He's bound to take it out on you, I'm afraid.'

Annette Morrell was aware she would not simply be able to tell Julian Temperley to go away and come back twenty-four hours later. His status ruled against that. She rang the publisher's publicity department and they admitted the size of her problem. It wouldn't be politic to tell him he'd come on the wrong day. However, if they held the signing session today and nobody came, there'd be even greater hell to pay. They wished her the best of luck.

Julian Temperley arrived at ten to one. He was a stern-looking man, with a flourish of grey in his otherwise black hair. He wore a trench coat and heavy-framed spectacles that kept the world at bay. Annette Morrell, pretending all was well, welcomed him, gave him a drink, showed him where the signing was to take place. She would have liked to leave him to his own devices while she set about solving the problem he had created, but that would have been unprofessional. Instead, Vita went into action.

She ran up the escalators to the crowded staff lounge where people on their lunch hour sat around, reading, talking, playing cards. She explained the situation and announced that she needed a lot of people to come with her and pretend they were members of the public and fans of Julian Temperley. In the absence of a real public, they would ask him to sign books for them. He would never know the difference.

Vita got plenty of takers. Some thought it was their duty to help out Haden Brothers in a crisis, while others just thought it was a bit of a giggle. She was a little surprised when Anton Heath and half a dozen furniture porters also volunteered to participate, but she needed every hand she could get. Charlie Mayhew was not amongst them, since he did not spend his lunch hour with the other porters.

The enlisted staff trooped down to the book department where Vita organized them so that they didn't appear all at once. She regulated their passage so there was never much of a queue, but neither was there a moment when Temperley didn't have someone waiting to get a book signed. Loz was the first of the porters to approach him.

'Very pleased to meet you, Mr Temperley,' he said.

'Thank you,' said Temperley, and he got down to the business of signing a book for him.

'Tell me, Mr Temperley, where do you get your ideas from?'

Temperley paused, looked up, and frowned as though contemplating this thorny question for the very first time.

'That's an awfully good question,' he said. 'Of course, one keeps one's eyes and ears constantly open, but you know there are times when an idea arrives perfect and fully formed. I suppose that's what we call inspiration.'

Loz smiled appreciatively and said, 'And would you agree with Michel Foucault that the coming into being of the notion of "author" constitutes the privileged moment of *individualization* in the history of ideas?'

Temperley frowned sincerely, said, 'You know, I think I would,' and moved rapidly on to his next customer.

Things went smoothly for a while as assistants from the soap shop or Spanish ceramics and casual dining got their books signed, but every now and again a furniture porter would come along and ask a rather more challenging question.

Douglas, the man with a penchant for thinking up names of rock groups, asked whether Temperley agreed that an author's name is not simply an element in a discourse (capable of being either subject or object, or replaced by a pronoun, and the like), but rather that it performs a certain role with regard to narrative discourse, assuring a classificatory function. Temperley said he did.

Another porter was of the opinion that the term 'author' was not a definitive source of all the significations which fill a work. The author, he said, did not precede the work, and was only a certain functional principle by which our culture limits, excludes and chooses. What did Julian Temperley think of that? Temperley said he found it a very interesting point.

Finally it was Anton's turn. He approached the table and said, 'Excuse me? Do you work here? I wonder if you can tell me the way to the house-plant department.'

'I don't work here,' said Temperley severely. 'I'm an author.'

'Oh, I see,' said Anton, apparently without guile. 'What's your name?'

'Temperley. Julian Temperley.'

Anton feigned puzzlement and took something out of his pocket. It was a newspaper clipping, an advertisement announcing that the signing session was scheduled for the next day. He pretended to be puzzled and to study it carefully.

'I don't think you can really be Julian Temperley,' he said at last. 'Julian Temperley won't be here till tomorrow.'

Temperley snatched the piece of paper from Anton, read the advertisement and for a moment looked furious, as though he was about to spit lava, but then he looked thoughtful and a sudden calming realization came over him.

'It only goes to show just how popular I am,' he said. 'I can turn up at Haden Brothers on the wrong day and still people come flocking to get their books signed. That's what I call being a successful author.'

24 · NEEDLECRAFT

It was Monday morning and Anton Heath was feeling good. He had spent the previous Friday afternoon querying his pay as usual, and that had passed a happy hour or two. However, over the weekend he had looked at his wage slip again and had spotted something else to query. It was a good way to start the week. He had seen an item called 'miscellaneous deductions and additions'. This, he knew, was a perfectly reasonable means by which tiny amounts of money were added to or subtracted from his wages so they were rounded up or down to the nearest pound for ease of calculation. Over a short period of time it evened itself out. However, whereas this sum was normally, by definition, less than fifty pence, a line of hazy computer printing made the figure appear as eighty-one. Furthermore, Anton had noticed that a couple of new clerks had started work in the wages office, and he was certain he could kill off several hours getting these new employees to work out and then explain to him the mysteries of miscellaneous deductions and additions, particularly if he used all his intelligence to pretend to be unutterably stupid.

He arrived at the wages office and was happy to find himself at the end of a sizeable queue. He looked around the room, exchanging greetings with people. They were mostly regulars. However, there was a comparatively new face, Vita Carlisle. He recognized her from the signing session and took the seat next to her and embarked on a conversation to help pass the time.

'You know,' he said to her, 'Haden Brothers used to have a fur department.'

Vita found this an odd opening remark but answered politely, 'Is that so?'

'They had everything in there,' Anton said. 'Mink, llama, leopard, zebra, tiger, giraffe.'

'Really?' said Vita. 'They really had giraffe?'

'No,' Anton admitted. 'Not really. It was just my way of getting your attention.'

'I see.'

'It used to be like a horror movie in there, like a slaughterhouse,' he said with lubricious disgust. 'It was evil. Beautiful, noble, wild animals had been tortured and murdered, their skins torn from them and brought there as trophies to hang on the back of some rich bitch who shopped at Haden Brothers.'

Vita didn't exactly approve of the fur trade herself, but she had no very passionate feelings about it, certainly none as passionate as Anton's.

'But it closed down?' she asked, trying to keep up her end of the conversation.

'That's right,' said Anton. 'People complained. They wrote letters, signed petitions, made representations, said they thought the fur department was an abomination. Do you think that worked?'

'Apparently, yes,' said Vita. 'There's no fur department now, is there?'

'Of course it didn't work. They had meetings with the Haden Brothers management. They talked about cruelty and animal rights, and Haden Brothers pretended to be very sympathetic and promised to review their policy. But they carried on selling furs.'

'Oh, really,' said Vita, for want of anything better to say.

'Then one day,' said Anton, 'some lone, heroic animal liberationist slipped a tiny little incendiary device into the pocket of a Black Glama mink coat in the fur department. The device worked. It caused a modestly sized fire, didn't put any lives at risk, but still managed to destroy about a hundred thousand pound's worth of animal fur. It was a very successful operation.

'It didn't hurt Haden Brothers directly, of course. They were well insured, they probably even made a profit, but the publicity wasn't exactly attractive. Nobody's going to go shopping for furs if they think they might get burned to death in the process. They had another meeting. The animal lib people never actually admitted responsibility, but they made it fairly plain that if Haden Brothers carried on selling furs, then expensive little fires were likely to keep breaking out.

'Oddly enough, Haden Brothers closed down its fur department. They issued a press release about how they thought a fur department was inappropriate in these conservationist times. Telling, huh?'

'Yes,' said Vita politely.

'So what exactly does it tell you?'

Keeping her composure, Vita said, 'It tells me that Haden Brothers know what's good for business.'

Anton snorted. It was partly with contempt, partly with ironic laughter, but Vita was not affected by his response. She continued, 'It also tells me that neither side was really interested in having a discussion about the actual morality of the fur trade.'

'I wouldn't have thought there was much to discuss,' said Anton.

'Then there'd be no point discussing it with you, would there?' said Vita dryly.

Anton laughed again. It was less ironic this time, and he had some admiration for the skill with which he'd been dismissed and condescended to. He left the question of Haden Brothers fur department. He asked Vita how long she'd been at Haden Brothers and which department she was working in at the moment, and whether she was enjoying it. He did his best to be charming and Vita was not wholly unmoved by his charm.

'I can't say I really approved of what you did at the signing session,' she said, 'but I think I can understand why you did it.'

'Good,' said Anton. 'We'll make a revolutionary out of you yet.'

'No, I don't think so,' said Vita.

A few more people came into the office. There was now standing room only, and the line was not moving.

'They're always making mistakes on the wages,' Anton said archly. 'I'm here every week querying something or other. Sometimes I wonder if they do it deliberately. What are you here to complain about?'

'They seem to have paid me three pounds too much,' said Vita.

'Turning you into a revolutionary may be harder than I thought,' said Anton.

Later, back in the furniture department, he was more robust. 'I met this crazy bird up in the wages office', he said, 'wanting to give money back to Haden Brothers.'

The porters, with the exception of Charlie, laughed riotously at this, though Charlie thought their mirth was something of a knee-jerk reaction. When Anton wanted his men to find something funny, they invariably did.

'I think she must be a Stepford wife,' Anton continued. 'She even had a crazy name. Vita!'

Charlie was pleased to hear Vita's name regardless of who said it. He didn't like the fact that she was being mocked, but it was probably inevitable that Anton would find her laughable. That didn't matter.

Simply knowing she was in the store somewhere and someone had seen her, was enough to cheer him up a little. Charlie was about to ask if Anton knew where she was working.

Then Anton said, 'But you know, the funny thing was, even though she's obviously a cretin and a robot, I thought she was extremely sexy. I could really enjoy giving her a good rogering.'

Charlie gave no thought to what he did next. There was a marble slab in his hands, the top of a console table. Without a moment's hesitation he dropped it on Anton's right foot. Anton roared with pain and careered across the floor as though participating in some avant-garde dance craze. Charlie instantly ran through a series of vigorous apologies and enquiries after Anton's welfare. He did not receive an immediate reply.

Swearing and cursing, his face contorted in pain, Anton at last slumped into a chair. He glared menacingly at Charlie.

'If I thought you did that on purpose,' Anton seethed, 'your life wouldn't be worth living.'

'I know that,' said Charlie. 'I know that if I'd done it on purpose you'd make my life not worth living. And you know that I know that. And I wouldn't deliberately make my life not worth living, would I? Therefore it's obvious that I must have done it by accident. Right?'

25 · OUTERWEAR

When Charlie got home from work the following Thursday evening he found Keith sitting alone in the living room. He was slumped on the sofa and he looked drunk. Sarah was nowhere to be seen. Normally a grunt would have been enough to acknowledge Charlie's presence, but this time Keith said, 'So how are you finding your job at Haden Brothers?' The voice was a little blurred and a little over-emphatic, but Charlie put that down to his being drunk.

'It's OK,' Charlie replied. 'In fact, you know, there are times when I almost enjoy it.'

'And have you found your art form yet?'

Charlie suspected he was being mocked here, but he thought it was only gentle mockery and so he answered seriously, 'Well, you know, it's not easy when you're working full time. But I'm still looking. I still have hopes.'

Charlie would have been willing to take this conversation further but Keith appeared to be having trouble concentrating on anything for very long.

'And how are you finding this sofa?' he asked.

'It's fairly comfortable.'

'Is it?'

'Well, I've got used to it.'

'Yes,' said Keith. 'I suppose you can get used to anything.'

It was only then that Charlie recognized a darkness, a coldness in Keith's voice. He couldn't imagine what the source of it was but he tried to be placatory.

'Don't worry,' he said. 'I'll be gone just as soon as I can afford to go. And I do appreciate your hospitality, really.'

'You find our hospitality acceptable, do you?' Keith said sarcastically.

'Like I said, I really appreciate it.'

'Of course you do,' said Keith bitterly and then he fell into reflection. It was some time before he said, 'And how do you find Sarah?'

'I like Sarah,' Charlie said, a statement that was not strictly true.

'I know you do,' said Keith. 'I bloody know you do.'

'Yes,' said Charlie guilelessly.

'And how do you find her sexually?'

'What?' said Charlie.

It was hard to believe that Keith was being serious and yet he certainly didn't look as though he was in a jokey mood. Charlie didn't know what to say. He hoped that if he said nothing Keith's mind might grasshopper away on to some other topic.

'Well,' said Keith. 'I'm glad that at least we don't have to go through the farce of you denying it.'

'Denying what?' Charlie said. 'I mean there's nothing to deny.'

'I'm not as big a fool as I look, Charlie. At least I'm not anymore. In my heart of hearts I suppose I've known for a long time that Sarah was fucking someone else. I had no proof and I had no idea who it was. Then it all fell into place. I hope you enjoyed fucking my girlfriend, you bastard.'

His words were fierce enough but as he spoke them they became increasingly weak. His initial anger drifted into morose depression.

'How could you?' Keith said softly, and then he began to weep.

'But I didn't,' Charlie insisted.

'Don't be a liar as well as everything else. I asked Sarah directly if she was having an affair and she said yes. She told me everything, about what you get up to on this sofa. At least you had the decency not to use our bed.'

Charlie didn't know what to say. Calling Sarah a liar was hardly going to help matters. Telling Keith that she'd been having sex with somebody *else* on the sofa would be worse still. Fortunately, Keith wanted to do most of the talking.

'It hurts me, Charlie, having my best friend betray me like this.'

Charlie had never suspected that Keith considered him a best friend, but it was a discovery that had come too late.

He began to say, 'Sarah . . . ' but Keith wouldn't let him speak. 'I don't want to hear her name coming from your filthy mouth,' he said.

Charlie knew how he must feel. It was like hearing Anton talking about Vita.

'Pack your bags,' Keith continued sorrowfully. 'Maybe one day I'll find a way of forgiving you, but until then you'd better stay out of my way. And if you ever try to see Sarah again, I'll kill you, I swear.'

Charlie saw no option but to pack and leave. This was not a big task. He gathered together his clothes, a couple of books, an A–Z, a couple of cassette tapes, and all too soon he was ready to be homeless.

'I'm not angry,' Keith said, as Charlie slunk out of the front door of the flat. 'I'm just terribly, terribly disappointed.'

Charlie was both confused and dismayed by Keith's behaviour, more so by Sarah's. But perhaps it was not so very hard to understand. Keith was trying to save his relationship, Sarah was trying to save her affair. This way they both continued to have what they wanted. Making Charlie homeless was a small price to pay, and they were not the ones paying it.

Charlie walked aimlessly for a while. It was still only eight o'clock in the evening. He thought that ought to give him time enough to ring round his acquaintances in London and talk one of them into giving him a bed for the night. But then he remembered how they'd all refused to do that when he first arrived in town. He thought there was every chance they'd say no again and he was reluctant to give them that sort of power over him. He had been in London a good while now and none of his old college friends had so much as asked him out for a drink. These days he seemed to have more in common with the furniture porters at Haden Brothers than he did with any of his old crowd. It was just about conceivable that one of the porters might have been prepared to put him up for a night or two, but he had no way of getting in touch with them. He didn't know where any of them lived and his relationship with them had got nowhere near the stage of exchanging telephone numbers.

He felt in his pockets and came up with about ten pounds. That was all he had in the world until he next got paid. In fact tomorrow, Friday, was pay day, but that wasn't going to help him much tonight. He had no credit card. A hotel room was out of the question. He knew nothing about hostels for the homeless, but he wanted to keep it that way. At eight-thirty tomorrow morning he would be able to return to the warmth and security of Haden Brothers. His task was simple enough; to kill a little over twelve hours on the cold, inhospitable streets of London. He could see the attractions of getting drunk. It could be used to bring about unconsciousness and insulation. But passing out drunk in the middle of London was a dangerous and stupid business, and he decided to go to the cinema instead.

He thought there must be some cinemas in London that had all-night showings. He went into a newsagent and riffled through a copy of *Time Out*, only to discover that all-nighters were confined to Fridays and Saturdays. Still, a good double bill would see him occupied until at least eleven o'clock, and so he found himself in a large, chilly cinema in King's Cross watching a couple of early Russ Meyer movies. The sound and picture quality were bad but those were the least of his problems. He was not there to lose himself in the films. He was there to waste time and, just as important, to plan what he would do once the films had ended and he was back on the street again.

If there weren't any all-night cinemas, surely there must be night-clubs that stayed open until the very early hours. Naturally he couldn't afford to pay to get into a night-club, but he had a notion that given enough charm and enough motivation a man could probably talk his way into a club, and once inside he could make one drink last all night and perhaps he could even find some dark corner where he might doze off and be left alone. As far as that went, this same man might also use his charm to work his way into the affections of some night-clubbing woman who would take him home and solve all his problems in one go.

By the time the movie ended Charlie recognized that he was not that man. He trailed out of the cinema as part of a crowd, and as they hit the street they dispersed each in their own direction, to their own homes. If he were truly the picaresque hero of his own imagination he would no doubt have fallen into conversation with some fellow cinemagoer who would offer him shelter from the storm. King's Cross, with its resident cast of violent drunks and lumpen prostitutes didn't look like the place to be a picaresque hero. He decided to do some walking.

He did not know his way round London at all well, but he headed south, reckoning that he would eventually come to the river. The Thames seemed a suitably romantic, not to say slightly corny, backdrop to his lonely wanderings. It was a cold night and he walked briskly in order to keep warm. He walked as though he had a purpose, although he deliberately took detours and diversions that made the journey longer and more time-consuming. He was surprised how deserted the streets were, how early London went home and to bed. He saw any number of dark, secluded doorways and passages where he might possibly have camped out for the night, but that would have defined him as a street person, a bum, and he was keen to establish, if only to himself, that he was a proper, useful, respectable member of society.

His meanderings meant that it took over an hour and a half to reach the river, a journey that might normally have taken a third of that time. But the walk seemed like decidedly hard work, and it was still only half-past midnight. There was a depressing amount of the night still to be endured, and his sore feet told him there was no way he was going to be able to keep walking around for the next seven or eight hours.

He sat on a bench on the Embankment and rested. A tramp of the old school and a young crustie both came by and attempted to talk to him. Talking to someone might certainly have made the night pass more quickly, but Charlie felt isolated, self-contained, and what could he possibly have to say to tramps or crusties? He ignored them as best he could.

It was obviously going to be too cold to stay immobile on the bench for very long. He soon felt chilled through and he walked again until he came across a bus stop and a line of people waiting for a night bus. He stood with them for a while. It made him feel better and less conspicuous. He had no real intention of getting on a bus, but his weekly travel card entitled him to travel free on night buses, and when one suddenly arrived, it looked so bright and warm and inviting that he boarded it with the other passengers.

He had paid no attention to where the bus was going, and it soon plunged into areas of south London where he'd never been before. At first he was frightened that he might get utterly lost, but, as he had the A–Z in his bag and the rest of the night to regain his bearings, he soon stopped worrying. Around him people were either falling asleep or being drunkenly loud and animated. He remained inert and uncon-nected.

When the bus reached its terminus everyone piled off. Charlie followed, and again felt that terrible gulf between people with somewhere to go and people with nowhere to go. He was in a local high street. It was cramped and unprosperous. There was a sort of rundown shopping mall, a few take-away food bars, a row of unsuccessful shops, all of which were closed and bolted. It looked like a reasonable place to get mugged. Charlie walked for a while, trying not to look like a victim. He wasn't sure what to do next, then he looked across the road, noticed a bus stop and a young couple waiting, and he saw that the bus he'd just been travelling on had turned round and was now about to head back for central London. He dashed across the road and got on board.

These two bus journeys took up the best part of a couple of hours. Time was gradually passing. He got off the bus near Waterloo and found a mobile caff. He had a cup of tea and a cheese sandwich with the thickest bread and thinnest slice of processed cheese he'd ever seen. There were a few taxi drivers hanging round drinking tea and they gave him some appropriately hostile stares. He did not belong there and he moved on again.

And that was how most of the night was eventually, laboriously, painfully, got through; by walking, sitting, riding the increasingly irregular night buses. He grew tired and yet he wanted to stay awake. He did not even let himself nod off on the buses. His walking and riding became utterly aimless and unplanned. Mostly he didn't know where he was or where he'd come from, and he certainly didn't usually know where he was going. However, it did not come as a total surprise when he suddenly found himself standing outside Haden Brothers.

Charlie had a mental image of what Haden Brothers should look like at night. He'd seen it on the postcards; a fantastic tower of illumination, spotlit, with rows of coloured bulbs that picked out the lines of the architecture. But it was now five in the morning, all the illumination was switched off and the place stood in eerie darkness. The lights in the window displays were out, and the ascending rows of windows on the upper floors were completely black. It somehow didn't seem right. It seemed to Charlie that Haden Brothers should always be lit by a kind of continual inner glow, should never sleep, never hibernate. At the very least he had imagined there would be emergency lights on inside, and he assumed there would be security men patrolling the floors. Charlie came to the plate-glass of the store's main doors, and he looked inside. Everything was still and dormant. There was no light, no sign of security men. The entrance was still inviting, it still beckoned, even though it was locked and impenetrable.

Charlie decided to walk around the store's perimeter. He knew that was good for killing half an hour or so, and he calculated that if he made seven or so such circuits, with perhaps five minute stops between, that would more or less occupy him until a time when he could enter the store.

In fact he only completed half a circuit before sitting down on the steps outside one of the distant rear entrances. He hadn't intended to sit for long, and he definitely hadn't intended to fall asleep, but suddenly his eyes closed, his head slumped, and the next thing he knew someone was shaking him to wake him up. It was a uniformed Haden Brothers commissionaire. For a second Charlie didn't know where he was, then he did know, and looking at his watch he saw that it was almost seven a.m. The commissionaire was brusque but not vicious. He just wanted Charlie off his steps, and when Charlie showed a great willingness to leave, the commissionaire was affable enough.

Charlie felt physically rough but emotionally not too bad. His body was tired from all the walking he'd done, and it ached from sleeping on the cold, hard stone step, yet he felt good to have survived a night in the wilderness. He had just enough money to buy himself breakfast. He went to a little Italian café, had bacon and eggs and drank as much black coffee as he could afford. Surviving the night was one thing; getting through a day's work on only a few hours' sleep was something else.

He clocked in and went to the staff washroom. He washed and cleaned up as best he could. He still felt grubby and he was sure he must smell. He saw himself in the mirror and thought he looked pretty bad, as if he'd been up all night. He didn't altogether mind. He wanted his fellow porters to see the state he was in. He wasn't stupid enough to expect sympathy, but someone might at least ask him what he'd been doing all night and he could tell his story. Then they would see that he was homeless, and one of them would offer him a roof over his head. That was the theory, anyway.

The moment he found himself in the company of the other porters he realized what a wild and unlikely theory this was. They didn't look at Charlie closely enough to tell how much or how little sleep he'd been getting. Even if they had, they weren't interested enough in him to ask what he'd been doing. And, of course, it became completely obvious to him that he could have been bleeding to death in some stinking gutter and still none of them would have helped him. Charlie was in need of another theory.

The workload wasn't too heavy that Friday morning. At lunchtime Charlie really wanted to go to the staff lounge and sleep for an hour, but he couldn't allow himself that luxury. Instead he bought an *Evening Standard*, read through the classified ads, and started looking for somewhere to live. It was a long shot but he hoped he might be able to look at a room that evening, accept it on the spot, find that the landlord didn't want a deposit, and move in that very night. It was a frustrating lunch hour. He phoned a lot of numbers but mostly got busy signals or no reply. One man did answer but he wasn't prepared to show anyone the room until Sunday morning. Charlie had no idea what state he'd be in by then.

The only consolation was that today was pay day. If all else failed he would have enough money to check into a cheap hotel. But a Haden Brothers wage wouldn't allow him to take a room in even the cheapest hotel for more than two or three nights. And if he did, then by Monday morning he would be truly penniless and out on the street again.

The furniture porters spent the afternoon querying their wages in their usual manner, and at four o'clock when that was done, Anton announced that they could all go home, all except Charlie who was to stay behind to do the clocking-out for everybody. Charlie didn't protest. He was left alone at the packing bench as the others trooped off to start their weekends.

The salesmen and consultants on the furniture floor knew better than to ask for a porter on a Friday afternoon, so Charlie was not disturbed for the rest of the day. He was dog tired and though he resisted sleep, a moment came when he could stave it off no longer. Charlie was still conscientious enough not to want to be found asleep at his post, so he searched out a corner of the packing area and slid down between rolls of bubble wrap and a Chinoiserie black lacquer cabinet that was ready for despatch. If he could snatch a couple of hours' sleep now, he would be in better shape to sort himself out that evening.

Sleep came easily. If he had any dreams they were calming and reassuring. Nothing could disturb him. He woke up gently and naturally some considerable time later. He was not disorientated. He knew exactly where he was. Only one thing was odd; he was in total darkness. Someone had turned off all the lights. That was a little strange, but it did not worry him at first. Then he looked at his watch. The time was – oh shit – ten o'clock at night. The store had been shut for hours. He was locked in. He thought he had every right to be furious. Couldn't they get anything right here?

He got to his feet, edged his way across the darkened space and found the light switch. The room re-formed itself around him. He opened the door that led out on to the furniture floor, specifically into the Raffles Room that specialized in wicker and rattan items. He shouted 'Hello' but was not at all surprised when nobody answered.

Just enough lights had been left on for him to make out the chairs and tables, and he crossed the department without walking into anything. He came to a desk belonging to one of the salesmen and he picked up the telephone. He put the receiver to his ear, and heard the reassuring burr of the line, then he stopped, having no idea whom he might phone or what he might say. He put the receiver down again carefully, and realized he'd better do some thinking.

He did a tour of the floor, stepping gingerly between coffee tables and standard lamps and swivel chairs and sofa beds, until he came to the swing doors leading out to the central escalators. They were motionless, of course, but Charlie could look down into the open space of the grand entrance hall below and see just a glimpse of each floor. There was not the slightest sign of life. He called out again and this time there was the hint of an echo, but still no reply.

He walked down the first escalator, then the next, then the next. His sense of indignation at being locked in gradually disappeared and he started to feel very uncomfortable, like an intruder, a burglar. It occurred to him that if there *was* somebody else in the store, a security man or a member of management working late, then explaining how he came to be locked in might not be so easy. He didn't feel he had done anything very wrong, except falling asleep, but he felt sure that must be one more offence for which he could be sacked. That really would be a disaster; no home and then no job. He started to think it might be as well if he were not found at all. He also realized that if anybody *did* find him, regardless of whatever else they did, they would certainly let him out of the store, in which case he would be wandering the streets again.

And yet, for all that the situation was alarming and uncertain, he somehow knew that he wasn't going to encounter anyone in the store. Something told him he was absolutely alone in the many rooms and floors of Haden Brothers. There was no other human presence.

Neither was there much heating. Charlie became aware of how cold he was. He was also hungry and thirsty. For a second this made him profoundly miserable, until he suddenly, recklessly, daringly saw that the store could solve all these problems for him. It wasn't his fault that he'd been locked in. The very least Haden Brothers owed him was supper and a bed for the night.

He went down to the ground floor, to the food hall and made his way to the chill cabinets. He picked an individual quiche, a tub of potato salad and a carton of orange juice. Of course he didn't really want cold food. He really wanted a plate of hot roast beef with gravy and all the trimmings but he wasn't that ambitious yet. However, if he was going to be cold on the inside he could at least stay warm on the outside. On his way back to the furniture floor he made a detour to the bedding department where he picked up a thick tartan blanket. He returned to the Raffles Room, drew the blanket around him and ate his 'picnic' from a long, low, glass-topped bamboo table.

When he'd finished he lounged on a sofa, put his feet up, and experienced a peculiar, and apparently inappropriate, sense of well-being. He felt strangely safe and contented. He had the sense that destiny was looking after him. This was a much better way to spend the night than wandering the streets and hopping on and off night buses. Somebody up there liked him, which was just as well, since down here everyone else was either hostile or indifferent.

Nobody knew he was there in the store, and nobody really cared. There would be nobody wondering where Charlie Mayhew was tonight. But this wasn't such a bad place to be. In fact, there was space for hundreds of people to spend the night in Haden Brothers. A solitary soul lodged in the furniture department would not be noticed tonight, or ever.

And that was when he had his Big Idea. If he could get away with it for one night by accident, why couldn't he get away with it for much longer by design? Haden Brothers could provide him with shelter and comfort, with all the food and drink, all the beds and sofas and tables and blankets; indeed just about everything else he would need. He didn't intend to steal things, he just wanted to have the use of them.

It was a mad and desperate plan, and yet the moment he considered it, he recognized its logic and rightness. He could live in Haden Brothers far more happily than he had ever lived anywhere else. He could become a sort of stowaway, a spirit of place. The idea delighted him. It was crazy, absurd, outrageous, and yet he was absolutely certain he was going to see it through, to make the store his natural habitat. He was going to become Haden Brothers' invisible lodger, its ghost. It was a wonderful prospect. It felt like coming home.

26 · CONTRACTS

'There are strange things happening,' said Arnold Haden to Derek Snell.

'Don't I know it?' Snell agreed, thinking of the recent bomb hoax, the problems at the signing session, Vita Carlisle's very public put-down of him.

But Arnold Haden wasn't talking about that. 'I think I'm in love,' he said.

'What?'

'I thought she was just a passing fancy,' Haden continued, 'but as time goes by I find that my feelings haven't passed at all.'

'Who?'

'Vita Carlisle. Who else?'

'I see,' said Snell, unsympathetically.

'Well, I'm not at all sure that I do. But I find myself thinking about her all the time. I find that I admire her qualities, when what I thought I'd always wanted was a woman without qualities. I really need some advice. What would you do, Derek?'

Derek Snell pretended to be giving the subject a lot of consideration, and after what he considered an appropriate passage of time he said, as though with enormous regret, 'Sack her.'

'Sack her?' Arnold Haden breathed.

'Yes,' said Snell. 'I think she's a bad influence.'

'Surely not. Surely she's a perfect employee.'

'She's a bad influence on you, Arnold. You're a man who likes a trouble-free existence. And I can see she's troubling you.'

'But I think it's the sort of trouble that I rather like.'

'I don't mean to be hard on the girl,' said Snell, 'but if you ask me she's nothing more than a little gold-digger.'

'But she turned down my offer.'

'I think she turned it down because she's holding out for a *better* offer.'

Haden could only see this as good news.

'That's all right by me,' he said. 'I don't mind improving my offer. As far as that goes, she can just about name her price.'

'That would be a very bad precedent, Arnold.'

'Well, no, not really, because my feelings for Vita are unprecedented.'

'I know you can afford her price, Arnold, but I see it as part of my role as your confidant to make sure that you get value for money.'

'It isn't really about money.'

'You're right. It's about something more important than that. Your peace of mind.'

'I really don't know what to do.'

'At moments like this, Arnold, you should do what you always do, throw yourself into some mindless sensuality. Do something empty, vacuous and without consequence.'

'Can you arrange that?'

'Of course I can. I've got a brand new intake of young, naturally blonde female shop assistants starting on Monday morning. You'll like them, Arnold, really you will. They're all very you. If they don't make you forget Vita Carlisle, nothing will.'

'Derek, I don't know what I'd do without you.'

'Frankly, Arnold, neither do I.'

27 · EXHIBITIONS

Charlie moved in to Haden Brothers. He felt immediately and entirely at home. His days were spent in the old routine as a furniture porter, and his nights were spent as a stowaway in the store.

Mornings were easy enough to manage. It wasn't so hard to make a sudden appearance, emerging when he heard the voices of others in the department. There was some banter about the fact that he was always early for work when the other porters took pride in being regularly late, but Charlie had an uncomplicated explanation. He said the sofa he slept on was so uncomfortable and the people he shared the flat with so unlikeable that he'd rather be at work. The porters thought this was plain stupid, but they didn't disbelieve it.

The end of the working day caused more problems. It was sometimes possible to stay behind as the others left by pretending he had some paperwork to complete, but the workload was rarely heavy enough for this to be convincing. On other occasions he would go into the Gents, lock himself in a cubicle and wait.

But that wasn't foolproof since from there it was impossible to tell whether everyone had gone or not. Besides, it caused talk to spend so much time in the toilets. But he had to lay low somewhere until the shop was empty, and he became very good at slipping away un-noticed, finding corners and cubby holes where he could hide away, places where he could see but not be seen. He'd watch as the cleaners hoovered and emptied the bins, then, when the store was quiet and the lights went out, he could take possession of his domain.

This worked well Monday to Saturday but Sundays were surprisingly difficult. The shop was closed and he felt he ought to have had the free run of the place, but all too often little groups of employees would be in the shop, rearranging a department, putting up new display units, building fake Italian plazas or Tudor cottages as part of some new promotion. He had to be very careful on Sundays, to lie very low indeed, to make sure he covered his tracks well on Saturday night.

He was amazed at how quickly he got used to his nocturnal world, and how bold he became. Whereas at first he had skulked around the store in dim light, like an intruder or burglar, he soon walked anywhere he chose, turning on lamps as he went. Whereas that first night he had camped out on a rattan sofa under a tartan rug, he now went to the bed department, made up a different bed every night and slept under fresh linen sheets. Instead of quiche and potato salad he had rapidly got used to fine cheeses, smoked salmon, the occasional small jar of caviar. He became adept at using the microwave ovens in the household appliances department to create entire roast dinners. He was not excessive. He was neither wasteful nor a glutton, but he had made the decision to live well, and expensive tastes were easily acquired.

The store was never quite as still and silent as he thought it should be. There were alarming creaks and settlings in the fabric of the building, eerie hisses and sighs from the plumbing and heating systems. In the beginning, every sound had thrown him into a panic and sent him running for cover, thinking it signalled another human presence. But he soon learned that it signalled no such thing and he came to accept these noises-off as part of the texture of his new existence.

He quickly lost any sense of danger. There were security cameras trained on all areas of the shop, and at first he skulked around trying to avoid their gaze. But it dawned on him that they didn't function at night. The light level was surely too low for them to create images, and even if it were not, would Haden Brothers really pay staff to sit up all night watching views of deserted, darkened departments?

Keeping clean was not plain sailing. On the one hand he had access to a whole galaxy of soaps and lotions, shampoos and shower gels, aftershaves and bath salts. On the other, there was nowhere he could comfortably take a bath or shower. He knew there must be several sets of bathrooms in the store, but he didn't bother to search for them. He would have felt too exposed and vulnerable if he had stripped naked and immersed himself in water, so he washed all his parts one at a time in the sinks in the Gents' toilets. Even this couldn't be done first thing in the morning for fear of being discovered, so he always abluted in the middle of the night.

Entertainment was not a problem. He would go to the hi-fi department and use the best equipment to listen to the best CD recordings. He would go to the TV and video department and watch the giant, flat-screen televisions with Nicam stereo. He had unlimited access to a full run of girly mags from the magazine department, and although he found these dreary, there were times when they were very useful. He tried out computer games, played with executive toys. Sometimes he even read a good book; something by James Joyce, Primo Levi, Georges Perec.

Of course he had no social life, but that was no great loss. His social life in London had always been non-existent. If he was going to have to spend his evenings alone and friendless, he was pleased to be doing it in the spacious, well-equipped luxury of Haden Brothers. The porters still invited him to go out drinking with them but he now had an even better reason to say no. Once out of the store he couldn't get back in.

He would go to the sports department and give himself a work out. He'd slip on boxing gloves and hammer away at a punch-bag, do a few miles on an exercise bike, have a session on the rowing machine, haul a few weights. He came out feeling invigorated and refreshed. He was shaping up, getting fitter than he'd ever been.

In moments of reckless absurdity he'd visit the men's outfitters department and try on top hat and tails, jodhpurs, kimonos, flying jackets, silk suits. He thought he looked pretty damned good, and he wished he had someone to share the joke with, someone who would admire him and laugh with him.

Sometimes he got lonely and then he would drink. He'd go down to the wine department and get a reasonable bottle of Châteauneuf-du-Pape, and swiftly knock it back. It boosted his spirits and made him feel confident and fearless. Then he would stride around the store like some conquering hero, king of all he surveyed. He would get careless and uncoordinated. He would occasionally knock things over, spill wine on to white damask table cloths. He regretted it but it didn't seem to matter. There was never any consequence. The only thing he really feared was falling into a drunken stupor and being found asleep next morning by a security guard. Then the game would be up and he'd have to face the consequences.

He was not sure precisely what crime he was committing, but he supposed it would be called theft and probably trespass. Nor was he sure what the punishment for such a crime might be; a hefty fine or possibly jail. Yet he thought that in the event he would probably get not much more than a good telling off. He imagined that Haden Brothers would be far too embarrassed to admit publicly what he had been up to.

He didn't wish discovery on himself, but he supposed it was bound to happen sooner or later. He didn't intend to spend the rest of his life living and hiding in Haden Brothers. And with luck he thought he wouldn't have to. Even though he never left the store, he still clocked in and clocked out. Now that he had no living expenses, no board and lodging to pay, no travel costs, his wages remained untouched. He was building himself a nice little stack of money, and when he had enough he planned to leave the store and buy himself the time to become an artist.

Given the amount of free time he had in the evenings and at weekends it would have been quite possible for him to begin practising his art straight away, but he preferred to think of artistic production as something for the future. What he was involved with at the moment was preparation, research, the gathering of material.

He did a certain amount of snooping; looking in private drawers and cupboards. It was not so very enlightening. He would find a box of suppositories, a birthday card with a salacious message, a pack of condoms. These things hinted at potential embarrassments and revelations, but he seldom knew the characters involved. He found his way into managers' offices and came across drafts of memos and letters that might have fascinated a student of office politics, but Charlie was no such student.

One night he entered Derek Snell's office and found some files labelled 'Confidential'. He looked inside but they contained nothing more important than job applications from female school-leavers. He shrugged. If the files had been genuinely confidential no doubt they would not have been left lying around like that.

If he had shared the same inclinations and motivations as Anton, he could have caused all manner of subversion and sabotage. He was in a position to steal or destroy documents, to wreck systems, to steal vital order forms and price lists and invoices, to create all kinds of confusion. But it never even occurred to him to do any of that. His snooping was done out of a kind of benevolent curiosity. He was exploring his environment, getting to know the place where he lived. The simple, surprising truth was that he liked Haden Brothers far too much to want to do it any harm.

Increasingly, however, it became possible for him to think of himself as some crazed despot and of the store as his own personal pleasure dome and treasure house. Of course he did not own any of the goods that surrounded him, yet in so far as they were entirely at his disposal, it was easy to think of them as his. He did not want to horde them or draw them to himself, and there was no sense in which he could take them home with him. It was enough to know they were there. He watched their comings and goings. He was aware of changes in the stock. Old lines sold out, new lines arrived. Seasonal goods had their day and then disappeared. He was aware that he had access to riches that other people only dreamed of. People worked hard to pay for those things that he enjoyed for free. This made him appreciative and yet he felt himself to be unmaterialistic. He took pleasure in the goods, but he had no desire to own them.

He went to the toy department, played with the model train layout, with a Scalextrix set up, with paper gliders and glove puppets. He visited a stockroom filled with Christmas goodies: artificial trees, musical fairy lights, several Santa Claus outfits. It was childish, but he didn't care, and not all his pleasures were so innocent.

He went to the pharmaceutical department to see what drugs he could get access to. The serious and recreational stuff was all locked away, but he was presented with a whole world of cough mixtures, cold cures, skin creams, antiseptics and hay fever treatments. Condoms too, but he had even less use for them than for the rest of the stuff.

He would go to the ladies' underwear department, look at the bras and panties, the teddies and basques. He'd pick them up, savour the fabric, rub them along his face and wonder who would buy these items. He'd imagine her getting them home, going to her bedroom, stripping naked, then lovingly trying on her new purchase, never suspecting that someone like him had already touched and fondled the garment. Or maybe she did suspect, maybe that was what she wanted, maybe their fantasies coincided.

Charlie was a frequent visitor to the pet department. At a certain time in the history of Haden Brothers, the pet department had contained all manner of exotic caged birds, cute puppies and kittens, marmosets, snakes, stick insects. But sensibilities had changed over the years and now the department sold mostly pet accessories and the only living things for sale were a few tanks of tropical fish. He would watch them for long stretches of time, their bright metallic colours flicking through the luminous blue water. They fascinated him. The aquaria were discrete worlds, tiny planets as complete and contained as Haden Brothers itself.

He watched the news on television, read the papers and sometimes went out in his lunch hour so he was not entirely cut off from the world, but a lot of it didn't seem to concern him any more. Rising prices, rail and bus strikes, unemployment, foreign wars, government policy, were things that passed him by. The staff newsletter, a Haden Brothers store plan, a mail order catalogue, these were the kinds of document that described and dictated his world.

He continued to work diligently as a furniture porter, but not so diligently as to offend his fellow workers. He hadn't become one of the lads, but that was fine by him, and if he was regarded as a bit of an oddball who kept himself to himself, that was fine too. The less they knew about him the better. Even Anton left him alone these days and Charlie was relieved.

Nevertheless, there were moments when he thought to himself, 'If only they knew.' One night he came upon the complaints department with its pool and parakeets, and he felt an overwhelming need to share this find with somebody. He was committing such a daringly brilliant scam that at times he could barely stop himself telling others about it, but somehow he managed.

Then one night there were unfamilar noises in the store, not the old reassuring creakings and settlings, but the mechanical noise of the central lifts being operated. Charlie was in the furniture department lounging on a Parker Knoll recliner, working his way through a jar of olives stuffed with anchovies, and sipping a Belgian fruit beer, and he happened to be reading Huysmans' *Against Nature*. It was fortunte that he was reading. If he had been listening to music through headphones or if he'd had the television on loud he wouldn't have heard any other noise at all. His chair was within sight of the lifts, so he gathered up his beer, book and olives, and scuttled behind a hand-painted Omega-style screen that separated the Italian decorative room from the Modern classics. He could still see the lift doors but he was well hidden. He listened intently and it seemed that he could hear not one lift in operation but two.

He thought the chances were that he had nothing much to fear. Even if the lifts were in operation there was no reason to believe they were coming to his floor, nor even that they contained passengers. However, he watched the lights above the lift doors and he could see that there were indeed two lifts in action, one descending a little ahead of the other. The first lift got to the furniture floor and stopped. There was a high-pitched bell chime and the doors started to open. Charlie felt a seep of adrenalin in his stomach, but then watched in some disbelief as a giggling young blonde woman ran out of the open lift. She looked drunk, excited, and she was completely naked. Charlie stared as she sprinted across the carpet, heading for the bed department. He was still wondering if he was hallucinating when the second lift arrived and an equally naked, middle-aged man dashed out.

Charlie had never seen this man in the flesh before but he knew perfectly well who it was: Arnold Haden. He was not so giggly, drunk or excited as the young woman, but he moved swiftly enough in pursuit of her. Charlie still distrusted his senses, but he also felt annoyed. Who were these people to invade his territory and spoil his quiet evening's reading?

He waited behind the screen, had another olive, another mouthful of beer. There didn't seem to be much doubt about what Arnold Haden was up to. He was using his store as a venue for a bit of late night slap and tickle. Rather than chasing girls round his desk, he was chasing them round the whole store. The girl was obviously happy to be chased and was entering into the spirit of the thing. Her delighted squeals could be heard ringing out across the floor. Charlie decided to get a closer look.

He went across to the bed department. There was a whole row of different styles and sizes of divan and mattress and headboard, and there were also enough obstacles, things to hide behind. He noticed how young and pale the girl was. Her hair was the colour of sun-bleached sand and she was wearing no makeup. Her pubic hair was a tiny, trim triangle. She was shapely and pretty, he supposed, but she seemed exceptionally bland. She let herself be caught by Arnold Haden and he pushed her down on to a queen-sized divan with teak storage drawers.

Arnold Haden was a lively lover. He stroked and kissed and stimulated his partner in all the right places. His body was white and soft and overweight, but he moved with a certain solid grace. And if he appeared to be enjoying the event rather more than the girl was, she did her best not to appear reluctant. They moved from bed to bed and Arnold Haden moved the girl from position to position. He went from above to below to behind, from lying to kneeling to standing. At one point he moved her to a spot in front of a full length wardrobe mirror so he could see himself.

He watched with almost as much fascination as did Charlie, but Charlie's response was rather more complicated. He had never been in exactly this situation before, in fact, if you discounted the incident with

Sarah and her lover, he'd never *remotely* been in this situation before – and it made him uneasy. It was embarrassing and distasteful and very possibly immoral. He wasn't feeling aroused by it; but he couldn't stop watching.

He noted details; an asymmetrical patch of grey hair at the base of Arnold Haden's spine, his appendix scar, his big flat feet. He saw that the girl had a pattern of honey-coloured moles under her left breast, that her nipples were scarcely darker than her breasts, that there was a narrow indentation around her left wrist from a recently removed watch.

It was an intimate and indecent display and yet it seemed a curiously innocent entertainment, like classical dance or mime or gymnastics. The pair of them were naked and untrammelled in this whole world of clutter and possessions, and Charlie envied them.

He watched until they had finished, or at least until Arnold Haden had. The climax was small scale, intense but undramatic, although as he came, Haden did shout something, some phrase that Charlie couldn't make out. Haden eased himself off the girl and the girl eased herself up off the bed. She was no longer giggling. She stood up, held herself shyly as though she wanted to find something to cover herself with. Slowly Arnold Haden pulled himself together. He patted her on the shoulder as he might have patted a defeated squash opponent and escorted her back to the lift. They got in and ascended to the Haden penthouse. Charlie's throat was dry and he was pleased to find that he still had a bottle of beer in his hand.

All was calm and silence again, but the sense of interruption remained. He knew it was crazy, but he felt that Arnold Haden had invaded his space and, what's more, he might do it again. It was another problem he'd have to live with. If Arnold Haden was going to start running around the store naked, there was every chance he might run into Charlie. They'd both get the shock of their lives, but Charlie was the one who would suffer.

At the same time, he saw how this situation might be used to his advantage. Seeing Arnold Haden in this state was another card to be held up his sleeve, not a trump card exactly, but it seemed to promise something. Blackmail hardly seemed a possibility, but if he was ever caught, it might be useful to have some inside knowledge about Arnold Haden.

Over the next few weeks Arnold Haden made a series of other erotic forays into the store. They were all more or less identical to that first one and Charlie learned how to cope with them. He would hear the lift coming and swiftly conceal himself. He no longer bothered to watch the action, though he did notice how similar all the girls looked, all young and blonde and apparently rather characterless. He realized that Vita Carlisle conformed at least partly to that type, although he knew for a fact that Vita was far from characterless. He almost expected to see her emerge naked from the lifts. The prospect filled him with dread. The spectacle of a naked Vita Carlisle would have pleased him well enough, but if he ever saw her in the grubby clutches of someone like Arnold Haden, it occurred to him that he might not be responsible for his actions.

However, having watched and heard Arnold Haden in action a few times, Charlie had finally worked out what it was that he shouted at the moment of orgasm: 'Hamnet is coming.' It didn't make much more sense as a cry of passion than it had as a graffito or as the name of a rock band, or, possibly, a password.

28 · TIES

Arnold Haden and Vita Carlisle have stepped out of the whiteness of the penthouse and are standing on the balcony, the place that was once known as Suicide Ridge. The night air is cool and moves across the skin like a chilling hand.

'You asked me why I wasn't frightened,' Arnold says. 'I think I can tell you, but it's a long story.'

'That's fine by me,' says Vita. 'It's a long night.'

Arnold Haden says, 'It was 13 June 1962 and we had all been drinking heavily. One did in those days, it was normal. There was my wife Patricia, my brother Timothy and myself, a fairly regular social unit. Timothy had just bought himself a new car, an Alvis, in metallic blue with a pale cream leather interior. He wanted to show it off so he took us for a spin into Oxfordshire. We went to a pleasant riverside pub, had Pimms and gin and tonics and beer, then decided to drive home.

'Tim and I were both in our mid-twenties, though he was older by a couple of years. We'd hated each other as schoolboys, been terrible rivals, bitterly jealous of each other, absolutely furious if one had something the other didn't. But by the time we went to university we'd learned to tolerate each other, and now that we were fully adult we had become good friends. It was just as well since we knew that sooner or later we would be jointly responsible for running Haden Brothers.

'As children we'd treated the store as our playground. Our parents were indulgent. We knew that within reason we could have anything we wanted from the store. Oddly enough, we were not particularly grasping children, which is perhaps only to say we were too spoiled to have developed the sense of values shared by the rest of society. We were as likely to be pleased by a cheap set of lead farm animals as we were by some vast and elaborate Hornby model railway layout. The store was also a fabulous place to play hide and seek. There was a time when we both knew every inch of it, all its secret corners and obscure hiding places.

'The line of succession, so to speak, at Haden Brothers had always been problematic. The founders of the store, Edwin and Clifford Haden believed there was something special and crucial about the fact that the firm was run by two brothers. They thought there was an empathy and kinship between brothers that guaranteed a successful business, and they believed there should always be brothers at the helm. Haden cousins would not have been acceptable. Haden sisters would have been unthinkable. Fate accommodated them. Edwin produced two sons, Clifford produced two daughters. The girls weren't treated badly. They were given shares and a trust fund, but the running of the store was left to the boys.

'Again it will seem odd today, but my brother Timothy and I were perfectly happy to continue that way of doing things. It was understood that we had a duty, or at least one of us did, to produce two or more male heirs. I suppose there would have been enormous difficulty had we *both* produced two male heirs, or had we each produced just one, but this was destined never to become a problem.

'As I say, we had been drinking heavily, and when the time came to return to London I, being marginally less drunk than Timothy, suggested that I should drive us back. But in our drunken state, a certain amount of boyish rivalry had returned, and Timothy insisted that he should drive. It seemed to me at the time that he simply didn't want me playing with his new toy. I acquiesced.

'Patricia and I had not been married so very long, a couple of months short of two years. I, of course, thought she was beautiful and perfect. It was a genuine love match, and yet I was well aware of the fact that she would make a suitable wife for a Haden Brother. She was charming and socially adept. She was good at meeting clients. She had an instinctive feel for the business and she loved Haden Brothers almost as much as I did. I little doubted that she would bear me two or more male children and I assumed we would be together forever.

'I thought this gave me a distinct advantage over Timothy. Despite being older than me, he was considerably less successful with women. He had never been in a serious relationship and it didn't seem to bother him. In fact he had often spoken, admittedly in a way that many young men do, of remaining a bachelor forever.

'We were on a by-pass outside Slough when Timothy said to

Patricia, "It's time you told him." Patricia giggled and tried to dismiss whatever Timothy was attempting to say, but he said to her firmly, "If you don't I will."

'It all seems so obvious now, so predictable; the stuff of soap opera, not of great tragedy. Timothy had decided that he had to have Patricia. He said they were in love, that they were lovers, that it was passionate and serious and that Patricia couldn't live a lie any more. She was leaving me for him. He knew I would be devastated but he was unapologetic.

'In fact, the alcohol numbed the effect his words had on me. I couldn't quite think straight, couldn't quite believe it, and yet I knew it was all true. Patricia said nothing and yet she denied nothing either.

'I was, and still am, absolutely convinced that Timothy only wanted Patricia because she was mine. He wanted her in the way he used to want my Dinky cars or my tin soldiers. I believe that if Patricia had been free and single, or simply attached to someone other than me, he would have been utterly indifferent to her. I was dismayed that she had let herself be seduced and used by my brother in this way. I was bitterly disappointed. I had thought she was more discriminating, better able to discern quality. Then she said, "This is silly. We're all drunk. Things will look very different in the morning." But I knew they wouldn't.

'Perhaps I should have fought for Patricia, tried to win her back. Perhaps I should have had more confidence in myself and in my ability to regain a woman's love, but I had no such confidence. I had been presented with a *fait accompli* and it would have been debasing to squabble. Besides, if Patricia really thought she loved Timothy, if she had really made love with him, then she was not the woman I thought I was in love with, and she was soiled beyond redemption in my eyes.

'I was seated in the back of the car. Timothy and Patricia were in the front, an arrangement that now looked all too stage-managed. In that moment I hated my brother more than I had ever hated anyone or anything in my life and I started to pummel him around the back of the head and neck. My fists were clenched so tightly they hurt. I was in a blind fury and I was unaware of my own strength.

'He was not expecting this cowardly attack and he was too slow to defend himself. I must have landed a freak, desperately hard rabbit punch on the back of his neck. Timothy's head dropped and his hands came away from the wheel, but the car ploughed on. The road had been clear a moment ago but now there was a huge lorry coming towards us. Patricia screamed and I realized the enormity of what I had done.

'Patricia was not a driver but she instinctively grabbed the steering wheel. It was too late, and if anything her frantic grab at the wheel drew us more directly into the path of the lorry. The driver was braking hard but the impact was certain and appalling when it came.

'Suddenly we were spinning through the air, lightly and inconsequentially, like a discarded tin can. The car landed on its roof. The windscreen and windows were shattered and there was a lot of blood. I heard Patricia moaning but Timothy was quite still and silent. I knew he was dead and I was in such pain that I thought I must be dying too. However, I remained conscious throughout the whole protracted business, as I waited for the police and ambulance to arrive, as I watched them cutting the car open to get us out, as we made the long jolting ride to the hospital.

'The doctors would eventually tell me I was lucky to be alive, though by then I couldn't agree with them. Patricia lingered on for the best part of a week. She was only fitfully conscious, and she was deadened by painkillers, but I was able to speak to her briefly. She asked me if I could forgive her, and I had to tell her that I could not.

'A doctor came to tell me when she was dead. He was only my age and considerably more callow. After he'd broken the news he seemed reluctant to leave. There was something else he had to say. He asked me if I knew that my wife had been pregnant. I had not. He seemed close to tears and I did my best to reassure him that I could cope with the news. I asked him if he knew what sex the baby was, but he couldn't or wouldn't say.

'I have always assumed that the unborn child was a boy, and I have tended to believe he was mine rather than my brother's. I know this is not strictly logical. I frequently try to imagine the boy and then the man he might have become, but it is all too vague, a picture seen through thick gauze in poor lighting. I am not so sentimental as to believe that he would have been a perfect son, a perfect man to take over the reins of Haden Brothers, but in his absence I do not know what will become of Haden Brothers, or rather I suspect I do. I think it will fall into the hands of managers and business specialists, into the clutches of glorified book keepers who have MBAs and who are computer "literate". And frankly I'm not sure that I can bring myself to care.

'The only piece of sentimentality I have allowed myself in all this is to give my unborn and unbearable son a name. I call him Hamnet, like Shakespeare's own dead son. He was on his way but he was never quite here.'

Only now does Arnold Haden become aware that there are tears flowing down his cheeks. A little awkwardly he looks at Vita and sees that she's crying too.

29 · MEN'S FRAGRANCE

It was another undemanding day in the furniture department and Charlie was wandering again. He had an official-looking piece of paper in his hand and had been killing some time by watching a demonstration of candle-making on the ground floor. Now he thought it was time to get back, and rather than use the escalators or stairs, he chose to return by one of the many lifts. He had entered a lift and the doors had closed before he noticed that the attendant was the same blind old man who had once taken him to the personnel department. The lift started to ascend and as it arrived at the first floor the attendant was about to begin his description of the goods available there, but Charlie stopped him.

'You don't have to do that for me. I work here. Remember?' he said.

The lift attendant inhaled sharply through his nose, taking in Charlie's scent.

'I remember,' he said, and Charlie expected a smile of recognition, but it did not come. 'How are you settling in?' the attendant asked stiffly.

'Fine,' said Charlie. 'Really fine.'

'Aren't you the one who wanted to be an artist?'

'That's right.'

'Do you still want to be an artist?'

'Of course,' said Charlie.

The attendant sniffed again, and this time it seemed to contain disapproval, though Charlie wasn't sure whether it was disapproval of his artistic ambitions or his person. Charlie thought it was quite possible that he smelled bad. His *ad hoc* washing and laundry might have left him less than deodorized. But then he wondered if it was more than that. Could there be something in his odour that might give the whole game away? Was the lift attendant's nose so sensitive that it could tell him Charlie's whole history and current situation.

'I have a problem with art,' said the attendant. 'It's supposed to please the senses: the eyes, the ears, the touch. Not many major works of art address themselves to the nose, do they?'

Charlie hoped this was the explanation for the lift attendant's coolness, that Charlie reminded him of his partial exclusion from the world of art.

'Perhaps that's what I should do,' said Charlie facetiously. 'Create olfactory art.'

The attendant grunted. The prospect of Charlie's future artistic endeavours did not make him any happier. Then Charlie thought of something the old man might be able to help him with.

'The last time I was in your lift, I was with a young woman,' Charlie said. 'Do you remember?'

'I remember.'

'I was just wondering if she was still around, whether you'd . . . ' he hesitated as he tried to think of a more elegant term than 'smelt', ' . . . whether you'd encountered her recently.'

'I haven't encountered her, but she's still around. She's still working here. I can tell. Why do you ask?'

'No reason, just curiosity,' Charlie replied unconvincingly, and the lift attendant was unconvinced.

'Believe me, she's not your type,' the lift attendant said, more forthrightly than Charlie would have liked. 'Don't even think about it.'

'Think about what? I never thought she was my type. I mean . . . '

'There's something very strange about that young woman,' the old man said ominously.

'About her smell?' Charlie asked.

'The smell is just a window to the soul.'

'Window?'

'Yes, window,' the attendant snapped. 'A door, a channel, the steam rising from the cooking pot.'

'And you can tell she's strange, that she's not my type, simply by sniffing?'

'There's nothing simple about it.'

'But you can tell whether people are compatible just by their smell?'

'I can tell everything. I can tell their age, their race, their class, their sexual preferences, their politics, and what they had for breakfast.'

Charlie laughed.

'You had bagels,' the lift attendant added. 'Onion bagels with cream cheese, from the Mr Bagel Cafeteria on the sixth floor.'

'That's good,' Charlie admitted.

'It's more than a parlour trick.'

'I know that, really I do,' said Charlie, and the attendant loosened a little. 'But what was so strange about Vita Carlisle?'

'Was that her name? Yes, it sounds like the right sort of name. She smelt very clean, if anything too clean, as though she'd been scrubbing and scrubbing at herself for hour after hour, as though she was trying to hide something, or obliterate it. Basically I thought she was a wrong 'un.'

'You could be right for all I know,' said Charlie.

'I know I'm right.'

'That's fine,' said Charlie. 'I don't care. I'm not offended. I mean, I don't know the woman, I was just curious; it's not as though I wanted to marry her or anything. All I wanted was to return something of hers, something I picked up by mistake. I wondered if you knew which floor she worked on, in which department.'

Charlie was not sure why he was denying that he found Vita Carlisle attractive. What did it matter if the lift attendant thought they were incompatible. Why did he care what the old man thought?

'You could always ask Derek Snell,' said the lift attendant slyly. 'But I can understand why you don't. He smells like a wrong 'un too.'

It seemed to Charlie that just about everyone he'd ever met in Haden Brothers had been a wrong 'un in some way or other, and he wasn't sure that the blind lift attendant was excluded from that category.

'There's not much point putting on a false beard to deceive a blind man,' said the attendant.

'I can see that,' said Charlie.

'Good.'

The lift had now arrived at Charlie's floor, but the attendant didn't immediately open the lift doors. He inhaled deeply again. 'I know you're up to something,' he said. Charlie was about to deny it but the attendant went on, 'Whatever it is, I hope you get away with it. But I don't think you will.'

He let Charlie out, and further conversation seemed redundant. When Charlie got back to the stock room there were eighteen footstools in deep-buttoned Dralon waiting to be moved.

JACK YARDLEY, lift attendant: I should have retired from this job years ago. You know the strangest person I ever smelt? It was a long time ago. I was just seven years old but I'd already lost most of my sight. It was 1933, on the opening day of the new Haden Brothers. There was a sort of party going on all over the store, with brass bands and barrel organs and free samples and demonstrations of folk crafts. I was with my mother but somehow we got separated. I was brave in those days. I wandered all through the store on my own, and found myself way up at the top on some sort of balcony out in the fresh air. That was the balcony that came to be known as Suicide Ridge but the name hadn't been given to it then. I couldn't really see where I was or what I was doing, of course, but I was aware there was a man standing on the balcony next to me. He must have thought I was in danger of throwing myself over the edge because he put an arm round my shoulders and pulled me back.

Even to a child he smelt really, really strange. It was a blend of all sorts of things, so complex: soda bread and coal dust, Vaseline and conkers, manila envelopes and paraffin, sorrel and lino and ear wax and old coins. I've never forgotten it. He was odd but he was friendly. He asked me if I liked the store; he called it his store. I said I liked it a lot, though of course I couldn't see what it was like, and I said I'd an ambition to work in it one day. And then the man said that his name was Edward Zander and he was the architect who'd designed the building and he was glad that I liked it.

I'd never heard of Edward Zander and I'd no way of knowing whether it was really him or not. Of course, he disappeared as soon as the store was open and if it was him, then I'm probably one of the last people ever to have seen him alive, which is a terrible shame.

But the most curious thing about all this is that however much time goes by, however much the store is spring cleaned and refurbished and air-conditioned, however much they rejig and redecorate it, there are moments when I swear, when I absolutely swear, I can still smell Edward Zander in the store.

30 · SEPARATES

Charlie had heard plenty of tales and rumours about Arnold Haden from the other members of staff. One or two people actually claimed to have seen him, but their descriptions bore little relation to the reality that Charlie had now seen. Charlie felt privileged to know about the man's comings and goings, and he would have been happy enough to report that, far from being a weird old recluse or eccentric, he was in fact just a randy old devil. But, of course, there was nobody to whom he could have made such a report, not without telling all. He had been thrown into a peculiar sort of intimacy and secrecy with Arnold Haden and, despite the obvious differences in their ages, class, incomes, jobs and sex lives, he gradually came to accept that he and Arnold Haden were kindred souls of a sort.

It seemed to Charlie that Haden Brothers was big enough for the both of them. He learned to avoid the bed department since that was where Arnold Haden generally took his women. But he also liked to use the rug department, and occasionally the bridal department where he would dress the women up in pristine white lace and satin before feverishly stripping them naked again. Charlie could see no reason why their paths should ever cross. Rather than being an intruder, Arnold Haden became part of the landscape, a feature of the place as much as the ornamental staircases or the marble floors. Sometimes Charlie would spot Arnold Haden and his latest paramour standing naked and strangely innocent in the furniture department and he thought they looked like Adam and Eve. This made Haden Brothers into some sort of Garden of Eden and they were its prelapsarian couple. The only problem with this scenario was that it tended to cast Charlie as the snake and the Devil, and he was reluctant to accept that role.

Inevitably Charlie became blasé about sharing the store with Arnold Haden. Although he tried to be circumspect, although he tried to cover his tracks, he inevitably got careless. He liked to spend time in a department called Future Worlds, a place that sold gadgets and gizmos that were at once high-tech and inessential: a massage chair, computerized diaries the size of a credit card, a ghetto blaster in the shape of a fifties Cadillac dashboard. In a store that contained a lot of more or less useless objects, this department strived to sell goods that had achieved a new higher form of uselessness. Charlie wasn't sure this department was a good thing. It was for people who had more money than sense, but why be puritan about it? In his current circumstances he could revel in it without having to approve of it.

Future Worlds was on the second floor, and Charlie was aware that several storeys above his head Arnold Haden was cavorting with one of his girls. He had heard the lift descending and made a quick exit. Once the happy couple had finished, he knew they would return via the lift to the penthouse. Charlie felt he was safe enough, but he was wrong.

Arnold Haden had packed off the girl and had decided to take a stroll through his deserted store. He had draped a crisp, white bedsheet around himself to cover his nakedness. The effect was comic. He looked like an extra in a very amateur production of *Julius Caesar*, and he moved inexorably towards the Future Worlds department. It was not a department he felt any special affection for, but it was as good as any other in his present mood. Sex with the young woman had not been particularly enjoyable. He was restless and his mind wouldn't settle. He kept thinking about Vita Carlisle. He was in need of distraction. At the very least he wanted to tire himself out so he could get some sleep.

He walked quietly into the department, feeling casual, nonchalant, and found an equally casual, nonchalant Charlie Mayhew standing by a display cabinet, examining the workings of an air ionizer. Arnold Haden couldn't at first believe his eyes. He thought there was no way anyone could be in the store, so he wanted to believe that the figure he saw before him was nothing more than a mannikin, a showroom dummy, and that his eyes were deceiving him into thinking that it was moving. But that delusion could not be sustained for long, and as soon as he realized there really was a person in the department, all his worst fears came upon him. He screamed in absolute, blood-chilling terror. Charlie spun round and also screamed but far less dramatically.

Arnold Haden was much more frightened than Charlie, and Charlie thought that was inappropriate. He was the intruder, he was the one who had been caught out. He was the one who should be scared to death. However, he saw Arnold Haden backing away, pressing himself against a mirrored pillar, holding his hands up as though Charlie was threatening to shoot him.

'What do you want?' Arnold asked, his voice wavering.

Charlie was still too shocked to speak, still too surprised at finding that he had the upper hand.

'You've come to kill me haven't you?' Haden continued. 'I knew you would. I knew there'd be somebody like you.'

'I don't want to kill you,' said Charlie.

'Then what do you want? And who are you?'

'I'm nobody special,' said Charlie.

'I think you ought to know, I won't negotiate with terrorists.'

The words themselves were brave and defiant enough, but the delivery was unconvincing. Charlie could see that all might not be lost. He knew he was in a position of some power here, but he wasn't sure he could think quickly enough to keep the advantage. However scared Arnold Haden was, it surely wouldn't take him very long to spot that Charlie wasn't much of a terrorist.

'All right, I will negotiate,' Arnold Haden said, his resolve disappearing. 'What do you want?'

'I don't want much,' Charlie said.

'Just tell me what you want and I'll do my best to get it for you, really I will.'

Arnold Haden was shaking and his face was iced with sweat. The white sheet was slipping down over his belly and he didn't dare hold it in place for fear that might be a 'wrong move'. Charlie took a step towards him and he fell to his knees.

'I'm not a terrorist,' said Charlie.

'That's all right. I understand. You'd probably prefer to be known as a freedom fighter; that's fine by me.'

'No. I'm not a freedom fighter. Look; I'm not even a burglar. I'm more a sort of lodger.'

Arnold Haden wasn't listening. His mind was running along its own desperate, paranoid channels. Nothing Charlie said made any impression. Arnold Haden began to cry. It was soft, miserable and completely beyond his control.

'I know I've not been a good man,' he said. 'I can understand why you might want to revenge yourself on me.'

'We could make a deal,' said Charlie.

'Yes, yes we could. Name your price.'

Charlie tried to think of a price. While he did so, Arnold Haden's sheet slipped off completely and he knelt in front of Charlie, wretched and naked.

'You're embarrassing me,' said Charlie. 'Pull yourself together.'

Arnold Haden picked up the sheet and held it in front of him gratefully.

'Stand up,' said Charlie. 'I can't concentrate with you down there.'

Arnold Haden did as he was told.

Charlie said, 'All I really want is for you to forget that you ever saw me.'

'All right, I'll do that,' Arnold Haden agreed through his tears and snufflings. 'What else?'

Charlie said, 'Nothing else really. That's all I want.'

Arnold Haden's wet face showed that he neither understood nor believed what Charlie was saying. He did not know what was going on, and he still thought Charlie was dangerous and murderous. He thought he was going to die, that he had nothing to lose. And that was why a hysterical, reckless bravery came upon him. He took the sheet from round his waist and threw it in the air so that it landed over Charlie's head. Charlie was taken aback, he couldn't see and Arnold Haden slapped him hard and repeatedly round the head before running off in a panic.

The slaps didn't hurt particularly, but Charlie was surprised and disorientated for a moment. 'Please come back!' he shouted but Arnold Haden didn't stop until he'd got as far as a counter in the adjacent minor electrical department, where, with remarkable presence of mind, he made a dive for the fire alarm.

'Oh no,' Charlie said. 'Please don't do that.'

It was too late. A number of sirens, each with different, discordant notes, were striking up all over the shop floor. Emergency lights that pointed to fire exits flickered into life, and above Charlie's head a row of sluggish sprinklers dribbled water on to the electrical goods below. It was Charlie's turn to run, although his course was far less obvious than Arnold Haden's had been.

He darted away from the direction of the fire exits. A recorded message crackled through the speakers advising him to proceed swiftly but calmly. He did not obey the message. His progress was impeded as a number of metal fire doors rolled down between sections of the floor, to isolate and contain the non-existent fire.

Charlie dashed into the towel department, to the winter sports room, to the luggage boutique, his options closing down all the time.

Then he heard voices, real ones this time, not recorded messages, and the barking of furious guard dogs. The voices belonged to security guards. They sounded loud but distant, though scarcely less alarming for that. He had never imagined in any detail the exact means and occasion by which he would be found out and caught, but he had assumed it would be a low-key affair. He was prepared to go quietly. But in the event, given the sirens, the dogs, the approaching guards, the attack by Arnold Haden, he could not avoid panicking. The desire to escape was instinctive and unquenchable.

He wanted to get to the furniture department. It was his territory. He knew the lie of the land and he knew plenty of places to hide there. He reached a little-used set of side stairs and ran up the five flights till he reached the furniture floor, emerging in the modern repro section. He circumnavigated tables and chairs and banquettes and took refuge in a small stockroom where damaged furniture was kept prior to being returned to the supplier. It was airless and pitch black in there. He squatted, his heart beating painfully, fully aware of the terrible absurdity of his situation, and yet reluctant to surrender, to take the simple steps that would bring the absurdity to an end. These had been good weeks, living high on the hog, courtesy of Haden Brothers, and he wanted them to continue, but in the present circumstances he couldn't see how on earth he was going to achieve that. And the longer he sat there in the dark, scared and inactive, the less likely it seemed that this would be the way. Assuming the security guards were systematically searching the building, it was only a matter of time before they found him.

Yet it was quiet now. He could hear no sirens, no dogs, no men's voices. It scarcely seemed possible they had given up the chase, but at least they were not too hot on his trail. Charlie was contemplating a move to some other hiding place, feeling ready for another sortie, when the door to the stockroom was savagely ripped open and the space was lit by the blinding light of an immensely powerful torch beam. He couldn't see who was holding the torch but a voice said, 'Oh Charlie, you've been such a disappointing lad,' and he knew it was Ray Chalmers.

'OK,' said Charlie, squinting into the white light. 'You win. It's a fair cop.'

'Is it?' said Chalmers. 'Is it really? Give me fifty!'

'What?'

'On the floor. I want to see you give me fifty press-ups.'

'Don't be ridiculous,' said Charlie. 'I can't do fifty press-ups. Just call the police and get it over with.'

'The police?' said Chalmers. 'I'm not sure the police would know how to handle a lad like you. I think they might be a bit soft on you. I won't be soft on you, Charlie.'

He strode into the stockroom. Charlie retreated, knocking over a broken card table as he went. He withdrew into the tangle of chair legs and table tops as the torchlight swept around the space, throwing hard, angular shadows. Charlie was much quicker on his feet than Ray Chalmers, but that only gave him a slight advantage. Chalmers crashed into the furniture, kicking items out of his way, tossing them aside.

Then Charlie saw his chance. There was a free-standing mirror positioned a few feet away from him. It was one of those with a wooden base and side struts, that tilts and swivels about its long axis. By pulling the bottom of the glass towards him he could make the mirror spin on its pivot and bring it crashing down on Chalmers' head. Timing was all. Charlie waited till Chalmers was very close, in precisely the right spot, then tugged the mirror. He heard the sound of contact, a stunned yell from Chalmers as he dropped the torch, toppled over and Charlie scrambled past him and ran out of the stockroom.

Charlie didn't know what the hell to do now. This was all going badly wrong. Beating up the head of security was nobody's idea of coming quietly. He knew he was in bad trouble, even more when he heard footsteps and dogs coming up some nearby stairs. And then he saw what he had to do. It was suddenly very clear and very obvious. He had to find the lift that Anton had used to convey them down to the hidden sub-basement. If he could get down there he would be safe. He had only the vaguest idea where the lift was, but it still seemed like his best chance. He made a dash in what he remembered as the general direction, but it was going to take some finding.

He searched with increasing desperation, turning down blind alleys, getting lost, going round in circles, searching for the William Morris tapestry that concealed the door to the lift. The security patrol was getting closer. His lungs hurt and he wasn't sure he could run much further. Then suddenly he turned a corner, found himself in a short, familiar corridor and, miraculously, the William Morris tapestry was there. At least it looked like the tapestry. He ran eagerly towards it, grabbed a corner and pulled back the heavy material, but instead of the welcoming lift doors he found a solid, oak-panelled wall.

'Oh, what the hell,' he said to himself. He'd done enough running, and none of it had been very effective. He decided to give up. He'd take what was coming to him. He stood quietly in front of the panelling and waited for his fate to arrive. Soon, half a dozen uniformed bruisers and their hounds entered the corridor. They whooped like a football crowd when they saw him and their dogs became dangerously sportive. The noise alerted Ray Chalmers and it was not long before he came lumbering after them. He had an open cut on his forehead and he badly wanted to hurt somebody.

Charlie stayed where he was, the panelled wall behind him, the row of security men keeping him at bay. He smiled wearily at Chalmers and gave a facile shrug, which only further incensed Chalmers. He pushed past the security men and said to Charlie, 'I think you're ready for some fist.'

He squared up, wound back his arm and delivered a big round-house blow to Charlie's chin. The force was immense and it threw Charlie off his feet so that he lost his balance and staggered back against the wall. However, the wall refused to support him. As he made contact with the wood, it immediately gave way and he felt himself falling through it. The security men were impressed that their boss still had enough fire in him to be able to knock people through walls. But they then saw that the wall had not been damaged, rather that a couple of the panels had simply flipped aside, that they were a sort of trap door that had opened up, and Charlie had fallen into a cavity beyond it. And as they watched, the trap door snapped shut, leaving Charlie safely on the other side, as though the wall had swallowed him alive. Ray Chalmers' disbelief was scarcely less than his men's. He started to beat and kick the wall, and he screamed, 'Someone's going to lose their bollocks for this!'

He looked about him for something with which to smash down the wall, and had just selected a cast iron fire extinguisher when Derek Snell arrived.

'What in God's name are you doing, Mr Chalmers?' he asked urgently.

'I'm going in!' Chalmers said. 'I'm going to flush out Charlie once and for all. Give me the tools and I'll finish the job.'

'That panel you're about to destroy,' Snell said softly but authoritatively, 'was salvaged from a fifteenth-century Bavarian monastery. It was chosen and fitted personally by Edward Zander, the architect of Haden Brothers. It is probably the single most valuable architectural feature in the entire building. While one would hesitate to put a price on it, I think it would be fair to say it's rather more than your job's worth.'

Chalmers looked as though he was being tortured by a coach party of devils.

'Besides,' Derek Snell continued, 'why in God's name would you want to smash it down?'

'Because he's in there. On the other side.'

Derek Snell tapped the panelling lightly with the knuckles of two fingers. 'It's a solid wall, Mr Chalmers.'

'No,' Chalmers insisted. 'It's a secret doorway. Ask them. Ask anyone.'

He turned to his security men who were desperately trying to avoid eye contact. They were not entirely sure what they had seen, and the more demented Chalmers became, the less sure they became. They did not want to appear as mad as him so they remained speechless.

'Why don't you go and have a lie down, Mr Chalmers?' said Derek Snell.

The search continued all night. More security men arrived, more dogs, a few not very interested police. Ray Chalmers knew it was pointless. They were not going to find Charlie Mayhew by searching the store since he had disappeared into the fabric of the building itself.

Meanwhile Derek Snell had talked to Arnold Haden, and Haden had given some limited support to Chalmers' assertions. Snell made it clear that he thought Chalmers and Arnold Haden were suffering from some shared hallucination. He was not convinced either of them had seen anyone at all. Snell thought that an empty, darkened department store was an eerie place at the best of times. If Arnold Haden chose to wander round it at night, semi-naked, in a post-coital daze, then he might well convince himself that he was seeing strange shapes, intruders, even ghosts. And as for Chalmers, well, in Derek Snell's opinion, the man was a deranged fantasist. He got a half-baked idea in his head and he was stuck with it until some even more crazy idea came along. For reasons of his own, he was choosing to believe that Charlie Mayhew was some sort of subversive, so of course he wanted to share in Arnold Haden's delusion that there was someone in the store. It fitted nicely with his conspiracy theories. Snell could not seriously believe that someone was in the store, even less that that someone could be the ineffectual, harmless Charlie Mayhew, a man he had hardly seen since the day of his first interview. The part about that someone then disappearing into walls, was absurd even by Chalmers' own high standards of craziness. Derek Snell would be glad when the whole nonsense was over and they could all go home to bed. He felt sure that Mayhew would turn up for work tomorrow in the usual way.

Charlie spent the night in a small dark chamber on the other side of the panelled wall. It was surprisingly comfortable. It was wood-lined, dark and dusty, but there was air circulating, a straw mattress, and he found candles and a box of matches. The chamber was hexagonal in shape and there appeared to be no way in or out except via the wall through which he'd entered. He could not see how the trap door was operated. There was no handle, no catch, no hinges. At the moment however, he was happy for it to remain shut. He had no wish to open it up and be confronted once more with a shopful of security men and dogs who were searching for him. He felt safer here than he had for some time, and he even managed to sleep a little.

For Arnold Haden the night had been something of a revelation. He wasn't sure who or what he had encountered. Charlie, despite his denials, could well have been a terrorist or a burglar or even an assassin. Arnold Haden was ashamed of the way he'd initially behaved, the way he'd begged and snivelled and caved in. But ultimately he'd had the strength to be able to handle the situation, and that pleased him a lot. He'd found inner resources, some bravery and guts that he'd never known he possessed. Yes, the world was frightening and dangerous, but perhaps there were strategies for dealing with it. He had been weighed, and he had not been found entirely wanting. He resolved that if a similar situation presented itself again, if he ever found himself confronted by an intruder, by some dangerous terrorist or would-be murderer, he would display that bravery and strength and guts from the very beginning. Moreover, he thought he understood the source of his newfound strength. It came from Vita. That's the way it was with love. It transformed you, it made you whole and strong. It made anything possible.

DEREK SNELL: A building can get sick just like a body can get sick. I used to tell Arnold Haden that the whole time, but he never listened. There had always been plenty of people who thought the entire Haden Brothers building was an abomination, an architectural monstrosity and the product of a sick mind, but over the years I came to see it was much more than that.

We always sought to make Haden Brothers a closed system. That way we could regulate it. If you have windows that let in fresh air and sunshine, you soon get into all sorts of trouble. By sealing up the building as much as possible, we sought to control temperature, humidity, light levels, traffic noise, and above all ambience. But unfortunately there's a down side to that.

You get a build up of stale air, of negative ions, solvent vapours, bacteria, radon, carbon monoxide. Before too long you get a sick building, and that can result in sick people. Staff get headaches, colds, allergies. They take days off sick. They get depressed. They take days off even when they're not sick. They get irritable and bad tempered. Morale drops. *Esprit de corps* sinks like a stone. There's a growing pool of human misery, and that results in a drop in sales.

I always said to Arnold that the future was in the suburbs, out of town, out by the ring road. In extreme moments I even suggested we should sell the Haden Brothers building to some smart developer who would turn it into trendy, overpriced designer apartments, and we should open a new Haden Brothers as the centrepiece of a mall on a spanking new retail park. But I knew it would never happen. I knew that Arnold would never give up the old building.

I'd heard the stories about Edward Zander supposedly having built a network of secret passageways through the store, but frankly I didn't believe them. And even if I *had* believed them, what difference would it have made? How could we have located those passageways without ripping open the building? And if we *had* located them, what would we have done with them? Turned them into a Christmas grotto?

When Arnold Haden claimed to have seen some intruder in the store in the middle of the night, and when Ray Chalmers said he saw the same person disappear into a solid wall, well, as far as I was concerned, that only confirmed that they were experiencing the effects of sick-building syndrome.

31 · BUREAU DE CHANGE

Time had been passing for Vita Carlisle. Her life had become a patchwork as she moved from one department to another, snatching a brief look at how things were in floristry or key cutting or the travel agency. There was a time when she would have told herself this was all 'good experience', that she was seeing tiny but profound glimpses of fascinating and diverse worlds. However, she became less and less convinced that this was so. A day or two in the glove department provided her with very much the same kind of superficial data as a day or two in the bakery, or anywhere else. There was never enough time and she never became part of the culture. Systems differed slightly from one department to the next, the stock was different, of course, and yet these differences were neither significant nor interesting.

Customers too were disappointingly similar. Vita felt they should have been colourful and fascinating and varied, but it seemed to her they displayed much the same traits and urges whatever they were buying. A man with a desire to buy a raincoat was not fundamentally so very different from a man with a desire to buy a pop-up toaster. The nature of his desires and the way he attempted to satisfy them were essentially the same.

And the other staff didn't help either. Some were pleasant and some not, but in each department they were pleasant or unpleasant in much the same ways. Vita tried to fit in, but she never felt at home, and how could she when she always knew she'd be moving on soon? The only person she'd met who seemed at all interesting or full of life was Anton Heath and she still didn't entirely approve of him.

The story of what had happened in the toy department preceded her wherever she went. How could it not? When a whole department gets fired, the rest of the workforce is inevitably going to take a deep and rather personal interest. It could happen to them too. And Vita, as the only survivor, was inevitably cast as the villainess. Bitchy and insinuating conversations would be conducted not quite out of her earshot. For a long time she tolerated it, but when she heard someone say, 'It wouldn't have happened if we had unions in this place,' she felt she'd had enough. Calmly and crisply she said, 'It has nothing to do with unionization. And it wasn't me who sacked them, it was Derek Snell. And it's good that it happened. If a whole department stands around laughing while a customer lies dying on the floor, then what are you supposed to do, give them a promotion?' The fact that this sounded like common sense did nothing to make Vita more popular.

It would have been easy enough for her to quit the job, to simply walk away from Haden Brothers and start again somewhere else. Other jobs weren't impossible to find. In fact, it would have been too easy. She wasn't a quitter, and besides, she felt a strange umbilical attachment to Haden Brothers, one that she wished she understood better.

Then came the moment when she phoned her mother who told her the terrible story about being picked up for shoplifting. They both wept down the phone, and then her mother told her much else besides; the family secret.

Something snapped inside Vita. She had truly had enough then. She could no longer tolerate the intolerable, and she knew she had to do something. And that was when Vita Carlisle had a brief, intense, life-changing conversation with Anton Heath, and then, at last, she rang Arnold Haden's secretary and said she wanted to see him at seven o'clock that evening, alone in his penthouse on the ninth floor of Haden Brothers.

32 · CO-ORDINATES

When Charlie Mayhew woke next morning, he hoped it might all have been a bad dream, but then it came back to him, nightmarish certainly, but he knew it had not been simply the work of his overactive subconscious. The hunters were really after him and he really was holed up in some secret chamber in the furniture department of Haden Brothers. The nightmare was going to begin all over again.

The candle had burned right down while he slept, consumed itself, and since there was no external wall or window nearby, it should have been pitch black in the chamber, but it was not. Soft bands of milky light were coming from somewhere above his head and he looked up to see three ventilation tubes in the ceiling. They were no wider than a man's hand but they went way up through the core of the building to the air and sky outside. He could see a patch of moving cloud. And at his feet there were three other holes, or rather continuations of the tubes above his head, taking air down to the floors below. He looked down the tubes but could see nothing.

In a way, the existence of this secret place in Haden Brothers did not surprise him so very much. The internal structure of the building was constantly being changed. False walls and partitions were put up every day. Screens and panels were frequently erected to hide inconvenient or ugly corners. The store was like a stage set; brightly painted scenery hiding a mess of botched wiring and ramshackle joinery. That these backdrops should create dead areas and hiding places was only to be expected, though there was nothing botched or ramshackle about the panelling of the room he was in at the moment. The presence of the bed and the candles was strange, but at a pinch this could be explained as evidence of bunking off by some earlier work-shy porter. He knew it was not a wholly adequate explanation, but in these unfamiliar circumstances he wanted to stick with the ordinary and the mundane.

Each wood-panelled wall of his hiding-place looked exactly like every other, and he did not know which of them was the one he'd come in through. And as he tapped them, judiciously and delicately, they all sounded equally solid. He could still see no joints, no edges. He concluded that judiciousness and delicacy might not be the best way to proceed. A full-blooded upper cut had knocked him in here and he suspected that something equally full-blooded might be needed to get him out. He decided to launch himself at the walls, at each of them in turn until one of them gave way just as it had last night, and then he could get back to the real world.

He looked at his watch. The shop was now open. He did not for a moment think that Ray Chalmers would have completely abandoned the search for him, but he surely couldn't still be conducting the full hue and cry complete with dogs. The powers that be wouldn't want the customers to see that. Furthermore, the many doors to Haden Brothers would now be open. That, along with a few customers to hide amongst, seemed to offer him his best chance of escape. There would be something very final about this departure. Once he left the world of Haden Brothers, he would never be able to come back. He would never dare show his face again. He would have to leave the area, maybe even the country. This filled him with a gigantic sadness, but what were the alternatives? He couldn't spend the rest of his life trapped in this chamber. And yet it appeared he might have to.

He took as long a run up as the room allowed, then flung himself at the first of the six walls. He bounced off it and it didn't budge. He tried the second, and again there was nothing, no movement, no give. In no time at all he had attacked all six walls and none had responded even slightly to his charge. There was not much air in the room. He felt dirty, weary, spent, and also pretty stupid. Throwing himself at walls didn't seem a very sensible activity. His shoulder hurt. He leaned into one of the corners of the room to take a breather, and the panels behind him collapsed like a house of cards.

He fell backwards again, further this time, into deep space and darkness. The panels that had moved were not the ones that led back into the store. It was as though he had been poured into the neck of a metal funnel that was narrowing all the time. He was falling, sliding down on his back, head first, into the gubbins and hidden workings of the store. Even as he slid, he had time to think that he must have fallen into a ventilation shaft or air duct, something commonplace and ordinary, and yet the inside of the shaft was anything but commonplace. The metal sides had been painted with huge poppies and marigolds. The flowers were wild and sketchy but they had obviously been painted by a skilled hand. They were all rich colours, bright reds and riotous yellows, but who on earth would ever have bothered to decorate the inside of a ventilation shaft?

Charlie's fall was swift but short and it ended in a tangle of dust and soft textures as he landed on a pile of old cushions, pillows and bolsters at the end of the chute. They smelled ancient and fusty. They were marked with what looked like human stains but they came from a long time ago. He was now in another enclosed chamber, somewhat larger than the first, but this one had brick walls and there was a small hatchway in one corner. The brickwork was shaggy with cobwebs and thick dirt.

This place was not pitch black either. A pattern of diamond-slashed light fanned across it at floor level, coming out of a narrow metal grille, a couple of feet long, a few inches high. Charlie kicked some pillows out of the way and flattened himself on the ground to look through the grille. He saw grey carpet, some full-length curtains, shopping bags and handbags, mirrors, women's feet, some bare, some stockinged; and there were lots of clothes festooned about the place. He realized he was seeing into the communal changing room in the Ms Haden Boutique. It was a rare and privileged viewpoint. He could see women putting on clothes and taking them off. Some had bare breasts. The scene was like something from an adolescent fantasy, and Charlie's adolescence was not so far behind him as to prevent him enjoying the sight.

If he had shouted, the women would certainly have heard his voice, though they might not have known where it was coming from; they would hardly be expecting a strange man to be hiding behind a tiny grille down by the skirting board. He was tempted to call to them, to ask them for help, but what could they have done for him? Even if they hadn't simply panicked and called security, which would have done him no good at all, there was no access between the changing room and Charlie's dust-filled chamber. Short of demolishing the wall, how could they possibly help him and get him out? He watched the women for a little longer, then prised himself away to investigate the hatch in the corner of his chamber.

It looked like the opening of a dumb waiter, with sliding doors that created a man-sized opening. They were shut now but Charlie prised them open and peered into the cavity revealed. It was not a dumb waiter. There was no shelf, no rope, no pulley, just a narrow, empty, vertical shaft that disappeared into darkness both up and down. It wasn't inviting, but apart from the metal chute that had delivered him there, it was the only way out of this room. He could see there were foot holes carved in the wall of the shaft and although they looked easy enough to negotiate, Charlie didn't know whether to climb upwards or downwards.

He decided to descend. He wasn't wholly sure why, but somewhere in his mind he still had the idea of finding the sub-basement that Anton had shown him. He remembered it as a safe place, a partly known quantity. There was food and drink in the sub-basement and there was a lift that could return him to the shop floor.

After a while the shaft was so dark that he couldn't even see where the foot holes were. He had to reach down with his feet and tap around until he found them. The blackness swallowed him up. He was disorientated. He began by counting the number of steps he descended, but he soon lost track. He knew he would have to descend seven or eight whole storeys of the building if he was to arrive at the sub-basement, but he had gone down nothing like that number when he ran out of foot holes and he touched down on a stone floor. He had come to the bottom of the shaft and he was aware of space around him, of cold, moving air. He had a sense of tunnels and corridors receding into the darkness, though he could see little of them.

He could, however, hear something, the sound of muffled speech. Two people were talking, two men, not so very far away. The owners of these voices did not promise to be allies, but he was drawn to them, nevertheless. He paddled out into the shapeless darkness, his hands touched a solid brick surface and he found himself in a low tunnel that was leading him towards the voices. They were getting louder. He still couldn't hear whole words but he could detect the tones of voice, one angry and frustrated, the other remorseful and pleading. And then he recognized one of them. The angry voice belonged to Ray Chalmers. Fortunately, it still sounded too distant to be threatening.

Then Charlie saw a point of light up ahead, a neat circular hole in the darkness at eye level, like a spy hole, which is what it was, a hole in the brickwork through to the other side of the wall, through into Haden Brothers. He couldn't resist peering through it. He was looking into a room he'd never seen before, not part of the shop floor but not an office either. It looked like a cross between a gymnasium and a display of Greek art. The walls of the room were painted Prussian blue and there was ornate coving and a dado rail. There were the shiny, complex mechanisms of fitness equipment, but they were interspersed with pieces of Greek statuary; male athletes cast in white plaster, naked and posed in the act of throwing a discus or javelin. One or two statues were missing arms or legs, but the torsos were impeccably muscled. In the midst of these structures Ray Chalmers was berating a young member of his uniformed staff. Charlie could not know what had been said but the young man looked mortified.

Then Ray Chalmers bawled, 'I want that blind bugger in here and I want him now.'

'Yes, sir,' the young man said. 'He's waiting outside. I'll send him in.'

The man he wanted entered the room. He walked slowly and carefully, but nobody guided him. It was Jack Yardley, the blind lift attendant.

'I need some specialist help,' Ray Chalmers said.

'Yes, sir?' asked the lift attendant.

'You see, I'm looking for a lad who apparently doesn't exist. A lad who can disappear through walls. A lad who nobody, except me, claims ever to have seen. Not even Arnold Haden is prepared to say he saw him now. He thinks he might have been mistaken. But I know he's here.'

'I see,' said the lift attendant.

'I understand you've got a good nose on you,' said Ray Chalmers. 'I hear that you can sniff out a traitor at two hundred paces.'

'That's a bit of an exaggeration, sir.'

'His name's Charlie Mayhew. Do you remember him? Do you remember how he smelt?'

'I think so. He seemed like a good lad, I thought he'd go far.'

'You know how it is with lads. Sometimes they go *too* far.'

'That's a shame. What's he done wrong exactly?'

'Never you mind, Jack. Suffice it to say the current situation is that he's hiding somewhere in this great store of ours and I don't know where. The tracker dogs have been useless, my security men have been worse, and now Derek Snell won't even let me carry on with the search. He says I'm wasting resources. That's typical. It's Vietnam all over again. So this has to be an undercover job, just you and me, Jack. You're my best hope, arguably my only hope. Are you up to the job?'

'I expect so, yes,' said the lift attendant. 'But what will you do when you find him?'

Ray Chalmers thought for a moment.

'I'll have his testicles for nipple rings,' he said. 'Not that I wear nipple rings, of course.'

'Of course,' said the lift attendant.

He took a deep, deep breath in through his nose, as though sucking in all the air in the room, and he walked across the space, avoiding the statues and the fitness equipment by some sixth sense until he stood by the wall where the spy hole was. Charlie, on the other side, could not look away.

'What is it?' asked Ray Chalmers. 'Have you spotted something?'

The lift attendant inhaled again then shook his head.

'No, sir, I must have been mistaken. It must have been your aftershave.'

Charlie knew the lift attendant's nose was too good, too sensitive not to have detected him, and he saw that at last he had found one friend in the whole of Haden Brothers. The lift attendant's sightless eyes continued to point in the direction of the spy hole. Charlie could have sworn the man winked at him, but then he turned back to Ray Chalmers who escorted him out of the room and off on a wild-goose chase round the store trying to sniff out Charlie Mayhew.

Charlie pressed on into the innards of Haden Brothers. Escape was still his ultimate aim. But equally he was involved in an act of exploration. There was something strangely wonderful and appealing about being in this dark, secret world, and after a while he found it wasn't so dark after all. Light filtered in through skylights, through more metal grilles, through other spy holes.

He was enmeshed in a system of tunnels and shafts, of spiral staircases, of rope and metal ladders, of sudden drops and tight spaces and low ceilings. It was maze-like and it was a sort of prison but it was also appealing. It bore the welcoming signs of a wild imagination at play, and every so often there were flourishes of highly accomplished art and craft. Long stretches of tunnel would be lined in William de Morgan tiles, elaborate Purbeck marble columns were used to support the flimsiest looking arches, staircases were decorated with gold and black mosaics. There were murals, some as crude as cave paintings, others detailed and obsessive, showing scenes of angels, mythological beasts and Hollywood stars of the 1920s.

This inner, nether world was an enclosed and illogical system. As far as Charlie could see, it had no function, no reason for existing, and yet it did not seem incoherent, certainly not meaningless. What's more, it regularly permitted glimpses into the real world of Haden Brothers. Charlie could look through grilles and holes and cracks and see the life that still went on in the store. He could see into stockrooms and offices and the photocopying department, into the press office, the baby changing room. He could look into the kitchens of the Rainforest Brasserie and see a drippy-nosed chef making Waldorf salads. He saw two of the invoice clerks having a quick wet snog among the ledgers. He peered into a corner of the kitchen co-ordinates department and saw an extremely respectable-looking middle-aged man loading his bag with matching aprons, oven gloves and tea cosies.

Once again Charlie could see but not be seen. He could observe but not interact. He was offered a series of places from which to watch and learn, to overhear conversations and revelations. And he wondered if this was the whole purpose of this alternate world, if it was perhaps a means by which staff and customers could be spied upon by the management of Haden Brothers. But if so, it must have fallen into disuse many, many years ago. He felt he was the first person to have passed this way in a very long time. And yet there was something that connected with the present.

He spent a long time in these dark, hidden places. Most of the day had gone and he had come no nearer to escaping. He was safe after a fashion, but it was not the sort of safety he wanted. He had moved rapidly through these tunnels and corridors, yet he had made no progress. He had not been aimless, yet he had drifted and meandered. There were too many dead ends, too many passages that led him round in circles, that promised much but delivered nothing, and none had even hinted at leading him to the sub-basement.

Haden Brothers would be closing soon and darkness would overtake it again. Lights were being switched off all over the store. He had found some more candles and matches in one of the stairwells, so he would be able to continue his wanderings all night if he chose. He lit a candle to be on the safe side. He was hungry and thirsty. His legs and feet hurt. The sheer frustration of his captivity was making him angry and blurred, but something still pushed him onwards.

He came to an intersection of stairs and tunnels. There were lead pipes and bundles of electrical cable, and set in the wall was a metal grille, perhaps nine inches square. Cool white light glowed on the other side of the grille and when Charlie looked through he saw that this light was emanating from the chill cabinets in the food department. The sight drove him half crazy. A whole department of luxury foods was waiting there for him: smoked venison and chilled gazpacho, Camemberts and lychees. Not that he demanded anything so exotic at the moment. He would have eaten almost anything. And not that it made any difference. It was all denied to him. He could see the food lined up on shelves and counters and in fridges. He could smell it. Without too much imaginative effort he could even taste it. But a solid brick wall meant he couldn't actually take it and eat it.

Then he saw there was a marble counter not very far away from where the grille came through the wall. There was a small pyramid of pies on the counter, game pies with a lattice work crust on top. He'd seen them before on his wanderings through the store. He'd eaten them and he knew they were good. They ought to have been put away and refrigerated for the night, but he was grateful for this bit of sloppiness. He thought that if he could dislodge the grille he'd be able to put his arm through the hole and he just might, just possibly might, be able to take one of the pies.

He reached up and took a grip on one of the lead water pipes above his head so that he could swing on it and bring his feet up to kick at the grille. It needed half a dozen attempts to knock it from its fastenings, but he succeeded. He stuck his arm through the hole, stretched and stretched, jammed his shoulder to the wall, extended his fingers, trying desperately to gain every millimetre and reach the pies. He was panting with effort and frustration, and when he pressed himself hard against the opening he could no longer see where his fingers were heading, but he knew he must be getting close. His fingertips were brushing the glossy pie crust, just a fraction more and he was sure he would do it.

At which point something hot and fleshy and unseen locked on to his wrist. He yelled out for the shock and horror of it. It felt as though he had been grabbed by something monstrous, and it took a while to realize he had been seized by nothing worse than another person's hand. That knowledge didn't reassure him. The hand was strong and very large and it wouldn't let go, wouldn't let him pull his own hand back.

A voice said, 'Got you, you smeg sucker!' and Charlie knew it was Ray Chalmers who'd got hold of him. He must have been making one last patrol of the store and seen Charlie's hand emerge from the wall. Charlie couldn't believe his bad luck.

Chalmers' grip was fierce and desperate but perhaps Charlie's desperation was greater. A bizarre bout of arm wrestling commenced. With enormous effort Charlie slowly began to reclaim his arm, pulling it back to his side of the wall. But Chalmers was still not letting go and the struggle continued until Charlie had managed to pull Chalmers' own hand back through the hole in the wall. Charlie knew what he had to do. With his free hand he reached down and picked up the lighted candle he was using to find his way. He brought it up and positioned the flame so that it was burning the back of Chalmers' clenched fingers. The skin began to blacken, to char, to smoulder, but Chalmers still wasn't about to release Charlie's hand.

'Let go of me, you idiot!' Charlie yelled, but the hand stayed tight.

The area of burned skin spread. Charlie could feel the heat of the flame through the gaps between Chalmers' fingers. Charlie's stomach was turning at the very idea. He couldn't look. Chalmers began to cry out in pain like a tortured cat, but it was a long time before he finally let go of Charlie.

When he did, they both fell backwards into their separate domains. 'I'm sorry,' Charlie shouted. 'I'm really sorry.' But he didn't wait to hear Chalmers' reply. He ran back into the complex heart of the store and Chalmers fell in a heap on the cold tiled floor of the food department. After a while, he dragged himself up and looked through the black hole where the grille had been. He could see nothing. For a moment he wanted to get a pickaxe, a sledge-hammer, a bulldozer, to smash down the wall and find Charlie Mayhew. If Haden Brothers got torn apart in the process that was a small price to pay. But at the same time he saw that it was no good, that nobody would believe what had happened. They wouldn't let him tear down the wall. Nobody would believe how he'd come to burn his hand. They'd probably say it was self-inflicted – just another good sign of madness. Derek Snell would be worst of all. He'd pretend to be understanding. He'd tell him to take more rest. Ray Chalmers began to weep helplessly.

RAY CHALMERS: And when the hand came through the wall, and after I'd grabbed it and got my fingers turned to charred hamburger, and when I looked through the hole where the grille had been into that blackness, then I knew it really *was* Vietnam. It was like the tunnels of Cu Chi and I knew all about that.

The Vietcong lived for years inside those tunnels. They had caches of weapons and explosives and food. There were munitions workshops, kitchens, field hospitals. Babies were born down there, men died there, they even had concerts and poetry readings.

More to the point, they had the whole network booby-trapped; trip wires that set off hand grenades, pits full of sharpened stakes for you to fall into, metal spikes that could snap out and pierce you at crotch level. It was the ideal place from which they could launch surprise attacks, and there wasn't a damn thing the US military could do against them.

And suddenly I knew that's what was going on in Haden Brothers, and it scared the life out of me. Charlie was in control. This was his domain, and frankly I was prepared to let him keep it. I wasn't going in there after him and I wasn't sending in any of my boys either. I'm no hero, no tunnel rat. If the might of the United States armed forces couldn't flush out Charlie from his tunnels in Vietnam, what chance did I have in Haden Brothers?

I put the grille back on the wall. I went to the first-aid room and bandaged my hand. If anybody had asked me, I'd have said I burned it putting out a fire in a waste paper bin. But nobody did ask. And again, if anyone had asked, I would now have told them that I could have been mistaken about ever having seen anyone in the store. I decided I wanted a quiet life. I made a tactical withdrawal. It's a good soldier who knows the right time to pull out.

But I said to myself, wait until this store really needs some security. Then let them see how they can manage without Ray Chalmers. I didn't have long to wait at all. The next thing I new, Vita Carlisle had taken Arnold Haden hostage. He can sort that one out himself, I thought.

33 · SEASONAL GIFTS

Charlie had not eaten for the best part of twenty-four hours. He was desperate to get out of the maze he found himself in, but he was even more desperate to end his hunger and thirst. The game pies were off the menu but he knew there was a sub-basement full of food and drink. Why was it so hard to find? He'd done his best to journey downwards but he didn't feel he'd even got close. In his mind's eye he could see all those tins of cling peaches and corned beef, fruit cocktail and red salmon, and it was driving him insane. How would he get to them? What was the secret? What was the trick?

Then he dropped his candle. The flame went out and he heard it hit the floor and start to roll. He scrabbled around in the dust and darkness and failed to locate it, but he did find a groove in the floor. He followed this with his fingers to discover it was continuous, the edge of something hexagonal; a trap door, a sort of manhole cover with a couple of finger holes in the centre, like in a bowling ball, and he inserted his fingers and was able to lift it up.

He peered down into the hole that had opened up and he could just make out another chute, smooth and metallic, twisting downwards like an enclosed helter skelter. It wasn't exactly welcoming. If anything it was sinister and threatening, but he was reckless and desperate enough to see something promising in this. At least it was heading in the direction he wanted to go, and he felt he had nothing much to lose.

He lowered his feet into the hole, sat on the edge of the opening, then launched himself and began another blind descent. The cold metal of the chute guided and supported him. He felt himself accelerating downwards, spun into helical motion, as though he was being passed rapidly down a dark curled intestine.

He was buffeted by the sides of the chute, made giddy by the swift but erratic progress. He spread his arms and legs in an attempt to slow himself down, but the surface was too smooth. His head was thrown backwards and he cracked his skull against the metal. The slide seemed endless but in a way that reassured him. The longer it was, the more likely it seemed that it might take him to the sub-basement. If only it would take him a little more slowly.

Suddenly the chute ended. Charlie had expected either to be launched into space or to make a crash landing, but, in the event, his descent came to a slow, gentle halt and he found himself deposited softly inside a metal sphere, about six feet in diameter. Suddenly it all clicked. He knew exactly where he was. He'd made it to the sub-basement and by some curious method he'd ended up actually inside the painted metal globe suspended from the ceiling; the one he'd seen with Anton.

From the inside he could see that the globe was made out of riveted segments. His weight was already putting a visible strain on the joints, and as he kicked deliberately at the weak points, the globe cracked open like an egg and he dropped out, through into the vestibule below, into a curiously familiar place. There it was, much as he remembered it, the sub-basement with its vaulted ceiling and its miniature railway, its water supply and shelves, and most important of all, its boxes of food and drink.

When he'd been here before with Anton, it had seemed scary and forbidding. Now it was like an Aladdin's cave. He dashed towards the shelves and pulled down a few cardboard boxes. They hit the ground and split open. Tins of food spilled out and rolled across the floor like tiny escaping animals and he swooped on a tin of prawns in vegetable oil. There was a tin opener hanging on a string by the shelves. It was the old-fashioned sort with one sharp, dangerous tooth that left the open tin with a ragged edge. He sawed away at the lid, pulled it back and scooped the prawns into his mouth with his dirty fingers.

He was ready to experience bliss. He didn't care too much about the taste, he just wanted to shove the food down to get it inside him. But the moment the prawns hit his tongue, he knew there was something very wrong. The prawns tasted foul; of all things dead and decaying, of rusted metal and industrial waste and other people's stale sweat. He spat the prawns out a moment before his throat gagged to prevent him swallowing. He now noticed a putrid smell coming from the tin.

He looked at it. The label had a design that he didn't recognize. From the lettering he knew it was old, very old, maybe even from the 1930s. If the tins were really that old then no wonder the contents had gone bad. He looked at the rest of them and they were all from the same era.

He opened a couple more and found they contained equally putrid food. Their sell-by date was ancient history. They came from a time before sell-by dates.

At least he knew there was some drinkable wine down here. Anton had proved that to him. He went to the shelves, opened a bottle and swigged it. It had flavour and body. It drove the bad taste from his mouth. It wasn't food exactly and since his stomach was empty it went straight to his head, but the act of consumption, of putting something in his belly felt blissfully good.

As he was savouring the wine, he looked down and saw another pile of tins, heaped up not far from where he was standing. They were empty. They had been opened and their contents had been eaten. He wondered how recently. And then he saw that they were resting at the foot of a door, as though someone on the other side had thrown them out. The door was a plain, wooden thing, solid, panelled and with an inviting brass handle. Charlie knew he had to look at what lay beyond the door.

34 · DESIGNER ROOMS

The year is 1933 and the room is still. For Edward Zander the great project is completed. The edifice and artifice of Haden Brothers is finished and Edward Zander, its architect and genius, is at peace. He is enjoying the satisfactions of a job well done, of clients satisfied, of a public eager to see and experience his masterpiece. He also knows that he will never work again, for within the outward, manifest construction of Haden Brothers he has built himself a home, a hidden resting place, a secret warren and world. Off the shop floor, away from the customers and the assistants, amid the internal workings of the brickwork and steel frame, amid the interstices and lacunae, at the heart of the ducting and services and supporting structures, he has made a structure of his own. He has built a world within a world, a maze within a maze, a more secret heart.

He knows he was fortunate to be given the commission for the store – he was not the first choice – and he knows he will never build anything better or greater. If history remembers him at all he thinks it will remember him for the excesses and contradictions of Haden Brothers, not for his earlier work of a few mannered private houses and the handful of stone follies he has built in Derbyshire and Dorset.

As he created the Haden Brothers building he also created a place for himself, a warren of hidden tunnels and staircases that meandered through the guts of the building, eventually trickling down to a deep sub-basement stocked with enough products to last him a lifetime. And adjacent to this vast storehouse he has constructed a small suite of rooms in which he intends to sit out his remaining years. He has seen the future and it looks cluttered and terrifying. It is a future of motorcars and aeroplanes, of movies and some newfangled thing called television. It is a world of bakelite and tubular steel, of synthetics and chemicals. It is a world for the masses: mass media, mass production, mass impulses.

He knows that something is over for him. He feels the wind of something as cold as history. He is a man out of place, a visionary, a dilettante, and there is no longer a market for people like him. He met Welles Coates at an over-populated cocktail party in Bayswater and he thought the man was mad. He spoke of moral and social principles, of synthesizing human needs. He quoted a Chinese poet. Zander is sufficiently self-aware to know he cannot cope with a Modernism that concerns itself with the planning and design of whole societies, that regards style as superficiality. And yet he knows that this too is the future.

These new philosophies and technologies perhaps ought to be a source of inspiration to a man like Zander, and yet it all makes him feel alien and out of place. This new world he has made for himself in Haden Brothers has been designed to his own necessary specifications, stocked with his own limited choice of goods, a telling selection, a brief sketch of the man and the times. He likes it here, away from people and spurious ideas of progress, away from fashion and novelty and daylight.

The suite of rooms is eccentric like its creator, but it is of its time. In the hexagonally shaped living room there is much that is mundane and ordinary; a polished oak dinner wagon, distempered walls, a herring-bone parquet floor, an overstuffed armchair. But elsewhere there is a lavishly ornate fireplace with panels decorated by Wyndham Lewis. The wool carpet has a design inspired by Sonia Delaunay. Beside the fireplace is one of Dali's Mae West sofas, its red satin impersonating her lips. And overhead, the ceiling is decorated with fluffy, heavenly clouds that Zander has painted himself.

There are some interesting objects, a Wedgwood tea set, a range of cocktail glasses and shakers, a Tiffany lamp, a Pye radiogram. He was not sure that a radio would work at these depths but he has other ways of entertaining himself. He has a violin, with a good supply of spare strings, a chess set, some self-made jigsaw puzzles showing work by Escher and Arcimboldi. And he has laid in a good supply of books and records, everything from Agatha Christie to *Ulysses*, from Bach to Bessie Smith, some bound volumes of *Punch* and *Vanity Fair* and *Picture Post*. There are pictures on the walls: seascapes and flowers, hunting dogs and English country houses; the outside world.

There is an austere but functional gentleman's bathroom with gilt mirrors, a marble basin and a cream claw-footed bathtub. The bedroom appears as a voluminous tent. The room is draped with pale orange silk, gathered into a bunch at the centre of the ceiling, so that the material ripples slowly down the walls. In the heart of the room is a small, hard, leather day bed that will be adequate for Zander's solitary requirements.

The rooms are warm, although he expects he will experience a chill in the depths of winter. He has running water, and that will be enough to keep his body and clothes clean. There is electrical lighting and in the kitchen are a Baby Belling in easy clean vitreous enamel, and an Electrolux refrigerator, Swedish designed, made in Luton.

He has always been known as something of a dandy. He has always dressed to prove his bohemianism. Nobody will ever again see him or be impressed by his outfits, but that doesn't mean he intends to let his standards drop. He has a four-piece corduroy suit with plus-fours. He has Reform shirts in scarlet, green and fawn, waistcoats in floral patterns. He has silk pyjamas and a smoking jacket. He has a soft felt hat and a mackintosh, but he cannot see that he will really need them. He even has a positively avant-garde lounge suit with one of those new-fangled zip flies.

Food will be something of a problem, of course. Fresh meat, vegetables and fruit are not to be expected, but he has laid in a lifetime's supply of canned, salted and smoked foods. There are myriad cans of herrings and sardines, pears and cherries, Irish stew, corned beef and prawns. But what he likes best about his food is that it has trade names. Never again will he have to go to a market and buy anything loose or seasonal, to risk being slipped some bruised or overripe goods. Here are names he can trust, Bisto and Oxo, Horniman tea, McVitie and Price's cheese assorted, Cerebos salt. These everyday names are so reassuring and homely. They are tokens by which life is measured and made safe. Heinz and HP, Lea and Perrin, Crosse & Blackwell: they are old familiars.

It was not easy to create this secret place. It was difficult to keep his intentions hidden. The tunnels and staircases and chambers had to be built, and he knows that builders are not a discreet or closed-mouthed brigade. He has had to be stealthy. Partly he disguised his intentions as mistakes. A passageway was built, then he would tell his charge-hands they had misread the plans, or that the Haden brothers had changed their minds. Since there was then no sense in dismantling the already constructed passageway, he told his men to brick up the entrance, and later he would find a way of joining it up with some other 'error' to form part of a whole, continuous system of such deliberate mistakes.

Even so, an intelligent project manager might have gleaned that he was up to something, so Zander fabricated fallings out with his collaborators. He was known to be temperamental and difficult. It added to his mystique. The turnover of workers was rapid. Men built blindly, following his instructions to the letter, ignorant of any final intention. Only he had a sense of the finished article. Not even Matthew and Frederick Haden knew what he was doing. The customer was deceived but satisfied. The brothers were overjoyed by their new building, and the budget was only slightly exceeded. And even if they had known that Zander had incidentally made something for himself as well, how could they really complain?

The concealed corridors and staircases that interlace the store will enable him to move around within it. The spy holes will enable him to look out on a malleable world that will reveal its changes by the goods bought and sold in the store. But he will be safe from these changes, and at the end of each excursion, after each spying mission, he will return to his sub-basement, to his suite of rooms and his hoard of products, to this place where it will always be 1933.

He has decided to hide here, to live in his bunker, to wait until the whole shooting match is over. He will have all he needs, and he will die here. In Haden Brothers he has designed a machine for dying.

35 · KILLING FLOORS

Charlie turned the brass handle and opened the old door. He stared into the darkness and could see nothing, but there was a decrepit old light switch at the side of the door and he flicked it on. Slowly a bedroom became visible. The silk that lined the walls looked brittle and frayed, and the leather of the day bed was like old, chapped skin. He had no idea what he was seeing, but it occurred to him that if it came to it, he might be happy to spend the night in these luxurious if faded quarters. But there was more to see. The floor was peppered with dust so that he left footprints as he walked across the room to another door on the far side.

He opened this one too and stepped into the living room. There was too much to take in all at once; the hexagonal shape, the clouds painted on the ceiling, the red satin sofa, and a strange, bad, unhealthy odour, though not nearly so bad as the smell from those cans of food he'd opened, and then he saw the room's occupant, Edward Zander, or at least what was left of him.

The corpse of Edward Zander was sitting awkwardly upright in the room's armchair, and he was little more than a neatly dressed skeleton, bones and skull projecting from the collar and cuffs of a Liberty's silk smoking jacket, his feet in leather monogrammed slippers. A hank of grey hair was draped down over one temple like a badly fitting wig that had slipped out of place. The effect was too comic to be immediately horrifying and it was a moment or two before Charlie recognized what he was looking at. And then he knew.

It was a long time since the doors to these rooms had been opened, since a living person had been there. A state of flimsy equilibrium had rested in this region and Charlie's presence had destroyed it. Air moved through the rooms, Charlie's footsteps reverberated across the floor. The scene was disturbed and Edward Zander's corpse pitched forwards as though it was making a lunge for Charlie. His light-headedness, his hunger and tiredness evaporated and he fled the room, slamming the door shut behind him, keeping all the horrors closed in. He ran through the bedroom, slammed another door, went out to the sub-basement, but he needed to flee further still.

His instinct was to climb, to ascend, to go up and up through the building, to get as far away from that dreadful room as possible. He needed air, though he knew that was asking too much. He went headlong. He could not have retraced his route even if he had wanted to. He just ran and ran, along tunnels and up staircases, the necessity to keep moving being more important than the logic of the journey. Where was he? What kind of world had he discovered, what place of death and decay, dust and darkness, skeletons and putrid food? And for the first time it occurred to him that this might be a place from which there was no return, no escape.

He stopped just long enough to wonder where he was. He had come a long way and he was now at the bottom of a narrow, circular shaft that was stitched with iron rungs. Without thinking and for no reason that he could have articulated he started to climb them. It was a long process. Up and up he went and as he got higher, the shaft got narrower still until it was scarcely wider than a man's body. He had a vision that he might get stuck here and starve to death, but he pushed on until he reached the very top of the shaft.

Light seeped in from some indeterminate source and the only way to go now was laterally, into a void above a suspended ceiling. He crawled on his belly into the space, through the dirt, over the metal supports and cables. He no longer had a sense of escaping but rather of hiding, of finding a place where his own fears and demons couldn't get to him.

He stopped again. He lay still and tried to catch his breath, and he thought he could hear more voices, though by now he could have been hallucinating. Yet he believed them to be real, a man's voice and a woman's voice, and although at first he couldn't tell precisely where they were coming from, they seemed to be below him. He listened hard, tried not to breathe and after a while he could make out words. There was talk of killing and Haden Brothers and somebody's mother, and he was fairly sure he picked out the name Vita. He became intensely interested.

He crawled further into the void, as quietly as he possibly could, until he found a place where a spotlight was fitted into the ceiling. A circular hole had been cut but the lamp was not a perfect fit. There was a thin crescent-shaped gap and Charlie pressed his eye to it to see what was below. At first he could see nothing at all, only whiteness, as though he was staring straight into a source of light, but then he realized it was an all-white room, and he moved his eye until he could see some of the room's features. Not only that, he could see the room's inhabitants too, and at least they were alive this time. Although he'd had only the briefest acquaintance with Arnold Haden and Vita Carlisle, as he looked down and saw them from his hiding place, they felt like his long lost friends.

36 · LOST AND FOUND

It is late now. Arnold Haden looks out of the window at the illuminated city. It has slowed down. People are in their homes, switching off their lights and televisions, turning in for the night, locking their doors and windows, checking over their properties, securing their territories. They will soon be asleep, falling into dreams and darkness until the end of the night, a night that Arnold hopes will end soon.

He says, 'Do you believe in heaven, Vita?'

'No,' she says without hesitation. 'If I did I wouldn't kill you.'

Arnold says, 'I do believe in heaven but I suspect that my idea of heaven is not much like other people's. People seem to think it will be like a party, a fun house, somewhat like a department store. They think it will be full of events; people to see, old friends and family and wives and children, a place of reunions with lots of things to do and see: the gardens, the angels, the music. They think that must be the alternative to oblivion. But I'm not so sure. If there *is* a heaven, and if I go there, I hope it will be an empty place, still and silent, without events or objects or emotions.'

Vita does not seem to be listening. She says, 'I liked your story about the death of your wife and brother and unborn child. Was it true?'

'Of course it was true,' Arnold says grimly.

'And what happened next?'

Arnold Haden says, 'I didn't know what to do. I didn't know exactly what a man was supposed to do having lost his wife and his heir and his brother. I knew of course that I should grieve, and I certainly did. But after that, what many people would do would be to "throw themselves into their work". It's an obvious solution and probably a wise one. Working at Haden Brothers could have become a sort of therapy, or at least an anaesthetic, something to fill my hours and drive out the pain. Then, after a few years of that kind of self-

226

obliteration, I would be expected to wake up, to find myself again. I would have lived and worked through my grief and I'd be ready to return to life. Part of that return would inevitably involve finding a new partner, a new wife. Together we could start again. She would give me children. There would be male heirs. There would be a new generation of Haden Brothers. All manner of things would be well.

'But it didn't work that way for me. I couldn't throw myself into anything. That seemed too obvious a course of action. I had to withdraw from life and from Haden Brothers. The store didn't need me. It never really had. I didn't need to work for a living, and I couldn't stand to be in the store. I no longer wanted to be surrounded by things. I rose above it all. I came up here to this penthouse, where I have tried to live an increasingly ascetic and monastic life.'

Vita snorts with derision but it doesn't knock Arnold Haden from his stride.

'I can see why you find that comical,' he says. 'I don't live exactly the way most monks do, it's true, but I'd argue that sex is holy. And I would say that what makes it holy is the fact that it is invisible. There is no product. Yes, sex can be bought and sold, but once you've paid for it, it doesn't hang around and clutter up the place. It doesn't need dusting or maintaining or insuring. It simply disappears until the next time.'

Vita's face shows an old, familiar contempt.

'I have rather mixed feelings about this situation, Vita,' Arnold Haden continues. 'Here you are threatening, promising, to kill me, and my basic human instincts are still intact. I'm not afraid to die and yet I do want to live. But if you asked me what do I have to live for, I'd have to say that I'm not at all sure. I have absolutely no sense of purpose, no great work or project I want to complete. I would certainly say that, day by day, I don't take any great pleasure in my continuing existence. But I would miss the sex, I really would.

'I can't pretend that intercourse with the female shop assistants of Haden Brothers is of any great depth or moment, and yet this direct, uncomplicated completion of a biological task makes me feel very alive indeed.'

'But,' says Vita, 'it isn't the *completion* of the biological task is it? The biological task results in babies, procreation. The task is to continue the line.'

'Well yes, you're right, I know. But I've attempted that task once, and it wasn't much of a success. I couldn't possibly dream of ever doing it again.'

'Oh, I don't know, Arnold, I think you could.'

He shakes his head in absolute denial.

Vita continues, 'You take some risks, don't you, Arnold?'

'No, I don't think so. I always employ safe sex techniques.'

'I'm not talking about disease, Arnold, I'm talking about procreation. Condoms break. Shop girls get pregnant. Suddenly there's an illegitimate heir to Haden Brothers. Suddenly you have a paternity suit, blackmail.'

'That couldn't happen.'

'Couldn't it?'

'No,' he says with finality, and then he tries to move the conversation on from this dismal subject. 'Look, Vita, I know you want to kill me, I know you intend to and I actually believe you will. If you want it badly enough, then I'm sure you can make it happen, and I'm certainly not trying to talk you out of it, but I sense an ambivalence in you, Vita. For some reason, you want me dead, but I'm not sure that you really and truly hate me. You're human, after all.'

She doesn't respond to that one, so he continues, 'But since you're going to kill me anyway, would it do any harm to grant me one last request?'

'You'll have to request it and see what I say.'

'Would you make love to me before you kill me?'

She gets up and walks over to him. Her bare feet are gentle on the white pile. She stands very close and hits him across his right cheek. It isn't so very hard, and he doesn't flinch.

'Or if not intercourse,' he says, 'how about some oral or manual relief?'

She hits him again in the same place. And again. And then she starts slapping him around the other cheek with her other hand, then across both cheeks with both hands in turn, and then her hands and arms are a blur and she is hitting him hard, as hard as she knows how, with all the strength and energy in her body. And her hands stray to his nose and mouth, clench themselves into fists and she is punching the living daylights out of him. Blood starts to trickle out of his nose and his lips are cut open. Vita keeps hitting and hitting him until she is exhausted, by which time her hands and dress are splattered with his blood. She stops. Arnold Haden remains impassive.

'I probably deserved that,' he says.

Vita is instantly calm again. The physical effort has released all her anger and energy.

'You know what makes me really mad, Arnold?'

'No.'

'It's the name of this store. Haden *Brothers*. I'm no deranged post-feminist, but it gets me very angry. Why not Haden Sisters? Why not Haden Brothers and Sisters and Daughters and Grandmothers and Wives and Nieces and the whole damn show?'

'Because it was two brothers who set up the store.'

'Then why not just Hadens?'

'I don't know, Vita. I didn't invent the name. I simply inherited it.'

'But you kept it. You didn't change it when you could have.'

'It's tradition,' he insists. 'It was a well-known name. We had a reputation. It would have been bad for business to have changed it.'

'A change of name would be bad for business!! You know, you're making it very, very easy for me to kill you, Arnold.'

'This is madness, Vita. You've had me here all these hours and you say you want to kill me but you refuse to tell me why. Now, at last, you seem to be giving me a reason and it appears to be because you don't like the name of the store! Is that right? Can I possibly have understood that correctly?'

Vita considers this carefully, weighing up the issues, wondering if that doesn't perhaps sound a little unreasonable, but then she says, 'Yes, that's about the size of it, Arnold.'

'I could change the name of the store if that would really help,' he says.

'Don't be pathetic, Arnold. That way there'd still be a Haden brother in the world, wouldn't there?'

'Yes, but not for so very long. I'm not young, Vita. Give me a decade or two at the most and I'll be dead. And then there'll be no more Haden brothers in the world. Nature will bring you my death just as surely as the dynamite will. It'll take a little longer, that's all.'

'And it won't be as much fun for me.'

'Fun?'

'Yes, fun. You know what fun's all about, don't you Arnold? You try to make out you're this tortured soul, but I think you're just a pathetic little soulless creep. I'm not saying you don't feel things. Of course you feel things. Dogs feel things, rats feel things. They feel hungry and they feel horny. And when they eat and when they fuck, then they have fun. But that's not the same thing as being human, is it, Arnold?'

'I *am* human,' Arnold insists.

'You probably don't even remember this particular bit of fun, Arnold.'

'What bit of fun? What do you mean?'

'It was a long time ago. She was a young, thin blonde. Just your type. She was naive, empty-headed, gullible. She was flattered by your attentions.'

This is sounding suspiciously, ominously, familiar to Arnold Haden, though he can't immediately think why.

'You had her a couple of times on a pile of Chinese rugs in the carpet department. You fucked her, Arnold. It wasn't a great fuck. It certainly wasn't very memorable for you, but she doesn't seem to be able to forget it.'

And then he recalls this is the same story that was told to him by the shoplifter who demanded to see him recently, the one he released.

'Yes, yes, I think I do remember,' says Arnold.

'Yes? What was her name?'

He shakes his head. He has no idea.

'It was Erica Carlisle. I'm her daughter.'

'Oh. Oh, I see. I'm sorry.'

'No, you don't see, not yet. The fact is, I came along precisely nine months after that sordid little event on the Persian rug. I'm *your* daughter too, Arnold. That's one of the reasons why I don't want to make love to you, though not the only one. I'm a Haden you see, a Haden daughter, a Haden sister. I've only just found out. My mother only just told me. After all these years she finally got round to telling me who my father is, and it turned out to be you. The boss who wants to fuck me. Like mother, like daughter. And now at long last you know why I'm going to kill you, Arnold. And maybe you can understand why I won't be too upset if I also manage to kill myself at the same time.'

'Are you serious?' Arnold demands. He looks at her and he knows that she is. 'Is that really what this whole stupid, murderous business is all about?'

'It's not stupid,' she insists.

'Your mother's a liar,' says Arnold Haden. 'Or you are. Or you're both fools, or blackmailers or maniacs or all of these things.'

This is not the reaction Vita was expecting to come from her revelation. This was surely the moment when they might both have wept, embraced, when anything might have been possible, when her mind and intentions might have been changed completely and forever.

Instead Arnold Haden says, 'You're just a stupid little shop assistant aren't you?'

She is ready to deny that vigorously but he doesn't give her the chance. Arnold Haden is across the room and inches away from her. He gives her a brief slap across the face, nothing serious, not exactly an act of retaliation for all the slaps she gave him, just something instinctive to silence a fiercely disobedient child. She is shocked and surprised by his sudden anger.

'I'm not your father,' he shouts, and he grabs her and throws her on to the floor, on to the soft white carpet, and he straddles her, his knees either side of her rib cage.

'I'm nobody's father, you silly little bitch. Not since the car accident blew away my chances of ever having any more children. I can fuck but I can't reproduce. I'm just firing blanks. Symbolic eh?'

And he slaps her again and she struggles but she can't move. He takes her by the neck. She fights and squirms but it's irrelevant. Arnold Haden is as strong as an ox now. Her neck feels so delicate in his hands, so deliciously fragile. The bones, the tendons, the windpipe, they could be snapped so easily. He enjoys this rare feeling of power. At the centre of this clean, white, featureless terrain, the red mist has descended. In this place without complications, his senses and instincts have narrowed down. He can see and hear and think of nothing but how perfect and satisfying it would be to kill this idiot girl who thinks she's his daughter.

He's so wrapped up in the tight focus of himself that he doesn't hear the peculiar noises going on above his head; a cracking sound as the ceiling sags and starts to give way, as muck starts to powder down, then the smooth surface splits, and finally there is a total collapse, a man's cry, and Charlie Mayhew falls through the ceiling from the void above, tumbles into this white world with a flourish and a crash and a hard, bone-juddering landing.

Arnold Haden turns to see what's going on. He can't believe his eyes, can't make sense of it, and in any case he doesn't release Vita's neck. Charlie gets up from the debris. His body and face are thick with dirt, and he advances on Arnold Haden, not that Haden seems to care. He lowers his head and goes back to his task, that of strangling Vita Carlisle. Charlie shouts threats, tries to get a response from Haden but it does no good. He hits Arnold in the back, kicks him, but the blows don't get through. Finally Charlie takes a handful of Haden's hair, pulls it as hard as he can and pushes something cold and metallic into the side of Arnold's neck.

'Let her go or I'll blow your head off,' Charlie whispers into Arnold's ear.

Vita looks up, sees Charlie, though she barely recognizes him. But she sees that the thing he's pushing into Arnold Haden's neck isn't a gun at all. It's the Parker pen her mother gave her, the Presidential International from the Duofold Collection, the one she had lost all that time ago.

Arnold Haden freezes, slackens his grip on Vita's neck but he doesn't release her completely. A stillness, an equilibrium settles on the three of them. A lot of time passes in the white room. It feels as though it might last forever.

Finally, Arnold Haden lets go of Vita, and Charlie takes the pen away from his neck, putting it swiftly away into his pocket so that Haden won't see that it's not a gun. They stand up. Vita straightens her dress, feels at the dynamite to make sure it's still securely in place. For the first time Arnold Haden sees Charlie's face. Yes, it's the intruder he saw in the store that night. He doesn't know what this means but he is no longer capable of being surprised.

'This solves nothing,' Arnold Haden says to Vita. 'He can blow my head off. You can now blow all three of us to smithereens. It seems to me we're right back where we started.'

Charlie doesn't know precisely where that is, but he asks no questions. He has arrived too late to demand exposition.

'Not quite,' says Vita. 'We're not exactly where we were. I've got it. I know what my demands are. I finally know what I want. I've thought of something that I think is going to give me more pleasure, more utility, than killing you, than killing either of us. And the strange thing is, I think it's going to give you a lot of pleasure too, Arnold.'

37 · REMNANTS

The big give-away is about to start. They come from far and near, many classes and races, many socio-economic groups, some with mixed feelings, some with mixed motives, but still they come; from the suburbs and the cities, from their town houses and tower blocks, from the streets. Some of them do not look like regular or typical Haden Brothers customers, and yet many do. Some have waited overnight. They stand many thick around the store, crammed densely around the entrances, waiting for the grand opening.

In the main, the atmosphere is good-natured. It's like a holiday. People are eager and excited by a common purpose and a sense of the absurd. There is also optimism and the belief that they will find what they want. There are some pockets of disbelief, one or two cynics and sceptics who think there has to be a catch somewhere, but even they are happy to take a chance on the promise of something for nothing.

'It will be chaos,' Derek Snell had predicted. 'It'll be mayhem, anarchy, bedlam.'

'What about crowd control?' Ray Chalmers had asked. 'What about discipline? You tell me it's going to be open house. You say it's going to be free shopping. I think it's going to be more like looting and pillaging. It'll be like a combat zone.'

Not that this prospect particularly displeased him. He still regarded combat zones as his kind of territory. And even if he couldn't save Arnold Haden from Vita Carlisle, or the building from the likes of Charlie Mayhew, at least he could save the store from its own customers.

'No,' said Arnold Haden, having been coached in what to say by Vita, 'I think a series of self-regulatory feedback mechanisms will come into play.'

'Run that past me again,' said Chalmers.

'Well, of course people will come from far and wide, but they won't

233

come all the way from, say, Scotland because they will appreciate that by the time they get here they may be too late, and the cost of coming all that way will be prohibitive. We have to find a market but we don't have to tell the whole world. Just enough to get the job done. A small announcement will kick the ball rolling, then word of mouth will do the rest.'

'That will still produce one hell of a lot of people,' said Derek Snell.

'Yes,' Arnold Haden agreed, 'the shop will certainly get full, but the very fact that it *is* so full will in itself be another feedback mechanism. It will deter a lot of people. If they arrive and see they can't get into the store they'll just go away again. And it won't go on for very long because as time goes by the store will contain fewer and fewer goods. It will be fine. Trust me.'

'Well,' said Derek Snell, 'you're the boss.'

'Yes, I am, aren't I?' said Arnold Haden.

It had not been the very easiest thing to achieve. When Arnold Haden telephoned his merchandise managers and floor managers and the members of the board, he met, to say the least, resistance. They thought he must be drunk or deranged or possibly both, though he sounded normal and controlled enough. Even the idea that he was being blackmailed by terrorists occurred to at least one board member, but Arnold had told him not to be silly.

But Arnold Haden didn't try to persuade or argue, he simply told them that he was going to give away the entire contents of his store and that was that. The suppliers, the salespeople on commission, those running franchises, were not to worry. They'd get everything they were entitled to and more. Yes, there might be some organizational problems, but that was why he had managers, to solve these problems for him. And if any of those he talked to insisted on knowing what was going on and why, he simply replied, 'Hamnet is here'. Of course, nobody knew exactly what he meant by that, but the words were potent enough, the invocation of something ineluctable. They knew it had to be done. That was the bottom line. Arnold Haden was the boss.

The doors are opened, thrown back, and the tide of people surges in, penetrating every department, rising up the store, up the escalators and stairs. They run and they leap. They have entered the fun house. They have broken into the winter palace. And once they get inside the store they see that there is indeed no con, no deception. It is a genuine free for all. First come, first served. If you can see it, you can have it. If you want it, it's yours. This is not a simple matter of ends and scarce means. The means are non-existent but the ends are limited. The store only contains so much.

They hit the clothing departments; all those suits and trousers and skirts and blouses, the sweaters and cardigans and shorts and culottes, the longline sweaters with delicate pointelle detail and shell designs on cuffs and hems, fashion jackets in sand-washed silk, underwired polka dot swimsuits in eighty-five per cent cotton and fifteen per cent elastane. They grab the windcheaters and blousons and sportscoats and blazers and overcoats and raincoats and waxed jackets and cagoules and parkas and trench coats. Casual and formal are snatched with equal delight. Eager fingers grab at the fabrics: jersey, denim, nylon, antiqued leather, seersucker, gabardine, acrylic, chambrey, goatsuede. All those features: raglan sleeves and faux horn buttons. All those colours: the aubergine and the willow, the contrasting mango and slate and wine, the complementary thistle and taupe and gunmetal. And then the underwear: the high leg briefs and the camisoles, the teddies, the tangas and thongs, the bras: padded and unpadded, front and rear opening, T-backed and criss-crossed and strapless.

People move around the store. It is not a flow exactly, more a restless bombardment of particles. Some are eager, some casual, some with an air of desperation that may be loud or quiet. They jostle and elbow each other a little, dash from department to department looking lost and excitable, but sooner or later they emerge, sometimes struggling beneath the weight or bulk of what they've obtained. Sometimes great piles of goods are precariously balanced in their arms so they look like jugglers or balancing acts.

Some have smaller desires and smaller packages. They may have come for one thing only; a gold-plated chronograph wrist watch with alarm, tachymeter, rotating bezel and automatic calendar, or a ball-bearing fishing reel with two-speed line lay and aero spooling system. They've got what they came for and are happy to leave.

Others dash into the store and grab the first thing they see, a thing they don't necessarily have any use for; a bentwood-style hat and coat stand, a triple action battery-operated cellulite massager, a durable car-wash brush with spray jet. They suddenly look very relieved. At least they know they've got *something*. Their trip won't have been in vain. Now they can wander through the store until they find something better, grab it and abandon the first item.

Elsewhere some curious bartering goes on. A man descending one of the staircases carrying a petrol-driven rotary lawn mower meets a man coming up carrying a five inch high torque sander and grinder. Both men are filled with envy. Their own acquisition seems suddenly dreary and inadequate. They have nothing to lose, so decide to do a quick swap.

The counter assistants, the employees of Haden Brothers, begin by trying to behave normally. It ought not to make much difference whether the customers are paying or not. The tills don't need to be operated, credit cards and cheques don't need to be accepted, but otherwise their roles might remain unchanged. People should still need help or advice, some information, some expertise.

But before long, normality doesn't seem to be much of an option. The customers don't want help. They don't want to be served. They just want to take. They don't care whether things fit them. They don't care about styles or suitability. When it's free it doesn't matter. Increasingly the assistants become redundant. They just stand and watch, but then it occurs to them that they too could become customers. They leave their positions behind the counters, they start taking one or two little items for themselves. Before long they are indistinguishable from the rest of the mass.

There are breakages, of course. In the excitement, displays of wine glasses and tumblers and vases get knocked over and smashed. A fifty-two-piece Royal Doulton tableware set in Olde England rose tree design is elbowed from the grasp of one customer. A twenty-four-inch, thirty-two-channel television set with tinted screen to reduce eye fatigue and a reversible remote commander, tumbles over a balcony from the third to the second floor, narrowly missing a child in a Beautiful Dreamer pushchair with floral frilled seat liner just that moment obtained from the pram department. The mother doesn't take much notice. There is nobody to clear up the mess.

Some of the goods, the washers and spin-driers, the cookers, freezers and dish washers, take some moving. Someone says, 'This is a rip off. There ought to be free delivery,' but most are more pragmatic. They arrange themselves into small groups, co-operatives, and they lift a corner each and struggle out of the department into the lifts or on to escalators and out of the store.

Elsewhere there is less co-operation and more humiliation. A frail shabby old woman is carrying two luxury-grade traditional Wilton rugs, one under each arm. They're big and they're cumbersome, and the burden is so great she can barely walk. It gradually dawns on her that she will never make it home with both the carpets. She could make it easily enough with one but then she'd have to abandon the other and she desperately wants them both. She drops the rugs and sits down on them and weeps at the enormity and the essential unfairness of her dilemma.

In an ideal world, of course, these goods might have gone only to the poor and needy, perhaps to people like this old woman; but how would Vita Carlisle and Arnold Haden have determined need? Would there have been a means test, forms to be filled in, a series of interviews, a bureaucracy to process the information? No, it had to be quick and easy, symbolic and metaphoric. To each according to their wants, according to their fitness and their ability to shop. Just like the real world.

On the seventh floor, in the furniture department, there are some slight problems. A twelve-foot-long oak dining table or a marble-topped sideboard is even harder to deal with than the washing machines, but somehow people manage. The free for all means that the three pieces of a three piece suite might each go to separate homes. Those twelve matching dining chairs may well depart to twelve unmatching destinations. But that doesn't seem to worry anybody. With much heaving and straining, every stick of furniture eventually heads for the exits; the bureaus and the TVs and video cabinets, the midi hi-fi stackers, cocktail and buffet units, the Windsor stools in yew and elm, the glass-fronted bookcases with adjustable shelves and drop handles. The beds go too: the sofa beds, the futons, the four posters. People struggle under the weight of chests of drawers, four door wardrobes with centre mirrors, shoe rails and tie racks. The tables with their glass tops and pedestal bases, the corner units with their block-foam cushions and serpentine springs, the Chesterfields and Chesterfield recliners, the twin-lidded ottomans upholstered in deep-buttoned tapestry-style fabric; they all depart. So too the drum tables and telephone stands, the ash veneer dressers, the console tables, the whatnots.

The furniture porters look on contentedly enough. They're glad to see the back of all this stuff. They encourage customers to go for it, to be bold, to take all that they need and a little more besides; although they stop some way short of offering to carry anything for anybody.

There are journalists and television crews inside the store. This event is news. They are there to film the crush of people and the effects of consumerism gone rampant. They find it hard work. The crowd builds and swirls, there are strange currents and eddies, and it's difficult to find a spot from which to film. There's nowhere that a reporter might stand alone away from the throng. Cameras, microphones and reporters all get jostled and knocked; although, in a sense, that makes for even better TV. Before long the crews reckon they've got as good as they're going to get, they decide to call it a wrap and they too do a little light shopping before they leave.

Into this curious set of relations and interactions comes Erica Carlisle. She moves through the crowds with a practised efficiency, past people burdened with standard lamps and kitchen stools and leather luggage and exercise bikes. She feels distant and detached from it all. Who are all these people? They look like invaders, not her type at all. She wants no part of this. When everything is free and easily obtained, she's not sure that she wants any of it. There's no pleasure to be had here, no thrill, no turn on. She leaves the store empty handed and wonders where her daughter is.

Other familiar faces pop up throughout the store. Carl Laughton, the former buyer, stalks the toy department, still disgusted and disgruntled; pleased to see the dissolution of the empire that has exiled him. He picks up a baby-faced female doll from a top shelf in the department and pulls it out of its see-through box. Rowdy children snap round his ankles and he deliberately kicks one of them. The doll's face is so trusting, so open, so big-eyed. He places the palm of his right hand over the face, holds the back of the head in the other, and pushes his hands together till the brittle, pink plastic twists and crushes. It feels good, but he still wishes the face belonged to Vita Carlisle.

Even the customer with the complaint returns, the one with the skin disease on his hands, and this time he selects a reproduction oil painting of a hunting scene set in an imaginary, historical England. He chooses it because, being flat and not too large, he can slip it under his arm without having to use his hands.

Of course there is pushing and shoving. People sometimes get kicked and knocked out of the way in the enthusiasm that overtakes the store. Some customers have their newly acquired goods snatched from their hands. A woven voile fitted bedspread with lace valance becomes the subject of a tug of war between two women. A couple of young men in primary-coloured tracksuits threaten each other over a racing bike with eighteen speed gears, cantilever brakes and cotterless chainset with alloy cranks.

A small scuffle breaks out between rival parties of youths who have their eyes on the same pairs of trainers. Ray Chalmers sees this and is briefly cheered up. He hopes it will get worse and Derek Snell will ask him to go in there, crack some heads, and he will have the great pleasure of telling Snell he's going for a lie down. But the situation is quickly defused when the youths realize that scuffling is only getting in the way of their ability to get their hands on the goods.

Arnold Haden and Vita Carlisle, Charlie Mayhew, Derek Snell and Ray Chalmers sit in the security control room watching the spectacle on a bank of video screens, each one showing a different part of the store, a different piece of the action. Vita is pleased by what she sees. Of course, it is a farce, but she still feels she has achieved something special and grand scale. Whether it is more pleasurable than killing Arnold Haden would have been she will never be entirely sure, but since she has now come to know that he is not her father, she thinks it wouldn't really be much of a pleasure at all.

Arnold Haden looks on in wonder. Vita was absolutely right as far as he's concerned. This is a vast pleasure for him, and one he would never have been able to devise for himself. It's as though he's watching a speeded up piece of film, a wildlife documentary perhaps, the locusts descending, the jackals picking clean the bones. But when all the flesh has been stripped away from the skeleton, when all the products have been dispersed from Haden Brothers, he will be left with something bare and beautiful. He will feel completely happy and completely vindicated.

For Charlie Mayhew these are bitter-sweet moments. He is witnessing the break up of something rather precious to him: his home. As the customers take away the goods it is almost as if they are taking away a part of him. They can restock the store, fill it with more and better items, but it will never be exactly the same again. After all this, things will have changed completely and forever.

In the store's cafés and bars, restaurants and cafeterias there is free food and drink on offer, but there aren't too many takers. As pleasures go, food and drink are too insubstantial, too fleeting. Today's customers want something that will last a while, something they can take home and show to their friends and families, souvenirs of this extraordinary day. Not that the food department is exactly neglected. The shelves are being systematically stripped, the produce falling into willing hands, the raw and the cooked, the tinned and the bottled, the smoked and the salted and the fresh.

Out from the musical instrument department go the guitars and electric organs and tambourines and trumpets and Jew's harps; the accessories – the strings and reeds and resin and tuning forks.

Out go all the familiar brands, the names you know and can rely on. Some sound domestic and trustworthy and dependable: Hoover, Kenwood, Burberry, Durex. Some sound like exotic foreign visitors: Givenchy, Lancôme, Cartier, Chanel. Others are more international: Zanussi and Kodak and Panasonic and Dupont and IBM.

Those eponymous brands that once seemed haughty and un-approachable now sound like just plain folks: Calvin Klein and Zandra Rhodes and Ralph Lauren and Jasper Conran. How can they be haughty when they're gratis and anybody's. Yes, a certain kind of democratization is going on. When everything is free then everything is equal. Which is not to say that certain things are not more desirable than others. There is still supply and demand. The Rolex watches are still more sought after than the own-brand plastic washing-up bowls and pastry cutters. The laws of diminishing marginal utility have not been entirely suspended. Nevertheless, it all disappears. It all ceases to be stock and is miraculously converted into someone else's property.

The day is, if anything, a long slow anticlimax, or at least the day's climax came at the beginning, with the first big rush and flourish, and it is followed by a slow diminuendo. The store is gradually denuded, cleaned out. There is less and less to interest the punters, less for them to want.

There are some disappointments. As the store is stripped of its merchandise, so the choice becomes increasingly limited. People have to settle for less than they hoped, or for something quite different from what they sought. Desires become transformed and muted, horizons are lowered. And eventually people have to settle merely for what they can get, when they have to take the dregs, the leavings, the sediment that others have refused or discarded; the shop-soiled, the mismatched, the useless. Slowly, unwillingly the crowd thins and goes home.

At long last a moment comes when the departments contain nothing but the counters and display units and the detritus that the crowds have left behind, and the cleaning staff are rapidly getting rid of that. There is nothing here now for anybody to want. The cupboard is bare. The few stragglers are very politely asked to leave, not that they need much persuasion now.

Arnold Haden decides the time is right to walk through the store, his store. This, he now realizes, is how he always wanted it to be, how he sometimes saw it in his dreams; spacious and empty and uncluttered, cleansed of humanity and its desires. He loves the stillness of the light, the rhythms of space and volume, the articulation of bare surfaces. The expanses of carpet are so broad and inviting. The departments are so clear, so free of secrets. He loves it. He thinks he might even spend the night here, camped between the pillars and display units, beneath the suspended ceilings.

It will be only a passing pleasure. Tomorrow things will start returning to normal. The store will gradually fill up with new goods and the status quo will return. It will be business as usual. All he has been through with Vita seems as nothing now. It was worth it for this one moment of stillness, a moment in and out of time, when both sides of the scales are completely, blissfully, empty.

He is standing in the pristine calmness of the homewares department, where the knife blocks and asparagus steamers and fish kettles are sold. Now that the store is so bare the sight lines are much clearer, and he becomes aware of someone bustling towards him from way over the other side of the floor. It is Derek Snell, and he has a spring in his step. He's smiling fit to bust. Arnold Haden hopes that Snell is sharing some of the wonder created by this sculptural emptiness, though knowing Derek Snell he very much doubts it.

'Isn't it exquisite!' Arnold Haden shouts when Snell is some thirty feet away.

'It's fantastic,' says Snell. 'Absolutely fantastic.'

Arnold is not surprised that Snell agrees; agreeing with his masters is one of Snell's great skills, but Snell's enthusiasm seems both intense and genuine. Arnold Haden has never seen him looking so happy.

'I was a fool ever to doubt you,' he blurts. 'You're a genius, Mr Haden, an absolute genius.'

Arnold Haden says, 'I don't think so.'

'Well, everybody else does. Haden Brothers is on every television channel, on every radio station, on every front page.'

'Just because we gave some things away,' reflects Arnold Haden. 'It's pathetic really, isn't it?'

'And everybody wants to interview you.'

'I'm no good at interviews.'

'That doesn't matter. People want to interview you because you're a marketing genius. This stunt of yours is worth untold millions in free publicity. It's a public relations coup of staggering proportions. The day Arnold Haden gave away a store full of free samples. They'll be talking about this for decades, centuries. You've made history.'

'That's not why I did it,' says Arnold.

'It doesn't matter what your motives were. You just have a pure instinct for retailing.'

Arnold Haden is uncomfortable with these compliments. He is no longer sure that retailing is a thing he wants to have a talent for.

'And do you know, they've started to queue up again outside?' Snell says.

'No, I didn't,' Arnold Haden replies. 'But why would they do that?'

'They're waiting for tomorrow morning. The new stock is arriving even as we stand here. Our suppliers are pulling out all the stops to make sure we have their goods as soon as possible. They're giving us better terms, bigger discounts. By nine o'clock tomorrow we'll have at least a representative amount of our core stock, then we let in the crowds again.'

'But why are they queuing? Hasn't someone explained to them that come tomorrow things will be back to normal and they'll have to pay for what they want.'

'Yes, we've told them. But they don't care. That's fine by them. They've got the taste for Haden Brothers. They want to come into the store and start spending their money. That's why you're a genius, Mr Haden, and that's why I bow down before your God-like prowess.'

38 · ACCOUNTS

LESLEY CRANE: I was there the day that Arnold Haden gave away the entire contents of his store. I wasn't there as a punter. I was still supposed to be a reporter but my career had been going really badly. My editor had spiked the interview with Arnold Haden. He said most of it was too boring and the part about 'Hamnet was here' didn't make any sense. I knew better than to argue. I suppose a real journalist would have got her teeth into the story and gone out there and investigated just what that phrase did mean, but I was never that real. I'd been very discouraged. I hadn't been getting any work. Even turning up at Haden Brothers on the morning of the give-away wasn't a real assignment. I was just a freelance hoping to spot something the official hacks missed. I badly needed a story.

When I saw all those people, those oiks and freeloaders, those spivs and parasites rampaging through the store, I felt absolutely furious. I wanted to say, 'These people shouldn't be allowed in Haden Brothers. They're spoiling it. They're destroying it. They're just looters. They don't deserve to have these goods.' Until then I never knew I had any such feelings for Haden Brothers.

Like everyone else I assumed that poor old Arnold had finally lost his marbles. That was very sad. I'd liked him well enough. And what was more, it seemed to me that the 'shoppers' were taking advantage of him, of his infirmity. I was disgusted by it. I didn't want to participate in it, but at the same time I wanted some kind of souvenir. I found myself in the book department and I found myself picking up a signed copy of Julian Temperley's *The Coldest War*. There was a whole stack of them and nobody was exactly fighting to get one. I still have it and it's a strange souvenir of that even stranger day but I've never read a word of it and I don't suppose I ever shall.

I staggered out of Haden Brothers. I didn't have a story, nothing I could sell. I didn't know what I was going to do next. I was more than broke. I was behind with my mortgage and the phone people were

243

threatening to disconnect me. I needed money. I needed a job. I made a really bold decision. The next day I went along to the personnel department of Haden Brothers, spoke to Derek Snell and begged him to employ me.

DEREK SNELL: I suppose you would have to say that I'm guilty. I was the one who arranged for the words 'Hamnet was here' to be painted at regular intervals on the windows of Haden Brothers. It was I who arranged for those same words to be left on Arnold Haden's answering machine from time to time. It was I who wrote an anonymous letter to Lesley Crane telling her to say those words to Arnold Haden and watch his reaction.

I did it because I wanted to keep him out of the way, out of harm's way. He was a loose cannon. He interfered with the smooth running of the store. The more he stayed in his penthouse the better I liked it, and the more efficiently Haden Brothers ran. It seemed to help just about everybody if Arnold Haden felt that the world was a threatening and dangerous place. And if he happened to believe there was some international terrorist group out there with the slogan 'Hamnet was here', and if he believed they were out to get him, then that happened to suit me just fine too. Yes, I'm guilty of terrorizing Arnold Haden, but I would say that I did it for good, sound business reasons.

I never wholly knew what significance the phrase 'Hamnet was here' had for Arnold, but I knew it must be something pretty important. I knew he shouted out 'Hamnet is coming ' at the moment of orgasm; I knew that because I'd been told by a number of the shop girls who slept with him. And this is perhaps another thing I am guilty of. I had sex with virtually all those girls, either before or after they had sex with Arnold Haden. I know that may seem strange to some people, but at the time it just seemed natural, just a way of keeping up with the boss. If he could do it, why couldn't I?

When Arnold telephoned me at home and told me he wanted to give away everything in Haden Brothers, I assumed he'd finally flipped. When I asked why he wanted to do such an extraordinary thing all he'd say at first was 'Hamnet is here'. Of course, I didn't know what he was talking about. Then he said he was being held hostage by a terrorist group and they'd kill him if we didn't do what he said.

What was I to do? I could hardly tell him that there was no such terrorist organization, that I'd made the whole thing up. Besides, he did manage to convince me that he really would be blown up by *somebody* if I didn't do what he said. I had to think about it for a long time. A dead Haden Brother and a vast hole in the top of the store, well that didn't sound very good for business at all. I did what he told me to do. That, after all, was supposed to be my job. The fact that it turned out to be the most astute piece of business Haden Brothers ever did, continues to amaze and confound me. And perhaps that is the main thing I am guilty of; underestimating Arnold Haden.

Having consulted my records, it does indeed appear that I did have sexual intercourse with one Erica Carlisle some twenty-odd years ago, slightly before or after she also had intercourse with Arnold Haden. And it was obviously around this time that she became pregnant with Vita. However, I'm far from convinced that Vita Carlisle is my illegitimate daughter. Miss Carlisle senior was obviously no angel. Anyone who would sleep with both her boss and his personnel director might sleep with just about anybody. And she probably did.

Nevertheless, since there is an outside chance that Vita may be my offspring, I suppose I have to be glad that I failed to talk her into having sex with me. And frankly, if by any chance I *am* her father, I'm even more glad that I failed to talk her into having sex with Arnold Haden.

VITA CARLISLE: Finding out that Derek Snell could well be your father, really isn't the best surprise a girl ever had. I know that fatherless children often fantasize that they're the illegitimate offspring of someone rich and famous. But this wasn't just fantasy. My own mother actually told me I was Arnold Haden's daughter. How could she get that so wrong?

And if she had to tell me, why didn't she tell me before I started working at Haden Brothers, before I joined the Flying Squad? I no longer have much idea why I ever went to work at Haden Brothers. Was it something in my genes? Was it because Haden Brothers was my mother's favourite shop? I don't know anymore, but I really did want to work there. I really did want to get on, to have a successful career. It sounds like complete madness to me now.

It all seems so long ago that I tried to 'blow up' Arnold Haden. It feels like a movie, as though I was playing a part, saying someone else's lines. I know now that I was never going to be able to *really* blow him up. It appears the dynamite wasn't real. My source, Anton Heath, if you really want to know, had given me fake explosives. But

245

I didn't know that at the time. And now that it's all over, I'm infinitely grateful to Anton Heath. He saved me from myself and I thank him for that.

I know that in lots of ways I was very lucky. I could have gone to jail for what I did, for what I tried to do. It was very good of Arnold Haden not to press charges, not to tell the police. I know I'll never do anything like that ever again. It was madness, all sound and fury. The only good thing to come out of it as far as I was concerned, was that at least I got my pen back.

ANTON HEATH: I met Vita Carlisle a few times while she worked at Haden Brothers. I found her a very closed book. I gave her my standard spiel about shopping and terrorism, about the inherent conservatism of department stores, about the commodification of people and their skills. I may well have talked about the virtues of blowing up Haden Brothers. She listened but I assumed she was just being polite. She was, after all, a very polite young woman.

The moment that Vita Carlisle asked me if I could get hold of some explosives for her was a crucial one for me. It signalled the end of theory. I felt I had to put up or shut up. I had to put my money where my mouth was. So I said, yes, no problem.

Of course, they weren't real sticks of dynamite. Where, in God's name, would I have been able to get my hands on real dynamite? I simply went to a Haden Brothers stockroom where I knew fireworks were kept between bonfire nights and stole three giant roman candles. I took off the colourful wrappers, wound pieces of tape and wire around them, tried to make them look serious and dangerous and I presented them to Vita. I think she was impressed. I would take no money for them. She didn't know they weren't real and neither did anybody else, and as all revolutionary terrorists know, blanks can get the job done too.

But it was a crucial moment because I knew then that even if I'd been able to give her real explosives, I wouldn't have. I may have been a coward, a windbag, a fake, but the simple fact is, I realized I was a theorist, not a terrorist. I didn't want to be responsible for blowing up anyone or anything. Vita Carlisle changed my life.

They're still out there, the men of violence, the bomb throwers, the wreckers. They don't need me. They still have their beliefs and their explosives. They're still trying to bomb themselves on to somebody else's agenda. But I am not one of them.

I wonder about them. Are they monsters? Do they have thoughts and feelings like us? Do they fall in love, give each other birthday presents? Do they like to go shopping? God knows I was only ever playing at revolution. I was being a naughty schoolboy. I feel I've woken up. It's as though I've been dead. It feels very good to have returned to the real world.

Of course the terrorists hate us, because we are not part of their solution. However, we are a necessary part of their cause; an anonymous, amorphous public that can be used and terrorized. We can only win by not being frightened, by pretending nothing's wrong. We go on with our lives. We tend our gardens. We get on with our jobs as furniture porters. We continue shopping.

Recently I was offered a significant promotion to become head of dispatch for the whole of Haden Brothers. I accepted at once. It was the chance of a lifetime. Even the doting parents, who'd always been a bit sniffy about having their son work in a department store, were really rather impressed, I think.

ARNOLD HADEN: If I've learned anything from all this, I've learned about love. There are so many things to learn about love. We talk about it in the language of exchange, of shopping. We talk about give and take, about possession and ownership. We say that money can't buy it.

I never wanted to own Vita Carlisle, but I did want to borrow her for a while. I wanted certain things from her, but I didn't want to shoplift them. I was prepared to barter. I wanted to give her things, but I wasn't trying to buy her affection. And in the end the final lesson is that love frees us, it detaches us from objects and things. And in the very end, because I loved Vita so very much I felt able to let her go.

When Charlie Mayhew dropped in through the ceiling of my penthouse, I knew that something had come full circle. I had suspected for some time that someone would sooner or later, by accident or design, gain access to the world of tunnels and staircases created by Edward Zander. For years it had been my own private domain. There was a hatch in the wall of my bathroom that connected with one of the main shafts. I frequently used to spend time in there. I looked out through the grilles and spy holes, into Haden Brothers, peering at a world I was too frightened to be a part of.

I had found Edward Zander's suite of rooms a long time ago. I had found his corpse. But what could I do about it? Who could I tell? I would have had to explain about the secret world, and at the time that was inconceivable. I kept it to myself. It's different now. I feel much braver these days. I've overcome so many of my fears. I appear in the shop all the time. I talk to my staff. I talk to the public. I lecture on retailing. I give informal tours of the store, and I talk about the building and its history. As a climax to the tour I always take them briefly into Edward Zander's secret world. They love it. I'm able to charge a lot for these tours, and it really is nice at last to feel that I'm contributing to the prosperity and success of the store.

CHARLIE MAYHEW: There are times when I wish Vita had succeeded. I think it wouldn't be a bad thing at all if Haden Brothers had been blown up or burned down. Or maybe it should have been turned into a hostel for down and outs. Or maybe a theme park or a brothel or an asylum.

Why do I feel so hostile? Well, you know, it was my presence that broke the deadlock, that ended the siege, the threat of Arnold Haden being killed. It was me who helped Arnold Haden and Vita Carlisle come to an arrangement. Without me they might still be in the penthouse threatening to murder each other.

And what did I get for it? Nothing at all. Absolutely nothing. Nobody said thank you. Nobody even said, 'We're giving away the entire contents of the store, why not go down there and take your pick?' No, I had to sit there with them and watch the whole event on closed-circuit television. Nobody wanted to talk to me. Nobody even wanted to admit that I existed.

I thought they could have given me some reward. I wouldn't have wanted much, but if they'd given me a choice I know exactly what I'd have asked for. I'd have come over all modest and dignified and said I simply wanted to be Haden Brothers' artist in residence.

Fat chance. Instead, they banned me from the store for the rest of my life. They told me that if I ever showed my face there again they'd be down on me like a ton of bricks. That hurt. That really hurt. What was I supposed to do? I had no money, no job, nowhere to live. What else was new?

And that was when I had a moment of great insight, a moment of epiphany. That was when I saw what my art form might be. It was more traditional, more conventional than I'd been expecting. But that was the moment I saw that it might be possible to write a novel about Haden Brothers, structured like a department store, with fancy window dressing, a bargain basement, loss leaders and all that stuff. I could see how it might be done, and I could see that it was worth doing. This was the big creative realization I'd been waiting for all my life. My art form had finally come. The only problem was, after what I'd been through at Haden Brothers, writing about the place seemed impossible. Sometimes it seems positively obscene.

The very thought of Haden Brothers makes me sick, but I can't think of anything else. I want to do the research but I can't get into the store. I can't write. I can't sleep. I can't do anything.

Of course, they can't stop me standing in the street outside, looking up at the Haden Brothers building, admiring the architecture and the window displays, doing some window shopping. But I suspect they're watching me wherever I stand, keeping an eye on me, making sure I behave myself. I don't know what they're so scared of. Anyone would think I was some kind of terrorist.

39 · DO IT YOURSELF

It is night, but the lights are on in Haden Brothers; a security measure, so there's enough light for the security cameras, so they can spot an intruder, so that nobody will ever again be able to 'do a Charlie Mayhew'.

The lights are particularly bright up at the top of the store, on the ninth floor, in Arnold Haden's penthouse. The place is a hive of activity, full of carpenters and tilers, painters and plasterers and carpet fitters. Arnold Haden is having his penthouse remodelled and redecorated.

The place is gradually coming into colour: earth tones and pastels and primaries, a purple bathroom suite, Majolica tiles in the kitchen, Afghan kelims, woodwork painted olive and azure, stained wooden floors. Something is being driven out; a coldness, a bleakness. There will be art on the walls. There will be pattern and texture. There will be soft, comforting furniture brought up from the seventh floor.

Arnold Haden knows more or less what he wants done, but he feels unequal to supervising the task himself, so he has called on expert help; on Vita Carlisle. She visits the penthouse often, carrying paint charts, catalogues, sketches and swatches. She was a good person to pick. Her experience in the Flying Squad has given her an unparalleled knowledge of Haden Brothers merchandise. She knows what there is, and what goes with what. As a result of this project Arnold and Vita have developed an easy if undefined relationship. It is not simple and yet it is not difficult. He no longer wants her as a sexual partner. She no longer sees him as the father she wants to kill. It is chaste and it is practical. It might even be called a friendship.

Neither of them is in a great hurry to get the penthouse finished. They are there for the process of change, for the sense of possibility and transformation, for things provisional and flexible, for things coming into being. Arnold Haden is appreciative of what Vita is doing for him and although he wants to express his gratitude, he will try not to do so by way of goods or money.

A little before midnight Arnold Haden sends the workmen home. He and Vita share a bottle of Rioja and a warm glow settles over them. He opens a window. Air and a smattering of traffic noise drifts in, but he welcomes it. It's the sound and touch of life.

Out on the street, at ground level, a long way below Arnold Haden and Vita Carlisle, there's a hunched, dirty figure standing outside the store. He is looking in one of the windows, at a curious display that consists of several hundred souvenir snow storms, each containing a tiny plastic model of the Haden Brothers building. He appears to be engrossed in the merchandise but then he looks about him furtively, sees the street is empty, sees that he's out of sight of the security cameras, and he takes a can of spray paint from his pocket. He shakes it, then, with a wobbly and unpractised hand, he sprays the words 'Charlie was here' all over the store window.